Edward Limonov is a Soviet émi[...]
the Soviet Union in 1974, had thi[...]
waiter, construction worker, furn[...] [...]
was born near Gorky in 1944 and at an early age got into
trouble with the authorities, eventually becoming a thief and
winding up in a psychiatric hospital. In 1967 he moved to
Moscow where he quickly became known as a *samizdat* poet.
His first novel, *It's Me, Eddie*, was published to great acclaim.
Limonov now lives in Paris.

EDWARD LIMONOV

HIS BUTLER'S STORY

AN ABACUS BOOK

First published in USA by Grove Press Inc 1987
First published in Great Britain by Sphere Books Ltd
in Abacus 1989
Copyright © 1984 by Editions Ramsay
Translation copyright © 1986 by Judson Rosengrant
First published in French under the title *Historie de son serviteur*

Printed and bound in Great Britain by
The Guernsey Press Co. Ltd, Guernsey, Channel Islands.

ISBN 0 349 10112 4

Sphere Books Ltd
A Division of
Macdonald and Co. (Publishers) Ltd,
66/73 Shoe Lane, London EC4P 4AB

A member of Maxwell Pergamon Publishing Corporation plc

HIS BUTLER'S STORY

Chapter One

I HAD BEEN completely captivated, completely enthralled by him for two months. Then on the twenty-eighth of February, 1979—I remember that day of my humiliation well—his limousine came to take him to the airport, since he was going to California, and in the last minutes before he left, he treated me to a nasty little show of hysterics. He stamped his feet and stormed up and down the stairs, screaming the same thing over and over again: "God damn you! God damn you!" His face turned red, his beard bristled, and his eyes seemed about to pop out of their sockets. There were times before that when I had heard him from the kitchen shouting at our secretary, Linda, but I had never actually seen him in that state. I had only heard him.

I stood with my back against the doorway and tried to figure out what I had done wrong. I had sent to the cleaners a pair of gray pants that he himself had put on the chest by the front door. The pants had spots on them and were lying on the chest with the other dirty things that were supposed to go to the cleaners, the chest being our special place for that. But it turned out he actually wanted to take the gray pants with him, since they were the ones he always wore on the plane. He didn't have anything else to wear, poor guy, except for a hundred or so suits in his closet.

So I stood there in the dining room doorway, while he ran up and down the stairs, hurling aside whatever got in his way and ripping open the doors and screaming the same thing over and

over: "God damn you! God damn you!" and "Ask! Just ask!"
He had shouted the first "God damn you!" while leaning over
me, since he, my employer, was much bigger and taller than me,
his servant—in fact, next to me he was a gorilla. He barked the
rest of his imprecations from a distance. Perhaps he moved away
from me because he was afraid he would lose control and hit
me? I don't know.

It was during those few minutes that I first began to hate him.
I was even a bit scared, but not that he would hit me. I would
have killed him if he had. I would have gotten the better of him
somehow, even rushing out of the kitchen after him with a
butcher knife if it had come to that. No, what scared me was the
obviously unhealthy nature of his hysteria and the insignificance
of the pretext that had provoked it. Well, go fuck yourself then!
I thought. Go scream at yourself! I know I haven't done anything wrong, and if you don't like it, fire me! Who cares! And
already gathering my things together in my mind, I walked
through the living room into the kitchen and went downstairs
to the basement, took a bottle of soda water from the box, and
proceeding to the farthest room, one heaped with broken furniture and the discarded or worn-out toys of his children, I sat
down on a broken chair, opened the bottle of fizzing soda
water, and started drinking it.

It was only then that I noticed my hands were shaking. That
observation infuriated me. Why the hell should I have to get
mixed up in somebody else's goddamn hysterics and inability to
control himself! Why should I? Visions of myself moving off,
suitcase in hand, into a yawning vastness of freedom both
calmed me down and cheered me up.

Upstairs I could hear loud stamping. Perhaps he was looking
for me? So let him, the asshole, I thought. I'll be damned if I'll
go back up there until he leaves. I've seen enough of his bloated
face and bug-eyes. What's he stomping around for, anyway? I
thought. Has he got flat feet? I put special rubber soles on his
shoes so his feet won't blister, even if they are flat. Actually, I

don't put them on; the Greek shoe repairman does. I just take the shoes to the Greek. And sometimes I shine them too. He keeps thirty or forty pairs in the house. Shining his shoes is one of my duties. I'm his servant, and that's what I'm paid for. When he's here in New York, I make breakfast and lunch for him too. For him and for his fucking businessmen. They frequently go over their papers at lunch.

The stomping and crashing continued. The house is probably fifty or sixty years old, so there was really nothing very odd about my being able to hear the hysterical Gatsby stomping around upstairs from the basement. The Great Gatsby. My employer. My boss. My oppressor.

Obviously I don't call him Gatsby to his face. Steven Grey, Multimillionaire, Chairman of the Board of Directors, Principal Stockholder, and President of Corporations, has no idea I call him that. But if he did, he'd probably be proud of the name; he's well-read and graduated from Harvard, and he has a grandmother who used to be a writer and a great-grandfather who was a friend of Walt Whitman's, and every room in our house has booklined shelves covering almost an entire wall. Mr. Grey knows who Gatsby is and would be pleased.

Actually, while hiding out in the basement from Steven's hysterics, I gave a completely different meaning to the image of the Great Gatsby. I suspected that Steven's Gatsby was merely an attractive façade he turned toward his women and his friends. It would have been interesting to be the other Gatsby's housekeeper too, to observe him from the kitchen, where I could have seen what he was really like.

Steven Grey, stomping over my head for the last time, slammed the front door and was gone. The throb of his limousine soon followed. After sitting another five minutes or so just to make sure, I went back up to the kitchen, drinking the soda water and trying to suppress the passionately indignant and condemnatory speeches I was reciting to myself. It was 8:15. The whole episode had taken only fifteen minutes. I walked

3

through the dining room to the hallway of our house, or rather his house, stepped into the elevator, went up to my fourth floor, or rather his fourth floor, entered my bedroom, which of course was really his, and started gathering my things together. The indignant speeches had stimulated my brain. I made them both to myself and out loud, appealing to an imaginary jury of arbitrators, whom I alternately called "guys" and "gentlemen," pointing out to them the correctness of my own behavior in contrast to Gatsby's hysteria, rudeness, and lack of self-control. Along with those thoughts, another, quite unexpected one suddenly occurred to me—that Soviet lads in faded battle tunics would soon be here, that my brothers would soon come to take revenge on everybody here, including my employer Gatsby, for all the insults I endured. Oh, what revenge they'd take. . . .

I hadn't gotten together very many of my things, had in fact only managed to dump them all in a heap, when the doorbell rang. I went back to the elevator and downstairs to the first floor, wondering who in the hell it could be so early in the morning.

It turned out to be Olga. I was so upset I had completely forgotten it was Wednesday. Olga is my one subordinate, a black woman of fifty from Haiti. She comes to our multimillionaire's little house four times a week. She changes the sheets, including mine, that being one of my privileges, and does the washing and ironing in the basement laundry room. She also cleans the house's bathtubs and toilets, polishes the silver, and wipes the dust from our surfaces, and does any other job that I, the housekeeper and therefore her immediate supervisor, ask her to do. I rarely ask her to do anything, however. I'm a shitty exploiter of other people's labor; I get embarrassed.

A well-defined morning routine was worked out years ago by Jenny, when she was still housekeeper before I took over, and it has been preserved during my time. I'm usually the first one to come down to the kitchen. I raise the window blinds, put the tea kettle on the huge restaurant-size gas stove, and wash out the grounds left over in the coffee maker from the night before. Olga usually arrives during that process. Then, sometime after nine, Linda arrives, the Great Gatsby's permanent secretary of eight years' standing. Just before or after Linda's arrival, the house echoes with the constant ringing of our four different phones.

I complained to Olga about our employer. Basically she agreed with me—after all, I'm her boss. I wasn't looking for any particular reaction, however; I just wanted somebody to complain to. Olga is a very kind woman, decent and hard-working. I inherited her from the above-mentioned Jenny, and I've never thought of replacing her. Olga shook her head at my story. She too thought that Gatsby had been in the wrong: if he hadn't wanted to send the gray pants to the cleaners, why had he put them on the chest with the other things?

"To hell with him! He thinks I need his job! I'll get another one. I'll work as a waiter in a restaurant where I won't have to put up with anybody else's hysterics. I'll work my eight hours and go home!" I told Olga, pacing back and forth in our immense kitchen. She stood leaning against one of the two long butcher-block counters that extend along its sides. I paced nervously, and she stood and listened. Then the phone rang. I picked it up.

"Hi, it's Steven," said the indistinct voice of the Great Gatsby. "I'm calling from the airport. Forgive me, Edward. Considering it logically, you were quite right to send the pants to the cleaners. They were in fact on the chest where we always put the things that are supposed to go out. Forgive me; I was just upset about my own problems and business. It wasn't directed at you personally."

I don't know why, but I let him off. Linda rebuked me for it later. "It's all right, Steven, I understand. Everybody's got problems. It's normal. It was my fault too; I should have asked."

"So long. I'll see you next week," he said. "Goodbye."

"Goodbye," I said.

"He apologized! That was him!" I told Olga in triumph. "He was calling from the airport."

Olga started smiling. She was glad it had all worked out so well, that Edward, who was already thinking about quitting his job, had managed to patch things up with Mr. Grey. I could understand her; from her point of view, I'm obviously a good person to work for. I frequently let her go home early, and I never tell her what to do, believing she knows what's expected of her, as in fact she does. If she sees that the carpet in the hall or in the solarium or in the living room on the third floor is dirty, she gets out the vacuum cleaner and cleans it.

Then Linda arrived, and I gave her my story. "It finally happened to me, Linda," I told her excitedly. "Steven jumped on me this morning. He finally did it!" I said. "I had heard him yelling at you so many times, I was pretty sure my own turn would come sooner or later."

"Only don't expect he'll always apologize, Edward," Linda said. "He only did this time because you're new here, and he's still kind of leery of you. With me he doesn't stand on ceremony that much; I'm lucky if he apologizes every other time. And there wasn't any reason for you to tell him it was your fault either. You should have let him know he was in the wrong, if only a little . . ."

Linda is brave enough with me in the kitchen whenever Gatsby's not around, but when he stays with us in New York, she trembles and worries. She's thirty-one years old, and she's worked for Gatsby for eight of those years. He has in that time trained her so well and gotten her so much under his thumb, that I'm sure that even at home in her nice, big apartment building in her not so nice neighborhood, she thinks about Gatsby's affairs. When she's in her light blue Victorian bedroom, or making love with her permanent boyfriend, David, or talking to her three cats, she remembers Gatsby. And Gatsby isn't all that reluctant to call her at home either—to use up her free time too.

6

Linda is the best possible secretary; otherwise Gatsby wouldn't have kept her for eight years. And the other businessmen too, Gatsby's friends and partners who come to our house, have told me more than once that Linda is very quick, reliable, and efficient.

She really is, as the piece of paper tacked to the cork wall of the clean anteroom where she sits surrounded by cigarette smoke puts it, "Able to raise buildings and walk beneath them. To derail locomotives. To catch bullets with her teeth and eat them. To freeze water with a single glance. SHE IS GOD." Next to this is written, "Linda."

Linda and her abilities are noted at the bottom of the list. At its top, by the name "Steven Grey," is the following: "Chairman of the Board of Directors. Able to leap tall buildings in a single bound. More powerful than a locomotive. Faster than a speeding bullet. Walks on water. Gives orders to God."

Steven has been giving orders to Linda for eight years. And shouting at her. Once he even tore a telephone book to shreds in a fury. Linda is expected to remember and know absolutely everything. Another time he lost his temper because she couldn't find the number of a girl he'd met on a plane a month or a month and a half before, according to him. "A month or a month and a half!" Linda said to me in an exasperated voice. "I found the number for him the next day. He had met her six months before, in November!" Everything that Steven doesn't remember, and as it turns out there isn't much that he does, Linda is required to remember for him—including the phone numbers of his girlfriends. She even classifies and files away the letters he gets from his mistresses.

I was completely enthralled, completely captivated by him when I was Jenny's "Russian boyfriend" and visiting the multimillionaire's little house. Even though Jenny complained to me about his hysterics, I always thought she was exaggerating. I was infatuated with him; he really did seem like a Great Gatsby to me—an overworked businessman, a living symbol of American efficiency and energy. I was delighted by his almost daily flights from city to city or coast to coast across the full extent of America, and from country to country. I was delighted too by the fact that whenever he flew to Europe, he always took that most fantastic of airplanes, the Concorde—and really, what else could he take! It seemed to me that for someone so contemporary, only the Concorde would do.

The corporations over which he presided as either Chairman or President were all very chic—businesses of only the most elegant kind. The extraordinarily expensive automobiles manufactured by one of his firms seemed then like automobiles of the future to me. That's how cars will look in the twenty-first century, I thought. The computers produced by another of his firms competed successfully with the best in the world, those made in Japan. Gatsby and his firm were involved in a real war with the Japanese over those computers and a tiny chip the size of your fingernail (the chip was capable of storing 60,000 bits of information). A secret war of industrial espionage and the theft of technical secrets and of bribery and buying and selling. Just like the high-tech films of James Bond.

My employer himself, invariably dressed in plain English woolens and very simple but impeccably tailored Astor shirts and low-heeled conservative shoes, bearded, and wearing glasses, a towering, energetic, loudly laughing, constant source of delight to all those who hovered about him, whether friends, women, or business partners, was for me a symbol, a kind of film hero—the young millionaire, the soul and hope of America. I could see only the façade then, and it was dazzling.

Even the fact that he had hired me, that he trusted me despite my being a poet and a writer and not a housekeeper at all, stood in his favor. Giving me the job meant sacrificing some of his own comforts. After all, I obviously had no experience whatsoever as a housekeeper, and I thought my service to him would therefore have to have its deficiencies and shortcomings. But he went ahead and hired me anyway, so that in the end it seemed to me that Steven Grey was, in a sense, patronizing the arts. And he had done so before. He was the producer of a film with excellent European actors, a very high-class film—"a piece of real art." Real art doesn't earn any money, of course, and as a consequence Steven Grey had lost "one point eight" million on that venture. I was extremely impressed by the loss of that "one point eight" million.

Just how much I liked him can also be seen in the fact that in that period of my life I sometimes excepted him from the theory of class struggle I had so thoroughly mastered during my first years in America. No, he's not a capitalist pig, I thought. A man who has thrown away almost two million dollars on an intellectual film and who laughs about it now obviously cannot be included in that crowd of faceless pigs. He deserves to be excepted.

I found a great number of attractive qualities in Gatsby then. He looked his brilliant best, for example, in the story of how he saved, saved in the most literal sense, the life of his friend Anthony by sending a special plane for him to Kenya, where Anthony had had an accident. Because of an improperly prescribed dosage of a new, untested medicine, Anthony had suddenly lost control of himself and in that condition had thrown himself through the plate glass window of a modern hotel. He was critically injured and unconscious—in a coma, in fact—when the plane sent by Gatsby picked him up and brought him back to the United States and one of the country's best hospitals, where several operations were performed. Anthony survived, although he remained a cripple. He had lost the use of one of his arms and both of his legs, and was no longer able to work, and had to give up the beloved architecture that took him to Kenya in the first place. But he was still alive. Thanks to Steven Grey. Steven had, moreover, for many years been paying the rent for the studio where Anthony lived, as well as paying for his food and a servant-companion, since Anthony was incapable of fixing his own meals or looking after his apartment himself. I, who still see so many unhappy events in my future, thought enviously of how fine it would be to have a friend like Steven Grey. I, who have looked so hard and long for friends and have so rarely found them, was deeply touched by that story. Even later, when my image of the captivating Gatsby had been filled in with certain less attractive details, the story of Anthony continued to have an effect on me.

Incidentally, Steven financed the film I just mentioned out of friendship too. Once, in one of those rare instances of real intimacy between us, while we were sitting in the kitchen for a half-hour's chat—and for Gatsby to waste a half an hour was like anyone else's wasting a month—he, the employer, told me, the unusual servant, how he had come to finance it.

"For three years, Edward, I played chess with a film director, and he played well. He was a good opponent. But during that time he continually complained to me about how he wanted to make that film, but that no one would finance it for him because it was too serious, so the poor fellow was forced to make commercial trash, which was not at all what he wanted to do. After three years I finally got so sick of those conversations that I told him I would give him the money myself, if he would just quit whining about it."

Mr. Grey smiled complacently. I'm not sure his version of how the film got made had much basis in fact. More likely, it was a legendary account of what had happened, but one that Mr. Grey himself believed. Yet the film did exist; that fact was indisputable. Gatsby then went into a complicated discussion of the financial reasons behind the loss of the "one point eight" million. According to him, the main problem had been a lack of control over ticket sales in most of the theaters.

"In those theaters where we had guards to keep track of how many people went in, and then compared that number with the amount of money we got back, we didn't lose anything," he said.

I don't know whether my employer was right; I don't know enough about it to say. Everything I know about economics comes down to the conviction that the best investment in the world is putting your money into revolution. It may be a very risky investment, but if you win, you win it all. I was therefore dying to say to him, "Why not put all those millions of yours into a revolution, sir?"

Thus we live. After that episode in February, there were still a number of other times when I found him delightful, but the shadow of that incident remained, until, supplemented by other shadows, it finally altered beyond all recognition the image of my employer as the superman, intellectual liberal, and best friend of servants, animals, and children that he very likely considered himself to be. My girlfriend Jenny used to call Steven Grey a limousine liberal, a name I grew to like very much. Here I am living in the most expensive neighborhood in Manhattan on the banks of the East River in a house worth one and a half million dollars, and in the service of a limousine liberal. I, a spoiled servant of the international bourgeoisie, as I jokingly, and sometimes not so jokingly, think of myself.

And it's true that I am spoiled. Or better, I'm spoiled for the time being. It could be—and I'm always ready for this, just in case—that I'll have to leave the millionaire's house and set off on my own again into a world full of poverty and the struggle for survival. But right now I live in a way that few people can in this city or this world.

In the first place, I am, as I've already said, the only one who lives at the millionaire's house continuously. Mr. Grey and his family live in Connecticut, in the "country" in the large manorial house on their estate. Mr. Grey's wife, the blonde Nancy, his four children, their staff of Connecticut servants, and his four automobiles are all there. As are their vegetables, their horses, their flowers, their swimming pool, and the several tenant farmers that Gatsby leases his land to.

Hanging everywhere in the little Manhattan house are land-scapes of Connecticut and the land owned by Gatsby lightly sketched in oils by the absolutely photographic artist Harris— Jacob Harris, I think. The frames are made of old, blackened, unfinished wood. Those landscapes remind me of the Russia I left five years ago—the same shallow brooks, country roads, spruce trees, and snow-covered meadows. The artist Harris painted countless picket fences, hedges, autumn trees, and red brick farm walls on commission from Gatsby.

Nancy and the flying Gatsby on weekends, when he isn't in his Asias and Europes, live there in very wholesome surroundings, with good milk (there are cows here and there in Harris's landscapes). It is assumed that their children will grow up there to become healthy, energetic, and authentic Americans too.

But I, Edward Limonov, live in the townhouse. My bedroom is on the fourth floor and looks out onto the garden and the river. Birds sing in the garden in the morning, and at any time of the day or night you can see ships, barges, and tugboats sailing by. The light of day enters my bathroom through a skylight cut in the ceiling. Every Monday Linda gives me money to buy food for the house, since one of my duties is to see that the refrigerator is always full, just in case, and on Thursdays she pays me my wages for the week. Going through the basement of the multimillionaire's house you come to the wine cellar—an object of real pride to my employer with its thousands of bottles of old French wine and stronger beverages too. All five floors of our house are filled with comforts, luxuries, soft beds, couches, books, and records. And it would all be good, a heaven surrounded by ivy and suffused with light—it would all be good, if its *master,* its real master, didn't visit it from time to time.

During the first few months of my employment, Steven's visits were fairly infrequent. Once or twice a week, say, he would appear at the front door in a taxi around six or seven in the evening, after rushing in directly from the airport. Often he was angry. He probably had his own private reasons for that, but the pretext was always that he could never find any money for the taxi, and he would run distractedly from me to the driver, coughing, continually taking his pipe out of his pocket, leaving it unlit, then putting it back again, and otherwise nervously fussing. His nervousness would at once invade our whole household, and I, who until then had belonged only to myself or to my regular duties, would suddenly belong to him. In the same way they have always done, his bad moods then would infect me and the house itself, but most of all they would infect Linda, if he happened to arrive during her working hours. Linda sits in her little anteroom on the second floor from nine in the morning until five in the afternoon.

I usually wait for him in the kitchen, keeping an eye on the street. When his taxi arrives, I run to open the door to spare him the extra annoyance he would inevitably feel at having to look for his key—as you see, I'm looking out not only for him but also for myself. After the commotion of arrival is over, and he has carried in, either with or without my help, his suitcase or suitcases and the invariable heap of tattered newspapers he has been reading in the taxi, he runs upstairs to his leather-and-wood-paneled office on the second floor and sits down at the telephone. The telephoning usually continues for about thirty minutes to an hour, although sometimes it goes on longer—two hours, or even three.

After he has finished with his calls, he comes back downstairs to the kitchen and appropriates my copy of *The New York Post*, always asking with old-fashioned courtesy if I have finished reading it and if I can have it. Finished or not, I always give it to him. It would be ridiculous not to. I ask him then if he would like a drink. By this I mean his usual glass of twelve-year-old Glenlivet Scotch with a quantity of ice and seltzer. If he is in a good mood, he makes the drink himself. I always put the bottle of Glenlivet out on the butcher-block counter in the kitchen, so he won't have to search for it among the other bottles in the kitchen cabinet that serves as our bar and once more become

13

irritated or lose his temper. These little traditions of putting out bottles and opening doors were established long before in Jenny's time as essential precautions against his bad moods. I don't know whether he's aware that both Linda and I, that all of us in fact, are at the mercy of his moods, but maybe he is.

After quickly skimming through the paper, he picks up his glass and goes to the master bedroom on the third floor, fills his deep, wide bathtub with water and a special variety of green pine scent, and lies down in it. When he takes a bath, he listens to the radio I recently installed on the night stand next to his bed. And while he takes his bath, we wait for him below.

We wait, the house and I, until he splits—disappears or goes out to eat at a restaurant and then somewhere else to get himself fucked. Sometimes, more often now, he comes back very late to do his coupling at home. I wait, and the house does too, because I have a feeling that the house likes me, but not him. Why me? Because I live in it and clean it and take care of it. And I really do clean it, since in addition to my housekeeping duties I've kept those of my old job, which was to do the "heavy" cleaning. Once a week when Jenny was still working and living at the house, I came to clean, vacuuming it from top to bottom and waxing its floors. Certainly the house does like me, the one who keeps it clean and neat and makes sure that everything in it is warm and dry. All Gatsby does is throw his towels and his dirty shirts and socks and underwear and his soiled suits on the floor, and track in chalk and plaster from the street, or wherever he gets it, and leave half-empty wine glasses and coffee cups lying around. In short, he brings disorder and dirt into our home—he uses it up, whereas I look after it.

The house and I wait for him to go. For us, his arrival is like an extraterrestrial invasion. Often, when we're expecting him, his girlfriend Polly arrives, a very nice but in my opinion harassed woman. Linda and I both agree that Polly is very nice and a benevolent and calming influence on Gatsby, our feudal lord, and we hope to God they won't quarrel.

The comparison of Steven to a feudal lord came to me only gradually, of course, during the many, many lunches I made for him. Usually he eats meat—lamb chops or steaks which I order by phone from the best butcher in the city, the Ottomanelli Brothers. It was only after seeing my fill of him slightly dulled with red meat and French red wine, a minimum of two bottles of which were always consumed at meals—it was only after seeing my fill of the puffy, flushed, red-bearded face of Gatsby with his paunch hanging over his belt—that I finally hit upon that very apt, as I thought, description of him as a feudal lord. That lord, a hunter, horseman, and dog lover, finishing up a joint of mutton and dressed in high jackboots and reeking of alcohol, dogs, and the stable, came to me somewhere out of medieval England. And Gatsby does in fact have a strange smell of leather about him from the closets where he keeps his suits and his quantities of footwear, a leathery smell with a pungent admixture of cologne and Dunhill tobacco, his invariable brand. Like all snobs—and it shouldn't be difficult to guess that Steven Grey is a snob—he has his own particular brand of Scotch, Glenlivet, his own shirtmaker, Astor, his own brand of underwear, Jockey, and his own brand of tobacco, Dunhill. In addition, there are other, more general principles of snobbism and the good life—his socks, for example, come only from Bloomingdale's and have to be a hundred percent cotton. And it is also at Bloomingdale's that I purchase the bow ties for his tuxedo and the bed linen for his house, for each one of its seven bedrooms. The bed linen too has to be pure cotton—no polyesters allowed.

When Polly arrives, she usually greets me with some thoughtful phrase like, "How's your book coming, Edward?"—the words change, but it's obvious they're all supposed to express her concern for me and her interest in my fate—and then she goes upstairs to see Steven. If he has gotten out of the tub by then and is dressed, he runs down the stairs to meet her. Whenever that happens, I withdraw to the kitchen or to my bedroom, impatiently waiting for him to go out to his restaurant. At the same time, I remain on the alert, in case he should ask me about some object, thing, or person it is essential I find at once either inside the house or beyond its confines. Although the owner of a small empire of firms and the master of the numerous people who work for him, he can never remember, for example, where the glasses and cups in the kitchen are, and inevitably opens every one of its twenty cupboards in succession looking for them. Even when I go up to my room to give him a feeling of privacy in his own home, I always leave the door ajar, in case he should suddenly need something or want me.

Scenes like the episode regarding my sending his pants to the cleaners have never again been repeated in such a blatantly obnoxious form, and there's a reason for that, as I shall explain in due course, but outbursts of hysterics still do rock the house on occasion, reducing Linda to a state of nervous shock and causing me to lose my temper. "You weakling, you hysterical old woman! Why can't you learn to control yourself!" I whisper under my breath while washing the dishes or drying them, or clearing the table.

Once he had to go to his place in Connecticut after spending three days at my, or rather at Linda's and my, house. We had gotten incredibly tired of him during that time and were counting the minutes. He behaved more or less decently, and with my help had already loaded the car with a box of French wine, his suitcase, and several incomprehensible electronic devices with tangled wires, but was still lingering somewhere in the depths of the house. I was sitting at my usual place by the kitchen window keeping an eye on his car so he wouldn't get a ticket, and waiting for him to finally get his ass out of there, and already savoring the moment when I would at last be able to kick off my shoes and lie down, since I'd been on my feet since six A.M., and it was now almost six P.M. . . . When from upstairs—Linda's little anteroom and Gatsby's office communicate with the kitchen by a stairway, so that if the door's open I can easily hear what they're talking about—when from upstairs I heard a sudden uproar: Linda's muffled and nervous answers and the hysterical bass of my employer. "It's been stolen! It's been stolen!" the deep bass voice repeated. I couldn't hear Linda's answer; they had moved away from the doorway well into the interior of the office.

I cringed with a sense of foreboding. After the initial quarreling, shouting, and other supplementary noises resembling the sound of furniture being knocked over, all of which took place well inside the office, it became impossible to make out any words at all, only the din of voices, and then Linda came running into the kitchen and asked in a hysterical half-whisper, "Edward, do you know where Steven's small black portfolio that he always keeps on the windowsill in the office is? It's gone, it's been stolen, and it has all his credit cards and his passport in it!"

"Linda," I said, "except for you and me, no one has been in the house for over a week now. I have no idea where his portfolio is, but if it was on the windowsill, then it's still there. I haven't taken anything from either the windowsill or the desk, since I don't like to touch the boss's papers. Maybe Steven put it somewhere himself?"

"No, he didn't move it," Linda said, but she didn't sound so sure. And then she added, "We'll have to go through the whole house, although it's almost certainly been stolen." She looked at me tragically and reproachfully.

I shrugged. "Who could have stolen it? Guests? His guests? Ghupta stole his portfolio, or maybe another one of his friends—the Hollywood screenwriter Jeff? Or maybe his wife took it? Or I did," I added resentfully. "That's it, it was me."

Linda was too frightened to say anything more, and I didn't say anything either, while upstairs Gatsby continued to thump and crash about. And then it was suddenly quiet. A light lit up on the kitchen phone, which, like the phones in every other room in the house, has a button for each of our four numbers and another for the intercom we use to talk between rooms.

"He's calling somebody," Linda whispered.

He quickly finished his call, and then there was the sound of footsteps. Flat feet, I thought maliciously. The flat feet were clearly on their way down to us. I was aware that at that moment I was thinking like a servant, that I was full of a servant's fear and animosity, and that like a servant who has done nothing wrong, I had no wish to see him. Society, civilization, culture, history, and what else?—books, movies, and television had all shaped our roles, those of master and servant. Like it or not, Edward, if you play the servant, if you live like a servant, even if there is much more intellect in you, intellect sufficient for a poet, say, it doesn't make any difference; nobody cares. You have to play the fool and tragically wait for him to come down. Curled up inside like a shrimp at the approach of a fisherman's net, or like what else?—like a hedgehog which a noblewoman reaches for and prods with the tip of her umbrella, the servant Limonov listened as the steps approached the stairway and then started down. Linda stared like a rabbit at the doorway's gaping maw.

And then he was standing in the doorway. One thing I have acquired in this world after many years of associating with people like myself is the ability to look and not look at the same time, or the ability to see without looking. I acquired that skill after several years of training in the New York subway system. It has proved useful. I saw Gatsby without looking at him. I sensed his psychopathic aura, and I felt his sweaty nervousness and tension, and I had the feeling that steam was whistling from him as from a teakettle and he was surrounded by a sort of red cloud. Perhaps his puffy red face produced this last illusion, or perhaps his red beard was at fault—that made me think he was surrounded by a hysterical red cloud. I don't know what it was, but I do know that I hated him, and that I hated him doubly both for forcing me to play that idiotic social role which required me to detest him, and for his not being able to rise to the level of ordinary human relations. For not even being able, the primitive bastard, to remain on the level of employer toward those who work for him and are paid for their labor. Instead, the cocksucker used that swollen cloud to violently shove the two of us, Linda and me, into the role of servants. With one thrust of his nerves, he shoved us out of the twentieth century and into the Middle Ages and history. In a few minutes, without resorting to violence, he turned me, a poet and lover of intellectual books on social themes, an anarchist and admirer of the raw New Wave music of Elvis Costello and Richard Hell, into a quaking servant. What was the use of my trembling with hatred for him? My hatred changed nothing; it remained merely the private affair of a servant. I could hate him if I wished, but a servant I would remain. I stood still, while he walked past me toward Linda, past his servant, his servant, his servant!

It might be said that Edward Limonov concocted all that himself, it was all his own invention, and he really didn't have any basis for his resentment of Steven Grey. That's true; there wasn't any basis for it, except that Steven Grey consciously and unconsciously and any other way you like felt himself to be the *master*, thereby automatically turning Linda and me into his servants. Paradoxically, Olga, shielded from him by Linda and me, wasn't one of his servants, whereas we were. He played that game, the fucking feudal overlord, the bloated bastard, and we had to play it too. He played it unconsciously, and I was included in it unconsciously, and the fact that I realized what was going on changed nothing.

I always knew, both then and later, that physically it was easy for me to work for him and with him. I had no objection to getting up at seven, or even at six, or to the fact that his friends or the businessmen he needed would sometimes arrive at eight—I even found that the morning's drill stimulated me and put me in a cheerful mood. Nor did I object to the fact that I had to spend the whole day on my feet and could go off to bed only at midnight. After all, he was only in the New York house two or three days a week; you could count on your fingers the times when he stayed longer.

But that extraordinary ability of his to transform both Linda and me into servants by his mere presence wrecked our relationship with him and turned every one of his visits into a calamity. And it certainly wasn't that I wanted him to sit and drink vodka with me in the kitchen—I would have been the first one to say no to that. It wasn't his friendship that I required, but rather a sense that my work was my own and wasn't merely "service" in the menial sense of the word.

In short, he walked over to Linda and blurted out something that must have come as a surprise even to him: "I called Nancy, and she has the portfolio with her in Connecticut."

Good God, how unhappy he looked! He was so disappointed, or rather not disappointed, but crushed! Why? Because it turned out we were innocent! He had already decided, decided as he always did, that it was *we* who were guilty. That it was *us*, us . . . To put it more simply, he wanted us, the other ones, the ones he could say it to, to be bad, guilty, and worse than him—stupid or undisciplined, but worse than him. Obviously, I'm only trying here to understand what his feelings were. Maybe they weren't quite what I'm describing, but his expression was unhappy.

After throwing open several cabinets with his trembling hands (and obviously blaming me that he had to do so, that he hadn't immediately seen the glasses and the bottle in the first one and had to open several), he found the gin and poured himself a drink, his hands trembling so much that the neck of the bottle rattled against the glass. And then he started jabbering about something. No, not justifying himself, but just trying to find something to talk about with us—a sentence about his car which stood gleaming outside the kitchen window. Then, glancing at the kitchen clock, he remarked the time out loud and happily muttered something else about the traffic on the roads he would have to take to Connecticut. In his barbarian code, all this was supposed to symbolize something like an apology, a retreat, but it's more likely that it was really the result of his own chagrin at the fact that he, the bastard, had been in the wrong.

It was so repulsive for me to look at him that I made a frankly contemptuous face and went upstairs to the second floor, passed through Linda's little anteroom, went into the TV room, and started looking out the window and thinking about what a son of a bitch he really was. Linda had already given in to him out of kindness, as she always does, and like him was drinking some kind of junk to calm her nerves, either whiskey or gin, who knows what. I heard only the ice tinkling in their glasses and their muted chitchat—a classic pair, the sadist and the masochist, the boss and his secretary.

Out of the window in the TV room I could see a girl of about ten dressed in shorts, with long skinny legs, a round ass, and little breasts under her training bra. She was learning how to ride a bike. Her frayed mama, worn out probably by the many thousands of love sessions she had had in her life, stood nearby and watched. The mama was my age, and her face, tensed with so many thousands of orgasms, was covered with little muscle lines and wrinkles. The wrinkles have developed on her face in consequence of her orgasms, I thought a bit mechanically, in the tone of an instructor of anatomy, and then turned my attention to the girl, whose skin and little body were still smooth and even and whose red mouth was stuck out capriciously in the pronunciation of inaudible words. I was so moved by the spectacle of that innocent child that I unconsciously started fondling my black "service" trousers in the vicinity of my crotch.

By virtue of a powerful imagination, my organ, the humiliated organ of a servant, found itself in the mouth of that child from a "good" and well-to-do family. Obviously, they were well-to-do and "good"; they lived next door. There are no poor people in our area. The poor come here only to work. Every morning around nine I see lines of them through the kitchen window, black women like our Olga for the most part, on their way to the houses and apartments of the neighboring rich. Around five or later, they make their way back to their outlying ghettos.

I got ten minutes' worth of pleasure from that wiggling girl on the bicycle. The only reason I didn't come was that Gatsby and Linda were still babbling downstairs, and either of those unbalanced personalities could have walked in at any moment.

Watching little girls is by no means my only hobby, the sort of hobby that lonely old gentlemen of a certain age tend to have and the sort that sometimes lands them in jail or even in the electric chair. No, I would never go after a child, but watching one out of the window is another matter, and of course I'd avail myself of the opportunity, if I lived somewhere in the country or in some provincial American town and found myself an arm's length away from some familiar and none too innocent-looking girl of that age.

But I would never under any circumstances take advantage of a child; grossness of that kind is for idiots who can't restrain themselves, whereas I, despite everything, am a person of culture and taste. A servant can be a person of culture and taste too, can't he? If the girl were to object, I wouldn't insist. Pleasure of that kind is merely a facet of my sexuality—a sexuality I understand very well—and nothing more. I long ago realized how society fucks everything up, depriving us of life's most interesting sensations and pleasures, fencing them off with prohibitions and taboos.

"Don't you dare!" But I do.

Then, taking the place of the little girl, who had glided off to the left on her bicycle out of the frame of my vision and into the wings, so to speak, Steven appeared in the window, opened the door of his car, sat down in its polished box, which since it was spring had its top down and gleamed luxuriously with the yellow of its new leather, pushed the seat back with his powerful ass, and turned the key. At that moment the girl came back out of the wings and glided past the boss's car, squinting at him with interest and then glancing back at him as she passed. I could see Gatsby smile complacently.

The bastard! Even there he got the better of me. The girl couldn't see the pale face of the servant high up in the second-floor window, but with a sweet and happy smile she took the hook of Gatsby's car. Women and girls and children, all females in fact, love whatever is brilliant or gleams or is shining with lights—Christmas trees, cars, diamonds, gold—and never trouble themselves with what is real or genuine, with the treasures of the mind, say. The girl on the bicycle proved herself a worthy representative of her sex, and spitting my prick out of her mouth, she rode over to Gatsby in his shining box, her eyes open wide with delight.

As you see, Gatsby still had his moments of hysteria, but they weren't directed at me personally, or if they were, then that was something he managed to keep to himself. And there was a reason for that, as I've already mentioned.

Once in March, after one of his typically long telephone conversations, Gatsby came skipping into the kitchen in a particularly good mood.

"Edward," he said, "we're going to have a very unusual guest this week. Can you guess who it is?"

"The Shah of Iran," I said, taking a stab. I didn't say that because I have such a wonderful sense of humor. The exiled Shah actually could have been our guest, since Mr. Grey really did know him and had at one time invested large sums of money in the development of Iranian agriculture, chicken or rabbit farms, I think, although I'm not sure. I'll add that Gatsby was pretty canny and got his money out of Iran long before "that" began—the revolution, I mean.

We have links with Iran. In our house there are a great many books on Iranian history and culture, as well as Persian-English dictionaries, and in the living room on the third floor is a table from Iran with a circular top made of tiny mirrors that was obviously cut out of a wall somewhere. The whimsical pattern produced by the mirrors is complemented by strange birds circling the table's marble edge. It is a very beautiful table. Mr. Grey probably vandalized a mosque or some other architectural monument to get it. There are also Persian miniatures hanging on the walls in the stairways of our house, and tasseled Persian pillows and cushions on the couches. And hanging on the wall in the third-floor living room is an immense hookah, which Mr. Grey's oldest child, Henry, on his last visit filled countless times with hashish and smoked with his college friends. We also have a Persian bronze brazier and Persian silverware and even Persian silver ashtrays with a crowned lion holding a saber in its hand. Or maybe they aren't ashtrays, since on their bottoms, on the reverse side, that is, there is a relief depicting a moustached man in a plumed helmet. I suspect this is the Shah's father, but maybe not. There's something written on them in Persian, but I don't understand Persian.

"No," the boss answered seriously, "it's not the Shah. It's one of your compatriots, a Russian. I already told him you're working here. It's Efimenkov," he said, speaking the name of a famous Soviet writer I had been on friendly terms with in my Moscow days, even visiting his house once.

How mixed up everything is in this world, I thought. I never expected to see Efimenkov on this earth again, and especially not in my—excuse me, in Gatsby's house. The news didn't particularly excite me, however; I had long ago forgotten that Efimenkov even existed. I had enough of my own worries.

But I felt that the boss would want me to be surprised, even astonished, and so like a good housekeeper I said in an excited voice, "You're kidding! Efimenkov? That's really amazing! That's really incredible!"

My master was evidently satisfied with my exclamations—he didn't require much from his servant. "I've known Efimenkov for several years now," Steven said. "We met for the first time at an international festival in Helsinki."

I had been aware that Gatsby knew Efimenkov, but the festival in Helsinki was beyond me. At that time in my life I had been quietly and peacefully breaking into out-of-the-way stores in my nice little provincial city of Kharkov. I don't even know what year that festival took place—when Gatsby and the Soviet Efimenkovs started hanging out together, when they all got together and made each other's acquaintance.

"He'll be here a month," my employer told me, "not the whole time, of course, since he'll be traveling around the country, but this will be his home base, so to speak." You could sense that the multimillionaire Steven Grey was proud of the fact that the world-famous Soviet writer Efimenkov would be staying in his home.

I realized then that the whole world is one big village for Mr. Grey, that for him a celebrity is a celebrity and that, snob that he is, a Soviet celebrity might be of an even higher rank, since as a Communist he would have the advantage of being exotic. In conversation with somebody, say the British Marchioness Houston, whom the boss is not indifferent to and who according to Jenny had once been his mistress, Steven will find an opportunity to remark importantly, "Efimenkov and I got really drunk yesterday. . . ." As you'll see in a moment, they really did get drunk on the one evening they spent together, but that isn't the point. In sharing his home with Efimenkov, Steven felt he was an international figure, someone who took part in international events and who had a place not only in the economic but also in the cultural life of the world, and that's obviously the reason why Efimenkov was so desirable a guest for him. He was one more confirmation of Gatsby's own importance in the world.

May God grant Efimenkov long life for making my time in the millionaire's house more bearable for me, and for raising me in the boss's esteem to the point where he no longer yells, "God

25

damn you! God damn you!" to my face, and where, if he loses his temper, at least he thinks about it before letting it take the mad form of biting his lip and snorting like a Cyclops before the nearsighted, bespectacled green eyes of his servant Edward Limonov.

The reason? Edward Limonov had written a book. A great many people in the world have written books, and among them a great many Russians, including Efimenkov himself, who so far has written and published, if I'm not mistaken, thirty-three of them, but Edward Limonov, "my new butler," as Steven Grey himself had called him in a telephone conversation with the Marchioness Houston that Linda had overheard and reported— that same Limonov a couple of years before had written a book that shocked and even astonished Evgeny Efimenkov.

Efimenkov had heard about the book but hadn't read it yet. Rumors about it had been circulating in Russia, where the new butler had sent it through a little American girl—the manuscript, I mean. And just before Efimenkov's arrival in my country, in the United States of America, Limonov's book had come out in condensed form in one of the Russian-language journals published in Paris, and caused quite a stir among all the Russians. Some of them loved the book, and others hated it.

Almost the very first thing that Efimenkov said to Mr. Grey's servant after he was helped out of the yellow New York taxicab by Jon Barth, the graying professor of Russian literature and, as I suppose, completely innocuous CIA informer (so that it's no accident he's always hanging around all the Soviet literary dignitaries who come here, that he's never more than a step away)— almost the first thing that Efimenkov said to the servant was, "Edik! I hear you've written a novel. How about letting me read it?"

If you take into account that Efimenkov was never really a close friend of Limonov's, and that the man getting out of the taxi was a Soviet writer who had come to America in connection with the publication of one of his books and was staying at the multimillionaire's house only as a result of his own relative independence, his status as one of the most famous writers in the world, whereas Limonov was that multimillionaire's housekeeper and an émigré and therefore presumably anti-Soviet— only if you take all that into account, will you understand just how interested in the book Efimenkov must have been, if he asked about it as soon as he got in the door. For you, perhaps, that might not mean anything, but in Soviet terms, it was a greeting with wide-open arms.

I let him have it. I gave it to him to read. And it blew him away.

And with good reason. The book talked about homosexuality, and about what it feels like when a man is the one who is fucked, and about the hero's other sexual experiences, and it did so openly, without hedging: A cunt was called a cunt without any concealment, and love was rendered in sharp outlines without any mincing or mawkishness. Moreover, it was clear that the hero was happy neither with the Soviet way of life nor with this one either, the one ruled by Gatsbys, although I still didn't know Steven then. In short, there was much that was pointed and stained with blood in that book. The hero didn't play at being macho when he didn't have anybody to fuck; he masturbated, and that's the way it was written—he masturbated. The hero wasn't afraid to lay himself bare, and that in fact was what impressed Efimenkov. And the most "awful" thing about the book was that the hero bore my name. He too was called Edward Limonov.

I didn't give him the book the very first day he asked, but on the third day, I think—the first time he spent the evening at home. Steven was off somewhere in Europe, and Efimenkov didn't go anywhere that night but stayed at home and read my book. The next morning he was supposed to fly to Colorado with Barth, and so when I gave him the manuscript, he had politely asked if he could take it with him. I told him he could, if he promised not to lose it. I had other copies—the translator had one, and there were more at various other places around the globe—so I nobly gave my consent.

When he came back several days later, Gatsby was at home, as Efimenkov was well aware. Nevertheless, the first thing he yelled from the doorway, lifting his head up after a quick glance into the kitchen, was, "Edik! Edik!" He knew if I wasn't in the kitchen, I would be in my room on the fourth floor. In response to Efimenkov's shouting, the boss came out of his office on the second floor and dashed downstairs to him, but Efimenkov waved him aside and headed up to my room. It was a complete triumph for me. A complete triumph over my boss. The servant was victorious. Art had leapt higher than his millions, if only for an instant.

I came out of my room onto the third-floor landing.

"Well, your book knocked me out," Efimenkov said, noisily gasping for breath. "I stayed up all night reading it. It's a scream of anger. The whole book's written in the genre of a scream."

"The only thing Zhenya would talk about the whole trip was your book, Edward," said Jon Barth, who had come rushing up the stairs after Efimenkov—our poor little stairway; Barth is as big as the Soviet writer. The two of them looked like sturdy airborne colonels come up through the ranks who had put on civilian clothes. The hands of both men stuck out of their sleeves as if their clothing belonged to somebody else. Sometimes, watching them reading together on the stage (Jon was Efimenkov's interpreter, for besides being a professor and a CIA informer, he also did interpreting), it seemed strange to me that they didn't suddenly throw off their jackets and start wrestling up there on the platform in front of the whole house—all those specialists in the Russian question, the Harrison Salisburys, the Updikes, the Ginsbergs, the Vonneguts, and the old Russian lady patriots of Russia without the Communists. They didn't take off their jackets and wrestle even once, which greatly saddened me. If Steven had joined them, that would indeed have been an impressive spectacle: The boss was just as powerfully built as they were, a real hulk, as we used to say on the outskirts of Kharkov.

Nancy had a supper party for Efimenkov that same evening, having made a special trip in from the country to meet him—you see what an important guest he was. Naturally I served. I placed the smoked salmon, herring, vodka, and various other delicacies from Zabar's on sterling silver trays and set them out on the dining room table. Several other people were invited, some of whom I already knew. They were all supposed to go to the ballet to see another Russian superstar, Rudolph Nureyev, so they were fortifying themselves beforehand. After the ballet they were planning to go to a restaurant where Linda, I knew, had already reserved a table for them, having herself been invited by Gatsby to make a "couple" with Jon Barth in order to neutralize him. Mr. Steven Grey couldn't stand Barth. He told Linda as much with his characteristic baronial candor: "You'll sit next to that ass Barth and keep him distracted so he won't disrupt the general conversation with his inanities."

Nancy, who I think was afraid she would be bored, invited another young married couple I wasn't acquainted with, and also present was a friend of Efimenkov's, an ugly scarecrow named Lydia, who, like Jon Barth, was for some reason an inevitable participant in the visits of all Soviet literary dignitaries to the United States. She was of Russian descent, but had been born in America and spoke Russian with an accent. Jenny and I used to laugh at Lydia and call her the lieutenant assigned to Major Barth. Maybe that's the way it really was, or maybe it wasn't, who knows, but the story of how I first met Jenny is also connected with the visit of another Soviet literary star to America—Stella Makhmudova. That was the first time I saw not only Jenny, but also the horse Lydia and the wrestler Barth.

But more about that in its place. On the evening in question they were all sitting in the dining room and chattering of one thing and another, with neither direction nor point—you know, polite conversation—which I in the kitchen found offensive to

29

listen to. Efimenkov was saying something about internal Soviet literary affairs, and Gatsby was talking about his business deals, and from time to time the hosts would ask me to bring them something, Gatsby in an exceptionally gentle tone of voice intended for Efimenkov, and Nancy in her usual one. Nancy has to be given her due; she was always fairly straightforward in her behavior.

You're probably thinking I was sitting indignantly in my kitchen and suffering from wounded pride, given the fact that here I was serving Gatsby and my compatriot Efimenkov even though I myself was a writer, and what a writer, since the literary superstar Efimenkov had just expressed his enthusiasm with my work in the most glowing terms. No, nothing of the sort. On the contrary, I was afraid that they would invite me to join them in the dining room and I would have to listen to all their horseshit, to Efimenkov's wooden accent and his naïve attempts to explain to my employer things he wasn't the least interested in hearing about. All the names of Soviet figures mentioned by Efimenkov were boring even to me—local celebrities; who the fuck cared. But of course Efimenkov didn't know that. Or if you think I was suffering from wounded pride and ashamed of the fact that I was serving them and that Efimenkov was there to see it, then that's wrong too. I had very healthy ideas about work and about being paid for it, and what Gatsby was paying me, in addition to my room and board and all the other privileges I enjoyed while living in his house, suited me just fine.

If I objected to Gatsby's exploitation of me, it was because of his unconscious desire to force my mind to take part in his business and his hysterics, and that wasn't a present I could give him. But to the exploitation of a part of my time and physical strength I was ready to give my consent, and had in fact requested that exploitation myself in exchange for his money. I needed his money in order to live and to write other books and to pay for the translation of those I had already written and to arrange for their sale and then to leave Gatsby and exploit my own labor.

I almost sighed with relief when they finally left for the ballet and I could start clearing the table. And although they had eaten all the smoked and pickled delicacies from Zabar's, including even the tiniest red morsels of the smoked salmon from Scotland on the silver dish, I still cleared away the dirty dishes enthusiastically. The last operation of the day. The end.

After putting the dishes in the dishwasher and making sure that the children had had enough television and gone to bed (Nancy had brought her two youngest children with her from Connecticut), I went off to bed myself.

I was awakened by bells. That is, I heard ringing in my sleep, but when I woke up, I realized with horror that it was the front doorbell. I got dressed as quickly as I could, but it wasn't easy. I didn't have a robe, and so by the time I got my pants and shirt on and had taken the elevator downstairs, whoever had been at the door was gone. I had almost decided that the ringing had in fact been a dream and had gone into the kitchen to get myself a drink of cold seltzer water before going back upstairs to my room and to bed for good, when the telephone suddenly rang. I looked at the kitchen clock. It was midnight. On the phone an old woman's trembling voice said, "There's a young lady at your front door. She can't get inside. I'm very concerned about her; it's cold outside and she has only a dress on."

My heart sank. It was Nancy of course. She and Gatsby both have the same idiotic habit of the rich of going outside without their coats on, sometimes even in winter. What do they care; they always catch the first taxi that comes along before they have a chance to feel the cold. And that fall evening too, Nancy had gone out with nothing but her dress on. Just as I was hanging up, there was another irritable ring at the front door. I rushed to open it.

"Everybody's sound asleep. I've been ringing for half an hour," she said angrily, but clearly restraining herself. "Everybody" meant me and her children, obviously.

"I'm sorry, Nancy," I said. "The children had already gone to bed and so had I. I thought you had a key."

"I didn't take it with me," she said, a bit apologetically, evidently beginning to recover from the cold and her vexation.

Gatsby and Efimenkov both had house keys, and I couldn't have stayed up all night waiting for them anyway, since they were coming back separately. Gatsby could have given her his own key.

I asked her if she needed anything, and she answered that she didn't and that I could go to bed. It was peculiar that she had come home by herself, but I could hardly interrogate the lady of the house; if she didn't want to say anything about it, I would have to be content with permission to go to bed. And so I went to bed.

I was awakened once again by an obnoxious sound, something like the domestic equivalent of a police siren—the sound of the intercom we use to call each other. I glanced at the clock. It was three in the morning. What is it this time? I wondered nervously. Another disaster, no doubt.

"Yes?" I said into the telephone in as cheerful and energetic a voice as I could muster. The tireless Russian, ready for anything at any time of day or night. Superman.

Efimenkov's drunken voice answered. "Edik," he said, "come on down! We're sitting in the kitchen and we want to have a drink with you. Steven wants to," he corrected himself. "I told him about your book, and he's very interested. Come on down."

I lost my temper. "If the 'boss' wants me to, then I will," I said, "but if it's you, Zhenya, then we can drink tomorrow or any other time, but right now it happens to be three o'clock in the morning."

32

"He wants you to, and I do too," said the persistent Efimenkov, calmly swallowing my resentment.

Swearing softly, I pulled on a khaki T-shirt with an eagle and "U.S. Army" on it and my black "service" pants and went downstairs. The two of them were sitting in the kitchen by themselves and talking, Efimenkov with his elbows resting on the table.

"Zhenya tells me you've written a great book," Steven addressed me as I came in.

I merely smiled in answer; what could I say? The modest Limonov. But Gatsby wasn't waiting for an answer and continued.

"I asked Zhenya if he meant you had written a 'good book,' but he insisted on his knowledge of English and maintained that you had in fact written a great book."

"Steven, let's drink to his book," Efimenkov interrupted. "Let's drink some very good wine."

"I'll treat you to something special, Zhenya," Gatsby said, and went down the stairway leading from the kitchen to the basement and the wine cellar.

"I told him all about your book," Efimenkov informed me, leaning toward me in a wearily confidential way. "I wanted us all to have a drink together, and maybe you'll stop hating him and he'll understand you better."

Efimenkov's simple face glowed from all he had drunk, but he wasn't drunk, and at that moment he wasn't playing any games. I decided to trust him. Only I couldn't remember ever having told him that I hated Steven. I had of course mentioned it in my diary, which I usually left lying around the house, since nobody else knew Russian. How do I know, maybe the inquisitive Efimenkov, maybe the Soviet writer had taken a look at it.

Gatsby returned with a unique bottle of German white wine that, as the label attested, was not intended for sale but only for collectors. I got up to get the glasses. Gatsby had made an effort to get them himself, but I stopped him by saying, "Excuse me,

33

Steven, but I'm still the housekeeper here." The joke was appreciated.

Gatsby opened the bottle, and the wine really was excellent. We sat and drank. After a few swallows, Gatsby turned happily and guilelessly to his favorite theme, himself. He spoke rapidly and fitfully about how tired he was of his countless responsibilities and obligations, about how little sleep he got and how much he traveled. Efimenkov listened attentively and even eagerly, I thought.

It turned out that Gatsby had found someone to take over for him as Chairman of the Board of one of the largest of his corporations, based in California, so that things would be easier for him and he could spend more time in New York, which he loves. That was exactly what Linda and I had been most afraid of, that he would be staying here more and more often.

And then Gatsby started talking enthusiastically about an offer he had received the week before to buy a satellite, "my own satellite," he said happily, and about how little it would cost, since it had already been written off by the government. He mentioned the sum, which I immediately forgot; it was so remote as to be unreal. He was, it turned out, undecided as to whether he should buy it. In his enthusiasm he looked just like a child. "Satellite" on his lips sounded like the name of a new toy. As it very likely was.

It was difficult to stop Gatsby. From the satellite he jumped to his war with the Japanese in the area of computers, and then just as quickly he turned to the story of "his" film, which Efimenkov obviously knew nothing about.

Gatsby continued to pontificate, and I wondered why the hell I was sitting there, if he wasn't going to let me speak. Oh, I'm so sick of these aristocratic whims. Efimenkov is a pretty brash type, and when he had something to say, he spoke loudly and persistently, not in the least concerned about his wooden accent. After all, he had spent his whole life reciting to huge auditoriums full of masses of people.

A break came when Gatsby left to take a leak.

"He really is overworked, poor guy. He doesn't look well; his face has an unhealthy flush. He obviously needs to take a rest; he's working himself to death," Efimenkov said with admiring sympathy. "And you see how he talks," Efimenkov continued, sipping some wine. "He's evidently suffering from nervous exhaustion."

It was clear he was delighted with the energetic American capitalist. In my opinion, Gatsby didn't really do all that much. For all his apparent energy, he accomplished a great deal less than Efimenkov imagined. He spent more time on traveling from Connecticut to Colorado and Texas and to New York and back, and to the West Coast and Europe, and on lunches and dinners, each of which lasted two or three hours and was always accompanied by French wine, than he did on actual work or business. The unhealthy flush on Gatsby's face could have been explained by the French wine and the lunches, and at forty Gatsby did have a paunch hanging over his belt, not a large one, but a paunch nonetheless, as for that matter did Efimenkov, although in years past he had been as thin as a rail. I couldn't explain all that to Efimenkov in the short time the capitalist was in the toilet. I couldn't explain that Gatsby was not as effective as Efimenkov thought he was, that the auto manufacturing and the other businesses he owned might in fact have managed quite well without him, without all his bustling and his lunches and his dinners, and that perhaps Gatsby was more concerned with gratifying his own ego than he was with working. I decided to explain that to Efimenkov some other time, but I didn't have a chance, and then he went back to the Soviet Union.

I had guessed it long ago, but it was only after looking at them then that it became absolutely clear that Gatsby and Efimenkov belonged to the same class, to the masters of this world, even though one was a multimillionaire and the other a Communist writer; or, if you like, that they both belonged to the same international gang, to the big brothers of this world, its elite. Not long ago there had been a note in a New York magazine about my employer with the absolutely incredible title, "Today's Working Class," and under the title a picture of Steven in glasses with his tie slightly askew and an incisively intelligent expression on his face—the image presented by the magazine to America was the same one he had of himself. But it wasn't the way I saw him. For me, from my vantage in the kitchen, he was a spoiled, capricious nabob who, if his father and grandfather hadn't left him millions, would probably not have been able to make even one dollar on his own. I knew that when faced with the simplest tasks in life, he was as helpless as a child. I didn't believe Jenny the first time she told me that, but now I knew that a missing button could unnerve him and deprive him of his poise. He could borrow a million, or even millions—that was his specialty, obtaining money; he had friends, or a bank could lend it to him—but he didn't know how to sew on a button. Everything he knew how to do was based on his inheritance, on the thing that gave him his place in the world, but not on himself. True, sometimes he was interesting.

Efimenkov has always maintained in his books that he is a working-class blue blood, a man of simple Siberian stock, in a way even flaunting his simplicity and sincerity. It's a naïve lie that he himself believes. He left Siberia when he was still a boy, and he hasn't worked as a laborer more than six months in his whole life, since the magazines and newspapers started publishing him when he was sixteen, and by the time he was eighteen he was already a famous writer. From that day on he never again had anything in common with ordinary people and has lived the rest of his life as a writer, a very famous writer and a member of the elite. He was given pictures by Dali, Picasso, and Chagall, and the only working-class thing about him is his musical comedy working-class cap and his fine leather coat which cost money—Comrade Mr. Efimenkov, although in general he's not a bad guy. It's all the same kind of phoniness as Mao Tse-tung's, who wore a blue cotton working-class tunic his whole life, or

Deng Tsao-ping's, with their banquets and their residence in the former Imperial Palace.

Gatsby and Efimenkov understood each other perfectly and needed each other, while I sat thinking unhappily about how I'd like to be with them, but unfortunately could not. I'm thirty-five years old and have earned my living by physical labor ever since I was seventeen, so that their pseudo-working-class slogans are just crap to me. True, we all work, but the kind of work Mr. Gatsby does is very different from the black woman Olga's or mine. Well, so maybe Olga doesn't measure up to Gatsby, the wrong education, let's say, but if you compare Gatsby and me, then who's better, who's more talented, who's more needed by the world? For me, that's the fateful question, the one I ask myself every day as I struggle and contend with my employer and rival, even if he's a beast and a devil, albeit a charming devil, a product of contemporary civilization, a brilliant devil in a gorgeous car. Edward Limonov and Gatsby. Which one will triumph?

Chapter Two

I OFTEN WONDER, while sitting in a lawn chair on the roof of our house on weekends, getting tan in the sunshine, reading the newspaper, and sipping a cup of coffee, what would have happened to me, what direction my life would have taken, if I hadn't met Jenny and grabbed on to her with all my might. What would have happened, if, on that rainy spring evening of April 24th, 1977, I hadn't gone with the Russian drunk Tolya to the poetry reading at Queens College where I met Jenny— Jenny, who didn't understand a word of what the Russian poetess Stella Makhmudova was saying, but who was there thanks to a happy conjunction of circumstances. What would have happened? Would I have survived or not?

I don't know. Probably I would have survived without Jenny, although sometimes it seems to me I wouldn't have. Many thanks to Tolya the drunk for coming by the hotel and literally dragging me out of my room. I really didn't want to go way the hell out to Queens College, as I remember, and I complained about it the whole trip.

Finally, after interminable bus and subway changes, we reached that seat of culture, purchased our tickets, and went into the auditorium. As we were looking for empty seats a little closer to the stage, I suddenly heard someone calling to me, "Edik! Edik!"

Looking around, I saw Vadimov, who, according to all my calculations, should have been in Russia. I walked over. With Vadimov were the ballet superstar Lodyzhnikov and a girl. The girl was sitting on Lodyzhnikov's right. A girl in a knitted sweater. A large girl. That's about all I noticed. Also that she had rather full lips, commonly called sensual, and a large, ridiculous gap between her teeth. There was something funny about her. Probably Irish, I thought for some reason. I spoke with Vadimov and Lodyzhnikov, and listened as she asked Lodyzhnikov about something. I decided she was the latest of Lodyzhnikov's girlfriends. He had a lot, none of them lasting very long.

It turned out that Vadimov was Makhmudova's husband. Vadimov had been the husband of a number of famous or beautiful women in the Soviet Union. That was his second profession, or perhaps his first, if you like. He was also a stage designer—by birth, I think. And now they were visiting America. A degree was supposed to be conferred on the poetess in recognition of the fact that the American Academy of Arts and Letters had made her an honorary member. She was forty years old, and she started out every morning with a headache and a hangover. In her past were a great many amorous adventures, just like Vadimov; she had been married to or the mistress of many of Russia's most famous men—poets and writers. And now she was married to an artist.

The auditorium noisily hummed and rustled as it waited for Makhmudova's entrance. Whatever you may say about her, she was considered to be Russia's number one woman poet. Old Russian ladies, Russian clods and nincompoops, and losers like Tolya and me had all come to hear her. Also represented in great numbers was the Russian-Jewish cultural aristocracy, a sort of international elite which had not forgotten the Russian language, or so it thought. They sat in the front rows, of course. I spotted people from two or three influential New York magazines, several wealthy widows, and a man from Odessa whom the great poet Volodya Mayakovsky had once called "Little Entente," a name that "Little Entente" was very proud of. A cunning and pushy little fat man with red hair, the energetic "Little

Entente" had made a fortune during the NEP period in Russia and gotten even richer here. He could, it was said, make money out of thin air. Just how much he understood about poetry remained an open question, however, especially in view of the fact that his hearing was bad. Actually, those people had all come there not out of any real love for poetry but rather to demonstrate their affiliation with culture. It didn't matter if it was Russian culture or even something as remote from them as Chinese culture, as long as it was Culture. It's the fashion in the United States now to be cultured, to go to classical music concerts or to the opera or ballet, and they all go; they're all cultured. If some fanatical practice, say scourging rituals, were suddenly to become the rage, I have no doubt they would all abandon themselves to the practice along with all the other members of bourgeois society.

It's only thanks to those big and little ententes that, for example, someone like Lodyzhnikov can even exist, I thought to myself, looking at him out of the corner of my eye. His art is ballet, which is in fashion among the bourgeoisie now, among the fat cats, so he's a superstar and rakes it in hand over fist. As little as twenty years ago he would barely have been able to make a living dancing in America. Twenty years ago it wasn't fashionable to go to the ballet. How the bourgeoisie spent its evenings then, I couldn't say. Probably they went to Broadway musicals. I don't know. I don't like ballet. It's contemporary life I'm crazy about, and all those sleeping beauties so dear to the hearts of the ruling classes both here in the US of A and there in the U of SSR (and, really, why is that?) irritate me with their sugariness. Just look at the dancers' thighs. If ballet does have a place today, then in my opinion it's the same one the stereograph has—in the wing of a history museum.

The poetess finally made her entrance. Dressed entirely in black. Although not in a black dress, but in black velvet pants, black boots, and a black jacket that failed to conceal her rather ample bosom. Her style of reading has always seemed vulgar and saccharine to me. She belonged to the generation of stern and staunch young Soviet men and women (as they saw themselves), the generation that had dared to enter the fray against falsehood at the beginning of the sixties. These youths—her friends, husbands, and lovers—thought it was possible to play the role of poet "in between"—in between trips to Paris and sprees at the House of Littérateurs and writing prose and verse that gave the finger to the authorities, but on the sly. Their great example, the one they chose themselves, was Pasternak, a talented poet but a timid man, confused and servile, a country philosopher, a lover of fresh air, old books, and the easy life. I, who feel like vomiting whenever I see a library, despise Pasternak. Yes.

But let's return to the poetess and the stern youths. The stern, uncompromising youths, reading their stern poems about the evils of making a career, or suddenly kicking in print the long-dead bloodthirsty tyrant Stalin, or full of indignation that somebody is beating a woman, were greeted with cheers by readers no different from themselves. Brusquely adjusting their sport coats or nylon jackets and carelessly pushing back their hair with manly gestures, the poets hurled their cant at university auditoriums overflowing with nincompoops, and the auditoriums burst into applause. The poets of that generation had tremendous followings. And then they suddenly lost permission for a long time to make their customary trips to Paris, or their books were published in editions of only a hundred thousand copies, instead of five hundred thousand or a million. And when those awful things happened, the world community at once stood up for them.

The years had passed, but there she was, a stern young girl of that generation. She was reading a poem about the poetess Tsvetaeva, who had killed herself in the provincial town of Elabuga, who had hanged herself. Well, such are the current idols of the Russian intelligentsia—the timid coward Pasternak, and Mandelstam, who died next to a prison camp garbage can where he had been foraging for leftovers, Mandelstam driven mad with fear, and the hanged Tsvetaeva. If only one of them had been a wolf and had died shooting back, had died with a bullet in his brain, but at least after taking a couple of the bastards with him. I'm ashamed for Russian literature.

Makhmudova had come. She was reading poems that had been written fifteen years before. She had come. They had elected her to the Academy. But why, if she hadn't hanged herself? You can't elect a hanged poetess to the Academy. It isn't nice. But why didn't you hang yourself? I wondered. Something, I don't know what, but something should have happened to you. Why didn't it?

The rebellious stern youth, the "bad boys" of Russian literature as they are still called by others just as "rebellious," the liberal American critics, those rebellious youth were punished for their virtues by the Soviet authorities—punished with dachas, apartments, money, and large editions of their books. Accept your Academy election, stern girl. The stern boys, approaching fifty now, have worn out their pricks with rubbing, from sticking them in the eager twats of their countless young admirers. Even when I was a kid, I used to think lustful thoughts about Stella Makhmudova, Russia's number one poetical cunt.

God, the stuff she was reading! Long-dead verses that reeked of insincerity and posing. And of course there was something about Pasternak, too. Pasternak, that obliging fellow who had translated from every conceivable language a whole book of "Songs about Stalin," had obviously once made a very considerable impression on the young Makhmudova. That coward whose only slip-up had been a decision that it wasn't necessary to cower anymore, and who had therefore written and published abroad his sentimental masterpiece *Dr. Zhivago*, that hymn to the cowardice of the Russian intelligentsia. But he was

42

deceived; it was still necessary to cower. And it scared him to death.

Vadimov was whispering something to me in an apologetic tone about how only the older poetry of his wife had been translated. "She's writing some very good things now, unusual poems," he told me, leaning in my direction, although I hadn't said anything either about new poems or about old ones. Maybe my face betrayed my thoughts.

"Sure," I said, "poets always like the new things better."

It was just a meaningless phrase. Obviously I couldn't tell Vadimov what I really thought of his wife and her poetry. When it comes down to it, I always feel sorry for people, and I couldn't tell the stern young girl that she hasn't been a stern young girl for quite a while now, but is just a sad middle-aged broad with big tits. And a fat belly. I'm sure if you took off her skin-tight pants, you'd find red marks where they cut into her belly. That whole generation went terribly wrong somewhere, and none of them has left behind a bloody track from his wounds. Everything was superficial, not really serious, done merely for "points."

The girl sitting on Lodyzhnikov's right kept asking him about something from time to time. He answered her, but I couldn't hear what it was. Only later did Jenny tell me what they had been talking about. It turned out she had asked Lodyzhnikov after I turned up who "that person" was ("You seemed funny to me, Edward"), and Lodyzhnikov had answered, "Oh, just another Russian!" The bastard! He knew I was a long way from being just another Russian. He'd read my first novel in manuscript and hadn't been able to put it down, had even taken it with him to rehearsal to read during breaks. My novel had shocked and impressed him, just as it later impressed Efimenkov. But Efimenkov was more honest. Another Russian! Don't be ridiculous!

43

Lodyzhnikov is a snob. Money made him one. He mainly associates with rich old ladies from Park and Fifth Avenues and with celebrities like himself. He fled Russia a penniless youth, the same as we all were then, but now he has millions. I haven't counted his money, but I think for just going on stage he gets from four to seven thousand dollars. Imagine, for one appearance alone! There's something grotesquely unfair about that. Even if he dances better than anybody else in the world, why should he get so much? Isn't the fame enough? Isn't it enough that his picture's in all the world's newspapers and magazines? Seven thousand dollars for one evening! There are families that can't even earn that kind of money after a whole year of hard work.

I know many dancers who do a completely different kind of dancing, not classical but contemporary ballet. Since that art is vital, the bourgeoisie doesn't support it; it only likes what's moribund and innocuous, and those dancers therefore haven't got a penny. To see them, you have to go not to the Metropolitan Opera, but to dark little theaters with slanting ceilings and peeling walls somewhere way the hell off-off-Off-Broadway or on the Lower East Side, or some place like that.

No doubt Lodyzhnikov is a decent fellow. I don't believe he's a mean or bad person. But he doesn't give a shit about the rest of the world and its poverty. Lodyzhnikov takes an animal pleasure in his fame and money, every day becoming, in the company of his rich old ladies, more and more of a snob. He's acquiring their habits too. For example, he has three dogs and two cats. What does he, a man in his "early thirties" living by himself, need with a litter of dogs and cats?

Give the money to the poor, you bastard! I thought ironically as I watched him.

I know I'm jealous of him. And I'm not ashamed of it, because I have a right to be. I'm more talented than he is; I know that too, although it has been enormously difficult for me. He's lying to himself when he says I'm just another Russian. He has always singled me out from the others. That I'm sure of. He's even afraid to associate with me, as mutual friends have told me. "He'll put me in his next book," Lodyzhnikov said to them. Actually, I wouldn't "put him in," since he's not right for the hero of a book; he's an ordinary creature, even though a superstar. It's television and the newspapers that make all these celebrities so important, whereas in real life they're usually shy and uninteresting little nothings. It's rare to find a real human being among them.

After the poetess had finished reading, there was a party given in her honor by Queens College at which I drank a lot and out of boredom shared several joints with Vadimov, who desperately wanted to be contemporary and American. I wasted quite a few joints on Vadimov and some other bumpkins, in fact, and the poetess smoked a couple too, but Lodyzhnikov turned them down; he was looking out for his body. Some crazy old couple took me for Lodyzhnikov and asked for my autograph. I thought it was hilarious, but Lodyzhnikov didn't, for some reason.

I knew from experience that if I wanted to continue the evening's entertainment, and it was still pretty early, I'd have to be pushy about it. And that meant I'd have to invite myself along with the rest of the company to supper or wherever else they were going. And so, like an experienced outsider, I attached myself to Vadimov and resolved not to let him out of my sight. I followed him everywhere until I was sure he wasn't trying to get rid of me and would take me wherever he was going. It turned out that the girl (Jenny) who had been sitting with Lodyzhnikov and Vadimov had already left, had gone home to the house where Makhmudova and her husband, Vadimov, were staying, and where they were all going to have supper. I wanted to have supper too, and so I took the bull by the horns and said I would go in the same car with them, justifying my persistence with a few mumbled words about my feeling for Vadimov and the poetess. It was a lie. I just didn't want to go

45

back to my hotel on Broadway and the filth and the stench and the loneliness.

Finally, after we had succeeded in wresting the poetess from her crowd of Russian and non-Russian admirers, we squeezed ourselves into Professor Barth's car, the same Jon Barth who would later escort Efimenkov and who in such situations was always on the very best of terms with Soviet writers—their guide and friend. "We" in this case meant Lodyzhnikov, Makhmudova, Vadimov, and I. The car set off down the road, while Makhmudova's admirers gaped and waved.

The professor's car happily chewed up the miles, and then, after about a half hour's drive, we came to a halt, emerging into the darkness and entering an open door, and thus began what was to be perhaps one of the most important events of my life. I found myself in the multimillionaire's little house, as I would call it later. Entering, of course, I didn't have the least suspicion that my subsequent fate would be tied up for several years with that house and its inhabitants or that I would live there. No, I didn't sense anything of the sort. It was dark, and I was stoned and drunk; after all, you've got to cheer yourself up a bit in this world to keep from drifting away out of depression and boredom.

I brutally abandoned Tolya the drunk that evening, although it was in fact he who had gotten me started on that journey in the first place. There was only one place left in the car—for me. "Bolivar can't carry two." Having played his part as an instrument of fate, he vanishes from the stage. Forgive me, Tolya.

The first thing I saw was the kitchen. Wide, like a dance hall. With a huge gas stove, as in a restaurant. With a thousand components, appliances, jars, boxes, counters, and shelves. It's difficult now to say whether I noticed all that abundance then, or whether it was simply the kitchen's sheer scale that impressed me; after all, I was stoned. And then I saw the dining room where the young girl Jenny, getting tangled in her long skirt, was preparing an American-style supper—putting out plates and knives and forks and numerous other things whose function was beyond me.

The poetess, out of Russian generosity (something that has always seemed suspect to me, even though I'm a Russian myself; it's more a lack of character than generosity), had invited some thirty people to dinner, which naturally shocked Jenny, although she had the good manners not to say anything about it. Several people helped her add a leaf to the table, which though large, still wasn't big enough for all that fraternity.

Above the table hung a spiral chandelier made of dark copper and no doubt very old, an elaborate structure of tubes and lamps that looked like the coiffure of a seventeenth century lady of fashion or a hat from a picture by Picasso. On one wall stood a high, open buffet with plates and dishes standing on end and painted with fishes, the various fishes of freshwater America, obviously. Depicted on the largest of them was an enormous pike. On another wall of the dining room stood a small old cupboard, and above it hung a painting, old too, with its surface even cracked in places, depicting a plenitude of different foods, from meat to fruit. A third wall was covered from end to end with the wooden lattices of windows and a doorway opening out onto the garden of the millionaire's house. Imagine, a garden!

It was all the more impressive for me, since at the time I was residing at a dirt-cheap hotel on Broadway in the nineties, a place where fires burned. That same April several rooms near mine on the tenth floor had been completely gutted, and I remember running down the hall with a suitcase containing my manuscripts under one arm and my white suit dangling from the other. Just think—after a hotel where the drunks urinated in the elevator and where they vomited too, where the stench of urine and excrement was never aired out of the filthy rugs, where it seemed that the inhabitants never slept and where at four o'clock in the morning they were still swearing at each other from window to window across the squalid courtyard, where

47

trash and empty bottles were simply chucked out of the windows, and where the police visited every day; after a hotel like that, you suddenly find yourself in a house with a garden. And a garden, as you later discover, that faces the river. That faces the river directly, and what could be more natural than that? And in the garden are trees and birds—as if you weren't in New York at all. And among the other houses facing the garden stands one that a couple of years before had belonged to Onassis, and next door is another that belongs, you are told, to a woman everybody calls "Mrs. Five Hundred Million." And among all those houses, Jenny's is by no means the worst, but one of the best.

At the time, obviously because we were keeping her from setting the table, Jenny had the door to the garden open, and I walked out into it with Lodyzhnikov and Vadimov and nearly went out of my mind from the fragrance of April grass recently and abundantly watered by the spring rain, and from the leadenly turbid East River with its whirlpools made by the huge ship or, more likely, barge that was floating silently and ominously by while Vadimov told me about some mutual Moscow acquaintances who, unfortunately, didn't interest me in the least, and Lodyzhnikov disdainfully interjected something in that skeptical way typical of people who are very successful but shy. I didn't hear a goddamn thing they were saying. Not far off the lights of a huge bridge shone like a Christmas tree, and on the other side of the river the cars were moving quietly and enigmatically along narrow little roads, while above a full moon had come out in the suddenly clearing sky. An immense tree in the center of the garden was still dripping with rain when we went back inside the house. It was a life so different that it seemed like another planet. I had sobered up.

Of that whole evening and of the "Russian party," as Jenny and I would later call it, I remember only the insane crush and the faces of a great many people who remained nameless, then as now. I remember too that I was very excited. After living for years in crappy, shit-smelling hotels, I was excited by the light and the talk and the food, although I was too excited to eat. Besides "Jenny's House" (one and the same for me then), there was yet another reason for my excitement. If only for an evening, I was again able to be what I am—a poet and writer. And although I valued only two or three people in that whole crowd, I was still myself again, and not that denizen of the benches of Central Park, that sullen, lonely Broadway transient with a knife in his boot who patronized pornographic movie theaters, that failure and half-dumb person who barely understood English. And so I was grateful to that crowd.

I remember that I helped Jenny clear the table afterwards, and I remember that I sat to her right (she was at the head of the table) and that I tried to talk to her, and that she gladly responded to me with amused curiosity. And I remember too that her front teeth with the large gap between them prompted a feeling of tenderness in me. I asked Vadimov, who sat next to me, where Jenny's parents were, why they were absent. "She lives here by herself," Vadimov answered curtly; he was talking to a beautiful woman sitting across from him, and I had distracted him. I had learned something about Jenny from my conversation with her, that her grandmother was a Pole, for example, but my impression of her, thanks to my rudimentary and slipshod knowledge of English, the alcohol (I had had more to drink), and the joints (I had more than enough of them that evening), was rather impressionistic and intuitive, although even in a normal state I'm more intuitive than reflective. And I sensed intuitively that it was very good for me there, and that I wasn't going to leave that house and its strange new life that day, that I shouldn't leave it, whatever the cost.

Jenny's girlfriend Jennifer, a somewhat heavy, pug-nosed brunette, sat across the table from me. She was dressed in dark, wide pants and something embroidered with tassels, and something else that was dark and shawl-like, as a result of which I concluded she was from Turkey. Jennifer smiled at me the whole time, probably because I was comical, a drunk and stoned

49

Russian, but I noticed that evening that they, that is, Jenny and Jennifer, gradually began to take me more seriously, perhaps because I was interested in them, and talked to them instead of to the Russians, and moreover helped them clear the table.

There were only two characters, Jenny and me, in the evening's concluding scene, which took place in the kitchen. I found a last joint in my pocket, to which Jenny reacted with unaffected pleasure. When I told her I had had dozens of them before that and had smoked them with the Russians, she was even a bit miffed. "Why didn't you give some to me?" she asked. I told her apologetically that I didn't understand myself how it had happened that she wasn't there when I was smoking the joints and passing them out, but that I wasn't being greedy; I just hadn't realized she smoked grass. Jenny informed me she had been smoking it for eleven years and answered my excuses with feigned severity. I could tell she was just kidding me; my English was so awful it made me look ridiculous. We smoked the joint.

There's a lot of the *muzhik* in me, and when I'm stoned it slips out into the light of day in all its abundance and often its vulgarity. I started grabbing her, and after stroking her hair I moved on to her arms and breasts, and then I started kissing her neck, and even though she laughingly pushed me away, it was obvious and understandable that our love play was not unpleasant for her, and it continued. She wouldn't let me put my hand very far under her dress, but she did let me stroke her large and beautiful legs and kiss her. I realized later that Jenny was perhaps an inch taller than I was, and when she wore high heels, she towered over me, but I still liked her to wear them—she looked imposing and a little ridiculous, with her soft round ass swinging back and forth and her long arms and legs that made her look like a woman in a Mannerist painting.

I don't know how long our love games continued, but laughing and looking me in the eye, she suddenly said, "I know what you want. You want to stay here and fuck me."

I'll admit I never expected such a declaration from a girl I barely knew, but delighted by her candor, I boldly and shamelessly announced that yes, I did want to, and that for all she knew maybe I loved her. Jenny said she could hardly believe that I loved her, since I didn't know her at all, but as to my wanting to fuck her—that she could believe, but it was already very late and she had to get up early and go to the airport the next morning. She was leaving New York for two weeks.

I certainly didn't want to leave. And I went on grabbing her the same way the peasants (to continue the art comparisons) grab their wives in Dutch paintings—just the way it probably ought to be between a man and a woman, once you get past the well-bred grimacing and prancing that civilization requires of us. Which is why I like marijuana. It doesn't increase my sexual potential, but it does take away my veneer of education and good manners, so that there's nothing left but a naked Russian lad.

We fooled around like that for a while, and she particularly liked it when I stroked her hair, or her head, if you like. But she continued insisting that I go home—it was already three in the morning, and the poetess and Vadimov were already sound asleep somewhere upstairs. I didn't want to go and quietly resisted, becoming alarmed only when she threatened to call the police.

"I'm calling the police," she said, and went to the telephone in the kitchen corner.

"The police don't scare me," I said.

"Then I'll tell them you tried to rape me," she announced with a giggle and, wiggling her ass, started dialing the number.

She actually could be calling the damn police, I thought.

"OK, I'm going, I'm leaving, but give me your phone number and maybe I'll give you a call when you get back and we can get together?"

"Fine, fine," she said, obviously genuinely tired and anxious to go to bed. And after writing her number down on a piece of yellow paper, she gave it to me.

"Or maybe I should stay?" I said, twirling my umbrella in the doorway.

"I really am going to call the police," she said, getting angry and moving towards the phone.

"I'm leaving, I'm leaving," I hastily agreed, and then after adding uncertainly, "I'll see you," I shut the door behind me.

That night in the elevator at my hotel a well-dressed *souteneur,* or pimp, as the locals say, tried to talk me into coming to him whenever I needed a girl or drugs. "If you're ready to spend twenty dollars, drop by; I have very nice girls—at any time of night. I'm in 532." Although the pimp was fancily dressed and I myself was wearing a velvet jacket, both of us were on welfare, and the elevator had just been used to take the garbage from the top floors downstairs to the basement and stank from the reddish slop that had seeped into the depressions of its old floor.

And now I'll tell you something that will probably make you despise me—my relationship with Jenny began as the result of a colossal mistake on my part. Unable to distinguish among the different faces and types found in the land of America, I took the housekeeper Jenny for the mistress, for the owner. I decided she was the mistress of the millionaire's house, and living there by herself, a wealthy heiress, while her parents were traveling abroad or residing somewhere deep in the American continent, eccentrically preferring the prairies of Texas or the mountains of Colorado to that little garden on the East River. I wanted, I'll admit, to worm my way into the house, of course I wanted to, and the thought of eventually marrying that rich girl also crossed my mind—to such things are we humiliated paupers driven by the circumstances of our lives. It was with that delusion that I called her from a phone booth one rainy day in May, and to my surprise, she invited me over. I had been sure she wouldn't want to see me.

Ah, dear Jenny, maybe you had your own reasons for taking in an unemployed foreign poet fifteen years your senior. Maybe you were satisfying your own inferiority complex, the complex of a housekeeper, by taking a poet for one of your lovers, even if he was a Russian poet.

But even if that's true, what difference does it make. The fact remains that you provided me with food and drink and gave me your body at a most difficult time in my life, and that that was enough to quiet and confound my proud soul, my proud and bitter soul, and to make me think, even with a kind of disappointment, that here was Jenny who for some reason didn't act like other people, who didn't keep it all for herself, but shared with others.

Yes, it all began with a mistake. Vadimov obviously didn't have any idea himself in the beginning who Jenny was—his English wasn't any better than mine—and when he did realize, it was too late to tell me; he had already gone back to Russia. I remember that Jenny mentioned Steven's name a lot in the first days of our acquaintance, although not long ago I found in my diary the following entry for that time: "Jenny's busy today, the little bitch; she has company, the sister of her music teacher Steven, or whoever the fuck he is." You can imagine how approximate my knowledge of English was if I took Steven for a music teacher. He was in fact the one who commissioned music! My guess now is that Jenny had obviously used the word "master" in the sense of "boss," and I had taken it to mean "teacher." Idiot! I called her a "little bitch" because I still didn't trust her. I didn't trust anybody then, nor do I now. There was only one person I ever had any faith in, and that was Jenny.

53

I showed up at her place after work. I had gotten a job for a few days painting the wall of an office on 42nd Street a disgusting yellow color. I remember that I walked along happily, almost rejoicing from awareness that I was on my way to the house of a rich girl and that she wanted to see me.

Jenny, clean, calm, contented, was sitting in the "solarium," although I didn't know then that that was what it was called. She was listening to music, calm, well-fed, old music, Vivaldi perhaps. She sat me down across from her on another green sofa with only a transparent plastic table between us, and we started talking. Or rather she asked me about my life, and I, getting confused and embarrassed, tried both to speak coherent English and somehow to make myself more interesting. I made up a lot of lies about myself, some of which I was able to put right later by referring to my then poor knowledge of the language, while others have remained uncorrected to this day, but I was, as I recall, very afraid that she would think I wasn't worth the effort and wouldn't want to see me anymore. In my pocket I had seventy-five dollars I had borrowed specifically for the occasion, and I involuntarily kept checking it, I think.

What did I talk to her about? I suddenly realized that in spite of myself, I wanted to make her feel sorry for me, and I remember that in telling her about my life, I mentioned my second wife, Anna, who had gone crazy, and my last wife, Elena, who had left me here because I didn't have any money. "Because of money" made an impression on Jenny; she even started blinking very fast and angrily muttered, "The bitch!" Inspired, and sensing in my bones that there wasn't very much time left and that if I didn't succeed in getting her interested in the next hour or so, I probably wouldn't have another chance like that again in my life, I informed her with fateful resolve that no one had ever loved me in my whole life, that my mother hadn't lived with me, but had left my father and me when I was only two, and that I had lived among soldiers until I was fifteen and had been raised by them. I sat there and told inspired lies about myself while looking out into the garden, where it was green and deserted and where a child's swing was swaying slowly and temptingly in the breeze. It's a good thing my super-decent mama couldn't hear, my mother who in almost forty years of living with my father had probably spent not even a single evening outside the house. Forgive me, Mama, but you wouldn't have wanted your son to perish, would you?

Mechanically staring into the garden, I clumsily struggled to pronounce the difficult English words, hurrying and stumbling over them, and wishing I had a glass of wine, some vodka, a joint—anything that would have relaxed me and helped me to make up even more and better stories. Watching her face, I had the sense that it wasn't working, that I was boring her, since she had grown very quiet and thoughtful, and was sitting there without moving, leaning back on the green sofa and lightly pulling with one hand at the strands of her chestnut hair parted on the side, her carefully washed chestnut hair. And she was moving her foot a little too—she was barefoot, and why not, with such soft carpets and such brilliantly polished parquet. I thought it wasn't working, but I was in fact saying then the full one hundred percent of what she needed to hear, she, Jenny Jackson, an American girl with English, Irish, and Polish blood in her veins. The point is, gentlemen, that she was unbelievably soft-hearted. But I only found that out later. I didn't know it then, and that's why those first hours with her have remained so painful a memory.

I blurted out all those admissions and then was suddenly quiet, physically aware, sensing it instinctively, that the sky in the garden was turning a dark blue. There was so much sky in her garden. And it was turning a dark blue and then graying and darkening.

Jenny sat half-turned toward me, wearing that evening the dress that I came to prefer over all her others, a dress with a little hood and narrow, very narrow gray-black stripes, a wide skirt that reached down below her knees, and a tight-fitting bodice—very pretty. She sat half-turned toward me and said nothing. Then suddenly she whispered, "Poor thing!" and faced me. A tear was rolling down her cheek.

Success! During the pause I had managed to conceive a hatred both for her mansion and for her "rich and idle" person, and in the infinite despair of my thoughts in that moment had already consigned the house and the garden to wholesale pillage, filling the place with my mythical comrades-in-revolution—I could already hear their footsteps and voices and the clank of their weapons.

"Poor thing." Even though I had lied about some things, it still referred to me. But wasn't I a "poor thing" in fact? I was. That meant she understood, that meant she was a human being, however unexpected and strange that was.

But poor Edward wasn't able to rejoice in his victory; he was too exhausted from an effort that had exceeded his strength. I remember dropping my arms to my knees and staring at the green rug, never imagining that more than once in the future I would have to vacuum it and even from time to time fuck members of the opposite sex on it when I was too impatient to go to my room. . . . And not long ago I happened to find on that same green rug the clothing, watches, bracelets, rings, and undergarments of a certain lady and my boss, Steven Grey, but not the owners themselves. . . . That all happened much later, however. On that May evening, as we were sitting there, the tear still rolling down Jenny's cheek, the doorbell rang, or rather it chimed, and sniffing like a baby, she said, "That's my sister," and went to open the door.

Sister Debby had brought a saxophone with her; she played the saxophone, as it turned out—little sister Debby, that is. The saxophone was placed on its legs there in the solarium next to a barrel organ and a music box—in the music corner. Sister Debby didn't resemble sister Jenny at all. She was very slender, with short black hair and olive skin, and thanks to her gaudily painted lips and eyes, she looked like a hoodlum and older than her seventeen years. Sister Debby had come up from Virginia, where the whole family lived, as it turned out—the first reliable information I got then. It also turned out that besides Debby, Jenny had three other sisters and five brothers.

"God," I said. "You're like Latin Americans; they're the ones who're supposed to have such big families."

"Ten children is really good," Jenny said. "You have somebody to play with when you're little and somebody to share your troubles with. An only child is always unhappy and lonely. You left Russia, Edward, and now your parents are all by themselves." Saying this, Jenny looked at me significantly and then continued. "If they had had more children, they wouldn't be so lonely now." Jenny was very sensible, it turned out.

That evening the three of us went out together. "Let's go somewhere for a drink," Jenny said carelessly. "Debby's tired of Virginia; she wants to go out."

"Of course, let's go out," I said, although inwardly I was terrified about what I would do if I didn't have enough money. But it was impossible to refuse, even though I would gladly have bought a bottle and drunk it there at home; that's what I always did.

And so we went out. The slender and insolently vulgar Debby put on a gray poncho, and I had on a checked jacket that the above-mentioned Tolya had once given me for nothing and that I had shortened and taken in, and a black cap from Paris I was very proud of that still had the label "Enchanted Hunter" in it. I had bought it for $1.25 at a used clothing store on the Lower East Side. Over her pretty little dress Jenny wore a long knitted cardigan with little knitted balls dangling from strings.

Once outside I took Jenny by the hand, and she walked along obediently without removing her hand, although she was in fact leading the way, not I. As a resident of the Upper West Side, I didn't know very much about their wealthy East. After we had looked into several small restaurants, our attention was drawn, I remember, to a crowded out-of-the-way place paneled in old wood where, however, a famous old harpist performed. We took our seats next to the stage, from which the harpist, who had a good figure but also the look of an outright lesbian and sadist, gazed amiably at the sisters from time to time. It was then that I learned of the existence of the drink called "tequila sunrise," which the sisters ordered, while I drank my customary J & B, a habit I'll probably keep until the end of my days. You have to have something to fall back on when people say, "What will you have?" and you're supposed to have a favorite drink. Well, I drink J & B.

Naturally the harpist started talking to the girls during the intermission, while a lanky, though suspiciously cultivated and considerate waiter addressed a few silly remarks to me I don't remember anymore. We eventually drank a fair amount there, and after Jenny and I had sufficiently stroked and squeezed each other's hands, and nudged each other with our knees under the table, and exchanged other displays of affection of the sort that are appropriate in public places, and the harpist had started to cover her harp with its case, Debby announced that it was time to leave, as indeed it was, and we tumbled out onto the street. I had enough money; the sisters didn't want to eat, thank God— or thanks to them, since maybe they just pretended not to.

For some reason we all laughed a lot on the way home, and Jenny ran away from me down the street, her cardigan flying behind her, and when I caught her, the little knitted balls on the strings were all rapidly swinging. I tried to kiss her, but she moved away from me, yelling something about Russians and how shameless her Polish grandmother said they all were, but she didn't move away very far. Debby, who was following behind, smiled a grown-up smile at all the commotion we were making.

After we got back to the house, Debby immediately went off to bed, while I sat with Jenny for another hour or so, kissing her again and putting my hands under her dress and taking hold of her legs, her belly, and her panties. . . .

She wouldn't let me. She wouldn't give in. I wasn't very insistent. I realized with Jenny it was better not to hurry; it would all happen in time. Of course, I would have preferred to fuck her then—I really wanted to—but I was afraid of pressuring her even a little; she might get scared and not want to see me anymore. But I left in excellent spirits, happy and exhilarated—the adventurer after a successfully concluded operation.

I called her the next day. Not too early, though I woke up very early myself and wanted to call her at once. I didn't have anything else to do anyway. My sole occupation then was to get up at eight after sleeping badly, collect my things—books and notebooks—in a plastic bag, and set off for Central Park to lie in the sun and read, given the fact that the park was only a few short blocks away. Lying there on the grass in my underpants among people as unlucky or crazy as I was, I tortured myself with books, teaching and coaching myself by reading my first English books with a dictionary. The selection was very strange: *The Philosophy of Andy Warhol*, which had just come out in paperback, and a book with a green cover by Che Guevara called *Episodes of the Revolutionary War*, which I'd swiped from somebody. I still have those books, and when I leaf through them on occasion, I unfailingly find tufts of dried grass between the pages, since I didn't lie quietly but turned over, presenting first my chest to the sun and then my back, while dreaming of my future, of my brave and glorious future, and of the ways I might bring it about.

I had been lying in Central Park since March and the loneliness was beginning to make me a little crazy. I usually went back to my hotel around five or six and cooked dinner on a hotplate—something quick, macaroni with hot dogs or chicken soup—and then after eating it, and maybe a brief nap, I rolled out onto the streets again.

As you see, it was a bleak and soldierly life, and its diversions were pretty much reduced to grass, which I regularly bought then for thirty-five dollars an ounce, obtaining another portion as soon as I'd smoked up the first, and one-night stands, which usually took place in a state of extreme intoxication from grass and alcohol.

I didn't attach much importance to the one-night stands, my drunken imagination easily endowing my partners with their merit, although as a rule not one of them survived the test of morning, or turned out in the light of day to be of any value to my life. But in the period I'm describing here, even those affairs had virtually ceased. The longest to hold out was Rena, an extremely ugly but incredibly horny middle-aged Rumanian Jew who lived near the Museum of Natural History and who taught ballet, I believe. I would always remember her unexpectedly somewhere on the street in the middle of the night, call her up, go over to her place, walk in, and start fucking her right in the doorway. I would simply step over the threshold, lift up her skirt, and, since her cunt was always moist and ready, brutally fuck her.

It was necessary to end that illicit affair, however, since she had unfortunately fallen in love with me. I was beginning to catch adoring looks in my direction, and I realized I'd better get out before it was too late. Vile aesthete and conceited animal that I was, aspiring to the best women in the world, how could I allow myself to go out with an ugly little hawk-nosed Rumanian Jew? Even granting that she was much better, more noble, and more spiritual than I, as in fact was probably the case, I still preferred in that time of extreme need to suffer without a cunt rather than suffer from an inferiority complex at showing myself in broad daylight with Rena. The last straw was her obsessive desire to meet Lodyzhnikov after I had carelessly let slip that I knew him.

So you can imagine how great was my need for Jenny. She of course had no idea of the role I had prepared for her, that I expected her to be my woman, my friend, my language teacher, and to support me, and that I had also decided to move in with her in time, since I still didn't realize, dolt, who she was.

But when I finally called on that May morning, having as a precaution first turned myself for three hours or so on the grass in Central Park, she told me to my surprise that she was busy and that we couldn't see each other. The "music teacher" Steven's sister from California was staying at the millionaire's house at the time. Imagine how disappointed I was. Who wouldn't have been? *An annoying obstacle on my way to the top*. I was in a hurry; I needed to prove to *everybody* just what sort of person it was they were neglecting. The rich Jenny and her house were substantial evidence.

She has guests, I thought bitterly. The cunt. As if there were anybody more important to her than me. Guests. I would have gone over and joined her guests, but Jenny didn't invite me. Maybe she's afraid to be alone with me. She wants to but is afraid; that happens sometimes, I reflected.

I went back to my hotel earlier than usual that day. I didn't feel much like reading. A black neighbor from my floor named Ken was sitting on a bench with a group of alcoholic friends, all black, in the dusty strip of greenery that separates the two opposing streams of Broadway traffic and drinking something. When he saw me, he jumped happily to his feet and shouted "Baby!" and beckoned to me. But I didn't go; I only waved to him from a distance and strode into the hotel's stinking maw.

It was probably a week before I saw Jenny again. She responded to my calls by saying that she was busy since Steven's sister was still there, and that she didn't feel well. I suspiciously thought she wasn't telling the truth, and lay in my hotel. Going to the park would have been silly anyway; the muggy spring rains had started. Even the sheets were unpleasantly damp, and I lay naked on the bed and gave myself up to despair, as only I, the psychopath Edward Limonov, am capable of doing. I even started crying. And from idleness, I also had a tremendous desire to fuck, and a dull feeling in my head. I even remember once howling quietly and mournfully for a whole evening, while I tossed and turned in bed and recalled Jenny's large legs, her long neck, her soft breasts, and her rather fat belly, which I had held in my hands. But I couldn't allow myself to masturbate; I don't know exactly why, but I couldn't. It was as if I felt some obligation to Jenny or to myself. I wanted to be a man, and not a pitiful masturbator.

Finally after the week had passed, Jenny called me herself. We had been talking about ten minutes, when she suddenly surprised me by saying, "Edward, I want to say something important to you."

Put on my guard, I answered, "Yes, of course, Jenny. What is it?"

"I have to tell you, Edward, that you're a very good, very educated, and very sensitive person, but I haven't 'fallen in love' with you." She was silent for a moment. I was silent too. "I like you," she resumed, "but I'm selfish. Very selfish. Very. If you want to be my friend, that's fine. But not love."

I had the presence of mind to agree with her. I said: "All right, we'll be friends. Can I come over in half an hour? We'll have a drink."

"Come over," she consented. "I have some company, Debby and her boyfriend, and some girlfriends of mine, if they won't bother you."

"No, they won't bother me," I said.

I left the hotel and set off through Central Park to the East Side, bitterly thinking to myself about her and about me and about how I would obviously never have any luck in life and about how foolish it was of her to reject me. Central Park after the week's rain was deserted, luxuriant, utterly beautiful, fresh-smelling, and without end, the way it is in May. It had just stopped raining, and I walked through that verdant paradise completely alone with the trees and plants; New York's tireless bicyclists still hadn't come out, nor had the drug pushers taken up their usual places.

By the time I emerged from the park on the East Side, I had already calmed down. Well, all right, what does it matter? I thought brightly. I'll find another way out, I'll still climb out of this shit. I'll still find a way out of it, even if Jenny won't be my springboard. There'll be other chances. Cheer up, Officer Limonov, I told myself, and even walked more energetically, firmly striking my heels on the pavement. Ah, what a fool Jenny is not to want to try somebody as unique as me.

Thus I walked along reasoning to myself, and when I had almost gotten to her house, I suddenly thought, Listen, Limonov, she's only twenty years old. Don't take what she says too seriously. Let her say whatever she wants to, and you try to change it. Have you actually forgotten Catullus? Remember the lines, "What a woman says to her ardent lover/should be written in wind and running water. . . ." That's exactly the sort of thing she said over the phone to you, and you came unglued.

Catullus cheered me up immediately, and when Jenny opened the door dressed in a belly dancer's costume—in a bra embroidered in bugles and shiny thread that had originally been made for Debby, as I later found out, and in very wide Moslem pants set low on her hips, I said, "Hi, Jen," and merrily kissed her. She looked suspiciously at me, sniffed my breath, and asked, "Have you been drinking, Edward?" I said I hadn't.

They were all sitting out on the terrace in the garden when the officer Limonov came in. Besides Debby and her Japanese boyfriend, Michael, there was a tall, slim Irish girl named Bridget, with auburn hair, as befits Irish girls, and unbelievably fair skin, as also befits Irish girls. After answering my "Hi" with her own, the first thing Bridget asked me was, "Do you have any grass?" I didn't have any with me; I knew Jenny had just given it up. She was allegedly suffering from back pain which she attributed to smoking marijuana since she was eleven. It wasn't her idea; she'd gotten it from her Indian homeopath, Dr.

Krishna. And maybe the doctor was right. During the period in question Jenny was fascinated with homeopathy and went to Dr. Krishna regularly not only as his patient but as his disciple.

I later calculated that Jenny changed enthusiasms about every six months. During the year and a half we were together, homeopathy was replaced by jogging—onward to health!—and jogging by the health food fad. Jenny, like tens of millions of other Americans, took up whatever was foisted on her by America's popular culture and its advertising machinery, eagerly exchanging enthusiasms as the popular culture dictated and, like every other victim, readily believing that they were her own. The roller skating epidemic fortunately took over the United States after we had split up, or I would certainly have been in on her smashed knees and broken arms.

I had to disappoint Bridget; I didn't have any grass. She kept her head, however, and very quickly got drunk.

When I arrived they were engaged in sporadic searching for the little bronze finger cymbals used in belly dancing. Jenny called them "zilts," or something. She had put her costume on and was all set to start dancing—the stereo was already scattering clouds of Middle Eastern music through the house—when the cymbals had suddenly disappeared and there wasn't anything to mark the rhythm with. Jenny got mad and started whining, while the rest of us looked in the drawers and moved the books on the shelves and finally found them, thank God.

Jenny danced several numbers, first wrapping herself up in a piece of Indian cloth I assume Dr. Krishna had given her, then unwrapping herself. I suspected then that the handsome, graying, seventy-two-year-old Dr. Krishna was sleeping with her, but he wasn't. I wasn't very far from the truth, however. Although Krishna wasn't sleeping with Jenny, he was sleeping with another of his patients and disciples, with that same girlfriend of Jenny's I had met on my first evening in the millionaire's house—with Jennifer. And she was only nineteen.

We know these doctors, I thought. Covered with the unearned glory of the hermits and gurus of old India, they come to the United States and put together whole fortunes, the swindlers, by relying on the naïveté of young Americans and their natural attraction to everything astonishing and unusual. At the same time, they don't forget to fuck the prettier and younger of their admirers and disciples, if such be at hand.

Jenny wrapped herself up in the cloth and then unwrapped herself, but I never did find out whether Krishna had given it to her. She danced very well, I thought; she had just the fat belly needed for that Arabo-Turko-Persian show. It moved exactly the way it was supposed to, twitching like a jackhammer. I tried it later on, but I couldn't do it; that kind of automatic abruptness of movement is possible only after years of training, and then only if you have the gift.

I only thought Jenny was a bit big for belly dancing. Those Eastern women with their fat bottoms and bellies who regale the eyes of Eastern men immediately after the hot mutton has been devoured are small, intentionally small. Jenny would probably seem awkward and clumsy to some Eastern men. Her other shortcoming was her chestnut hair. A belly dancer's hair should be jet black, as should her cunt hair. I noticed long ago, by the way, that cunts with black hair are always red, that is, of vivid hue. The cunts of blondes, on the other hand, are paler in color, pastel, so to speak. The black-haired cunt should be more appealing to Eastern men; it's red like the mutton they've just eaten.

But it's quite possible I'm wrong, very possible in fact, since Jenny was even invited to dance nightly at The Oasis, an expensive Middle Eastern restaurant where you can watch women's fat bellies gyrating while you're eating your dinner. That means her dancer's art was worth something. It often happened later that when Jenny lost her temper with Steven the "music teacher," she would threaten to quit her job and go to The Oasis, where she could make lots of money. "A lot of money, every night!" she would say angrily. "I'll manage!" she would add with conviction. I too thought she'd manage. She had worked as a babysitter for about ten years and was already out on her own when she was sixteen.

Everything was proper enough in the beginning, but then we all got drunk. There was as much wine as you could want, and "hard drinks" too, as in the best liquor store.

Jenny had apparently forgotten all about our phone conversation, or else her expressed desire to remain just friends had been only a passing whim or was perhaps merely her way of flirting.

The whole party stayed over at Jenny's, and I remember her sleepy voice as she assigned everybody a place in the house. By one o'clock, they had all gone off to their various floors. Jenny didn't put me to bed, however, although I do recall that as I returned from her house to humid New York, I was smiling and sure of my future.

We started seeing each other almost every day. In the evening I would come to the millionaire's house and usually we would sit in the kitchen or in the solarium and talk quietly, telling each other the stories of our lives and getting to know each other. Sometimes I would even buy Jenny roses, and once I brought as a gift an English translation of a very beautiful poem of mine. It began with the words, "As if a silent branch had traced a line/ And in memory gently bended down,/ A southern alpine glade with rooted tree,/ like the steps of someone dear in water. . . ."

Even though I had written the poem five years before my arrival in the millionaire's garden, it for some reason seemed to me that with my poet's vision I had seen not only the garden, which really did look like a southern alpine glade with a huge tree in the center from which a swing was suspended, but also the leather chairs in Steven's office and many other details besides.

Jenny didn't seem to pay attention to the poem then; she skimmed through it and put it aside, and I had already decided she was indifferent to art, which offended me a little, but very late that night she called me at my hotel after I had gone to bed and asked me to recite my poems to her. I explained that the poem I'd given her was the only one that had been translated into English, but unperturbed she answered: "It doesn't matter. Read them in Russian, Edward."

The funny part is that she liked it. She listened over and over for half an hour at a time without understanding a single word, and after that she would call me up in the middle of the night and ask me to recite to her.

Sometimes when she was barely awake.

But we didn't sleep together or make love. Often we would lie on the grass in the garden for hours after dark, hardly speaking, but caressing each other like infatuated adolescents. Then, in the summer of 1977, I thought that there were times when I was in love with her in the most sincere way; I didn't have to pretend. But maybe I wasn't so much in love with her as with the empty green garden, the passing ships, the gray water of the East River, and the big house filled with books and elegant things, eh, "Comrade Limonov"?—as the manager of the Hotel Diplomat used to called me.

But I did fuck her soon after the first and last time she visited me at the hotel. That completely unexpected visit was to play an important role in our relationship.

Chapter Three

I'VE ALREADY mentioned how soft-hearted Jenny was. I often had the sense later on that she was studiously playing the role of my mother, despite me and possibly despite herself as well. It wasn't her fault; nature made her do it, and nature is unyielding. The effect was often comical, although fifteen years younger than me, almost young enough to be my daughter in fact, she took me under her wing. It may be that Jenny became attached to me because that was what she needed—her nature required her to worry about somebody, to feed him and buy him clothes and press medicine and vitamins into his mouth. In that sense, I was a real find for her, the little mama!

I had, however, been neither very close nor very communicative with my real mother, and cut out on my own the first chance I got, cut out to wherever it was more interesting. I remember that I never even kissed my mother and was considered surly and unaffectionate, and was always being compared with the boy Valya Zakharov, who was not only affectionate with his own mother, but with mine too, and always came to kiss her whenever she visited his family. Where are you now, model boy Valya Zakharov? And really, where do all those model boys go?

By the time I was three, I had, according to my mother's accounts, already ceased to trust her, and once, as she was carrying me home from a hospital in Kharkov after a bout with the measles and we had to cross some railroad tracks, I started screaming in a terrible voice, begging her not to throw me under a train which just happened to be racing past. A hysterical child, you say? Yes, maybe I did grab hold of my mother's neck not out of love but in the same way a drowning man grabs on to the neck of the one who's drowning him. Fifteen years after the episode with the train, my lack of faith in my mother was fully vindicated: She betrayed me.

There isn't much to tell. We'll pass over the reasons, but in the fall of 1962 I found myself locked in anguish and terror behind the walls of a neuropsychiatric institution. Like any energetic and lively youth who has suffered several weeks in the torture chambers of the "violent" ward, I made up my mind to escape. I called a meeting of my pals, my band of hoodlums, and they brought me the necessary equipment—a hacksaw blade and some clothes. In a couple of evenings I had managed to saw out two bars in the window grating, and then, after changing clothes, I jumped out, and disappeared into the darkness. And it was then, I remember, that I learned what an incredible pleasure it is to *disappear into the darkness*. Nothing can compare with it.

I made my escape alone; the several other "lunatics" who had planned to go with me got frightened at the last moment, although thank God they didn't turn me in. It was my mother who did that the next morning. And from the best of impulses, from concern about me, as it turned out. "I really thought you were sick. The doctors told me that you were."

My mother took the hospital orderlies and the police around to every one of my friends until, on what I think was the seventh of those visits, they finally found me sound asleep. I could have gotten away even then. As that gang escorted me downstairs, my mother walked along beside and assured me that although they were taking me back to the hospital, it was just to fill out the documents for my release. I looked down the flight of stairs and realized that if I suddenly jumped over the railing, the orderlies and the police wouldn't be able to catch me, and that once I was downstairs, they would never find me, since I knew all the backyards and blind alleys and empty lots. But I trusted my mother, for which I paid with another three months of horrors and insulin shots, and was driven to such a state of rage and genuine insanity that I talked a giant, the handsome seventeen-year-old paranoid Grisha, who always went around naked out of reverence for his body, into killing the orderlies and escaping. Which Grisha agreed to do.

If you woke up every morning from the wheezing of a catatonic lying next to you who was being fed liquids through a hose into his belly and from the howls of a naked red-haired Bulat who kept screaming, "I'm the chief Soviet whale! I'm the chief Soviet shark!" then your faith in your mother, or anybody else for that matter, would soon perish. Probably my misfortune was that I had managed to land inside a psychiatric hospital at a still very tender age. My mother, of course, had never in her life been committed to a psycho ward, and so I made no attempt to tell her what I had seen there. I just kept silent. What was there to tell her? Like everyone else, she had her own life to live and was looking out for herself, mother or not. When the orderlies knock somebody down at the foot of your bed and start beating him until he's bloody, then you do what's necessary and draw your own conclusions about the world and mankind. I drew them.

And so when I saw Jenny's motherly little ways, my feelings were mixed. On the one hand, I needed Jenny's help and concern and company, and on the other, her mothering irritated and intimidated me, and I felt uncomfortable whenever I encountered it. In the beginning that happened rarely; after all, we'd only just become friends.

It was only a month after we first met that I finally learned that Jenny was the housekeeper—that it was her job to keep the house in order, that she had been living there for four years, and that she began as a live-in sitter for the "music teacher" Steven's children. The "music teacher" grew from his initial innocuousness into something on the order of God the Father looming

70

over our cloudless life in the millionaire's little house and capable of ending it with a single word. Watch out, Edward!

And now that I am myself his housekeeper and servant, I find that my life is in a sense divided. One life I lead while Steven's away, and the other I lead when Papa Steven's at home. He's only five years older than I am, but the sense never leaves me that he's my father. When he's not around, I commit "illicit acts" and carry on a "dissolute and sinful life," which I carefully conceal from him out of fear of punishment. But when Steven's at home, I go around with my lips pursed, an exemplary servant, and I retire early, don't drink, and get up at seven, before he does, in order to have time to make him coffee.

Not only king, count, lord, and "master," but also father, as in the Middle Ages. Not only tsar but father too. In his office, where you make your appearance every morning along with a throng of the other members of your trade, the boss hardly seems like a father, yet Steven Grey, someone to whom I am linked by a complex system of particularly intimate "employer-servant" relations, is necessarily a father too. And that's why I fear his comings and tremble in panic. Terrible is the wrath of the father Abraham.

I can't remember anymore exactly how I found out that Jenny was a housekeeper, a servant. Maybe she even told me herself, since she certainly didn't conceal it from me—that she was mistress of the house was something I imagined on my own. Externally I didn't react; my expression remained unchanged, but internally I was dismayed. "Edward is the 'lover of a governess.'" Or more accurately, the admirer. I remember that the words "housekeeper's lover" and "servant's lover" made a deep impression on me, and that henceforth I thought of myself as such, sometimes with bitterness and despair and sometimes with the defiant pride of an outcast. The pride of an outcast, in my view, can be even more passionate than that of an aristocrat or lord, however the hell ancient his family.

I later met European aristocrats in Steven's house. Some of them traced their genealogies back to the times of Saint Louis and the Crusades. Just recently Lord Charley stayed with us, a likable alcoholic, one of whose ancestors had in some way distinguished himself at the Battle of Hastings. During his visit at the house, I made an instantaneous improvement in my knowledge of how Scotch whisky is made and of the various ways it may be employed. To start with, the lord rebuked me for drinking it with ice. Scotch, it seems, should at the most be mixed with a couple of drops of water. The lord mixed his one drop with his finger. He started drinking in the morning.

So now, having seen my share of aristocrats close up, I believe myself to be much prouder, morbidly proud in fact. But for me, as a proud man, there was also a kind of distinction to be found in the acknowledgment that "Edward is the lover of a housekeeper." Well, all right, go fuck yourselves, so she's a housekeeper, what of it? I still needed Jenny. And I stayed.

By the end of May I finally succeeded, patient pilgrim, in reaching her cunt. In the solarium toward morning after one of the usual bashes at her house, when she and I were both very drunk, I pulled off her pants and started fondling her pussy. A nice pussy to touch. Actually, in Jenny's case it would be more accurate to call her organ a cunt. Jenny was a large girl, and she had a cunt, a childbearing organ, whereas pussies are found on girl-women, flat-chested and debauched androgynes who look like Olympia in the famous painting by Manet—you recall. My ex-wife Elena had a pussy. Jenny had a cunt. For me, unfortunately, it was somehow second-class. There's a vast difference between a pussy and a cunt.

At first Jenny resisted, twisting and whimpering, but then, after turning on her side and raising her leg in what I have to say was a most indecent way and holding it there, she started to help me. Almost simultaneously with the appearance of a rosy strip of sky in the garden, she had an orgasm, during which she sobbed quietly like a rabbit. And at that moment I sincerely pitied her, a big baby, sick and drunk with a fat ass and thighs and that hole, that wound torn in her for some reason.

I don't know why, but I didn't stick my prick in Jenny that dawn; either I didn't want a cunt but a pussy, or more likely I was simply too drunk to get it up. In any case, I didn't even try to lodge it in her. After it was completely light, we stood up without speaking, like utter strangers, without even a kiss, and I went back to my hotel, not even wondering what it meant. The supermarket near me on Broadway was open, and I bought some beer and sausage that desolate morning, took it home and ate it, and then crashed.

I was awakened by the telephone ringing. "Yes!" I said in my usual way.

"Did you call me?" Jenny asked.

"No," I answered, "I didn't call."

"Linda said somebody asked for me, a man who spoke English with an accent. Linda thought it was you."

"With an accent?" I mockingly asked. "That's all I have. I don't have the language, but I do have the accent," I said.

"You speak pretty well, Edward," Jenny objected, and added, "Debby and I are on Broadway not far from your hotel. We're coming over, all right?"

She had never visited me at the hotel before. I was alarmed. My room really was so dirty, dismal, and poor. And glancing about my wretched little abode with its stained red bedspread, its peeling walls covered here and there with posters and drawings, and its hot plate on the windowsill, I thought, What will be will be! and I asked Jenny if she would give me half an hour.

"Why half an hour?" she asked, a little offended. "We're right nearby."

"My . . . translator, Bill, is here," I lied. "He was passing through on his way from Massachusetts. . . . We've been working on a translation, and we're almost finished. He's leaving in about half an hour."

73

"All right," Jenny answered, satisfied. "We'll be there in half an hour."

I rushed out to the store for some wine. I didn't have any food either, but I didn't have enough money to buy that, too. I had just enough for two bottles of wine, and then only the cheapest. And of course I didn't know very much about wine then. It's only now, after living in a house with probably the finest wine cellar on the whole East Coast of the United States, that I've become such a specialist, but then I didn't know anything.

I had barely managed to return with the alcohol, had only just taken the bottles out of the paper bag, when the sisters arrived. I heard Jenny's laughter coming down the corridor and the almost boyish voice of Debby, and I opened the door before they got there. They were smiling broadly and Jenny was shaking her head disdainfully.

"Somebody offered to sell us heroin on the elevator. Very cheap. When we said no, he offered us angel dust. 'Very nice, ma'am, the best in town, ma'am,' said this black guy without a shirt."

"'Whatever you want, ma'am,'" Debby continued. "And then he put his mouth right up to Jenny's ear and quickly whispered, 'Wanna good fuck, mama?'"

The sisters laughed. The black slang sounded very natural in their imitation, as they drawled and sang the words. I could imitate the blacks, but I was a long way from their skill.

"So this is the way you live, Edward," Jenny said, taking in my room with a mockingly squeamish look. "We had to wait fifteen minutes for the elevator, and in all that time we didn't see one white person. Are you the only one here?"

Jenny sat down on the edge of my bed, on the red bedspread. On the wall above the bed was a huge slogan from Bakunin that I had written with a thick felt-tipped pen on separate sheets of paper and glued there: "Destruction is Creation!"

"Well, no," I objected to Jenny, "I'm not the only white here.

There's an old Chinese man on my floor, and there are several old white women on Social Security, and our manager is white."

I was even a little embarrassed that there were so few whites at our hotel. I offered the sisters some wine.

"Yes, we want some wine," Jenny said, and stretched out on my couch, kicking off her shoes. "Give us some wine, Edward. We've come to visit you."

Jenny made a face at the wine but drank it. We all sat on my bed, and after finishing the first bottle of wine, we opened the second and started arguing about revolution. The seventeen-year-old Debby took my part when I pronounced Steven an exploiter and declared my disagreement with inheritance laws that made it possible for idiots and half-wits of every kind to live in luxury and get on in the world just because their fathers and grandfathers were talented people. "I don't object to people who've made their own way, who have gotten rich on their own—I even respect them," I said, "but their children should start from zero like everybody else."

Jenny said that Steven was neither an idiot nor a half-wit but a talented person in his own right and even a liberal.

I said that I didn't mean her boss when I had been talking about half-wits, since I didn't know Steven, but the system itself. "We need to completely reorganize society, our whole civilization; we need a world revolution, and the new history of man should start from zero," I told the sisters.

"A revolution means blood and killing people," Jenny said with conviction.

"What?" I said. "Read the history of any revolution carefully, Jenny. They all begin with flowers and fresh hopes, in a festive atmosphere, and it's only counterrevolution that makes it necessary for a revolution to take up arms!"

Then we all started yelling and interrupting each other and lighting cigarettes, until Debby and I somehow finally managed to convince Jenny. She admitted that her boss had very specialized talents, such as, for example, a talent for obtaining money to invest in his companies, but that he himself, without his inheritance, would never have been able to acquire a house and garden like that by the time he was forty, or his estate in Connecticut and all his millions of dollars.

"Even his grandfather was a millionaire," I said heatedly, "but I'd like to see how he would have done if he had had to start out here at the Hotel Diplomat. Would he have survived or not!"

We all started laughing, and Jenny suggested getting out of the Diplomat and going somewhere for coffee.

"Then you'll have to lend me some money, because I haven't got a cent," I said.

"Don't worry about it," Jenny said. "It's our treat."

We sat for a long time on some cardboard boxes waiting for the elevator. Dirty and squeaky though it was, it was the only one in all three wings and nine floors of the Hotel Diplomat.

We set off down Broadway, and they didn't like it or anything it had to offer. Finally, after going almost as far as Lincoln Center, we took our seats in a little restaurant called "La Crêperie." I ordered something to eat and drank some wine, while the sisters had dessert and coffee. I ate while Jenny sat beside me and stroked my knee, which she had never done before. Something had clearly changed in her attitude toward me. The ice had broken somehow. Maybe the sight of my room and my awful slum hotel had persuaded her that I was real. I was just as honest as my hotel was. And just as straightforward.

Most likely that's just what it was. She had seen that all my bullshit about revolution wasn't entirely baseless, and she had seen my books and the typewriter and the sheets of paper. It was clear that I really was struggling, and that I had never had a fucking thing in life.

All three of us came out of the restaurant with our arms around each other, feeling very close. It was a warm evening, and the idle stoned were wandering up and down Broadway. Everybody wants to make that one life slipping continually through his fingers more beautiful and interesting, even if it's only in marijuana dreams. We have only one life, after all, and there's always less of it.

We walked along, and I could feel Jenny's warm, living body next to mine and her large hip, and my prick started to rise, and I took her by the breast with one hand like a country lad, embarrassed neither by Broadway nor by Debby. Jenny laughed.

Debby left us at Columbus Circle and started looking for a taxi, and I said to Jenny, "You realize of course that I want you very much."

"Yes," she said, "and I really, really want you. And you'll have me, but not now."

"Why not now, Jenny? When?" I asked.

She pretended to get angry and said, "I have to explain to this Russian ten times that I have a vaginal infection and that it hurts me."

"Is it dangerous?" I asked.

"Not for you," she said, "but it's painful for me."

I didn't remember her telling me about an infection. Maybe it was the night before, or when I was drunk. Probably it was when I was drunk.

"How long have you had the infection, how much time?" I asked.

"Eight months," she answered in embarrassment.

"When will you get over it?" I asked in dismay.

"Maybe I already have," Jenny said. "I'll find out tomorrow. I'm going to the doctor's."

Before getting into the taxi she patted me on the cheek and then suddenly took my hand and kissed it. And then they drove off, and I remained standing on Columbus Circle. Then I went back to the hotel—where else was there to go? My mood was pensive. She's a good girl, I thought. We could buy a farm and have children. We could live . . . I could become an American. . . .

Back at the hotel I discovered I was out of cigarettes and I badly wanted to smoke. Usually in such circumstances I went down to the street where without any trouble along the edges of the sidewalk I found thick butts or even whole cigarettes lost by some goof or drunk. This time for some reason I didn't feel like waiting to take the elevator down and then back up again. My window was open, given the fact that it faced not the courtyard but open space, open all the way to Central Park in fact, since the buildings in that direction were all lower than the Diplomat. In the room above me they were stamping and yelling something to repetitious music, and so I went to close the window.

At that moment, carried by a gust of wind from an upper floor, a thick butt touched with lipstick plopped heavily on my windowsill. It wasn't even a butt, but a barely smoked cigarette. Oh, these women! I burst out laughing, picked up the butt, lit it, and while pacing around the room, sang:

> *On the deck the sailors*
> *Were smoking cigarettes,*
> *And pauper Charlie Chaplin,*
> *He gathered up their butts. . . .*

I was then supplementing my welfare checks by making *piroshki* and *pelmeni,* or Russian ravioli, for Madame Margarita. Madame Margarita spoke beautiful Russian, lived on Park Avenue, and was manager, secretary, and mommy to Sashenka Lodyzhnikov. For nothing, mind you—he didn't pay her.

Madame Margarita, God bless her, paid me three dollars an hour—a bit more than an illegal immigrant. I and another man of letters, the haughty homosexual snob Volodya, made the *piroshki* and *pelmeni* in her kitchen, narrow as a pencil box. I, however, was the only one working for three dollars an hour. Volodya was Madame Margarita's partner. They sold what we made to private clients, usually rich old ladies from Park and Fifth Avenues, and to the snack counter at Bloomingdale's.

Volodya had the highest regard for the manuscript of my first novel, the same one that had knocked Efimenkov out, and although he called me an "underground man" and was a little afraid of me, I think, he treated me very cordially. While we made the *piroshki* and *pelmeni,* a tediously mechanical activity, Volodya would, when he was in the mood, recite poetry to me, sometimes for hours on end.

Occasionally Lodyzhnikov would drop by for a little bite of something good to eat, say a meat patty with mushrooms, since he lived nearby. To Madame Margarita, he was dearer than if he had been her own son. The only thing I didn't understand was why she had chosen Lodyzhnikov for a son and not some obscure youth—me for example. And really, why not? Especially considering the fact that before Lodyzhnikov, Yakovlev had been Madame Margarita's son for a while, as had the just recently emigrated Bulgakov, along with his entire family. Sashenka became her favorite and the most prominent of her sons. Moreover, Madame took care of all his affairs for him, so that Sashenka was the spoiled child of the family. "Don't eat the cherries, boys; they're for Sashenka. Sashenka loves cherries. And the patties in the refrigerator are for him too." Madame Margarita took sweet tea in a thermos and cherries to him at the theater.

Sashenka's a nice boy, I thought, while I made the fucking *pelmeni.* He dances. But Limonov is mean and bad. He's not entitled to cherries. Limonov makes *pelmeni* for three dollars an hour.

A few days after Jenny's sudden visit to my hotel, I took a great quantity of *pelmeni* I'd made by myself from Madame Margarita's to the millionaire's little house—Jenny was going to have a party with Russian food and had invited all her friends. Besides the *pelmeni,* I also made a huge pot of *shchi,* or Russian cabbage soup. I tried to make a fruit *kisel* for dessert using Madame Margarita's recipe, but I botched it and it wouldn't set for some reason. I still don't know how to make it. Jenny was obviously planning to introduce her new boyfriend to her friends. That meant she had finally accepted me.

I arrived from Madame Margarita's with the *pelmeni,* and as

usual Jenny had company. Sitting in the kitchen with the blinds
down were Bridget and her boyfriend Douglas, a drummer with
a very well-known New York rock group, and Jenny, who was
rolling them a joint(!). She had no intention of smoking it herself, but she couldn't deny herself the modest pleasure of at least
rolling it.

Jenny didn't care much for Douglas. "From beating his drums
for so many years, he's turned into a complete dummy; he's
started to rattle his brain," she said and laughed. She and
Bridget had been friends since high school, however, and for
Bridget's sake Jenny put up with Douglas in "my kitchen," as
she said with pride.

Bridget was sarcastic and cynical. Jenny was sarcastic too, but
not nearly as much as Bridget. Bridget thought the whole world
was shit and never had anything good to say about anybody.
She was even planning to write a book about her life entitled
Shit.

I had the sense that Bridget respected me for some reason.
Perhaps because I didn't care too much for people either and
made fun of them. Or maybe she believed in me, to put it in
more pompous terms. I don't know, it's always an elusive thing.
Some people like you; others don't.

They started smoking, and I took a drag too whenever my
turn came. After a few joints we were all doing just fine and
starting to laugh a lot, and then we went out onto the terrace in
the garden. And we laughed there too. The stout Mr. Robinson
was walking past us from the river to his house with several
guests, and he looked at us in alarm. After Robinson had disappeared into his house, Jenny said, laughing, "Mr. Robinson
doesn't think servants should use the garden." It should be said
in Steven's favor that he didn't check up on or in any way forbid
anything either to Jenny or, later on, to me, but whether that
was from indifference or a genuine respect for liberty, I am unable to say.

Two children, a boy and a girl dressed in white, suddenly ran into the garden, ran into it as if out of a newsreel at the beginning of the century, clad in wide pants reaching to their knees and wide shirts the same shade of white, and started turning somersaults on the grass. They were about ten, no more. Later on another boy came out, a bit older than the others, slender and handsome, with long dark hair, but dressed in the same white clothes. . . .

"Isabelle's children," Jenny said to me. "She's the only friend I have in this neighborhood. That house over there belongs to her," and Jenny pointed to a four-story townhouse partly hidden by a huge magnolia tree.

The children hurtled past like phantoms from the beautiful life back into their house and then returned with little orange plastic rattles which they started beating each other with as if they were clubs. Jenny and Douglas got involved in the mayhem too, and the garden was filled with squeals and laughter.

Out from behind the magnolia tree in response to the laughter came a woman dressed in a lilac smock patterned with crimson flowers tightly girded with a broad flowered belt, and wide lilac silk trousers and spike heels. "A beautiful Jewess," as our Pushkin would have said. A very beautiful Jewish woman. She walked over to us and stood next to a flowering azalea bush on the terrace, on purpose probably, and to very good effect.

Jenny introduced us: "Isabelle, my neighbor and friend! Edward, a Russian poet!" Jenny pronounced "Russian poet" with pride, it seemed to me. Isabelle and I lightly shook hands. Her hand was covered in gold and jewels. A small hand.

Then, calling the children over, Isabelle introduced them to me:

"Edward, this is my daughter Chloe." The plump but graceful Chloe held out her hand, then withdrew to the grass and started spinning the wheel of a toy—showing me that she knew how. Silently.

"This is my son Rudy," said Isabelle, showing me a plump

boy with a provocatively insolent face who firmly shook my hand like an adult.

"And this is my oldest son, Valentine."

The oldest boy was gentler, slenderer, and more delicate than the others. He had large, sad black eyes, perhaps just like his Portuguese father's. I liked Valentine best—he was independent, like me, although he seemed to take part in all their games. And, as I later found out, he liked me too.

"Valentine said, 'Edward's a very good person,'" Jenny told me later on, adding, "and he doesn't say that about everybody. I have a lot of respect for his opinion; he's very smart."

I think that I'm not a very good person, or that I was a good person, but I stopped being one from being worn out by people who forced me to live by their rules. Or maybe I never was a good person either. I'm capable of being good, but I'm also very capable of being mean. Valentine, however, died not very long ago, surviving to the day before Christmas. He was thirteen years old, and he died of cancer. Neither chemotherapy nor the best doctors in the world could save him. "Whom the gods love dies young."

A year after that scene in the garden, he suddenly didn't feel good, and after tests and a check-up, the doctors discovered that he had cancer, and the family moved to California, to a climate better than New York's. They treated Valentine, and one hope was replaced by another, and it seemed that there was still reason to hope, and then he died.

Did I pity the boy? Yes. The usual horror of life. Valentine was unlucky.

I'm still alive for the time being. If there is "another world," Valentine and I will meet there and we'll be friends. We were kindred spirits.

But then, standing and sitting in the flowering garden, we suspected nothing. All the trees were in bloom, every one of them, except for the magnolia, which had already finished. Isabelle was saying that she planned to come to the party that evening too and would bring the children with her and something Russian to eat, some caviar and vodka she had bought. "I'm always by myself," she said, neither to Bridget nor to Douglas but to me. "I don't go anywhere, only to my neighbor Jenny's when she has a party." She said it, and then went sadly back along the path to her house.

There are special moments in life that are much more deeply inscribed in the memory than others. It is that day that I remember Jenny, although there were many other episodes in the garden, and we spent two summers, two springs, and one fall there together. Still stupefied with grass, I sat in the garden with her and felt an extraordinary tenderness toward her. A tenderness toward her cheek, and her little hands. A tenderness toward her friends and those others close to me who were sharing with me my time on earth. Tenderness toward her as one of them.

Her combs were the same color as her eyes. And the embroidery on her East Indian dress and her shoes with their long straps tied around her ankles were the same color too. There were little mirrors sewn on her dress, a great many mirrors sewn on by the Indians, and when Jenny moved, rays of sunlight were scattered in every direction. How young she is! I thought.

Then we had supper on the terrace, steaks that Jenny had prepared, and drank red wine. Wasps circled the food, and everybody was intimidated by them, even the punk rocker Douglas—everybody except me. Bridget and Douglas admired my intrepidity and presence of mind in the face of the clear and present wasp danger, and Jenny snidely remarked, obviously making fun of me, that I had been as steadfast as a real revolutionary. She followed that with caustic remarks about bourgeois society, wondering how we could ever coexist, she being so bourgeois herself. I couldn't even answer—I was still stoned—and merely grinned sheepishly.

Bridget and Douglas got ready to leave, since they were supposed to come back to the party that evening. Jenny walked them to the door. "I'll make a speech when I return," she said in a tipsy voice. "I need another glass of red wine."

After she came back, we uncorked another bottle and sat down in the kitchen.

"You talk about inequality, Edward, about the rich and the poor," she began seriously. "But God, Edward, God loves everyone. And I, if you want to know, am happier than my boss. Whenever people come here, to my kitchen, I'm happy that I can feed them. God commands me to help people. My father is not a rich man. He was a naval officer in the war, and then served for twenty-eight years as an FBI special agent. He did his duty—he worked in order to raise and feed and educate us, his ten children. And we had everything. If you work, then you can have everything. But you want to destroy that peaceful life!" she surprised me by exclaiming. During all this we had been kissing and embracing each other from our chairs. But at that point she freed herself.

"Right now, right this minute, I'm going to show you something!" she suddenly cried and dashed out of the kitchen. She came back with a large-format book. "This is my favorite book," she said, and started quickly turning the pages. "Come over here and look," she demanded.

I moved to the chair next to Jenny and looked. There wasn't any text, just pictures. In picture after picture the artist showed the successive destruction of mankind by war until there was nothing left but a man and a woman and a flower. And then life began again and once again revolutionaries and soldiers appeared, and war again destroyed the whole world, except for a man and a woman and a flower.

"Here!" Jenny said, slapping the book shut and extending it to me. "I give it to you. So you'll remember how it all ends. If I have a baby, I want him to be happy," Jenny exclaimed. "But you, Edward . . . !" and she jumped up and started pounding her fists on my back.

Thus we talked and fondled each other, and then after eight

the guests started to arrive. The party was a definite success. Many of the more than thirty people who had been invited had never tried Russian food before, and for them it was very exotic. Each guest drank a shot of vodka with me. I turned nobody down, and obviously got drunk as a result, since I couldn't remember later on how the party had ended.

Coming to, I didn't understand at first where I was. Only after looking around for a few minutes did I realize that I was in Jenny's room. You never know the time in the houses of the rich, or what season of the year it is. The air conditioner had been on all night and had made the room so cold that it felt like winter. The room was dim, since the blinds were down, and only the light of an unknown season showed through the crack. Then I remembered and scowled in disgust.

I've always been poor, ugly, and short. In any case not the sort that women throw themselves at. And now my prick won't stand up either, I thought pitilessly. Probably a little too pitilessly and a little too certainly, but honestly nonetheless.

An unsuccessful morning after an unsuccessful night. And now my prick won't stand up either, I repeated to myself and scowled again. "You ought to go to a doctor. I want to take you to my doctor," Jenny's words came back to me.

The next day after her dance lesson, her belly dancing lesson, that is, she went to her doctor and probably said to him, "I have a boyfriend. I like him, but he can't get an erection." That took place at 2:30 or 3:00 in the afternoon. And then she told the doctor my "case history"—what she knew about me. "His mother left him when he was a child. He was raised by soldiers until he was fifteen. His first wife was a prostitute. The last two years he has had sex only with men. He won't say how old he is, but I think he's about thirty."

From her bed I heard noises resembling the smacking of parched lips. She was waking up. And she had been awake several times during the night. That does her credit, even though she hadn't touched me or in any way tried to break down the wall that had arisen between us after my one unsuccessful attempt to fuck her. Or if she had tried to, it had been very tentative.

Actually, I did remain a few minutes in her "womb," as that place is pompously termed, or even more idiotically, her "vagina" (continue the sequence, if you like: "angina," "regina"...). I entered it, yes, but I didn't remain very long. Nothing lewd or particularly exciting—a twenty-year-old girl with a clean, slightly heavy body equipped to bear children and love a husband. Fresh young breasts, a long beautiful neck, everything fresh and smooth. And a cunt that was probably a bit wider than necessary. . . .

And I, that twisted monster who had been lying next to her, had woken up in another bed, although one close to hers. A feeble monster. My body wasn't twisted; on the contrary, it was dark and spare, but inside . . . My God, inside it was a pathological jumble of nerves and terror. . . .

Thus I quietly lay there, despondent yet at the same time thinking, But what about Rena, the Rumanian dancer? How am I to explain then my bestial, hour-long fucking with her? Of course, it had been several months since I'd quit fucking her. Maybe something had happened to me in the meantime? I didn't believe there was anything wrong with me. Probably it was something else, say a temporary aversion to Jenny. Or that I wasn't used to her yet? Yes, that's what it was. I was still getting used to her.

I didn't succeed in reassuring myself but returned very awkwardly that morning to my hotel—retreated to my hole, ashamed to even look at Jenny. You know, masculine pride. There is nothing more painful than wounded masculine pride. A prick that won't stand up or one that's too small are devastating discoveries for a man. Even a small child's first discovery of the existence of death doesn't compare in horror. I was crushed. My prick wouldn't stand up! And I have to say that no sensible references to bestial fucks with Rena or other beings of the female sex more remote in time could reassure me, although they did help to salve the wound a bit.

An old man was riding up on the elevator with me, and I glanced at him and shuddered. His ear was a bloody abscess covered with scabs, and there were ulcers on his cheek too. His nose was half rotted away. Why on earth do they let such creatures walk around on the streets and in hotels? I wondered. And then I had a sudden ironic thought: His probably stands up every time like a stick. I even broke out laughing at my own black humor.

I didn't call Jenny for two days. She called me herself.

"Come over, I have a surprise for you," she said to me in her usual voice, or even, I thought, in a slightly mischievous one. I went. Another wouldn't have, but I always go, even if disgrace awaits me. I'm brave, or maybe stupid, but I go.

A surprise. The surprise turned out to be a questionnaire from Dr. Krishna consisting, if you can imagine it, of about three hundred questions; I'm not exaggerating. The Indian quack wanted to know everything about his patient, the better to devise his Indian-Gypsy tricks later on. After you'd already forgotten what you'd written down on the questionnaire, he would suddenly but gently announce, looking into your soul with his piercing eyes, "Well, sir, your mother's uncle was an alcoholic or your grandmother on your father's side was insane. . . ." Despite the shitty state of my affairs, I had a good laugh while reading the questionnaire, as did Jenny, although she still declared in a severe tone of voice that we would start filling out the questionnaire the very first thing next morning.

There wasn't any food in the house from Jenny's point of view, and so we went to a restaurant. From my point of view, the refrigerator was full, and it would have been possible to live for a good several weeks on the food that was there. But I didn't argue with her. Hers was the consciousness of an American girl, mine that of a foreign writer struggling with poverty.

In the restaurant, Jenny suddenly started feeling bad and complained about a pain in her back, and we returned home immediately. Aware of my own guilt, I offered my unfucked girlfriend a massage by way of compensation, and we went up to her room, I in terror, to tell you the truth.

By morning Jenny had forgotten all about the questionnaire, as had I, because by then I had fucked her, three times at least. "What's happened to you, Edward?" she asked happily on her way to the shower that morning. Nothing; I had simply gotten beyond my usual tangle of feelings.

She sang happily in the shower, and I listened to her voice while lolling on the bed like a kind of lazy person, one leg hanging over the side, and reckoned up my feelings. The reckoning wasn't very comforting. I suddenly realized distinctly and clearly for the first time that I didn't love Jenny *(I don't love Jenny)*, and that I never would.

I wanted very much to fall in love, wanted it, I realized, more than anything. I liked Jenny, but she didn't even suit me physically. She didn't know how to fuck, and would just lie there like a big unhappy dummy, a female animal waiting for sperm to be deposited in her. There are men, no doubt, who like specimens of that kind and find them exciting, but I unfortunately do not. She was patently a mama, and I even felt something a little like shame in fucking her, as if I were fucking my own mother. Maybe she was my mother in my last incarnation?

Although I had fucked her a rather long time all three times, I don't think she had an orgasm even once. Licking her cunt would have been no problem for me of course, and she would probably have come if I had, but if you're going to lick a cunt, you at least have to feel like it, but with her I didn't. Even though I have more than once in my life risked licking the cunts of prostitutes.

88

Jenny wasn't the least erotic. She was a healthy animal, healthy despite her continual indispositions and complaints about a pain in her back, or in her stomach, or in her "vagina," as she would say. But if Martha must bear children and bake bread, they will go to Mary Magdalene to fornicate.

Thus I lay and drowsily mused. Jenny came out of the shower. "Lazy boy!" she said in the lisping voice she had probably used with children when she was a governess and a babysitter. "It's time to stop idling and get up. I'm going down to the kitchen now to make us some coffee and an excellent breakfast. Do you like bacon and pancakes with maple syrup? I'll make bacon and pancakes with maple syrup and you get up and take a shower."

Jenny was obviously in a good mood. Later on I became convinced that the knowledge she was "making love" was more important to her than any pleasure she got from the act itself. How nice! I'm doing it. I'm making love just like all the other girls! she probably thought. Her God, and she had gone to Catholic school, no doubt encouraged her to feel that way. Well, it doesn't matter if I don't enjoy it; Edward does.

I was sure she would later tell her girlfriends in detail how her new boyfriend had fucked her three times, and how afterward "we drank coffee and had delicious whole wheat pancakes with an extra cup of barley flour; the pancakes turned out really well. And maple syrup . . . It's hard to get real maple syrup now, but Nancy brought some from Connecticut. She got it herself—you know, they make holes in the bark." Jenny was fond of all the pleasant little details.

I'm not making fun of her; I still respect Jenny, and there aren't many people that I do. But, good Lord, she was such a little Martha that she would regularly bake her own bread! Various kinds: unleavened, sweet, raisin, and even with zucchini or whatever else she could think of. Incredible homemade bread that even Steven would proudly serve his guests now and then. She ground the flour from grain herself; that tells you some-

89

thing, doesn't it? In a real flour mill given to her by her friend Isabelle.

We had breakfast on the roof, where we had taken a small folding table, and we sat across from each other and drank coffee out of red ceramic cups and poured maple syrup over our pancakes. Then Jenny brought a cassette player up to the roof and a cold bottle of champagne, and we took our places in lounge chairs, drank the champagne in the blazing sunshine, and listened to music.

The tape was called "After the Ball," the name of one of the songs included on it. They were old popular songs: "I've Got Rings on My Fingers," "Good Bye, My Lady Love," and "Will You Love Me in December as You Do in May?"

Those melodies both then and now evoke in me a kind of festive melancholy. Perhaps because they really are about our lives in this world—my life and Jenny's and the lives of other people who lived before us—about our private little stories and tragic mistakes, our whims and our passions. The song "After the Ball" tells how at a ball "he" mistook her brother for her lover, and so foolishly lost his happiness, and how "she" soon caught cold and died. "After the Ball." I'm writing this too after the ball.

Chapter Four

I'M VERY ASHAMED to admit it, but I gradually came to hate her, quietly and feebly. Maybe it was the hatred of an adventurer for an escapade that hadn't lived up to his expectations, that hadn't come off, an irresolvable subconscious bitterness at the fact that she was a servant and not the lady of the house. I don't know. One thing is certain; along with the gratitude I felt to Jenny, I also detected in myself the first twinges of antipathy for her. She had revived a corpse, and the corpse, having come back to life, at once resumed its nasty little tricks, as you see, and instead of gratitude, concealed a bitterness toward the girl who had found him on her doorstep.

The first time I remember being ashamed of Jenny was when she and I were sitting in the kitchen and I was introduced to a young woman who had unexpectedly walked in holding the hand of a blond boy of about five.

"The Marchioness Houston . . . Edward Limonov, my boyfriend," Jenny said proudly, introducing us.

The nicely perfumed and beautifully coiffured marchioness, obviously no older than I, smiled benignly and extended a cool hand to me. To say that "we exchanged a few words" would be an exaggeration, since, like an idiot, I said nothing and stupidly gawked at the guest from across the sea. It wasn't that the marchioness was particularly beautiful—after all, I had once been married to a very beautiful woman, Elena—but that she was a lady from head to toe. I glanced at my girlfriend, who unfortunately was sitting in the kitchen barefoot, with her hair uncombed and a mess and a white pimple breaking out under her nose. She stubbornly refused to squeeze out her pimples, letting them burst by themselves since she was afraid of blood poisoning. She was wearing a blue skirt I had made for her, and not very well either—it was my first attempt, and the skirt stretched across Jenny's fat stomach, emphasizing it, and the wide ruffles, which were inappropriate for such heavy material, made her backside look so heavy that she seemed to me at that moment to resemble nothing so much as a large goose.

Looking at Jenny and comparing her with the Marchioness Houston, I returned from the realm of dreams and the petty everyday details of my struggle to the harsh reality of today: *I was the lover of a servant*. The full wretchedness of my situation loomed before me in the guise of the unkempt Jenny, and there in the kitchen, responding to the unaffected questions of the Marchioness Houston, to the simple courtesy of a well-bred lady, while Jenny was giving the little Lord Jesse a glass of milk, I swore to myself that I would leave Jenny that day and never return.

Fortunately I didn't keep my word. The fact is that I had nowhere else to go except back to what I had known before. And returning to Central Park to read and dream was something I simply could not do. Madame Margarita, the fairy Volodya, and the superstar Sashenka Lodyzhnikov hadn't accepted me as one of them. They might have, but on terms that would have been humiliating to me, and I didn't want that; I wanted to be treated as an equal and with respect. And anyway they didn't interest me.

My casual sexual relations had been a passing thing, and I had no wish to prolong them. I had derived something from them, a certain kind of knowledge, but the main thing, gentlemen, is that my partners were all poor homeless creatures like myself who had been cast out into the huge city either by their own volition or against it, but poor! Like me, they had their own struggles, on a much lower level, but struggles. For a good job, for success in their own narrow area of life, or perhaps for a better lover. Often I was a lucky find for my partners, but they never were for me. I didn't want to associate with poor people; they depressed me. I needed a psychologically healthy atmosphere. That was the secret.

More than Jenny, it was the millionaire's house I needed. *I loved the house;* it was good for me, it and its carpets and pictures, its parquet floors and thousands of books, its huge leather folios with drawings by Leonardo da Vinci, its garden, and its children's rooms—they were what I needed. Both nature and instinct had shown me the way, for the only means of getting into the house, the key to it, was Jenny. Not even through Steven Grey could I have gained entrance to it and lived there, unless he had been gay, but he wasn't.

I know what you're thinking; go ahead and ask: "Why didn't you, Limonov, who prattle so much about world revolution and the necessity of wiping a whole civilization off the face of the earth, why didn't you take even one step in that direction? Why have you been so busy with your dick, as we've seen, and with every other kind of thing, some even directly opposed to your 'goal'? Why didn't you join a revolutionary party, for example, since they exist, even in America?"

I'll tell you why I didn't. In the first place, those puny little parties would only have taken me as a minor little member, a mosquito, and I would have been handing out little newspapers and tracts on the street and going to petty little meetings, and maybe after about twenty years of party discipline and demagoguery, I would have become, say, a provincial Trotskyite boss. And then what?

And in the second place, I want action. Not one American leftist party has any chance of success now, and I don't play games that are already lost. My life is running out; I can feel it in my bones.

And then, gentlemen, you've obviously got me mixed up with somebody else. I have my own ideas, you see, and the well-fed face of the proletarian is no less unpleasant and repugnant to me than the well-fed face of the capitalist.

There was another way out—I could have let myself go and exploded in rage and left for somewhere in Beirut or South America where there's shooting, and taken a bullet in the brain for something that had nothing to do with me, something I didn't understand at all or understood only partly, and walked around with a submachine gun and felt free and alive. I have never been afraid of getting killed, but I am afraid of dying in obscurity; that's my weak point, my Achilles' heel. What can you do; everybody's got one. You'll forgive me, but I'm ambitious, even incredibly ambitious. And greedy for fame.

And therefore I would, like Lord Byron, have gone off to fight to free the Greeks, or, in my own case, the Palestinians, if I had already made a name for myself, if I had already become known to the world. So that if I were cut down by machine gun fire somewhere among the sandbags and palms of Beirut, I could be sure that the fat *New York Times,* which always leaves your hands so black that you have to wash them with soap and water after reading it, would come out the next day with my photograph and four lines on the first page (with the rest in the obituary section)—"Died: Edward Limonov, poet and writer, author of several novels, including *It's Me, Eddie.* Killed in a fire fight in the Moslem sector of Beirut."

But I knew that those lines wouldn't appear anywhere. And that's why I didn't lose control.

I think after that encounter with the Marchioness Houston, I wrote a poem, a ridiculously bitter poem, only part of which I remember, but containing the lines, "You won't make a lady out of a servant,/ Never, never, never. . . ." To be honest, I wasn't trying to; I realized I would have to grit my teeth and endure Jenny and take advantage of the millionaire's house. The typical reflections of an opportunist, I admit, but is that against the law? Who says it is?

It turned out that at home in England the Marchioness Houston lived in a thirteenth-century castle with three hundred servants(!). Not too shabby. I hadn't even suspected that such castles exist. They even had their own zoo, with tigers and bears, as I learned from an illustrated tourist guidebook to the castle. The marchioness had brought a certain number of the guidebooks with her to America to give to friends and acquaintances, and she gave one to Jenny. She also gave Jenny, if I'm not mistaken, two hundred dollars for looking after the young Lord Jesse and serving him breakfast.

I too did a little work for the marchioness—I shortened three pairs of pants for her, one of them yellow and all bought in America. Neither Jenny nor I particularly cared for them; one pair was even made of polyester instead of cotton or wool. The fabric should have been natural—cotton, wool, or silk—as the housekeeper of that advanced and well-to-do American home knew, and as I, her boyfriend, did too. When Bridget came over, we all sat in the kitchen in various postures and condemned the marchioness for her polyester pants, deciding that the English were still very provincial, even the lords.

I too went along with what they were saying, although I was wistfully thinking too about the freshly bathed marchioness and her rather impressive bottom lying upstairs on her bed on the third floor, obviously wearing one of the red night shirts our black Olga had laundered for her.

I had gone into the laundry room and had looked at the marchioness' night shirts—I just couldn't help it. The marchioness is lying in her bed, I thought dreamily to the monotonous chatter of Jenny and Bridget, my eyes half closed . . . fragrant with the warmth of her body and the odor of her fashionable perfume, a smell like the one the ordinary Soviet cologne White Lilac used to have. Maybe she's stretching and rearranging her pillow. . . .

I'm sitting here in the kitchen with my servant girl and her friend, I thought dejectedly, while my place is upstairs, in bed with the marchioness. Wherever else an opportunist's place is, it is in any case not in the kitchen.

Jenny, of course, couldn't have been aware of my treacherous thoughts, but seeing that I had suddenly grown sad, she got up from the table, came over to me, and bending down low said in a lisping whisper, her governess' whisper intended for children that I found so incredibly irritating, "Silly man. Just be patient, my period will be over tomorrow and you can go inside me then." She thought of course that I was in an agony of desire, that I wanted her. That I craved her insipid charms.

Not likely. It was the marchioness I wanted! The marchioness, wife of a lord, the marchioness who lived in a castle with three hundred servants, a castle where tourists were admitted several days a week from ten until three and where there were pictures by Goya and Velázquez and Titian. What was I put on earth for, if I couldn't fuck the marchioness!

I think the Marchioness Houston liked me. Well of course she liked me; she had mentioned my beautiful hands and my beautiful shoes several times. Obviously it was clear from my face that I wasn't born to be the lover of a servant. Maybe I was born to be the lover of a marchioness? Houston even pitied me for living in a foreign country and outside my natural surroundings. It's unlikely the marchioness was thinking it would be nice to fuck Edward, but running into her on the stairway and in the kitchen, I desired her passionately. But not so much sexually, I think, as socially. I had a social inferiority complex; that's all. If fate had presented me with an opportunity to fuck her then, it would no doubt have been very therapeutic for me. How proud I would have been. But there wasn't any such opportunity. Whenever important guests like the marchioness and her husband stayed at the house, I spent relatively little time there, because then Steven Grey was home a lot. During such periods Steven and his guests relegated Jenny and me to the kitchen, to the servants' quarters, so to speak. I was intimidated.

After the departure of the Marchioness Houston and the young Lord Jesse, Jenny's parents came up from Virginia for several days—her tall, lean, sharp-nosed, dependable, tolerant father, and her thin mother, dark as a grackle. Jenny gave a dinner party for her parents, inviting another couple—a former FBI colleague of her father's, now a New York police official, and his wife—and me. Inspection of the groom.

I arrived a little late for dinner in order to give myself a certain weight in the eyes of Jenny's parents, coming as if from work, although I had no job then of course. I had simply gone to the movies to kill time.

Tall like an awkward tower, the warm, tipsy Jenny met me at the door and immediately started hugging and kissing me and telling me how much she loved me, and then she dragged me into the dining room. She was wearing a flowered crêpe de Chine dress and new black shoes from Charles Jourdain, and her hair was curled, although it was virtually the only time that she ever did anything with her hair.

They had already finished eating and were drinking champagne. Jenny entertained her parents no worse than Steven did his lords and businessmen. Champagne and candles.

After eating the lamb and artichokes left for me, I partook of the champagne and the conversation. The champagne with a vengeance; the conversation with caution.

The three of us—the men—had a lot to drink, and I've forgotten many of the details of our conversation, but I formed one unshakable opinion that evening, which later acquaintance with Jenny's father only confirmed. Both retired FBI men were terribly like my own retired father, an ex-Soviet army officer and employee of the NKVD, MVD, and so on. The same memories of the past and of colleagues and opinions about their subsequent fates, and the same view of life as something that had been entrusted exclusively to *them* to preserve and protect.

"Where's John now?" father Henry asked.

"Which John, little or big?" the New York policeman asked, seeking clarification.

"Big—you remember, he worked in the diamond department."

"Oh, big John's a wheel now; he's director of security for IVTA."

"Jiminy, he's really up there!" father Henry exclaimed in delight. "That's a giant multinational. . . ."

The wife of one unfortunate had cancer and was slowly dying at home, while the daughter of a certain Nick, nicknamed The Kid, had given him a grandchild—a constant stream of such information came from both rivers.

Just ordinary people, I thought in amazement. I had some more champagne with them, and then started drinking whiskey. The New York cop was an Irishman and a heavy drinker, and when they were finally filled with respect for my manly drinking skill, I told them, for my part, that they reminded me of my Communist and ex-secret police agent father and his friends. I thought it would astonish them, that they would be shocked.

"Probably so," father Henry answered calmly and reflectively. "People who share a profession resemble each other in a certain way. It's easier for you to see, Edward; you've lived both here and there."

"My father was and is a good person, despite all the ill fame of the organizations he worked for," I said.

"And why not?" the New York cop said. "You're a good fellow, as I can see, and Jenny loves you, so why should your father be a bad person?"

Later on the New York cop started asking me about the kind of books I write, and how much writers are paid before they become famous. The policeman and I continued drinking for quite a while after papa Henry had stopped, and I started complaining to the New York cop about how hard it is to make a name for yourself in literature.

98

"You stick to it," the policeman told me. "Jenny says you're very talented. It's difficult for you now, but be patient, persevere. The beginning is always hard in any profession, but later on your books may become best sellers, and you'll be famous like Peter Benchley, and they'll make a movie in Hollywood. . . ."

A journey of thousands of miles across the white hot desert of the literary business separated me then from a film, as it separates me now, and anyhow I wouldn't want to be a Peter Benchley. I'd like to have his literary agent, the famous Scott Meredith. His agent's a treasure, but Peter Benchley is a shark and marine horror specialist—no, spare me that.

I would have enjoyed talking to the New York policeman some more, but remembering my promise to Jenny not to stay late, I hastened to leave. It was already around one o'clock in the morning.

Jenny walked me to the doorway, where she sighed with relief. "I was afraid you would get drunk," she said. "It's a good thing you didn't; you were very cute tonight. I love you very much," and she kissed me. "Tomorrow I'll tell you what my parents said about you."

Her mama said I was "cute" too, and when I met her Polish grandmother later on, she wanted to know what kind of Russian I could be—Russians are always big, even huge, and have beards, but that even so Jenny should watch out for me; you should never trust Russians. And furthermore they beat their wives.

Jenny wanted a husband. As you've seen for yourself, fucking was a less important need for her than having a man in her life. She was always raving about how strong my body was. I think that despite my strong body I wasn't an ideal object for her purposes. I had neither the money nor, what is more to the point, the desire to build a happy future in the form of that family of ten she was very likely planning after her parents' example, but she liked me, and she indulged her heart in my case, even going against her maternal instincts. Thank you, Jenny.

I fucked her whenever I felt like it, fucked her brutally, without tenderness, preferring the dog position so I wouldn't have to look at her face. I didn't bother about her pleasure at all, leaving it to her to satisfy herself by masturbating if she wanted to have an orgasm. Sometimes I fucked her as many as five times, if I was inspired, but not finding any response to my prick in her body, I grew less and less interested in that activity, so that after I had fucked her a little while, my prick would tire of that meager pleasure and withdraw. Whenever that happened Jenny would start bawling, "Edward, I love you! You're not well. How unhappy we are!"

Edward was in fact as strong as an ox and giving the once-over to the scrawniest whores on the street, but then something strange started happening to Jenny, and once when I tried to stroke her cunt with my hand, to give her at least some kind of pleasure, she suddenly jerked away in pain. That happened at the beginning of August, and after that she complained about discomfort for a couple of weeks, but quietly, and then during one of her regular belly dancing performances, she suddenly doubled over and rushed with a yell to the elevator. When Bridget and I got to her room, she was lying curled up on the bed and groaning, "My vagina! My vagina!"

I didn't understand anything about women's diseases then, nor do I understand anything about them now, but something was clearly wrong with Jenny. I gave up sex with her for a while, and she went to Dr. Krishna, who applied himself to finding out what was the matter with her. We now slept soundly on separate beds, and she changed her refrain a little. "Edward, I love you. We're both not well. How unhappy we are!" she whined, and asked me for such innocent pleasures as remained to us—massaging her back or playing with her hair.

While with one hand I unwillingly stroked her hair and held a glass of wine in the other, she chattered incessantly. "God sent you to me," she said. "I love you because you're nice to me." I can imagine how her usual men must have treated her, I thought to myself, if she regards my almost indifferent attitude toward her as something special.

"Keep stroking my hair, don't stop, I like it," she said, using her lisping tone again, and I stroked her hair some more while sipping my wine, an excellent 1966 Bordeaux. She continued babbling: "As soon as I get better, Edward, we can do *it* again, but we'll have to take precautions, since we don't have enough money to have a baby—can you imagine you and me and a baby in your hotel?" Jenny spoke the last sentence very seriously. "No," I said. But I could imagine it very well—she and I and the baby covered with shit walking down Broadway, and a bottle of cheap wine sticking out of the pocket of my torn jacket— and it seemed so wildly funny to me that I could barely sip the expensive wine.

"We'll have to take precautions," she repeated.

"Uh-huh," I said, "but I thought you already were taking precautions, that you were taking pills."

"No, that's against my principles." (Abortion was against her principles too.) "I only recognize mechanical means," she said severely.

What kind of mechanical means? I wondered, reviving. What does she mean, a condom maybe? Ugh, how disgusting! I thought. I tried fucking with a condom one or two times in my life—it just didn't work. "All right," I said out loud, "we'll use mechanical means."

"We'll have money someday, Edward," she said enthusiastically. "We've got to!"

But how? thought Edward, the heel. I may have money someday, but live with you, my poor little kitchen angel, is something I will never do. You already bore me, and the prospect of spending my whole life with a woman who has to make such an effort to come doesn't appeal to me at all. I like expensive whores, lascivious kittens who tear you up inside and arouse you. But you're a country girl, a stupid girl with a big fat ass and fat thighs, a twenty-year-old girl. And you don't get under my skin, and you don't smell of perfume.

"I love you very much, Edward!" she whined again.

It was starting to annoy me. She needed to be told off, to be put in her place. I turned off the light and lay down on my back. "Jenny," I said, "I want to ask you something very important."

"What is it, Edward?" Jenny answered in the darkness in a cautious voice.

"You see, Jenny, I want the kind of love in this world where, if they sent me to prison and gave me a life sentence, say—and what the future holds for me is still very unclear—my woman would get herself a submachine gun and free me. Could you love me like that?"

After a moment's silence, she said, "Edward, that's ridiculous. Just because you get into trouble, that doesn't mean I should too. I'll still love you, I won't disown you, but," and then she said the fateful words, "it's your problem."

Jenny went on to explain, but I wasn't listening anymore. I had in an instant managed to secure for myself the moral right to think whatever I wanted of her, had done so because I was serious about life and had asked her in all seriousness, even though I knew she wouldn't pass the test. I was weighing and planning my future, and I needed people who were real. She wasn't one of them.

Though the inner distance between us was becoming ever greater, on the surface we lived almost like husband and wife. I would arrive at the millionaire's house on Friday evening, and begin Saturday morning on the roof, sunning myself and drinking coffee, or pretending that I was sunning myself and drinking coffee, while in fact digging around in the rooms. When there weren't any guests around, Edward, the housekeeper's lover, became complete master of the house and liked to be left alone and undisturbed, and of all the rooms in the house he definitely preferred those that belonged to the children.

I was envious. I had never had my own room either as a child or as a youth, although in the best dreams of my boyhood, I had envisioned one in the form of a steamboat cabin—a white, happy childhood with white curtains stirring in the breeze and a gleaming river visible through all the windows, and a colored bed and my own dresser for my clothes, and booklined shelves, and a white washstand with a round mirror.

Our whole family—my father and mother and I—shared a single room. It was the fifties, in a country that had been utterly destroyed by war, and there was a housing crisis. All I had was my own little "corner" where I kept my things—my father's old knapsack, an old topography textbook of the same age, a few books on foreign lands and plants, and some maps. I was so hampered by the adults and wanted a private place of my own so badly, that, being an energetic boy, *I resolved to excavate myself a room*. With my characteristic practicality, I immediately set about it, digging a hole in the communal apartment house basement where we and our neighbors stored potatoes and coal. I dug in the evenings by the light of a kerosene lamp and carried the dirt outside in bags which I emptied under the huge elderberry bushes that surrounded the building. In the daytime I covered up the hole with boards on top of which I piled coal. I imagined submachine guns hanging on the walls of my dug-out (from hooks, I think) and bunks for the other "kids," although I had no clear idea who they might be. I might perhaps have finished my hole and finally enjoyed the privacy of my somewhat strange children's room (let's call it a children's room on the "Russian model"), but our family moved to another building, and I know nothing of the subsequent fate of that vacuum in the heavy Ukrainian clay. I hope nobody fell into it.

While looking over the room belonging to Henry, Steven Grey's oldest son, I started to feel terribly sorry for myself and my unfinished dug-out. Christ! I thought, you've reached the age of thirty-four and have never even once had a decent place to live. I looked in the drawers, stared at the amateur color photographs of happy children, sniffed the crab claw, felt the little Chinese figurine, turned the pages of a vacation book about a bunny rabbit, and jealously examined a cowboy hat from somebody else's childhood, a huge eraser, modeling clay, and some foil, all those little things that no child can possibly manage without. A piece of old wood stood on a chest and a stuffed owl scowled from a top shelf. The yellow floor, the blue shag rug, the cork wall on which was thumbtacked yet another sunny photograph—green and sky blue, with four children on the grass, one sticking his tongue out, and an azure sea visible through some rocks in the background. It's been many years now since Steven Grey and his family settled permanently in Connecticut, and the New York house has remained much as it was when they lived here. And the children's rooms have too.

On one wall in an old frame hung a copy of the last issue of a newspaper published, as it turned out, on board the unfortunate *Lusitania*. The issue was dated May 7, 1915. The headlines were "The Dardanelles," "The Italian Crisis," "An Important Japanese Operation," and "Extensive Use of Gas against the British by the Enemy." There was also an announcement of an upcoming concert in the ship's saloon: "Concert in Saloon!" And there was a report by Sir J. French from the European front, written in the unvarying style shared by military communiqués the world over—the attempt to conceal and downplay a fucked-up situation: "The same morning three units carried out a concerted attack on a position in the Bois de Pally recently captured by us. This attack achieved the enemy's goal of gaining a foothold against our front line, but our counterattack permitted us to retake half of the hill almost immediately. . . ." You're screwed, Sir J. French, I thought. They'll throw even more men at you at night, since the main thing is to gain a foothold, and in the morning your front line will become their rear.

Next to the relic from the *Lusitania* hung a portrait—an old gentleman in a pince-nez and green tie, probably a grandfather or great-grandfather. In another frame on the same wall was a group portrait of some gentlemen who had received the Edison Prize, with Edison himself in the center. The prime movers of progress, so to speak. To a significant degree, it is thanks to these fine-looking gentlemen and their boundless curiosity that the very existence of *Homo sapiens* is in jeopardy.

On the opposite wall was an art nouveau poster depicting an auburn-haired, bare-shouldered woman who was covered with flowers, who was bedecked with flowers. This lady, unlike the Fausts in their stand-up collars, was completely innocuous and didn't even have a name.

Hidden behind the door was a surprise—a yellow 1919 newspaper, framed like the other one of course, with a portrait of the same old gentleman in pince-nez and what were evidently his words printed in huge letters underneath: "People want us to be efficient and to provide service of the highest quality. That is impossible without capital investment. There must be an equitable interrelation here. If costs go up, then prices must too!" Golden words from the old gentleman, I thought to myself. He's right. Prices have been going up to this day and will continue to do so until the entire system collapses. And if it collapses, then everything else will too—both prices and costs, and the portrait of the gentleman in the green tie, and the millionaire's house, and maybe the whole world.

Then a white children's bed stood next to the doorway leading to the roof; now it has been replaced by a large adult bed Nancy brought from Connecticut. I have accustomed myself to fucking my women on the adult bed with the door open, so that the sunlight in all its vitality falls directly on the victim's cunt and on my own organ, which is tremendously stimulating, and heats both cunt and prick to incandescence. Then, however, a children's bed stood by the door, and next to it (and still there) a maned rocking horse from India embroidered in gold.

I sat on the horse and rocked and quietly thought, Why couldn't I live here? It would be a fine thing to remain living in this little house for the rest of one's life, and sleep in the children's bed, and throw children's books on the blue shag rug. Thank you, Jenny, I thought as I rocked on the horse, clasping it between my tanned legs. I have no right to be here, none at all. Thank you, Jenny. I'll have to give her a kiss when I get back downstairs. She doesn't feel well. Besides her vagina, her back hurts. She sleeps on the other bed, but next to me, obviously creating the illusion for herself of a normal life with a husband. Last night there were light blue sheets with butterflies on our beds. She does everything she thinks she's supposed to do so that sex will be pleasurable for Edward, and obediently sucks my organ. What can I do? she probably thinks. Edward must have an orgasm, and my vagina hurts me now. She makes an effort for my sake, but doesn't get any pleasure herself, the angel.

I've stopped dreaming about complete happiness, I thought, continuing to rock and watching through the open doorway a sudden gust of wind blow my Sunday *New York Times* from the roof to toss it in the river, no doubt. I've become calculating and don't worry about Jenny anymore, and always leave her in bed in the morning without regret, without even a glance in her direction; I leave her and the butterflies on the sheets and come up here to this children's stateroom. Downstairs sleeps a woman who is alien to me, a twenty-year-old woman who oppresses me with her plans. Down there lie her heavy bottom, her breasts, and the rest of her dubious charms, while I sit up here, a boy who has risen early and already contemplated an old geographical map. I have existed and I shall continue to do so, I thought, as usual full of boundless faith that morning in my own exceptional destiny. And when my hour comes, I shall leave this house for other women and other lands and return to my own destiny. Here in the children's room of the millionaire's house I've found an unexpected respite from my struggle, a place to hide out for a while. But enough of resting, I said to myself, and sliding off my Arabian courser, I went downstairs, where Eastern music and the voices of Jenny and somebody else could already be heard.

That somebody else turned out to be Jennifer, whom I had mistaken on my first visit to the millionaire's house for a Turk. She was in fact a Jew. I didn't care much for Jennifer; of all Jenny's friends, Bridget was my favorite, but Jenny liked Jennifer for some reason. I suppose it was because they were both cows and crazy about babies, and each eventually had one, Jennifer first, then Jenny a little later.

After I came downstairs that morning, Jennifer revealed to me and Jenny that she had "fallen in love" with the seventy-two-year-old Dr. Krishna.

"Congratulations," I said.

"I'm so happy!" she exclaimed, and jumping up from her chair, she embraced Jenny. Then she embraced me, giving off a strong odor of pot, and said that she and the doctor were planning to get married in the fall.

I even started to respect her for her "originality" and daring and her craziness. A difference of fifty-two years isn't exactly trifling, I thought. What a people these Indians are. He's never been married until now. He's just starting out. His first wife.

It was very hot, around a hundred degrees. After taking her bra off very nearly in front of me and something else besides that looked like panties—New York girls have an extraordinary simplicity about these things that is on occasion even offensive—the idiotic Jennifer ran out into the garden and started twirling about in nothing but her Indian blouse and her skirt. She leapt up and down, holding her arms high, and pointlessly waved her hands, performing something in between a belly dance and a gymnastics exercise. A Jewish chicken, I thought derisively. Pimply, happy, and satisfied with her Krishna, who was an "excellent man," as she had told Jenny. I could see that she really was happy, only it all looked so silly.

While this was going on, the other fortunate, Jenny, was jabbering on the telephone in the kitchen. I had just given her a gift, the Virgin Mary on birch bark, the work of my friend Borka Churilov and the only Russian thing I had left.

"Thanks for Jenny," said the sweaty Jennifer, who had just come in from the garden, distracting me from my thoughts. She kissed me.

Jenny was going out with Jennifer; they had things to tell each in private. Both were contented with life. One had "fallen in love" with a seventy-two-year-old Indian doctor, and the other with an ambitious Russian guy who was a writer, only the sort of writer of which there are so many around, since who the fuck had read his books? For my part, I immersed myself in a book by Virginia Woolf I'd just discovered on the dining room bookshelf.

At the end of August Jenny and I visited her parents in Virginia. I remember her striding energetically ahead through the crowd at the Port Authority bus terminal dressed in a long skirt like the mother of a family, and myself dressed in white pants and a black cap trudging along after her with a vacant expression on my face and loaded down with bags. Among other things, the bags contained loaves of Jenny's own freshly baked bread. Hot as it was without that, the bread gave off an additional steamy warmth.

Once underway on the bus, Jenny happily dozed on my shoulder, while I read a book on anarchism, from time to time gazing at two attractively jaded teenage girls sitting on my right, both of them blondes, both drinking cans of Budweiser, and both chewing gum with their beer.

I had just started a chapter on anarchism in Spain, when the bus came to a halt. We were, as it turned out, already in Washington, D.C. I reluctantly took leave of the Spanish anarchists, sturdy fellows all, smiled in farewell to the insolent teenagers, with whom I would very gladly have gone, and picked up our bags. The bread, thank God, had finally cooled.

Unemployed blacks were hanging around the spit-stained bus station as if waiting for a miracle, and just as in all the other waiting rooms of the world, on the red chairs of that waiting room sat the usual crowd of idiots as if brought in and placed there, while nearby somebody was kicking a machine that was obligated to dispense gum to people but wouldn't. In short, a bus station like any other. Jenny's father, who was supposed to meet us, naturally wasn't there, and she started making calls to Virginia, on the other side of the Potomac.

Then they arrived, Jenny's father and mother, in a huge swamp-colored car meant for a large family. They'd gotten mixed up about the bus schedule somehow. I'd never been to Washington before, and they therefore showed the future husband of their daughter a little of the empire's capital. The first thing her father took me past was the FBI building, of course, and why not, since half of his life had been connected with that organization. Jenny, for her part, observed that Mr. Herbert Hoover always sent her mother official congratulations on the birth of each new child, and that if I would remind her when we got back to the house, she would find the letters and show them to me.

"Didn't he send any money?" inquired the practical Limonov.

"No," Jenny's mother said with regret.

"If you had lived in Russia," I said, "you would have been a mother-heroine, and the state would have given you a medal for your children and paid you money."

"That would have been nice," her mother said.

To myself I thought what I usually did, that there was no fucking need for all those children, since there wasn't enough to eat on the planet anyway, and that there were already so many people running and crawling over the surface of the globe, both in the huge cities and the rural districts, that the crowd was impossible to bear even psychologically. And furthermore, if one was going to be objective about it, I already knew two of their children, Jenny and Debby, and neither had yet distinguished herself in the world in any way, nor was there any hope that they ever would. All of your ten children, mama, I thought, will tread the earth for another half-century, devouring its meat and grain to sustain themselves, but that's all they'll ever do, mama, that's all. The only thing mankind can brag about is its history, and history, mama, is something your children will never have any part in. They're outside history, mama . . . I thought to myself, while our car, driven by a former special agent of the FBI, crossed the Potomac and the family joyfully showed Limonov the Pentagon and Arlington National Cemetery.

Why, even Kennedy's a minor figure in the historical scheme of things, I thought, a local bureaucrat-hero of no particular mettle. You'd have to be feebleminded to be born into such a family and not become President. Whereas your children, mama, are just rabbits, unfortunately just rabbits, I thought pityingly, since I wasn't malicious and had myself made a gigantic effort not to be a rabbit, and even though my own destiny was unclear, I understood that making an effort was half the battle. I had, however dimly, always known that, and for that reason had even in the toilets of the world stood gazing suspiciously at my face, distancing myself from their human din, their rabbit commotion. I wanted my own face, and not the flushed face of a rabbit. My own, however fucked-up, bitter, and tear-stained, but my own!

Their house stood on a hill, a split-level house built into the hill with most of the rooms on the upper of its two floors. The house stuck out into the middle of an orchard, or, excuse me, not an orchard, since for the most part its trees weren't fruit trees but pines and other varieties that I, an inhabitant of asphalt jungles, didn't know the names of in either Russian or English, and so we'll abstain from old-fashioned landscape descriptions and merely call them trees. In short, then, there was a house, trees, as much as an acre or more of greenery, hammocks, a small vegetable garden cultivated mainly for pleasure by the children, a dog named Achilles given to the family by Isabelle as a gift, a drum set in the room belonging to Robert, another of the Jacksons' sons, pictures of rock-and-roll stars, children, and her parents in Debby's room, and, in the evening, fireflies on the property outside.

An abundant American dinner awaited us: the inevitable steaks and salad. They drank wine in the house, not to get drunk, but they drank—the tip of Jenny's mother's nose was a suspicious red, but it's possible too that she had a cold. During the meal all the children and their father got after Jenny in a friendly way for her boundless admiration for Dr. Krishna. Even Debby scoffed at her. I supported the children cautiously, afraid that Jenny would take offense. Her mother took a middle position.

Soon afterward Jenny herself started laughing at Dr. Krishna and his medical knowledge, but not then. She got very, very angry then and suddenly started shouting, "Cut it out! Cut it out, people!" an expression I liked so much that I at once added it to my own vocabulary.

So we "cut it out" and started talking about something else. As soon as we'd finished dinner, the children started showing me family photographs, one album after another. In the beginning there were two—the young mother and father. The father wore a military uniform; it was wartime. Then a wedding: the men in jackets with enormous shoulders and flared trousers, the ladies in hats worn to one side. Everybody looked so old then, I remarked to myself. A peculiarity of the times, perhaps? Then came the babies, lying on their backs or sides and dressed in white or pink. Almost all the more recent pictures were Polaroids. From album to album the children gradually grew until they finally assumed their present-day form. I looked at them as they crowded around me and said, "Good kids! You did that very well; you grew up fast." They all laughed.

In keeping with the proprieties, they gave me a separate bedroom. After all, I was Jenny's boyfriend and not her husband. They had set aside a place for me in a huge room downstairs, a sort of second living room whose door opened directly onto the garden. Before going to sleep, and after their parents had gone off to their own room, we all went up to Debby's room and smoked a joint. The grass belonged to Debby and Robert—the brother and sister were good friends—and turned out to be very strong. We lazily sat or lay in various corners of the room among the dolls, the pictures of rock stars, and the photographs of Debby's former boyfriends. There were a surprising number of the latter, despite her seventeen years.

The next morning I woke up before almost everybody else in the house and went out into the yard, where I made a careful reconnaissance of the whole territory. I carefully examined the vegetables in the garden, tested the hammock, though I was soon driven away from there by the mosquitoes, and then re-turned to the house, where I noticed a tangle of bicycles in the room where I'd been sleeping. I got on one of them and rode off, but after circling the house, I came back, since I had no idea where to go. At that moment, Debby came out of the house yawning. For some reason, I was especially glad to see her and no one else, and I went over to her and like a curious tourist started asking her all about the garden. It turned out that she was raising the tomatoes, whereas the pumpkins belonged to her thirteen-year-old brother, Ronald. After properly manifest-ing my delight in regard to her tomato plants, I remembered the bicycles again and suggested we go for a ride. "Okay!" she said. She was very easy to please.

We went into the house and had a cup of coffee. Her parents hadn't yet made their appearance, and I didn't even know where their room was, there were so many doors. We had already taken our seats on our bicycles, when at the last moment we were joined by Robert, who, as it turned out, had just taken his car to a garage. We set off: Robert first, then me, and then Debby on a little bicycle that obviously belonged to the youn-gest of the children, the eleven-year-old Kevin. After we had climbed to the top of the asphalt road high above the house and were already resting on our pedals, I heard an anxious voice call, "Edward!" Looking in the direction of the voice, I saw Jenny standing in her nightgown at the front door. She was standing on one leg and scratching it with the other. The mad Edward merely smiled at her and waved.

Our jaunt was not without its minor incidents. From a house with a cement swimming pool painted a dark blue and hidden deep in a gully among the trees some shaggy dogs rushed out at us, barking furiously. Robert and Debby put their legs up on the handlebars and I put mine on the frame, and we quickly coasted downhill to a green bridge crossing a little brook, and left the disappointed dogs behind. Eventually we reached the place where all the Jackson children had gone to school. Robert and Debby laughingly showed me, as if it were one of the sights, the special building where the defective children studied. I laughed at the defective children too, and regretted that it was Saturday, since they had probably all been taken back home to their families and it would therefore be impossible to see their defects.

It was very hot, and so we decided not to ride any farther but to remain in the school yard and spend some time there. Each of us taking quiet pleasure in the fact that he wasn't defective, we rode on the swings, and then when he saw somebody he knew throwing a ball in the basketball hoop all by himself, Robert asked me if I wanted to play. We played with the other guy for a little while, and then switched from basketball to soccer, which I'm a lot more partial to. Debby played soccer no worse than Robert did. After we had exhausted ourselves and the ball, we rode back home. I was already getting tired of the American hinterland, even though I was also making an effort to "study" it. Since you're here, Limonov, ask about everything; stick your nose in all the details. . . .

And stick my nose in all the details I did. On a shelf in the living room I found *The People's Almanac*, went out into the garden, sat down in the sunshine, and began to study it. It contained more than a thousand pages of different kinds of information from every domain of human endeavor. I of course was most interested in the lists of criminals "most wanted" by the

FBI, lists going back many years. After 1969 the "most wanted" were political criminals, especially those belonging to certain organizations—the Weathermen, the Black Panthers, and still earlier, the Students for a Democratic Society. Obviously, the two giants, America and the Soviet Union, had undergone a process that was still not quite clear to me but that was the same in both countries, since at the end of the sixties in the Soviet Union too the most important criminals for the KGB had been the dissidents. The mosquitoes were biting me, and the sun was roasting me unmercifully, but I read on and on, reading until lunchtime, unable to tear myself away. Papa Henry even came out and said he would give me the *The People's Almanac*, and I could read it in New York. Papa Henry was obviously hinting that I was being "unsociable."

After lunch I decided to be more sociable for Jenny's sake. And so, when they invited me to go to a baseball game between two school teams, one of which the eleven-year-old Kevin played for, I said it had always been my *dream* to see a real baseball game and I was dying to go.

We piled into two cars, the big car belonging to Jenny's father and a small blue one belonging to Robert, and set off. On the front seat next to his father sat the grave little Kevin, chewing gum. He was nervous, but he chewed his gum like a grown-up, pretending he was a tough guy.

There were already quite a few cars parked at the site of the upcoming event, and many of the seats on the wooden benches had already been taken. All of us—the more than ten members of the entire Virginia-based Jackson clan and I—took our seats higher up where it was more comfortable, in the center, so to speak, of the bleachers that partly surrounded the main part of the baseball field and that were separated from it by a high fence, and got ready to cheer Kevin on. And then it started. . . .

I thought it would be insufferably boring and had already begun to steel myself for the ordeal. How wrong I was! There was nothing boring about it. In just a few minutes, the solitary figure Limonov found himself caught up in a vortex of local hysteria. "Our team"—that is, Kevin's—was called the Yellow Socks and was playing the Tigers, and, gentlemen, it was the championship! And so all the relatives of the Yellow Socks and all the relatives of the Tigers were there, plus all their friends and acquaintances, and everybody else who cared about the reputation of the town and the school, as well as all those who were merely curious, and all those locals who had come simply because there was nothing else to do in town, and all the local hooligans and local intellectuals, and . . . All of them had clambered up onto the benches with cans of beer and Coca-Cola and other soft drinks and with cigarettes between their lips, and were waiting for the action to begin. Underneath the bleachers wandered very young children ready to pick up balls coming over the fence, if there were any.

Children of eleven, twelve, and thirteen are exceptionally different in size and form. On the same team were giants and dwarves, men and babies. All of them took their turn at bat and struck at the ball thrown by the opposing team's best pitcher, and when they swung and missed, the crowd roared and whistled indignantly, but when a lucky batter swung and hit it and threw down his bat and took off round the bases, the crowd roared and whistled in delight. I was afraid for the catcher the whole time, since I was sure one of the kids would hit him between the eyes with the bat or knock his brains out—the bat was a serious weapon—and spoil the whole game, but the kids were up to it and didn't hurt him.

A fat blonde, her tanned shoulders bared and the straps of her bra and pink undershirt cutting into her ample flesh, shouted to her son, a small blond boy with his hair cut in bangs just like Prince Valiant's, "Bobby, be aggressive! Be aggressive!" And Bobby was, insofar as his size and strength permitted, and he hit the ball well, and took off around the field, while his mama grabbed hold of the fence in raptures and screamed, "Bobby-y-y-y!"

I looked at the Jackson clan. Papa Henry at the far end of the bench was yelling something and slapping his hands on his knees, Debby had stuck two fingers in her mouth and was whistling, and even the usually morose Betsy was yelling too, although in the general uproar it was impossible to tell what she was saying. But when Kevin came up to bat, we all started wildly applauding and yelling, "Kev-in!" as if shouting encouragement to our own champion in single combat—me too, as I suddenly realized to my own astonishment. Our man did no worse than Bobby had—he was even better, thanks to the fact that Robert had coached him for several hours before lunch by throwing a ball to him. He was in good form, our champion, and he hit the ball brilliantly, and we all started shouting again, I don't remember what, and whistling, and in my enthusiasm I struck Jenny on the shoulder with my hand and screamed something else along with all the others, and then we applauded our Kevin while he circled the bases.

When I finally recovered from that collective paroxysm, I heard Jenny choking with laughter and pointing at me and shouting, "Look at Edward! Look at how Edward's screaming and waving his hands! Ha, ha, ha!"

Jenny was obviously very happy about my sudden manifestation of normal human feelings. Maybe she was thinking that Edward, like all normal men, like our American men, likes baseball too and gets carried away and starts yelling, and despite his eccentricity and aloofness, he'll be a good husband for me. And we'll have children, and we'll get in the car just like Mom and Dad do and take our whole family to baseball games, and Edward will write his books and make money with them, and it doesn't matter if it isn't very much at first, as long as he's doing what he likes. And he'll soon stop raving about the destruction of civilization and forget about all that, and I'll be a good wife to him, and on weekends I'll bake bread and the children will play in the yard, and we'll have lots of flowers—Edward likes flowers.

Probably that was what she was thinking, and I could understand her. I didn't hate her there in that American town; she suited me much better there where there weren't any Marchioness Houstons or sweet-smelling and fancily dressed and painted whores to compare her to. There Jenny had the advantage of being on her own ground, where the electric lights they had turned on at the baseball field worked to her benefit, as did the fragrance of the nearby grass and trees and even the smell of the pipe of the portly gentleman sitting next to me and of Debby's and Robert's cigarettes.

And it was then, on that field, that I suddenly realized that I didn't hate Jenny, but rather something much bigger, maybe the very arrangement of the world, or maybe nature itself for what it had given me at birth, for that enormous and eternally dissatisfied ambition that was in my blood and that wouldn't let me stop and catch my breath—wouldn't let me stop and live with Jenny on a farm and be happy and perhaps mow hay and maybe even write books, but different books, books full of tranquility and happiness rather than anxiety and the need to escape. Jenny was someone I could have been happy with, and maybe it was just that which made me hate her?

I had looked for love for so long, had wandered in chaos trying to find it, to find Jenny. And now that I had found her, and with all that was genuine and false in me had made her fall in love with me and had won her, I was going to reject her and turn away and tell her I didn't want her or need her. Or even more monstrously, that *I hated her*. And hated her because she was an ideal, the girl I had in fact dreamed of for two years while lying alone in my filthy hotels and choking on my own hysterical sobbing or fucking with prostitutes or other men. . . . It was *she* I had been seeking in all those bodies, thinking that this is the one, that here she is, or even that here he is. And now I had found her.

The Yellow Socks lost to the Tigers that evening six to eight, but what difference did that make? Jenny had lost to me on her own ground, but then I was somebody who didn't play by the rules.

Chapter Five

THEY STILL hadn't caught Son of Sam then, and sometime around the beginning of August at three o'clock in the morning he again wounded two victims, the girl later dying in the hospital, the guy surviving. The city was overcome with terror, not so much in Manhattan as in the Bronx or Queens, where the Son of Sam "worked," but the streets of Manhattan too emptied earlier than usual, and it would happen that coming from or going to Jenny's at night, I would suddenly find myself completely alone. Even the number of ordinary crimes diminished, the thieves and robbers probably afraid that the insane murderer might shoot them down too "by mistake," after silently appearing out of the darkness as he always did, so that you wouldn't even have time to defend yourself or shout that you were a robber, although it was unknown whether he had a sense of solidarity.

I walked in those legendary times through the sticky, spectral city, at first a little frightened myself, but then seeing that nothing had happened to me, I got bolder and even took my usual route through Central Park. The air was fresh there, not as hot and much nicer for walking than the foul West Side, but the main thing is that it was more direct. I didn't even walk into the park, but jumped over a fence into its green darkness and strode through the trees toward the East Side. I came out of the park in the neighborhood of the Metropolitan Museum, and I often brought Jenny fragrant branches or flowers as evidence of my bravery. True, I still took off my glasses, so I wouldn't look like an intellectual in case I encountered some lowlife, and I also carried a knife with me, and sometimes even two—one in my boot and the other in my pocket.

We lived quietly then. Jenny sucked my cock and tried to cure her vagina. The story of the curing of her vagina (it really is an awful word, isn't it?) is interesting and instructive, and I shall therefore permit myself to dwell on it.

You have to pay for everything, gentlemen, one way or another you have to pay. It's an undeniable truth. I didn't want to be merely an idle boyfriend for Jenny, and so the honorable and hard-working Limonov himself volunteered to sew her some rags and alter a few things from her vast wardrobe of skirts, blouses, dresses, and pants.

Once when I was in the house alone, with neither Steven nor his guests around, thank God, and had been rooting in Jenny's things for several hours at least, humming something to myself as I did the alterations, Jenny and Jennifer arrived. They had just come from the quack Krishna, with whom they were both studying homeopathic medicine. Even more pimply than usual, Jennifer disappeared to make a phone call, and Jenny, after sitting down on the bed in the room where I was seated at the sewing machine with her skirts strewn about me, suddenly announced, "You're going to get very mad, Edward, but both you and I have gonorrhea. Dr. Krishna finished his examination of me this morning."

I have of late become a very even-tempered man—very cool. I therefore continued to press on the pedal of the electric sewing machine, and its speed didn't even waver. I kept on sewing; what could I say to such an idiotic statement?

"Why don't you say anything?" Jenny asked irritably.

Making a wry face and pulling her skirt out of the clutches of the machine, I said, "I'll kill you at five."

"Why at five?" she asked in puzzlement.

I didn't say anything, but thought to myself, Well, gonorrhea then. It's even fair—I have to pay the price, don't I, for living here and fucking Jenny and having the pleasure of seeing the children's room and not having to suffer the heat thanks to the air conditioner . . . and for the expensive French wine she brings me from the cellar, and for the garden and the other pleasures? Obviously I have to pay the price. . . .

"You'll have to see a doctor," Jenny said.

"Uh huh," I answered, and pressed down on the pedal again, stitching the next seam.

"You're not being serious, Edward," she said.

"What am I supposed to do?" I said, turning toward her for the first time in the whole conversation. And really, what did she want from me? Gonorrhea is just gonorrhea; nobody dies of it, and if they do, so what?

And I left her to go to the bathroom—there was a bathroom in every bedroom in the millionaire's house. I pissed, and afterwards washed my cock in the wash basin while standing on tiptoe and stretching, and then wiped it with satisfaction on a face towel. "You get it too!"

Jenny didn't say anything to me after I came back to the room, and we went downstairs to the kitchen to get something to eat. Another friend of Jenny's had come over too—Martha, a stocky blonde just as pimply as the others. I knew from Jenny that she was pregnant and was planning to have an abortion soon. I sat down with them and ate some *shchi* I had made a couple of days before, and they had some too. I sat there and fumed. The *shchi* was very hot; even the potatoes in it were overcooked and falling apart.

If you're going to infect me with gonorrhea, at least don't overcook the *shchi*. Why the fuck was it left on so long! She forgot about it, the cunt! I thought to myself.

I was sitting at the table with three defective sluts and dreaming about how I'd like to chase them all out, the pimple-faces. Jennifer was particularly disgusting—pug-nosed, with a rose in her hair. She had on a yellow skirt that day too. She had her feet up on the air conditioner; they all went around in their bare feet. They were drinking beer. Fat. And then they complain in *The Hite Report* about what a poor job men do of fucking them, I thought resentfully. What kind of man would you have to be to get it up for a fat, pimply creature like that?

As soon as I finished eating, I went upstairs to Henry's old room without saying anything, opened the door to the roof, and sat down in the doorway. A few minutes later Jenny came in.

"If you won't go to my doctor, I'll never fuck you again and I won't see you anymore," she said angrily.

Go fuck yourself, I thought. She gave me gonorrhea, and now it's my fault too. I'm fed up with your fucking house, you servant, and this whole musty summertime story. You peasant cunt! And I walked out, saying, "I'll come back when you calm down."

Neither Jenny nor I could hold out in proud solitude for very long. Two days at most. During that time I managed to make the rounds of the darker Broadway dives and visit two prostitutes. There was never any doubt in my mind that I didn't have gonorrhea, and if I had, the prostitutes would probably have detected it, since they always carefully examine the client's penis before setting down to work. After rolling in the mud a little, I at once felt better and freer, and in two days was again sleeping on "the other bed," while Jenny groaned in her sleep nearby—the air conditioner was on, and it was cold.

Autumn came. I remember peering out the window at the wet terrace and its wet chairs with the usual autumn thoughts going through my mind, as if looking timidly out at chaos from the comfortable nook I had wrested from life—the millionaire's town house. Sometimes I would open the door to the terrace and stand confidently on the threshold, while chaos whistled around my feet. Looking at it from the millionaire's little house, it didn't scare me—it wasn't intimidating but defeated, not what it had been from my hotel. Seen from the hotel, it was a genuine, epic, old-fashioned, invincible *chaos*. But in the town house I just poured myself a shot of cognac, put a slice of lemon and a piece of Camembert on a red breakfast tray, sat down in the solarium with some quiet music on and maybe a book in my hands, and gazed into the rainy garden undismayed.

You see, the rich have over us poor not only the advantages of property; they are also freer from the onslaughts of chaos. It mounts its attacks, but the rich man merely lights a fire in his fireplace or orders somebody else to do it (I light Mr. Grey's fires for him), and sits down, warms his hands, lights his pipe, and puffs a pleasant tobacco. Chaos is frightened away by the fireplace and the pipe. And it's frightened away most of all by beautiful women. Whereas all the poor man can do is hang around the streets, so that whenever the weather is bad, his whole life comes to pieces.

So my life was sweet. My only duty was maintaining good relations with Jenny. And, as you see, I did maintain them, upsetting them only occasionally, but never seriously. Whenever she started in on her favorite topic—the children she wanted to have with me—I nodded with enthusiasm, "Sure, sure, Jenny, of course we'll have children." But at the same time I thought that to merge my sperm with her ovum, or whatever it's called, would be contrary to nature.

It was during this time that Dr. Krishna finally had the sense to examine Jenny thoroughly—I don't think it was his idea alone; somebody had obviously suggested it to him—and a huge tumor was discovered in her vagina. So much for obscurantism. You can believe in whatever you want, in forms with three hundred questions or in gonorrhea, and never have the sense to conduct a simple medical examination, to look inside her cunt. In any case, Jenny now thought she had cancer (!) and was undergoing treatment. Whatever sexual relations I had with her came to an end. She didn't feel like sucking my cock anymore. First, we were already pals; second, how could a person do that if she had cancer? . . . It wouldn't have bothered me.

I really wanted to fuck, but I did my best to sublimate, to transfer my sexual energy to some other domain. I became furiously active, and after several setbacks finally found a literary agent with Madame Margarita's help, or more accurately, a female literary agent, and she agreed to work with me. Unfortunately, Liza's still working with me, and the book that so delighted Efimenkov remains unsold. . . .

I also did all the things the classic failure's supposed to do. I wrote long letters to the newspapers and magazines, on political topics mostly, and I even sent a letter to President Carter, which nobody answered of course. The newspapers and magazines didn't answer either. I used Jenny to check my clumsy translations into English, and she either laughed or got mad, but she still helped me. In exchange I got some patterns and made her skirts with ruffles, which she had grown increasingly fond of. I have no illusion the skirts I made were masterpieces of the tailor's art, but Jenny liked them and they made her happy. So, as you see, we worked together excellently in life, even if not in bed.

From time to time Jenny would buy me presents. Knowing, say, that I liked beautiful boots and that my own were starting to wear out, she would with a smile suddenly hand me a box— "Surprise!"—containing just the kind of boots I wanted to replace my old ones with. Once she bought me several pairs of jeans and some sweaters all at once, which, given the dilapidated state of my wardrobe, were very much to the point. In general she took care of me like a mother.

At that time I was still going to Madame Margarita's to make *piroshki* and *pelmeni,* although less and less often. Unfortunately, the very good cook and gay man of letters Volodya and the enthusiast Madame Margarita turned out to be poor businessmen, or rather, not poor businessmen, but unable to devote all their time to *piroshki* and *pelmeni*. Volodya was writing a book about ballet and seeking and rejecting new lovers and in the evenings going either to gay baths or to the parties of the rich. Madame Margarita was busy with Lodyzhnikov's business. . . . You need to be a harassed little person who knows that if he doesn't sell a certain number of *piroshki* and *pelmeni* each day, his family won't have anything to eat. Then the business will succeed. After shuffling through their papers, and counting and recounting, and adding, multiplying, and dividing, but mainly subtracting, they decided to quit.

But as so often happens, another way of making money suddenly appeared on the horizon, this time in the form of one of Madame Margarita's friends, the French woman Christine, who already owned one restaurant that gave her an appreciable income, and who had decided to open another on the corner of Fifty-seventh and Third Avenue with a Russian evening bar serving appetizers. Volodya, who had already squandered the advance on his ballet book, planned to go to work there as the head chef, taking me on as a cook, to which I agreed, although not without reservations, to be honest, but I still agreed, having decided at the same time to get off welfare. The fact is, I really wanted some sign of visible progress in my life, and I wanted it soon. What made up my mind was the fact that we would be expected to work evenings, from five until one in the morning, so I would have my days free and could still write. But the restaurant still wasn't open, and on my way to and from Jenny's, I would peer into its chalked-over windows at the workmen rushing urgently about.

On one of the last days of my *pelmeni*-making I got involved in spite of myself in a heated political argument with Madame Margarita and Volodya. I didn't really want to argue, but I lost my head. Somehow they egged me on imperceptibly, to the point where their placid philistinism irritated me so much that I jumped in. Basically our positions were these: Madame Margarita and Volodya believed that only Russia was shit, while the rest of the world, and the United States in particular, was beautiful. Whereas I said that the whole world was shit, the United States being no exception, and that our civilization deserved to be destroyed, since it had enslaved man and deprived him of himself, of his sense of freedom. "We, the whole world, have been living in Orwell's 1984 for a long time, only we don't realize it," I said.

Volodya smirked, which only made me madder.

"Thanks to the training and education the Soviet government gave you, and gave you for nothing, by the way," I said to Volodya, "you occupy a privileged position here. Just as you did there, in fact. You wrote and published books on ballet there, and you write and publish them here."

"And who stops you from publishing your books?" Volodya said maliciously. "Haven't found a publisher for your pornography yet?"

"No, I haven't," I said. "You know perfectly well how hard it is for me to find a publisher, and you know why. . . . Maybe I'll never find one."

"Limonchik," said Madame Margarita with inimitable calmness, "what can you do; it was your bad luck to be born in the Soviet Union and come to America too late. All the places are taken now. If you had come here in the thirties, it would all have been different. Maybe your children will be happier. Certainly they'll be happier," she concluded sympathetically.

"Can you imagine that?" I answered. "What am I supposed to do now, lie down and die?"

Madame Margarita shrugged.

"Maybe I should wait for rebirth?" I asked sarcastically. "It's my 'bad luck.' But I don't believe in rebirth. I know everything is happening *now*. There's nothing ahead but a dark pit. And there isn't anything in it. It's just a pit!" I was silent for a moment. "To nobly make *piroshki*, and haul somebody else's furniture and paint somebody else's walls, and live in the Diplomat, and drink and grow old and merely accept it," I continued, "while all around you is the odor of money, and expensive cars are speeding by, and morsels of young female flesh are displayed in the picture magazines. No thank you. I'm much too passionate and ambitious for that. I don't know how, but I'll be successful here. Me, and not my children, whom I don't intend to have anyway," I said angrily to Madame Margarita. "If I have to kill, then that's what I'll do!" I added in a facetiously calm voice.

"You're a typical Soviet, Limonchik," Madame Margarita said, "a typical Soviet. . . ."

Madame Margarita is very smart, and in her youth was very pretty; I've seen photographs. She had once been married to a wealthy businessman—had engaged, in short, in the usual business of females and sold her cunt for a profit. And not very long ago she had a millionaire among her lovers, a publisher. She still lives alone in a beautiful apartment on Park Avenue and doesn't have to go to work, having already earned everything with her cunt. Her only work now is going down to the bank, and whatever she does for Lodyzhnikov, or the *pelmeni* and *piroshki,* she does for her own pleasure and not for money. I'd make the same bargain with the world too. And of course it wasn't unpleasant for her cunt either. Pleasurable and practical.

I walked from Madame Margarita's up the broad expanse of Park Avenue, past the doormen in full dress uniform, and swore in two languages. "Limonchik, what can you do, it was your bad luck," I bleated, parodying the sympathetic voice of Madame Margarita. Ah, you whores, I thought. You're all members of the same gang—Gatsby and Efimenkov and Stella Makhmudova, and Volodya and Solzhenitsyn, and Madame Margarita and Lodyzhnikov and the poet Khomsky, and Rockefeller and Andy Warhol, and Norman Mailer and Jackie Onassis, and all the designers and hairdressers and blue bloods and party secretaries, whether they live in a country pompously calling itself the "leader of the free world" or in another that no less vulgarly pretends to have a monopoly on the "bright future of mankind." You all make up a cruel international mafia, a union of strength and capital with learning, art, and intellect. And the millions and billions of us simple people are required to submit to your cruel whims, to your games of the mind and imagination, to your caprices which cost us so much, since from time to time you push us into war. Fucking Big Brothers!

I reached the millionaire's house and complained about the Big Brothers to Jenny.

"Edward," she said, "don't pay any attention to the fucking politicians. They're the same everywhere, in all countries, and no doubt they'll push us all over the edge someday!" And then she started making soup, the most peaceful activity imaginable.

Life is an indistinct affair, utterly diffuse and formless, and it is only those principles that you yourself introduce (or that are introduced for you by others) that give life whatever order it has and a kind of purpose and coherence. Jenny was of course a very important stage in the process of "my struggle," as I envisioned it, the struggle of Edward Limonov against the world and everybody in it. Yes, that's the way I conceived it—as *one against all,* and it was a struggle in which I had no allies. I just recently happened to overhear my employer Gatsby shouting in his office during one of his regular fits of hysteria, "You're all against me! The whole world's against me!" I was astonished to find that he perceives the world exactly the same way I do.

I lived invisible to everyone but Jenny. And I lived intensely; I was in a hurry. Unfortunately, nobody else was. I badly wanted to get ahead. Onward! I shouted to myself in an agonized voice. But the world held me back with a firm grip, not wishing to let me leap with such sudden ease into the next category of life, or, if you like, to climb up onto the next rung of the social ladder. Up, I'm sorry to say, from the very bottom. There weren't any rungs below me. Unless it was jail.

I wanted to get out of the hotel and move somewhere else. I

sensed from everything that I needed to get the fuck out of the Diplomat, that the time had come to move. If for no other reason than just to move.

My first attempt proved a false start. After one of my arguments with Jenny, I decided to strike out on my own, and tried to find myself an apartment. The ballet writer Volodya rummaged through his vast circle of acquaintances and introduced me one day to a little twat named Mary Ellen. This dwarfish little bag of bones lived in a two-room apartment near Lincoln Center and was studying ballet for the fun of it. Mary Ellen had a rich homosexual dad who lived in Washington, D.C., and who paid for both her apartment and her two two-hour classes a day. "Mary Ellen's apartment is too expensive for her and she's looking for a roommate," Volodya told me. "Talk to her. If she likes you, she'll take you and you'll pay her something. Or you won't have to pay her anything," added the cynical Volodya, "if you start fucking her; then you can live there for nothing. In my opinion, she doesn't so much need a roommate as a prick," and he laughed in distaste.

Mary Ellen did in fact need a prick. The first time we met, she looked very intently and significantly at me, and passionately informed me of her desire to learn Russian. Her apartment was spacious, in a huge modern building with mirrors in the lobby and several doormen who used special televisions to watch what was happening on every floor. The lobby even had its own newspaper stand.

I liked the building and I liked the apartment, but I didn't much care for the circumstance that I'd have to sleep on a little couch in the living room. And write there too, for when I asked Mary Ellen where I would work, it turned out I'd have to do that in the living room too on the only table in the apartment. The upshot was that I would be renting a "corner" of her apartment, as they say in my native land, and not a room. Naturally, if I start fucking her, I thought, then I'll sleep in the bedroom with her and work wherever I see fit. But after looking at her gray, sunburned, bony little arms with their skin strangely cracked like crude leather, I had no desire whatever to fuck her. That is, I wasn't excluding the possibility of occasional copulations with her, once a month say, after I'd had something to drink or smoked a couple of joints, but to become dependent on her wasn't something I wanted to do.

After spending about an hour with her at her place and drinking several cups of instant coffee without sugar, since Mary Ellen didn't offer me anything else, I took my leave, solemnly promising to think about her offer and decide during the week. I also recommended that she think about it too and make her own decision. Riding down on the elevator with a well-dressed elderly woman and listening to the soft music emitted from somewhere in its ceiling, I talked myself into moving in with Mary Ellen, citing to myself the example of the "real opportunist." A real opportunist, Edward, I said to myself, would move in with Mary Ellen without hesitating, and fuck her with his eyes closed. And so must you!

I called Mary Ellen several days later and told her I was ready to move in if she hadn't changed her mind. "As a roommate," I emphasized diplomatically.

"Fine," she said. "You can move in anytime from tomorrow morning on, or any other day." I said tomorrow, of course; I was impatient, and immediately went back to my hotel and started getting my things together, books for the most part. I only had one suitcase, so I packed the books in shopping bags with handles.

I must have looked like a bag lady when I climbed onto the bus going down Broadway the next morning with two of my sacks, both very heavy. But what could I do—I didn't have any money for a taxi, nor anyone who could have helped me move, so I was forced to move my things piecemeal by bus.

Carrying my shopping bags, I made my way past the self-important doormen in braid with a timidly defiant expression on my face and went upstairs to Mary Ellen's floor. To my floor, I thought proudly, as I pressed the buzzer. She didn't answer for a long time, but then she finally opened the door. Her face was sleepy and, it seemed to me, a little guilty.

"Did something happen?" I asked, already aware of what it was.

"I'm terribly sorry, Edward. My father just called from Washington and said you can't stay here; he's against it. I called you at the hotel, but you'd already left. . . ."

I stood in the doorway like an idiot with my shopping bags. I didn't even lose my temper, since I've grown quite used to fate's little tricks. I just borrowed five bucks from her, left my shopping bags, telling her I'd be back for them later, and hopped onto the elevator. She called after me that she was sorry about it and apologized and something else, but I couldn't hear anymore. Outside it was a blindingly sunny autumn day and the wind was blowing some flags, although, since I was in a hurry to find a bar, I don't remember exactly what kind they were— whether the flags of countries or just for decoration.

I had to call Jenny from the bar several hours later, since I was drunk and didn't have any money with me. Jenny arrived in a taxi with Bridget, and they took me away. "Bad boy!" Jenny said several times with a maternal smile. The bartender was pleased it had all worked out without his having to call the police, and I felt like my relatives had come for me. It really is a good thing to have relatives, and know they won't leave you in the lurch, even if you have been a "bad boy." And as we rode in the taxi back to the millionaire's house, the sun was still out, and the wind was still blowing the flags, whatever they were.

In order to compensate for my failed attempt at moving, I soon afterward resolved to get off welfare. As I say, I was anxious for evidence of my progress in life. I remember with what astonishment and delight the clerk at my welfare center on Fourteenth Street looked at me—as if I were somebody who had just come back from the dead—when I informed her of my intention to give up welfare assistance, since I had found a job and was now able to support myself. That probably didn't happen very often. The black clerk shook my hand and wished me luck in my new life, and I gazed for the last time at the immense sea of my now ex-comrades in misfortune sitting in the large hall waiting for their appointments. Goodbye, comrades! I thought cheerfully, as I strode out the door.

Okay, I thought, we're on the next level now. I was the only one who realized it of course; the people on Fourteenth Street carrying on their unruffled trade in plastic sandals, polyester dresses, and suspiciously large cans of tomato sauce certainly had no idea that I was already on the next level, that I had climbed up a little bit from the bottom where I had been. I couldn't even share my happiness with Jenny—I'd concealed the whole welfare business from her.

Is that something I should do on the next level? I wondered, passing by a porno theater. It was, and I went in and watched a porno film. Even on the new level I still had some of my old bad habits. The porno film turned out to be shitty.

It's always the way that either nothing happens, or if something does, then the first event is immediately followed by a second and then a third; obviously they come in batches. A couple of weeks later Jenny and I went to Southampton for Jennifer's and Dr. Krishna's wedding. Not only was he a crazy Indian for marrying a twenty-year-old girl, but a rich one as well, and the wedding therefore took place in a large restaurant with an ocean view.

Looking back at that momentous occasion from the present, I can see that the wedding was one of the most boring, but at the time it seemed to Limonov, with his then great yearning need for throngs of people, to be grandiose and significant. I even managed to be, if not at the center of attention, then at least on its periphery, since I was by no means the least attractive man in that crowd and could actually dance better than anyone else, which earned me the attention of the ladies and I suppose the bitter resentment of the men. I was dressed, I remember, in my white suit. The day was sunny and warm, fortunately, although I had in fact been following the weather reports for a week, afraid it would turn cold and I wouldn't be able to wear it, the only impeccable item in my wardrobe. The lively, smiling Limonov, surrounded by ugly girls and women, and as breathless from dancing as a young virgin at her first ball—you know, Natasha Rostov. "Are you a designer perchance?" asked a fifty-year-old-lady, puffing away at her cigarette and rendered even happier and more interested when I told her I was a writer. Another lady of the same venerable age took me for a ballet dancer; obviously, such ladies think that all Russians living in the United States are ballet dancers.

What can I say? I was flattered by their attention, and although it would have pleased me even more to be surrounded by a flock of young actresses and models rather than by a motley crowd of slightly crocked married women jealously watched by their paunchy and sullen better halves sitting at their tables with loosened ties, or by a crowd of Jenny's pimply friends selected as if for their complexions, a gaggle of twenty-year-old girls of various sizes, even those groups stimulated me somehow, although I realized it was all very silly. This is silly, Edward, really silly! I thought to myself, and then grabbing my next partner, I rushed onto the dance floor, desperately seizing from life whatever it was capable of giving me that day, and in fact did give me. The orchestra (certainly Krishna had hired an orchestra) was a jazz ensemble, with saxophones, drums, and a piano—what else; I couldn't expect him to invite Richard Hell and his group, could I? The orchestra liked me too, and even started to accompany me, keeping time to my movements.

I used to have a Polaroid picture taken that day by Raj, a relative of Krishna's, in which I am sitting at a restaurant table in my white suit with the sea behind me and a happily romantic expression on my face. I later gave that picture to Elena, who no doubt has lost it, which would be a pity. Behind me you can make out the head of a woman, or her hair at least; that's Andrea, the girl I danced with the most that evening and who won me, having prevailed over all her rivals. That is, I fucked her, or more accurately, she fucked me, or even more accurately, we fucked each other a few days later. I was at the wedding with Jenny, after all, and had come in the same car with her, which she drove. Besides, I had no intention of abandoning her that evening or of hurting her; I still cared about her, and anyway it was enough that I had hardly danced with her that day. Andrea and I merely exchanged phone numbers.

Despite my expectations, the bride and groom, or rather the husband and wife, didn't look all that incongruous, didn't seem like grandfather and granddaughter. Even though Jennifer was only twenty, she was stocky, robust, and swarthy, with a coarse blunt nose, and looked older than she was; I would have said she was thirty. Krishna, on the other hand, was just the opposite: he looked much younger than his years, and was tall and well-built for his age, without any wrinkles to speak of on his tanned face, so that I would have given him fifty-five instead of his seventy-two. And so they looked quite normal together—nothing particularly shocking.

Among the guests was a whole clan of Indians: men, women in saris, and even Indian children, and not one of them got drunk, and I noticed too that the men danced, but the women didn't. It also seemed to me, as I looked at the Indian women, that Jennifer very much resembled an Indian girl—it was no accident I'd mistaken her for a Turk the first time I'd met her. Her face was of a generally Eastern type, and if you had taken off her clothes, she would have looked like one of those squat women with fat thighs you see held on the pricks of their grinning Indian rajas or non-Indian sultans, those well-built women sitting or lying in various positions, sometimes very uncomfortable ones, on the pricks of their rajas in Indian colored miniatures tinted in red and in gold. Who knows, it may have been that very resemblance that tempted Krishna into thinking they would be happy together in bed.

Andrea and I met again only a few days after the wedding, both of us waiting a bit, as if out of decency, although we both knew what we wanted. Finally, after a phone call, I went down to her place on Chambers Street in an unfinished loft which she had bought with several friends. Each of them had a separate bedroom but shared a huge kitchen and a gigantic hall, empty and uncluttered, which they planned to use for concerts and dance performances and for teaching and studying dance. Andrea was in fact a student of modern dance, and I soon had my fill of sweaty youths and girls in tights or wide pants and T-shirts portraying snakes or a Chinese theater or whatever while rolling on the floor with significant expressions on their faces—which all seemed so second-rate to me. Nevertheless, during the months I spent fucking Andrea, I posed as a passionate admirer of modern dance, and even went to some of her performances. Andrea was either the seventh or the fifth dancer in "The Silences of the Night," or maybe it was the "The Scream of Day"—I don't remember exactly what, although it had a pretentious title and reminded you of something halfway between therapeutic group gymnastics and a theater for the deaf and dumb.

I didn't burden myself with any any special efforts on Andrea's behalf; we just went to a place called the Ocean Club near her place on Chambers Street for drinks, and I told her, just as I had told Jenny, about how unhappy I was. I told her I didn't want to be a homosexual and had therefore become friends with Jenny, although I couldn't have sex with her because she was very sick. "Jenny and I are just friends. I merely play the role of being her boyfriend," I said, "only please don't tell anybody, Andrea," and Edward made a noble face. I don't use that pitiful technique anymore; it seems unworthy of a man. And I very much want to be a "real man," as indeed I am.

Andrea wasn't required to believe anything I told her—it was just the usual love song of the male; any noises would have done. She wanted my hands on her little body and my prick inside her, and I wanted just as calmly and confidently to see her naked; she probably had short legs and a hairy crack. A twenty-year-old cunt, I thought with a certain aversion.

Andrea told me in her turn how unhappy she was. She had had an affair for a year and a half with a guy who also did modern dance, who crawled on the floor, in other words, and sometimes she thought she still loved him. Pronouncing the word "love," Andrea's face assumed a tenderly bovine, dreamy expression.

Realizing that we were both unhappy, we drank some more, and she suggested going to her place for a smoke—she had some grass at home. We returned to the unfinished loft, went into her bedroom, and lit up. A few minutes later I found that I was fucking her without even taking her panties off but just pushing them a little to one side, and with my own pants in a tangle around my ankles, that I was fucking her and that it was extremely good, as if I had come home again—and doesn't it seem to you, dear reader, that a cunt is a home, warm and cozy? Her sticky cunt followed my prick wherever I wanted it to; if I went to the side, her cunt did too, and if I pressed down, her cunt inclined downward too, softly and benevolently enveloping my prick as it did so. I lifted her dress as high as possible until it covered her face, took her large breasts in my hands, large for a girl so small, and lay down on her as heavily as I could and stroked. She was submissive and only panted, and then she softly moaned. I liked the way she fucked—I don't care for women who are too vigorous—and especially that feeling of domestic tranquillity she gave to me. Her cunt was a home, cozy and warm. She came with me, later admitting she had waited.

We lay still and I surveyed the field of battle. Strewn on the floor and bed were singles and ten-dollar bills belonging to her, my glasses, and various other feminine junk that had tumbled out of her purse, which also lay nearby. We both burst out laughing. On tiptoes, trying not to make any noise, we took turns going to the cold bathroom at the other end of the loft, and then we undressed completely and lay down, and I grabbed her luxuriant hair and pulled her head onto my prick. . . .

I was awakened at dawn the next morning by a sweet odor of decay in the room, as if outside they were doing something with corpses under the window. Looking out the window, I saw the backyard of a butcher shop. . . .

I had become a full-fledged member of American society with surprising speed. The French restaurant opened at last, and I started working there with Volodya and Kirill, a young guy from Leningrad and one of the characters in my first novel. Kirill and I were no longer friends, however. As you know, I had completely left Russians behind and set off on my own path.

I had left, but they still came. The two intellectuals, while making dough or shaping *kulebiaki, pelmeni,* or *pirogi,* the delicacies that were the basis of our menu, chattered nonstop, reciting Russian poetry together or suddenly breaking into *Les fleurs du mal* in French. Both of them, you see, had received Old World classical educations. Both were terribly, shamelessly cultivated, and their fastidious intellectuality at once created a distance between them and the rest of the kitchen. Otherwise they wouldn't have avoided sharp conflicts with the populace, even though the main kitchen was upstairs and we worked in the basement where the bouillon was made and the dishes were done in a special wing, and where the only other person besides us was the restaurant butcher.

I had listened to Russian poetry every day in fabulous quantities for a dozen years without a break, and the pompousness, vulgarity, and artificiality of Russian verse made me sick, and I therefore obstructed them by swearing, banging pots together, or reciting my own recent verse out loud, poetry which was frequently unbearable to them. Our little skirmishes had a rather benign, even friendly character, however, and neither they nor I took offense. But what really irritated me was their casual and misplaced disdain for our fellow workers. Neither Kirill nor Volodya called them anything but "cattle." I've never considered myself a model of altruism, but to hear insulting Russian names spoken every day right to the faces of our completely unsuspecting co-workers was for some reason offensive to me. As a result, I started swearing at them in earnest.

Taking advantage once of a convenient moment, I swiped several gallon bottles of cheap wine and a couple of bottles of whiskey from the bartenders upstairs—theft or expropriation? Expropriation without a doubt, I told myself, and just like Robin Hood I shared my booty from time to time with the people, including the puffed-up intellectuals, who of course called me a thief but who refused the wine and the whiskey neither the first time nor the last. On one occasion I also treated a black guy named Victor from the upstairs kitchen, who had come down to us to make a meat filling with the huge meat grinder located in our territory, and I'll admit he looked like a hoodlum—a broken nose and a raspy voice. I poured him a half a glass of whiskey—I knew how to make friends—and we jabbered awhile about his Antilles islands, where he was born. After Victor was gone, Volodya and Kirill started protesting:

"Don't start bringing your black friends down here, Limonov," Volodya said. "We know how much you like them, you wrote about it in your book, but we haven't got any use for them."

"Yes, Limonov," added Kirill, getting so angry he even turned red, "go upstairs if you want to hang around with them. We have a nice quiet place here, and we don't want them coming down. We don't need a crowd of blacks around here. This isn't Harlem."

"You disgusting intellectuals!" I said to them. "It's my business, and I'll make friends with anybody I want. You squeamish pansies!"

"If you don't stop bringing him down here, we'll tell the manager that he's been hanging around and that you've been drinking," the intellectual informers said maliciously.

I got my way. Victor came to visit me frequently after that, calling me "brother" and laughing very loud, and we had a good time. The intellectuals grumbled and muttered but in the end got used to Victor and even found him to be witty in his own way. Later on I heard something completely unprecedented—Kirill bragging in my presence to one of his girlfriends that he had a black friend at the restaurant named Victor!

Not unfortunately, but not fortunately either, life in the restaurant basement didn't last very long. Despite our grand beginnings—several parties organized by the owner Christine for publicity purposes during which well-dressed young whores with young men of the *Playboy* type toured the kitchen, and my two countrymen turned red and tried to keep their dignity though dressed in cooks' uniforms, and I imagined myself knocking one of the long-legged, sweet-smelling cunts over onto the potato sacks—despite those beginnings, the restaurant was poorly patronized. Despite all the ads in the big New York newspapers and magazines and the enthusiastic reviews in the restaurant sections of the *New Yorker* and *Cue* arranged by Madame Margarita, the restaurant declined, Christine lost money, and every night the dining room was three-quarters empty and the handsome waiters were spending more time combing their hair and bickering in the cloakroom than they were waiting on customers. There were rumors that we would soon be closed.

It wasn't so much that I liked working, no, but that with Jenny's help I had started looking for an apartment. I wanted to become a normal person, a member of their society, and then we'd see, maybe fate would toss something my way. Maybe a publisher would buy the book, since my agent, Liza, had finally received from my translator, Bill, the first chapter in English to go with the other two he had already finished and was now setting down to work with enthusiasm—and now this obstacle in my path.

Fucking unsuccessful businessmen! I needed their two hundred and ten dollars a week; I needed it badly. Believe it or not as you wish, but it was on the very same cold November day that Jenny found me an apartment on First Avenue and Eighty-third Street that the Russian section of the restaurant was closed. "We can't have such a large menu. It just isn't paying its way, unfortunately," Christine told us. I put on my leather coat bought used some time ago in Italy, picked up my old umbrella, said goodbye to Victor from the Antilles, and left behind yet another basement in my life. I went to Jenny's, of course.

She told me to take the apartment.

"Edward, how long can you go on living at the Diplomat; that's a very depressing situation. You'll feel a lot better as soon as you get out of there. I'll help you," she said. "I've already spoken to Linda about it. We're very tired of the Chinese couple, you know, the Chus, who vacuum and wax the whole house once a week. They go around the house the whole day without saying anything, and you can't communicate with them," Jenny went on. "If you want, we'll can let them go, and you can do the cleaning instead. Even though she pays the Chinese thirty dollars a week, Linda is willing to pay you forty, and that will be exactly enough for your rent—one hundred and sixty dollars a month! Do you want it?"

I said, "I want it," thereby depriving a Chinese family of rice. The struggle for existence. Neither the first mean thing I've done, nor the last.

You'll say something about how a hundred and sixty was too little, right? The fact is that Jenny found me two little rooms in a three-room apartment, the third and largest room of which was occupied by Joe Adler, a twenty-three-year-old Jewish-American boy who was trying to live independently of his mother and become a painter; he even had a beard. The apartment actually cost three hundred and twenty dollars. And so we made our decision. "If it ever happens you can't make your rent, Edward, I'll always be able to help you out," Jenny assured me encouragingly.

Jenny borrowed a car from one of her friends, and on a cold, snowless first of December, I dragged all my shopping bags, my pictures, and my suitcase out of my hole in the hotel and took my leave of the manager, who said, "Good luck, Comrade Limonov!" Dressed in an ankle-length black coat with a caracul collar that had belonged to her grandmother and, for some reason, in a black dress too, Jenny stepped on the gas and we set off for a new life. The "Destruction is Creation!" poster I had left hanging in the hotel. Looking back for the last time I saw standing in the wind next to the hotel a little crowd of our black brothers, including I think my neighbor Ken. He had a long and passionate conversation with somebody in the hallway on one of my last nights in the hotel. When out of curiosity I opened my door a crack to see who it was and what was going on, Ken was alone. Poor guy, he was evidently already suffering from delirium tremens.

"Hurrah!" I shouted when I was finally alone after Jenny had left and the boy Joe had gone to a meeting of the building association. I had succeeded in climbing out of that shit after all. Congratulations, Limonov! I said to myself seriously and triumphantly.

I started enjoying life a lot more then—it was a new period. I became exceptionally zealous about equipping "my" new apartment, as I affectionately called it. By New Year's, I had completely furnished my two rooms; I even had a large desk given to me by Jenny—who else?—and for the first time in my life had the pleasure of my own desk with a great number of drawers into which I at once put all my papers. I had a bookcase too, old and slightly rotten, more a shelf than a case, but exceptionally pleasing to me, and I started buying and stealing books in order to fill it up as quickly as possible, and when I did fill it up, the books made their way onto the windowsills and other convenient places.

I didn't fight with Jenny anymore; my apartment brought us together. Its appearance in her life provided a new object for motherly concern and practical activity. Every time Jenny visited, she brought something along with her: kitchen towels, or a skillet, or some dishes she had picked up very cheap—"Guess how much they were, Edward?"

Once she dropped by with Bridget, Martha, and Douglas, Douglas out of breath from dragging in a box of French wine, and the girls carrying between them about twenty bottles of different kinds of alcohol quite essential to any decent home. A small loan from Mr. Grey, who would never notice this drop in his sea of bottles. I couldn't even begin to count all the stuff Jenny dragged over to the apartment, including such things as linen and even a huge quantity of various Mister Cleans and Spic-'n'-Spans and the other poisonous liquids and powders with which my new homeland is so richly endowed.

But I got the bed myself. I too had certain practical talents, not to mention a super I knew in a huge stone box on West End Avenue.

I even went so far as to get myself a Christmas tree. I didn't have anything on it except for lights, that being as far as my money would go, unfortunately, but it didn't matter. The main thing was that I had my own Christmas tree reaching to the ceiling as in my childhood. It was as if a war had ended and everything was beautiful once more and life was set right again. I put the Christmas tree in the corner of my study, or my office, as I called it, and frequently turned on the lights and lay down by it, by my own tree, and enjoyed it. I had a home. Not a hole into which a tormented animal retires only to sleep, but a home. For the first time in many difficult years. A *home*.

It's natural that when you acquire an apartment, you acquire expenses too, and so I took whatever work I could find—anything to keep from sliding back into the past and its mode of life. And when Seva, a photographer I knew, asked me to help him turn some empty industrial space he had just rented on Madison Avenue in the twenties into a loft for four dollars an hour, I happily agreed, and we started knocking down partitions. Jenny was very glad I had found work. She was in fact an exact clone of my mother, who had always been very happy too when after getting stuck in some shit, I found myself a regular job. Even if it was difficult, dirty, mindless work.

After breaking down the partitions, we began putting up new walls, after which there was plastering and painting to do. As a consequence of the close working relationship that developed between us, Seva once asked me to go with him and his wife to a party given by a photographer friend of his, a woman who also taught at the School of Visual Arts. I went with Seva, since I have never turned down a party, neither then nor now, and we had a lot to drink.

Sarah was a pupil of the lady photographer, and I remember she was the first to talk, provoking me and laughing at me. . . . The result was that we left together. It was a rainy New York winter evening, and I suggested she come with me. And she did. . . .

The most distinctive thing about my new girl was her wig. In the process of fucking or, if you prefer, the sex act, I was suddenly amazed to see that her wig had slipped down over her eyes. Or more accurately, I was astonished to see that her scalp had slipped down over her eyes, and at once realized that it was a wig. Unembarrassed, Sarah rearranged the wig with one hand; the other was busy holding my balls. We fucked all night lying on the floor by the Christmas tree, on a mattress brought in from the bedroom. Sarah's cunt wasn't too big, her skin was white, and the little Jew humped like a nanny goat. Twenty-two years old, a little shorter than me, hook-nosed, slender, and with large dark eyes, she was a true daughter of the Jewish race, a seeker of adventure and collector of the most diverse experiences, including even the lesbian kind, and was ready at any moment to go wherever you liked. All she needed was to grab her small but voluminous shoulder bag.

Around midday we crawled out of bed and went down to the Village, having decided to get something to eat there. Snow was falling, fluffy and light just like in Moscow, falling and melting on the dark New York sidewalks, while the inadequately dressed New Yorkers pulled their hoods over their heads, or wrapped themselves in scarves, or opened their umbrellas. Our insolent New York children packed the wet snow into snowballs and threw them at people. The skeleton of the Great City stood out vividly against the snow storm.

Sarah and I walked arm in arm, and she gazed at me lovingly the whole time—you know, with that satisfied and sated look a woman gives you when you have fucked her well, have fucked her unbelievably well. I was her man, her male, in the most direct and unashamed sense of the word, her prick that had taken and untied the knot of her passions and tensions, so that they had all flowed out of her, leaving nothing behind, and it was good for her to be with me, and she was calm and easy, and her body didn't torment her anymore. How do I know all this? I saw it all in her loving gaze. I know that fawning feminine gaze.

We came to a little restaurant called Johnny Day's I've visited many times—unlike inquisitive New Yorkers, I'm conservative—and where we ordered steaks and Beaujolais Villages and talked animatedly. After all, we still didn't know each other and there was a lot to talk about, although during the conversation too I caught that fawning, submissive look again from time to time. I enjoyed myself, I'll admit—we drank two bottles of Beaujolais and I sat there and made up some boastful lies, I remember, and she knew I was making it all up, but we didn't care. We were "having a good time"—I love that charming expression—and laughing, while outside the large picture window of Johnny Day's, the snow was falling.

After lunch we rolled out of the restaurant into the snow.

143

Women are boastful too, and Sarah immediately dragged me off to show to one of her friends, a photographer and sadist. She wanted to parade me in front of the sadist, of course, and to show the sadist off to me. I didn't refuse her that pleasure, especially since the sadist lived close by and we could walk there.

"The walls of his studio are black. Don't be scared, but he has chains and whips hanging on the walls," Sarah told me hurriedly, starting to run ahead in the snow and looking back at my face.

"Do I really look like somebody who's afraid of chains and whips?" I asked her, laughing.

"No," said Sarah, "but I didn't feel too brave myself the first time I went there, and I'm not afraid of anything either."

There really were both chains and whips. The sadist was a stocky fellow of middle age and very tired-looking.

"Are you a photographer?" he asked me almost at the front door.

"Sorry, no," I said. "I'm a writer."

"A writer," the sadist repeated with evident satisfaction and asked me to sit down. "You're a lucky man," he continued. "Write your books and remember that you're very lucky. You're not in this shitty business—photography, I mean. I detest it."

At that moment a half-dressed honey-blonde model with butterflies painted on her cheeks emerged from a barely noticeable door, also black, and said:

"Raphael, I can't do what he wants me to. For this money let him get somebody else. I'm leaving!" And she disappeared through another door.

"Calm down, baby," Raphael called after her. "You think I want to do anything for the money I get?" He turned to Sarah. "I take it this guy is your new boyfriend?"

And not waiting for her to answer, he addressed me. "You aren't an American, what are you? "No, wait, let me guess. French?" he said, doubtfully.

"No," I said, "Russian."

144

"Ah, a Russian . . . a Russian. . . . You're lucky, Sarah; they say Russians are very good lovers. Does he fuck you good?" asked Raphael, turning toward Sarah on his revolving chair. I forgot to mention he was sitting on a revolving metal chair.

"God, Raphael," Sarah said, "why do you have to be so obnoxious?"

"I'm a tired old professional sadist who earns his living in the shitty business of photography. The shittiest business imaginable. You're only a young cunt," he said. "How old are you, twenty-three?"

"Twenty-two," Sarah said.

"Aha, twenty-two, but I'm fifty-four. I'd like to see what you'll be like at my age."

"At least I'll never be so cynical," Sarah said.

"Russian, what's your name?" Raphael asked me, once again not giving Sarah the satisfaction of an answer.

"Edward," I said.

"Listen, Edward, hold on to this Jewish princess. She's a very talented photographer, even though she's still a young little cunt. In a few years she'll make a lot of money at photography once she gets this crap about photography being an art out of her head, and she'll be able to support you very well. All you'll have to do in return is give her a good fuck from time to time; nothing more is required. Based on what I hear about Russians, that shouldn't be too hard for you."

"I refuse to make money doing fashion photography. I want to do what I like," Sarah angrily protested.

"Oh please!" he said, waving her away. "Don't talk such rubbish." And then he stood up. "If you want coffee or something to drink, help yourselves; if not, I am unfortunately going to have to kick you out. Fucking business!"

We turned down the coffee and rolled back out onto the street.

"Don't worry, he's not as bad as he seems. He gives me work and helps me make a living," Sarah said, starting to talk very fast. "I'm a good printer, and he often asks me to do printing for him and pays me pretty well. The first time we met, he invited me to join his harem—he has a harem of several girls, models—but I refused to." Sarah ran ahead again and looked back at me anxiously. "I've never slept with him," she added uncertainly.

"Sarah, you don't have to justify yourself to me," I said. "Raphael's fine as far as I'm concerned. I like crazy people. And I even enjoy the fact that he talks out loud about things that ordinary people don't. I can't stand polite conversations about the weather. Raphael's all right; he's a good fellow."

"Yes," Sarah said, relieved. "I'm glad you liked him. He's very kind, even though he pretends to be mean."

We went to her place in Brooklyn. Ordinarily I wouldn't go to Brooklyn for any reason, but now I was following a cunt there, was being led there by a cunt hidden beneath a brown wool skirt.

Back at her apartment, we immediately lay down on her huge metal bed with brass knobs and several tiers of lattice work of various kinds, and started fucking. . . . By the middle of the night I was trembling all over from just the touch of her fingers on my skin, and we were completely covered with sweat and semen. When I looked at my prick while we were taking a shower together, it was torn and bloody, or more accurately, worn out.

You think she took her wig off in the shower? Shit no; she just tried to keep her head dry.

"What's wrong with your hair, Sarah?" I asked, trying to put the question in an indifferent tone, as if by the way. How did I know, maybe she had a complex about it; maybe the wig was her Achilles' heel.

"I'm crazy," she said, a little embarrassed and turning her head a little to the side with a lightly apologetic smile. "I tear out my hair sometimes when I get depressed. It's growing back now."

146

Jesus, I thought, is it really necessary to tear your hair out, and how much do you have to tear out before it becomes necessary to wear a wig? You really are crazy, Sarah. I used to know a girl who had the nervous habit of pulling out her eyelashes and who sometimes went around without them, but to pull your hair out . . . All of it?

Maybe Sarah lost her hair as a result of illness, say a thyroid disorder; I've heard of things like that. Actually, the absence of hair on Sarah's head didn't bother me; I had always rubbed shoulders with freaks and crazies, and anyway I didn't consider myself exactly a paragon of mental health. If she didn't have any hair, then she didn't. . . .

All the same, I spent New Year's Eve by Jenny's side instead of going out. I was fair and not without a sense of gratitude, although I took the addresses and phone numbers where I could reach either Sarah or Andrea—just in case. I say I spent it "by Jenny's side" because the poor girl was sick in bed with a bad cold or the flu. However much I wanted to be out in the noise and the crowds, I stayed with her; she deserved a Happy New Year.

At exactly twelve midnight I drank some champagne with the patient, bought obviously with her money, and we toasted with Gatsby's very best champagne goblets, made of German crystal. "What do you wish?" Jenny sniffled, and I told her: "I want to be famous and I want the whole world!"

I don't know what she wanted, maybe ten children and me, a husband in pajamas. After our toast we chatted a little more, and then she let me go into the TV room to watch a New Year's program. "You're probably bored, Edward," said the noble Jenny, letting me go.

I went downstairs to the TV room with my goblet, watched *Yellow Submarine*, had several martinis, and then around three, I went back up to the bedroom, feeling very calm and majestic. Jenny was asleep and breathing heavily in the midst of clouds of water vapor from two round electric humidifiers. They were her latest fad. She had heard somewhere that there wasn't enough moisture in the air in wintertime and that it was therefore a good idea to sleep with humidifiers on. Grinning like a hoodlum, I unplugged them and went to bed.

The time flew by, January and then February—it was already 1978. I worked every day with the photographer Seva, remodeling his loft, and then rushed off to see my girls.

In the spring, my roommate, Joe Adler, gave up his dreams of a free and independent life as an artist after all. His mama had won. She found Joe a well-paying position in Yonkers, and he decided to give up his part of the apartment, and I, mad fool that I am, was suddenly overcome with a desire to take the whole place for myself.

At first Jenny didn't approve. "How are you going to pay for it, Edward?" she reasonably observed when I first told her of my intention. "You don't have a regular job."

Jenny didn't realize that she was in fact going to pay the one hundred and sixty dollars for the other half of the apartment. For I was sure I could easily hook her, so to speak, on the idea of our sharing the apartment together, the apartment serving as a kind of prologue to our shared family life, a place where our children could perhaps play someday. "Our own apartment."

Ours or not, I still had no intention of giving Jenny a key to it. Hell no!

Mama Jenny's maternal heart was of course unable to resist the temptation of having her own nest. Within a few days I had, in addition to my study and bedroom, my own living room with four windows.

My relations with Sarah developed, unfortunately, along the same lines they had with my other girls; that is, she gradually started to irritate me. I was tired of her. When we fucked, I sensed even through my marijauna or alcoholic stupor that she was giving herself to me and was moved by me, which is something I can't stand, in fact. I hate it when other people love me but I don't love them. Looking at her with as unprejudiced and sober an eye as possible, I suddenly realized that she wasn't pretty enough for me. Maybe I understood that earlier too, but the feverish state of mind I was in whenever I grabbed whatever cunt happened to be available just to keep from being alone and masturbating, and suffering the anguish of not having anybody to stick my prick into or take at least a modicum of animal warmth from—that state of mind had passed.

Sarah now seemed to me to be just a crude little slut from Brooklyn—crude and uncultivated, fussy and loud.

She would flop down in my apartment and throw on the floor her trashy boots, underpants, stockings, and other awful things which I turned away from in embarrassment and distaste, just as I had from my mother and her feminine secrets when we lived together in the same room.

Once Sarah appeared at my door in a very agitated state. Rushing in, she immediately demanded bourbon and announced that she was very hysterical that day. She was pretty hysterical every day. Downing the bourbon and pushing her wig back from her forehead, she told me with an insane gleam in her eye that she had gone to see about a job and that the man doing the hiring had made her pull up her skirt and expose more of her bosom.

I said, "I hope he was satisfied; you have nice breasts." And she really did have nice breasts, small and well-formed.

"Really, Edward?" she asked, becoming excited. "You really think I have nice breasts?"

"Yes," I said, "you really do." I didn't add that in my opinion her temperament was too loud and screwed-up; I just said, "Sarah, I'm hungry!" And that was the honest truth too. I didn't have any money and had been dreaming since morning of how nice it would be to have a piece of meat. I could have gone to Jenny's, but I couldn't take that crazy woman with me.

Sarah didn't have any money either, as she happily informed me.

"Let's fuck then," I said, and we went into the bedroom. But it didn't work; Sarah simply radiated craziness that day, and she kept giggling in a silly way. I gave up trying to fuck her and went back into my living room to make myself a drink. When I came back, she was naked and bending over like a monkey to cut her toenails.

"Sarah, it's vulgar to stick out your cunt and cut your nails in front of somebody you love."

"Edward, you're so petit bourgeois!" she retorted, continuing to cut her toenails.

"All right, so what if I am, but you look gross," I said.

She continued to cut her toenails anyway, chattering about something which I stopped listening to, and then she sprawled out on my bed, covering herself up a little, and put her dirty feet on my pillow. I'm not particularly squeamish, but I thought in puzzlement, What the fuck is the little slut lying around here for? What is she doing here? And then I said out loud that I had to meet some friends for dinner and that I couldn't take her with me.

Sarah grew sad and said that she was leaving too, but she had to make a phone call first. "Is that all right?" she asked.

"Of course it is," I said, and sat down at my desk as if I were going to write something. . . .

Despite my indifference to her, Sarah still continued to play a role in my life for a long time. Long after Jenny had left and the traces of other less remarkable girls in my life had grown cold, Sarah still turned up in my bed now and then. Maybe the hope of obtaining me blazed up in her again from time to time. She really tried to win me. Even after I had grown completely insolent and sent her as a sort of living present to a friend of mine who had just arrived from Europe and was living by himself on Madison Avenue and didn't know anybody in New York and didn't have anybody to fuck, Sarah went obediently. I've already said that Sarah was open to any experiment.

We broke up just recently. After supper at P. J. Clark's, we came back to the millionaire's little house and climbed into bed, either to fuck or to sleep. But Sarah was so drunk and stoned that her Brooklyn upbringing started to come out. She accused me of greed (!), of having a middle-class mentality (!), and of other terrible sins as well, and shouted "Shit!" and "Fuck!" and laughed hysterically. She drove me into such a rage with her crazy behavior that I threw her out without fucking her. I am, when it comes down to it, the servant of millionaires. I have rich neighbor-whores living next door to me who sometimes even allow themselves to call up on the phone during parties given by my employer and complain about the noise. I don't much care for noise myself, and so in a fury I hit her naked body and threw her out on the street at three o'clock in the morning. I made her pick up all her rags, and I threw her out without even screwing her. I said, "Get the fuck out of here right now!"

Sarah looked at me with reproachful, sobered eyes and said over and over again, "Edward, aren't you ashamed of yourself! Aren't you ashamed of yourself!" I was ashamed, but I had decided to punish her.

A few days after that episode, I received a letter in the official envelope of the Metropolitan Museum of Art, where Sarah was working as a photographer. The letter was a remarkable one, and it was obvious that Sarah really did love me, so bitter was her farewell:

> You're a big, gaping, empty zero. You're a synonym for permanent failure. You're a failure in friendship, you're a failure in love, and as far as your career is concerned, you're nothing but a self-deluded jerk. You're unlucky in everything you do because all you care about is your own superficial, insensitive personality.
>
> The real reason your book isn't making it in the United

States has nothing to do with its so-called controversial theme. The reason nobody will touch your book here is that the United States has much higher standards for literature, and your book just isn't good enough. Carol [her deadly dull, gray friend who works as a drudge at a publishing house] actually told me that your book is self-indulgent and boring, and that she couldn't even think about showing it to her publisher.

In the last analysis, your ideas are all on the surface and don't mean very much at all. You're just a pretentious idiot.

I doubt you have even one friend in this world you could show this letter. Nobody who would laugh at how silly all this is.

Go on living like a servant and moving from one servant's job to another and intoning your clichés.

Nobody will ever be affected by anything you do.

You're a baby with a huge ego. You're masturbating your way through life.

There wasn't any signature.

Chapter Six

I BROKE UP with Jenny very unexpectedly, although it was exactly the way I had always wanted to break up. She found herself another guy, got pregnant by him almost immediately, and went to live with him in another city—Los Angeles. God gave her a baby and established her in the life that was most befitting for her; with me she had obviously violated both the divine and the mundane orders of things.

After meeting my ex-wife Elena, Linda said to me, "Edward, I just can't see what Jenny and Elena have in common. Elena is a very stylish woman, but Jenny was almost a peasant." I explained to Linda that Elena had been the wife of the Russian poet Eduard Limonov, whereas Jenny was the girlfriend for a year and a half of another person altogether—a poor, unemployed welfare recipient and tenant of a single-room-occupancy hotel, the New Yorker Edward.

Jenny did the right thing in leaving me, or nature did. She wasn't getting anything new from our relationship, and even though we had started making love again, there were times when she was indifferent to my prick, and she was only very rarely happy; sexually, we just weren't compatible. Occasionally, she would start talking about marriage, and I, attempting to look sad, would say that we couldn't afford to start a family yet, and she would agree and drop the subject for a while.

I don't know if she ever suspected that I was having affairs with other women, or if she believed I was satisfied by the meager diet she provided. I just don't know. She did, I remember, find women's things in my bathroom several times—a little watch, a necklace, a ring—and there were several other times when she found hairpins on my bedroom floor. But either she preferred to believe me when I told her that one friend or another of mine had spent the night there with a girl or when I made up some other, sometimes rather clumsy lie, or perhaps, reasonably enough, she just didn't want to make a scene about it. But I don't think that she ever did suspect just how frantic my sexual life was, so frantic that I even had a little green book in which I wrote down my amorous meetings so I wouldn't get them mixed up. Sometimes I had two or even three different girls in a single day, and I was as proud of my Don Juanism as any adolescent.

Be that as it may, by the time Jenny suddenly left me, I had gotten used to the constant oscillation in my feelings for her between friendliness and gratitude and aversion and irritation. You already know what I had to be grateful to her for, but what irritated me about her was her plebeian manner. For example, whenever she was sitting down with her fat legs spread wide (she had begun to put on weight, gentlemen), so that you could see her cunt, or not her cunt itself, but her underpants with her cunt underneath, she was too lazy to pull down her long skirt or straighten it. She wore long skirts in imitation of Nancy, her employer, who was always arrayed in the same uniform—skirts so long they even dragged in the snow and mud.

I would say to her, "Jenny, what do you dress like an old woman for? You're only twenty-two. (She was already twenty-two! Time had passed.) And why do you have to sit in that vulgar way? Are you too lazy to move your legs?"

She would laugh, but if I continued to insist, she would get irritated and yell her invariable response: "Cut it out, Edward! Cut it out! Stop criticizing me. I'm sitting the way that's natural and comfortable for me, and other people don't have to look if they don't like it!"

Once I drove her to tears that way. It was on a day when she looked particularly disgusting to me—her jaw was swollen from having her wisdom teeth removed and she had another pimple under her nose. She offended my aesthetic sense. That's the sort of person I was then, gentlemen, but really, how could I help it! She was after all a sturdy and likable girl and could have looked a lot better; she could have used a little makeup, say. I told her all that then, and she started crying.

"Why do you keep criticizing me! You act like you're my teacher!" she said. "Instead of encouraging me, you make me feel like a nothing."

I told Jenny that I didn't always do what other people told me either, but I listened to what they had to say and considered it, and if I found something useful in their criticism, then I tried to bear it in mind and change. And that I wasn't criticizing her to humiliate her or show that I was better than she was, but only to make her better, since I cared about her. The crafty liar Limonov.

"And really, Jenny," I said, now completely into my didactic role, "how much longer are you going to waste your time with Martha, Jennifer, and even Bridget, when it comes down to it? You need to spend more time with cultivated people and read more and maybe even go to school somewhere. Even at my age, I've thought at times of studying at Columbia University. You're a smart girl, Jenny, and you aren't going to be Steven Grey's housekeeper forever. The people you go around with now are much less than you are. You're obviously much brighter than they are and much more talented."

Jenny stopped crying and perked up and started making plans. "You're right, Edward, I should go to school," she said enthusiastically, and we began discussing where she could go. But having made her plans, Jenny didn't have the strength to carry them out. She was lazy and given to inertia. She had an innate intelligence and was streetwise the way simple people are, and she was very sarcastic, but God, what did I want from her anyway, that she'd become another Marie Sklodowska Curie and for my sake turn herself into something diametrically opposed to what she actually was? No one can leap higher than their ceiling, and you can't make a lady out of a servant girl. And I didn't. All Jenny would ever be was a mama cow. If only she'd had ambition, but unfortunately no, I never found a drop of it in her, except for a certain pride in me, her boyfriend, if you can call that ambition. Once Jenny told me, "You're a typical poet, Edward, with long wavy hair just like you're supposed to have," and she touched my hair. "Just like Lord Byron." She said this last phrase with pleasure and respect. Yes, perhaps I was her ambition, and she was doing her best to win me, but what if she couldn't, and went down in defeat?

The next day she was sitting barefoot and unkempt in the kitchen of the millionaire's house once again and chattering with her usual Jennifer, Martha, or Bonny, who lived next door, and drinking beer, with her feet so dirty that Linda still remembers it now with horror.

The days and months went by as usual, one weekend replacing another on the roof of the millionaire's house, and then the summer was gone. In August 1978 Jenny took me to California. It was her vacation, and mine too in a way, the first one I'd had in the three years I'd been in America. We had in the meantime tried to put some money aside. "Save your money, Edward," Jenny told me. "Saving money" sounded ridiculous in my case. I had plastered and whitewashed two apartments, the full extent of my earnings for the summer, so that Jenny ended up paying for my part of the trip, which made me sick. Even though she was my girlfriend and I was an opportunist, it still made me sick; it's better to have your own money and not depend on anybody else for anything.

We flew to California with Jenny's friend Martha; it was her vacation too. And there in California, with the participation of Martha and the poet Alyoshka Slavkov, a friend of mine who at the time was living in Michigan and working for a publisher of Russian books, the final act of the story of Jenny's and my romance was played out—a story that had begun by error.

I, who sometimes view my life as the labors of Hercules or the travels of Odysseus, was glad when after several days in gigantic Los Angeles and depressing circumstances in the vast, beautiful home of Isabelle, who had only just moved there with her dogs and Valentine ill with cancer and Chloe and Rudy, we finally went to live in a redwood forest, an arena more fitting for Herculean labors. Jenny's father and mother owned a little piece of warm California land that in its own way was quite wonderful—a redwood grove and a real saloon built a hundred and fifty years before by the first California loggers. The four of us tumbled out of the car and into the saloon one splendid August day and distributed our things in the upstairs rooms that had once belonged to prostitutes. The fact is, the saloon had stood virtually untouched for its whole one hundred and fifty years; nobody had remodeled it, and Jenny's parents only went there once every couple of years. On the first floor, just as in all the saloons I'd seen in the movies, there was a bar and an immense fireplace, to the left of which a wooden staircase led upstairs to the second floor—to the prostitutes' rooms. It's obviously very symbolic that the last time I fucked that peasant angel was in one of those very rooms.

We had picked up Alyoshka Slavkov in Los Angeles and taken him to the forest with us immediately after renting an idiotically uncomfortable beige Toyota that looked like a piece of soap in shape and color and that stank like a toilet inside.

If you've never been in a redwood forest in your life, it will be very difficult for you to imagine. Darkness reigned there. A little sunlight fell on the small meadow where the saloon stood, but the rest of the Jackson property lay in the shadow of the giant trees and therefore in a kind of permanent green darkness. In the evening packs of husky raccoons would come out of the trees to the campfire Alyoshka and I had built near a rude fireplace made of stone, and beg in the hope of making off with something. If I turned the beam of the flashlight toward the huge tree that was closest to the fire, the whole band of them, sometimes as many as five or six raccoons, would freeze in place in their fur coats with only their eyes gleaming. If we left the kitchen door open, they would come in there too, unafraid of its bright electric lights, and after taking whatever food was offered, would run heavily away. At night we could hear them walking on the roof. I liked the raccoons. There was also a kind of dark blue bird living in the redwood forest, which I fed bread and called a "blue jeans bird," since it was exactly that unbelievably artificial color.

Jenny's brother Robert was the only one living at the saloon when we got there; I had met him, you'll recall, at their parents' house in Virginia. This young man lived an easygoing and carefree life, accumulating an immense quantity of trash in black plastic bags. The only reason he didn't have problems with rats is that the raccoons would probably have gobbled them up if they had come. The raccoons had chewed through the bags which were heaped in a pile under a tree next to the kitchen, and the whole area around the saloon looked like a dump.

Robert's morning began at six. At least whenever I would get up very early myself, I would find the young man sitting in the kitchen next to the already lit iron stove, his morning joint gaily glowing between his lips. As the day progressed, he smoked more and more, and when evening came, he would cook himself up on the same stove a stinking paste of hallucinogenic Mexican mushrooms. Sometimes his friends would come to visit him from the nearby college campus in old cars, and they would all sit out on the veranda and take turns scraping out mushrooms from the pot with an aluminum spoon. What Robert was trying to do remains a mystery to me. The only food he ever ate in front of me was carrots. He was a vegetarian, and there was always an inexhaustible supply of carrots in the refrigerator, which Robert and his friends and Jenny and Martha made juice with, and then drank. They must, I think, have consumed dozens of pounds of carrots. Jenny claimed that Robert ate our vegetables too, our vegetables and our bread, since he didn't have any money of his own—or so she said. But it's also possible she was exaggerating.

The skinny, likable Robert, with his utterly vacant, ethereal gaze, was the mildest of creatures. True, the only time he was capable of grasping anything, in my opinion, was in the morning. Whenever I opened the refrigerator to get my morning can of beer—which is how I started my own day, since Alyoshka and I were drinking heavily—Robert would always ask in amazement, "Beer at eight o'clock in the morning, Edward?" and grin and shake his head. And I, motioning at his invariable joint, would say, "A joint at eight o'clock in the morning, Robert?" and shake my own head. He was a very "cool dude," this Robert, and later on, when Jenny and I started having our arguments and disagreements, he couldn't understand at all why we weren't getting along with each other.

"What are you arguing about?" he said to me one morning. "Jenny and you, Edward, are getting upset over nothing. You should take it easy; after all, you don't have anything to argue about. I eat my mushrooms, and then everything's fine with me. The world's really beautiful, you know. . . . Do you want some mushrooms, Edward? They're cheap—five dollars a bag. You can even order them by mail. . . ."

For us Robert was something like God's own representative in the redwood forest. He had a calming effect on us, but of course not even he could keep us from dividing into two camps.

Sometimes it seems to me that if it hadn't been for Alyoshka, I might not have lost Jenny then, but it's possible it only seems that way. I realized even in Los Angeles that with the four of us in one car the trip wasn't going to be an easy one. We could never agree about anything. If Alyoshka and I wanted to spend the day at the beach, the girls wanted to go to a restaurant and then to a movie, and so on. If you also add to our continual disagreements the fact that Martha was a complete stranger to Alyoshka and that during the whole trip he never had, as far as I could tell, the slightest desire to fuck her, as well as the fact that Jenny's and my sexual relations weren't giving us any pleasure, then you can imagine how we, a group of strangers irritated with each other, felt in that tin can of a car. Jenny, moreover, did all the driving. Alyoshka still didn't know how to drive then, I wouldn't have trusted myself with the car, and Martha didn't drive either for some reason, and so Alyoshka and I found ourselves completely at the mercy of their coalition.

Once enclosed in that small space, we discovered that we were all very different. And not just because Alyoshka and I were Russians and the girls were Americans—no. After all, Alyoshka's English was excellent and he was moreover already enrolled in a graduate program, while I myself had in fact forgotten more of Russia than I remembered. But the girls had their own interests, and we had ours.

Health food, for example. Alyoshka and I laughed heartily at their passionate faith in health food and made fun of it every chance we got. Whenever we stopped at a health food store, and there are a great many of them in California, I tried to find out from Jenny how she knew that the food—shitty tomatoes, the famous carrots, and rotten onions—had in fact been grown without the use of chemical fertilizers. And what if they had? Jenny got mad when I laughingly maintained that the owners of all the health food stores were crooks, and that they bought spoiled produce from the supermarkets around the corner and sold it to her as wholesome food. I would have kept quiet if the shitty health food hadn't cost twice as much as the much more wholesome-looking "normal" food.

The girls also had huge jars full of various kinds of vitamins with them, which they would constantly bring out during the trip and share with each other. "Do you want to try some B-2, Jenny?" or, "Why don't you give me some C with A-6, Martha!" So went their little conversations.

I might have put up with the girls better by myself, much better—I wouldn't have paid any attention to them, but Alyoshka and I continually egged each other on, and since we were speaking Russian, we unfortunately had the fatal ability to say whatever we wanted about our opponents in their presence. If we had had only one common language, we would necessarily have restrained ourselves and spoken less, instead of spinning a web of hysteria together.

The girls' conversation was little more than gossip. They chattered incessantly about Steven and his lovers, about Nancy and her love affairs, and about their own mutual acquaintances and their love affairs, but never about books or politics.

Alyoshka and I discussed Russian and English and world literature for three days or so until we got tired of it. I'm not saying our conversations were more interesting than theirs— you can chatter boringly about literature, too, and I in fact talk less and less about it now than I used to—but only that our conversations were of no interest to them, whereas to Alyoshka and me theirs were merely the primitive babbling of servant girls. Yet the fact remained that we were divided into two hostile factions, and that I was in the worst position of anybody, since both Jenny and Alyoshka came to me whenever they were unhappy about anything at all, and Alyoshka moreover told me whatever was on his mind in a language the girls didn't understand, thereby implicating me in his hysteria too.

He said that they were stupid country girls, but I already knew that they were simple and dumb and boring. But I couldn't tell Alyoshka in so many words that those girls were in fact just what we deserved then—if we had deserved any better, we would in fact have been traveling with them. That was something I had always understood very clearly; it was an objective reality. Just as the fact that I was traveling at Jenny's expense was an objective reality.

In short, I had several fallings out with Jenny because of Alyoshka, during which she screamed that it was her first vacation in almost four years and that she had the right to rest in whatever way she liked, even if it only meant not being criticized every minute. "I don't care about your literature! Fuck your literature and politics!" she screamed. And for the first time in my life I heard her say, "I'm paying!"

I told her that there that was no question about her right to rest any way she liked, and that, yes, she was paying, but since she had taken me with her—I hadn't imposed myself on her—I had certain rights too. . . .

We couldn't reach any agreement and drifted further and further apart. In the evenings, Alyoshka and I sat by the fire, and I made *ukha*, or Russian fish soup, and drank vodka from a huge bottle, while Jenny and Martha made a point of going to restaurants in town, first Japanese and then something else. We were virtually enemies.

Seeing the state of affairs, Alyoshka decided to go back to Los Angeles and stay there with a friend for a while, especially since he was also finding our health food diet expensive—he was a student, remember. Once more I found myself caught between two fires. I understood Alyoshka, who was complaining that he was running out of money too fast—I myself had scraped by for several years, and many of my more impoverished friends got by on very small amounts of money, so that it was possible to understand him. The standard of living of the millionaire's housekeeper was much higher than that of the student Alyoshka. But I could also understand Jenny's point of view when she complained to me that Alyoshka hadn't given her enough money, and that he obviously expected her and Martha to feed him at their own expense. If I hadn't known Jenny, I would have thought she was cheap, but she wasn't. It was just that we had all driven each other to the point of hysteria while rolling along the highways of California inside that tin can. We should never have gotten together in one group, or at least we shouldn't have taken Alyoshka with us. Then I would have been able to take an ironic tack with the girls and we wouldn't have become enemies. . . .

I breathed a sigh of relief when we deposited Alyoshka on one of Los Angeles' little green streets. I embraced him, and he trudged away. The girls too were much happier when I got back to the Toyota, and I hoped the remainder of our trip would be more pleasant.

And so it was for a while. After leaving part of our things at the saloon in the redwood forest, we turned the nose of our Toyota northward and set off for the town of Carmel, where an automobile "concours d'élégance" was supposed to take place. Steven Grey and his whole family were there—he was an exhibition sponsor, of course.

God, how some people in the United States live! Racing along the Seventeen-mile Drive on our way to Carmel, I saw green golf courses with men and women dressed in linen golf clothes taking aim at the ball with their clubs or crossing the greens in little white electric cars. And I saw buildings surrounded by virtual fortress walls, one as big as the Mauritanian Citadel or the Novodevichy Convent in Moscow and perched on a cliff, so that it would have been possible to jump from the windows of that little house into the crashing Pacific below. Everywhere were walls of flowers, palm trees, grape arbors, and then again along the road the extraordinary dwellings of the rich receding into the distance.

The exhibition had been organized on the grounds of a very expensive hotel, on an unnaturally green golf course, one edge of which came unexpectedly and abruptly to an end right above the ocean. A happily murmuring, well-dressed crowd surrounded the automobiles, and as it moved the crowd changed its form, composition, and color from moment to moment like a kaleidoscope turned by the skillful hand of a child. The white, pink, and light blue summer dresses of the women, the white pants of the men, the handsome, respectable judges sitting at a table covered by a white tablecloth with the beard of Steven Grey flashing among them, the extraordinary automobiles themselves passing in front of the judges' table before returning once again to their assigned places at the exhibition—all of those things and people, that whole palette, struck me at once. I was lost in wonderment in much the same way, probably, that Robert was from his hallucinogenic mushrooms. I knew that it was that world that I belonged to, and not the world of our vulgar Toyota and Jenny and Martha, or even of the student Alyoshka.

Steven Grey's oldest son, Henry, came over to us, a tall boy dressed in white linen pants and white shirt and a dark blue club blazer and a tie of the same color, and wearing delicate glasses and a name tag with the word "sponsor" on it—tall, cultivated, and happy. I very quickly attached myself to him and followed him away, leaving my girls, who had suddenly grown much less sure of themselves, somewhere behind.

I walked among the cars and admired them. All around shimmered the hot California midday. Sitting in a white Rolls-Royce that according to its placard had been made in 1906 was, to my very great astonishment, a tall, erect, completely gray woman in an old-fashioned white dress, lace hat, and gloves reaching to her elbows. With the infrequent golden spokes of its wheels and its bicycle tires, the Rolls-Royce looked exactly like the carriage that took Cinderella to the king's ball. Its body was made of wood and painted white, and its doors and fenders were edged in gold.

Following my Virgil—Henry, that is—I walked through the exhibition grounds, passing by the most unbelievable structures, some more reminiscent of mausoleums and parthenons than contemporary automobiles, and others gleaming in gilt and lacquer and sometimes the size of small Victorian living rooms. Some of those extraordinary cars even seemed to have parts of churches or public buildings attached to them, and one marvel produced at the beginning of the century even had columns!

Standing nearby a cylinder-shaped racing car of the thirties under a gorgeous tree whose species I didn't recognize, and next to a small white table containing only two sweating glasses with a few ice cubes and the dregs of something rose-colored on the bottom, was a couple—a well-groomed man in a white linen suit who looked like a spoiled writer or actor, and a girl. The girl was like a creature come to me from one of my dreams—in a white hat with a black veil, and behind the veil a young, beautiful, shining face made uneasy by something. Pink stockings, a dress whose black skirt was covered by a transparent white one, and furs of some absurd kind—several little beasts, chinchillas perhaps, hanging from the upper part of her body, although I can't say whether they were actually hanging from her dress or stitched to her wrap—fool that I am, I just don't remember. Her outfit was obviously from the twenties, and the girl, nervously young and bold, belonged to that rare order of young women whom I liked unconditionally and had dreamed about in all my hotels and shabby apartments. She was the one I dreamed about, and not Jenny. . . .

At that very moment Jenny herself touched me on the sleeve. I pretended I was looking at the ocean. The girls had found me all the same. They had, as it turned out, already said "hello" to Steven—the reason Jenny had come to Carmel in the first place. And they led me from the exhibition like a prisoner or some doomed person back to our vulgar Toyota and took me away, although I would have preferred not to go, would have preferred to stay there forever.

Sitting in the car I closed my eyes from time to time and tried to visualize the "girl in chinchilla," as I called her, although I wasn't at all sure that the little beasts she was wearing were in fact chinchillas—I had had no more chance in my life to learn to distinguish among furs than the majority of the population of India, poor people, has had to distinguish among the different kinds of meat—lamb from pork, say?—without ever tasting either one or the other.

The girl in chinchilla. Good Lord, I thought, how has it happened that I'm already thirty-five and have only twenty years or so left, and that I've got to fit into those twenty years all my pleasure and delights, and all the books I still have to write, and all my women? I don't have the girl in chinchilla! Even if she's mean, even if she is disgustingly silly, it doesn't matter, because she's beautiful and out of a fairy tale, and if I don't have her, then what am I? Nothing! I bowed down to beauty then, gentlemen. I was ready to fall down on my knees before beauty. Where did I, a boy from the ugly and boring outskirts of Kharkov, contract that infection, that love of beauty which makes life in this world a hundred times more difficult? Do you actually think it was easy for me with my love of beauty to live at the Hotel Diplomat, where the best-looking faces, or at least the healthiest, were the faces of pimps? Do you think that abasing myself before beauty as I did it was easy for me to fuck the Rumanian dancer Rena with her monkey face, or to ride in the Toyota with those crude girls?

I know, gentlemen, that you will immediately start vying with each other to tell me all about spiritual beauty and to explain to me that that very Jenny, the one driving the Toyota, possessed a beauty of the spirit, which I, miserably ambitious person that I am, as you'll say, don't understand. I do understand, but there was nothing, absolutely nothing I could do about it. Before physical beauty I was and am ready to fall down in the dirt and let it walk over me—its little feet won't soil me. Beauty makes the tears well up in my eyes. It's awful! I place beauty higher even than talent, for talent is given for the world's benefit, is it not? Talent is a sort of applied thing, whereas beauty is endowed at birth both for the world to admire and to be adorned by.

Then the last act began. In Los Angeles, a place I had no desire to go (but who pays the piper calls the tune, and Jenny was paying), we stayed with a certain Mark, who was a childhood friend of Jenny's older brother Donald. Mark was a large, slightly heavyset guy who always went around dressed in checked shirts and jeans. He had, in my opinion, not so much a California look as that of somebody from deep in the American hinterland, from the middle states, conservative and landlocked. Mark was the owner of a printing shop. He had, in other words, a certain affiliation with culture, and dreamed of opening his own publishing house someday. May God grant that he does.

Martha was at that time obsessed with the idea of moving to Los Angeles and was looking for a job, something I was required to take part in too. From morning on, Martha, Jenny, and I would set out on a tour of the city's hotels, trying to find Martha something at one of them. We went on like that for three days during a tremendous heat wave, and those drives around the hot, sweltering city among the crowds of people tremendously irritated me, as did the fact that we were staying with Mark and sleeping on the floor in sleeping bags. By the fourth day I couldn't take it any longer and in spite of my desire to remain on good terms with Jenny, I suggested returning to the redwoods. If, however, they wanted to stay on in Los Angeles instead, I would go back to New York, since I was tired of sleeping on Mark's floor and couldn't see any reason for it and was uncomfortable and bored.

To my amazement, Jenny agreed to go back to the redwoods again, but in order to thank Mark for his hospitality, the girls decided to have a party. The girls were so lackadaisical and tedious that even the sight of them plunged me into a deep depression, but it was in a California supermarket where we had gone to buy food and alcohol for the party that it finally dawned on me for the last time, so that I was left without the slightest doubt, just how great the distance separating us was. It's only in California that you find such vast supermarkets, so large that your friend at the other end of the hall looks like a tiny point. It was there in the supermarket that I suddenly saw myself in a huge mirror and was astonished to discover just how alienated and strangely isolated from them I looked.

Fat-assed with big calves and both dressed in skirts with ruffles that I myself had made (Jenny had lent Martha one of her skirts to wear), the two girls laughed and gesticulated crudely while waddling like geese down the aisle and loading the cart up

with chickens and whole sections of greasy lamb ribs. Butchers'
or bakers' wives? I thought to myself. I, on the other hand,
dressed in a checked summer jacket, a cap (the same one from
Paris with the label "The Enchanted Hunter"), white pants, fine
boots, and glasses, and with an astonished look on my face,
didn't fit with them at all, but looked like a creature from another movie perhaps, if you imagine that huge supermarket mirror as a motion picture screen. Precisely as if an editor in that
same Hollywood, say, had in his haste mistakenly spliced into a
sedate, realistic family movie about the American Midwest a few
frames from a European existentialist film about an outsider. An
editor who was drunk.

The party took place that evening, the guests arriving gradually. The first to appear was Jenny's older brother Donald. He
obviously couldn't wait; a romance was apparently developing
between him and Martha. The second person to arrive was another relative, Mark's brother, his younger brother John. It was
clear that the exclusive source of their parents' imagination was
the Bible, since they had given their children the names of the
famous evangelists. I didn't ask them where Matthew and Luke
were, but I wanted to. The last to arrive was a certain Peter, an
aging failure whose life was brightened only by his recollections
of the 1969 student disturbances at Berkeley. Whatever he was
talking about, he would sooner or later make his usual leap into
the past: ". . . whereas when I was at Berkeley . . ." or, "in
Berkeley we had . . ." Peter reminded me of our own Solzhenitsyn with his eternal camps. Fuck you and your Berkeley, I
thought angrily. You can't live on memories all the time. Do I
start bullshitting every five minutes about "Russia . . . Now
when I lived in Russia . . ."?

They all had their Berkeleys. Jenny's brother Donald, who
was already about thirty, was trying to become a rock star—the
world of the music business, the unjust, treacherous, sinister
Berkeley of music. Brother John, short and stocky with a dark
beard, was stuck on reincarnation. After we had smoked some

grass, of which brother Michael had more than enough—he was as the owner of a printing shop the most successful among us—younger brother John sat down next to me and started methodically ramming reincarnation up my ass. If he wants his soul to transmigrate so he can once again waste his life in arguments about trashy ideas that two million Americans have lifted from glossy mass-market paperbacks, then he needs no better reincarnation than he has now, I appealed both to Nature and to God. I trust they heard me.

Later on there was dancing in the living room. I stuck my head out of the kitchen to take a look. Martha was lovingly intertwined with the lanky Donald. My Jenny was dancing with Mark of the invariable checked shirt, and both had taken off their shoes and were in their stockinged feet. I glanced out of the kitchen for just a moment, and although I'm sure that Jenny didn't see me, I did notice that the two of them, Jenny and her brother's friend, were very well-suited to each other. Her face even had an entirely different expression than it did in my presence—completely calm and self-assured and cheerful. They stamped their feet in unison whenever that was called for, and no less harmoniously they stepped to the side or forward, whenever the music required them to do that. For some reason they reminded me of a painting by Brueghel—dancing peasants, I thought. And although Mark looked like a complete hick to me, his printing shop notwithstanding, I was still a little envious of the way they fitted together.

I went back into the kitchen, where Peter and John at once fell on me again with their Berkeley-reincarnation jumble, and since I haven't known for a long time what to do at parties, and was altogether lost at that one, the only recourse available to me was to get drunk, which is what I did, and with the addition of a goodly quantity of grass managed to get through the evening.

The next morning, suffering from a terrible hangover and the slowness of the girls—who weren't in any hurry to pack their stuff, whereas I, in proper soldierly fashion, had already quickly gotten mine together—I sat dully in the living room and examined Mark's books, the only thing there that interested me even remotely, and quietly bickered with Jenny and Martha. With equal bitterness on both sides, we climbed into the Toyota around noon and set off.

Once on the road, they chattered for hours on end about Mark, John, and Donald, and even about Peter, of whom in my opinion there was nothing to say except that he was an old loser. "And then Donald, Donald goes . . . Ha-ha-ha . . . And John, John comes over to me and he goes . . . Ha-ha-ha . . ." came to me in the back seat.

God placed you among simple people, Limonov, even though you have fled them your whole life, I thought, pushing myself into a corner and suffering from my hangover. "God!" I appealed to Him. "You saw how I tried to save Jenny from her friends, from the warm bog she's grown accustomed to, but she simply refuses to understand what's going on, and is boldly and resolutely going down the drain with her peasant friends. Even though she's better than they are, their society is swallowing her up," I said to God. To which God replied that all human beings are equal in His sight, and that He didn't appreciate my snobbish little jokes—that if Jenny spent her life in the company of Martha and Jennifer as a housekeeper or as a mama cow, that was for Him, God, no different than a life in which she became terribly intellectual and read every possible book and spoke with Alyoshka Slavkov about literature for six hours straight, in the end driving him into a corner—an intellectual Jenny peering derisively at Alyoshka through recently acquired glasses: "What was that, Alyoshka?"

"No, no," I said to God, "that's not what I meant. I know it's a primitive idea, but I still think that man makes his appearance in the world for just a short time, that he is, as a philosopher once said, a corpse on vacation, so that it's probably necessary to try to do your utmost and be exceptionally vigorous."

"Listen!" said God. "You go ahead and be vigorous—you're ambitious—but Jenny has a different agenda. If it doesn't interest you, it still interests her. And anyway, she tried to be vigorous. She has lived with you almost a year and a half, and you yourself know what a difficult person you are—I don't need to tell you that—and I just don't think she should try anymore. It's all clear now—actually it was all quite clear to Me at the very beginning, although not to you, of course: The two of you just don't make a couple. You've had your rest and regained your strength. Now it's time to give Jenny her freedom. She deserves it."

I didn't give Jenny her freedom; she took it herself. Haven't I been saying that she was a strong girl? We stayed in the redwoods for a while, reemerging every other day to go to the beach, and although the girls irritated me, we got along somehow. Remembering my conversation with God in the Toyota, I was lenient with them. In addition to everything else, a whole family of farmers had taken up residence in the saloon, real peasants this time—a high school friend of Jenny's and her husband and their two children. The husband, however, didn't refuse to sit around the fire with me in the evenings and drink, beer for him and vodka and beer for me, and we talked about crops, land improvement techniques, Soviet grain purchases, fishing, and horses. . . .

I endured it all and looked forward to the day when we would finally have to leave: we had bought round-trip tickets with a specific return date. Cheap tickets. But early one morning, Jenny informed me with a yawn that after discussing it, she and Martha had decided to stay for another week, and that she had called Linda in New York the day before and warned her she would be delayed, and did I want to stay on with them too?

Good old honest Jenny. I could tell by her face and eyes that she was weary of me, that she wanted to stay on without me, and be free of me and my ironical, intellectual look that judged and criticized everything, of my spying look that made her uncomfortable, and spend the week at her own simple peasant amusements—in conversations about nothing at all, in gossiping and sitting with her legs spread as wide as she pleased, in dancing and prancing and gobbling down health food, in drinking her gallons of carrot juice along with handfuls of vitamins A, B, C, and D, and the like.

And so I said, "No thanks, Jenny, I need to get back. I've got unwatered plants at home, and I've got to finish my *Diary of a Loser,*" the book I was working on then. And Lenya Kosogor, a friend of mine who was repairing X-ray machines for the B & B company, had promised to take me on as his assistant. I needed the money; my rent was coming up soon.

Jenny and Martha took me to the airport. It turned out there weren't any economy seats left on the plane, and they put me in first class for the same price with my beloved and hated big brothers. "Lucky man!" Jenny said, and I kissed her and then, like one caviar grain among the rest, I resolutely took my place in the dark passenger mass.

In the seat next to me was a large, sturdy, well-groomed fellow with his tie loosened who looked like Steven, and who spent the whole five hours of the flight shuffling through some obviously very important papers bound in a dark leather folder with a gold imprint—the image of a lady tenderly feeding breakfast to a huge cat through a doorway—while I read a greasy copy of *Interview* the whole time and bitterly thought that someday they'll have to do an interview with me, and their Bob Colacellos or even Truman Capotes can go fuck themselves—I'm still more interesting than the people they interview.

Jenny arrived in New York not a week but about ten days later. She didn't call me; I called her, or rather I called Linda to find out whether she had heard anything from California, and got Jenny instead. It seemed odd to me that she hadn't let me know immediately that she was back, and I even got upset about it. "But why," you ask, "why, Edward? You, an opportunist, got upset because your servant girl didn't call you when she got back from vacation?" I'm a live human being, gentlemen, and not an opportunist from a psychiatry textbook case. Besides, we opportunists and ambitious people are just as sensitive and egoistic as anybody else, and we suffer from life even more keenly than normal people do, and get nervous and depressed, only we still find the strength to take action when we need to.

The next day was Saturday, the day I was supposed to clean the millionaire's house. I vacuumed and waxed and polished the floors, and didn't cut corners then as I do now, but did what I was supposed to honestly, working by the sweat of my brow for eight hours, and during that whole time suppressing the vague anxiety I was feeling. After washing the kitchen floor and thereby finishing my work, since that was always the last thing I did, I sat down in the kitchen with Jenny and had a drink. I tried to persuade her to have something too, but she refused for a long time, until I forced her. I was in an alert state of mind and sensed that something had happened to her.

After a few drinks—lemon and rum toddies with cinnamon sprinkled over the top of the steaming drink; there's nothing better than that awful mixture if you want to get drunk—I said to her, "All right, Jenny, let's have it. What happened?"

"Nothing special," she said timidly, obviously trying to keep her composure. "Martha and I have decided to move to Los Angeles to live. Martha found a job at a hotel, and I'll make batik. You remember when I gave Isabelle that dress, Edward? It turned out really well, didn't it? Well, I'm going to make dresses or blouses like that and sell them to a store. Isabelle knows somebody who has a women's clothing store and she promised to introduce me to her."

"When did you decide to move?" I asked, sipping my hot elixir. The steaming rum entered my nose, making it hard for me to drink.

"In January," Jenny said and paused. "Right after New Year's," and she was silent again, not saying anything else, not asking me if I wanted to go with her or how I felt about her decision. I didn't say anything either and drank my rum, and when I had finished it, I stood up and walked over to our huge kitchen stove, poured myself some hot water and more rum, took her empty glass and poured her hot water and rum into it too and added a slice of lemon to each glass, and then sat down again. Without saying anything. We drank our two toddies, and then I said to her, "Well, if you really do want to go, who do you have waiting for you there?"

"Well, who do you think?" Jenny asked, making an effort and looking not at me, but out the window.

"Mark, who else?" I said, not looking at her either.

And then she burst into tears and fell down on her knees in front of me and begged me to forgive her, and said she had hurt me, as well as a lot of other things you're supposed to say in such situations. To which I calmly replied, patting her on the head and in fact exulting in the vileness of human nature, that nothing had happened, that it was normal, and that she shouldn't take it so hard. The noble Limonov.

We poured ourselves some more rum, no longer bothering to mix it, just plain, incredibly strong dark Meyer's rum from Jamaica, and before we drank it, Jenny proposed a toast in a quiet, piping voice:

"To the greatest guy in the world!"

I wondered who that might be, since she couldn't be so tactless as to drink to Mark in my presence.

But no, thank God, the toast was for me. "To you, Edward!" Jenny added fervently. And then she asked me what I thought about him—about Mark. I answered something to the effect that I thought they would make a good couple, which in fact was what I thought; you remember my thinking as they were dancing together in Los Angeles that they were well-suited. She shed a few more tears, and we agreed to be friends, the best of friends, of course we would be friends, and I kissed her and went home.

I walked along and thought. What had happened was of course no great tragedy, but it was very unpleasant and even painful for me, gentlemen. I thought dejectedly of the fact that this one too had betrayed me, this Jenny whom I had sometimes called a saint to myself and whom I had finally begun to trust, so that it would never have occurred to me that she, that Jenny would betray me. I walked up York Avenue, repeating some lines of Apollinaire's to myself: "Even she who is ugly/ May cause her lover pain,/ She's the daughter of a constable,/ Who serves on the island of Jersey. . . ."

And for some reason I also remembered the time my mother betrayed me, and the medical orderlies took me away as if to be executed, and then, when I was eighteen and already a completely different person and still wobbly from an insulin injection they'd just given me, my return home from the mental hospital with my military father. And as I walked the thirty blocks back to my Eighty-third Street, I remembered too that cruel, hopeless New York winter when Lena had betrayed me, and I recalled all the grudges I had against people; I remembered them all and tallied them up and drew my conclusions.

Go your own way, I told myself; don't trust anybody. People are crap. It's not that they're bad, but weak, feeble, and pitiful. They betray more out of weakness than from malice. Go your own way. Strong creatures hunt by themselves. You're not a jackal; you don't need a pack.

And then, as I was already nearing home, I suddenly discovered in the midst of my pain joy that I had been betrayed—it was, ultimately, proof of my solitariness, my specialness, and, if you like, of a kind of success. Before I had had the sense that Jenny was somehow superior to me. Now, thanks to what had happened, she was just like all the other girls and women. In itself, the fact that Mark was fucking Jenny meant little to me. Only that Saint Jenny no longer existed. And that was good. Order once more reigned in my world. It's terribly hard to live with saints. It's better to live with prostitutes; they're more honest. It's better to live with bandits; you can defend yourself from them with a knife in your boot, or even better, a pistol stuck in your belt under your T-shirt. The hardest thing is to defend yourself from people who are good.

You will say that I'm not being objective, since I myself had in fact betrayed Jenny with numerous other women, and even hated her, and was planning to leave her at the first opportunity. Exactly, I was *planning* to, but what if I wouldn't actually have done it? What if it was all just empty talk and bravado?

Thus was I betrayed by my servant girl, my peasant angel.

The next day I did something I would never have expected of myself. And you too will probably be just as surprised to find out what the next turn of events was. I went to the millionaire's house and proposed to Jenny—asked her, Jenny Jackson, to marry me. She started crying, but she turned me down, although she respected me tremendously for it and said, "Thank you, Edward!" and kissed my hand. And then I left, breathing a sigh of relief.

I walked back up York Avenue again on my way home to the plants and the bookcases and the tables and chairs that Jenny had dragged in to build a nest that was never to be, and as I walked, I thought once more, Go your own way, Edward. Strong animals hunt by themselves. You don't need a pack, Eddie baby, you don't need one.

I spent the next two weeks almost continuously fucking and hash smoking with a poetess named Diane at her dark, many-roomed labyrinth on Third Street crammed with idiotic furniture and hung with pictures painted by her own hand, since before becoming a poet, she had been a painter. We woke up every morning to an awful rumbling and roaring just outside our window: the street was the headquarters of the Hell's Angels, or at least of their New York chapter, or whatever they call it. At any time of day or night there would always be dozens of motorcycles drawn up on the street in ranks, with the Hell's Angels themselves sitting in the building doorways with cans of beer in their hands. In the mornings they warmed up their bikes, or something.

Only once, in the company of Diane, who swayed like a sleepwalker and had painted her fingernails with black lacquer and was wearing a short coat just as black from under which her skinny legs stuck down like two sticks, did I take the subway back to my place to water my plants. For some reason we preferred fucking at her place, to the roar of the Hell's Angels' motorcycles while lying under a huge portrait of a headless half-man, half-woman. Diane had for a long time been the girlfriend of a certain punk rock star who was either insane or merely pretended to be, and although she was only twenty-five, she was ready for the scrap heap.

After two weeks, having sufficiently recovered my self-esteem, I summoned my strength, and leaving Diane alone with her headless portrait, I returned to a normal life. I called Jenny to inquire about the state of affairs at the millionaire's house and to find out if I still had my job as cleaning man, even though I'd missed two days of work.

"Of course you have, Edward. Don't worry about it, everything's fine," said the decent Jenny over the phone. "You haven't lost your job, and you'll still get your eighty dollars for those two Saturdays. I told Linda you did the cleaning, and anyway, she only notices the rug in her office, which Olga vacuumed."

Jenny also said that Madame Margarita had been looking for me. But she didn't ask me where I'd been for the last two weeks, not wanting to pry into my private affairs.

I called Madame Margarita and heard her perpetually cheerful voice say: "Limonchik! I'm glad you called me. I've got masses of work for you to do. Only I'll tell you beforehand that the work is very hard—you've got to dig in the ground and do a lot of other kinds of construction things. I've just started remodeling my house in the country, and I've hired a contractor who has his own local workers, but then I remembered you and that I had promised you some work," Madame Margarita said, very proud of herself, "and the contractor has agreed to take you on.

I'm going up there tomorrow. It's in upstate New York, and if you like I can take you along with me."

It turned out later that she hadn't just happened to remember me. It was simply that one of the hired workers had made off with a goddamn antique clock of hers, and she'd hired me to replace him. But everybody likes to seem like a benefactor. When after living in America for five years, I finally obtained a green card, four people immediately told me that it was because of their efforts that I got it.

I packed my bag and went. They promised forty hours a week at four dollars an hour. One hundred sixty dollars. I went—I didn't have any other work.

I spent two months in a town near the Hudson River working as a common laborer and bricklayer and returned to New York at the end of November, there being no more work for me to do in the country.

The whole month of December I spent doing clothing alterations for rich ladies on Fifth Avenue and Park Avenue—skirts and pants. I charged them five dollars an hour for the sewing and cheated a little on the time, so that I started to pick up some money—at least, I was able to make my rent and live after a fashion, but I was bored. I was alone once more.

Once after sewing all day, I was sitting and eating and mechanically watching television, trying various stations, and irritably thinking, How long will I have to keep doing alterations on all their old shit? I'd spent the whole day repairing a torn coat with a fur lining of the sort that any bum would wear, although it belonged to a lady who lived next door to the Guggenheim Museum. Who would have believed that these rich ladies would be so cheap and have their old coats altered or have me patch their husbands' old trousers? I thought. And then on one of the programs I suddenly saw the sweet little face of Lodyzhnikov, so that instead of switching stations, I lingered for a moment, whereupon I was afforded the opportunity of beholding Drosselmeier himself—my former lover Leshka Kranets. Tall and imperious, Leshka strode about the stage in a huge black batlike cloak. The lead. Leshka was a drunk with a heart of gold. He not only slept with you, but worried about whether you were satisfied, or drunk enough, or whether you needed something to wear. As brief as our romance was, he still managed to give me some gold cuff links and to send me money in beautiful envelopes with the tenderest of inscriptions and anticipations and apologies, lest I be offended by the money, which was intended as a gift. But my prick takes me to those who don't love me, which of course is why I remained neither with Jenny nor with Leshka or Sarah, nor with any of the other, by no means bad people, with whom a generous fate has brought me into contact.

At that moment, Leshka happened to be tying a scarf around the neck of the nutcracker. You remember the part where the head comes off? I started smiling and then burst out laughing. Leshka had always been a healer and a doctor, and it had been my lot from time to time to feel the benefit of his healing organ in the days when I still considered myself bisexual.

But who will heal me now? I thought. Jenny was leaving on the fifth of January and already had her ticket. The millionaire's little house had provided me with a great deal of healing, and now I wouldn't be seeing it anymore. And then it suddenly occurred to me, why in fact shouldn't I see it again? Why shouldn't I offer to take Jenny's place? She had tried to find somebody, but hadn't been able to. I would have my favorite garden again, and the house with the children's room where I could take refuge from calamity, and a reliable income—every week. Let's look into it, I thought. I still wasn't ready then to live on my own.

And turning off the television, I erased Leshka from the screen and called up Jenny.

Chapter Seven

YOU CAN reproach Steven Gatsby with probably just about anything you like, including the lack of a sense of humor, but he does enjoy showing off, and his snobbery is something you won't take away from him. Therefore, when Jenny arranged an interview for me with Gatsby in the same long-suffering solarium three days before she left, she was certain he wouldn't take me, but I understood her boss better than she did. We looked each other over, chatted for ten minutes, and I knew I could work for him as long as I wanted to. A housekeeper-writer was something he required the same way he required bread, and I believe that my sojourn in his house will in time inevitably take its place in his family chronicle.

Jenny finally rolled out of the house on the fifth of January, 1979, taking with her a heap of cardboard boxes and other assorted trash, and accompanied by virtually the whole Jackson clan, by the timid Martha, who hadn't left for Los Angeles yet, by Bridget and the weeping Linda, and by numerous other tertiary figures—friends and acquaintances of Jenny's—as well as by the shrieking of children and an otherwise indescribable bustle. Jenny's friends also managed to pilfer a number of other absolute essentials, including a fair quantity of alcohol, which she let them haul out of the basement and stick in among the clothing and furniture that did in fact belong to her. I didn't intercede on behalf of "our" alcohol at the time; I didn't want to ruin her leave-taking.

I was genuinely happy that she was going. She was actually

moving only her body to Los Angeles; her mind and thoughts had already been there for a long time with the proprietor of the printing shop. She was an appalling sight the last days before she left, her pregnancy having made her even more animal-like and bovine. Like any real American girl raised on mass culture, Jenny, as you already know, firmly believed that everything natural was healthy, and behaved accordingly, burping, letting out mooing sounds, and unfortunately even smelling bad. I'm ashamed even to pronounce the word, but, yes, she did that too, although it's true she first gave a warning, saying, "I'm going to fart," although the warning didn't in fact change anything. In short, she really let herself go after she got pregnant.

How is Mark going to put up with her? I thought. "Goodbye, Jenny Jackson," I said at the door.

"Goodbye, Edward Limonov," she replied with a smile. Nobody asked me to go to the airport, and so I didn't. The door shut behind her.

Only then, gentlemen, did I realize how lucky I was that Jenny was gone from my life. It's good, I thought, when your whole future is open to you, wide open again, and you can do whatever the hell you want. For a start I went up to her former room, now mine, and thoroughly washed it and threw out everything I thought should be thrown away, with a firm hand clearing away all her trash and her dirt. I worked on that project for the next two days—Saturday and Sunday. As I've been saying, Jenny hadn't done anything for the last several months, except read books on babies and how to raise them.

On Monday Linda arrived and my working life began.

"Edward," she said, "the basic thing you need to know about Steven is that he's not a detail person. He pays other people, people like you and me, to work out the details for him. He only gives general instructions, and he likes you to anticipate his thoughts."

"Okay," I said, "I'll anticipate his thoughts." I didn't have any idea then how I was going to do that, and I still don't, but I was already well beyond that other Edward, the naïve Russian, and was saying "Yes!" to everything, and somehow it has worked out. It's an easy thing to say "yes," and it doesn't cost you anything. And so I said, "Yes," "Of course," and "I'll do it."

"The fact Steven hired you means you're more than halfway there, but were you aware that Nancy wanted to hire Marilyn," Linda said, lighting a cigarette, "a girl who used to work for her on the farm in Connecticut? She's taken Marilyn under her wing, and Steven hired you against her wish. Just between us," Linda continued, "that's the main reason he took you. Nancy wanted a spy in the house, but Steven can't stand Marilyn—she's fat, ugly, and pimply—and he won't have a spy in his home; he wants to keep his personal life private."

"Yes, I know all about Marilyn; Jenny told me," I replied, although I had never suspected that my being hired as housekeeper concealed such complicated behind-the-scenes machinations, intrigues, and struggles. "I thought Steven hired me because he's a snob," I said, "so he could brag a little to his friends about his butler being a writer."

"That too," Linda nodded, "but you'll still have to try to please Nancy, if you don't want her undermining your position here. My feeling is that she still hasn't given up the idea of Marilyn. So be careful!"

"What should I do?" I asked.

"You'll have to try really hard, and when they see that you're indispensable," Linda said, "they'll leave you alone. You'll have to straighten up the house, clean out the basement, rearrange the tools, check each room individually, and fix all the little defects. . . ." And she gave me an extremely long list of things to do, including scraping and repainting the front door.

"And after I've finished taking out all that rubbish, they'll hire Marilyn," I said.

"What do you want?" Linda asked irritably.

And, really, what did I want? I went downstairs to the basement and worked there until six in the evening, and I did so because I wanted to remain in that house and be for a time a servant of the world bourgeoisie, at least until I got tired of it or until something else turned up. What else could an opportunist do? We always like to get ourselves in as tight as possible with the rich and famous. Maybe I'll find myself a rich woman here, flashed feebly through my mind. Then we'll see, I thought, as I cleaned out those Augean stables. The labors of Hercules and the cleaning of the Augean stables—you remember. It was only then that I realized what a shitty housekeeper Jenny was. The basement obviously hadn't been cleaned for years, while she sat warming her ass in the kitchen and nurturing her "tummy," as she called it, tending it and pampering it for her belly dancing efforts.

I, the diligent whore Limonov, licked it all up and even found in the basement some remnants of the orange carpet that covered the hallway and stairs, and used them to repair the first three steps, which were completely worn out and torn. I knew how to serve—the first thing was to cover up the most conspicuous holes and let your boss see that you were working and make him aware of the results. And I also sorted out all our tools, electrical tools in one drawer and mechanical in another, and even sorted all the nuts and bolts and put white labels on the drawers so you could tell where everything was.

But the three steps made the biggest impression, naturally. When about ten days later Steven made his first appearance at the house after hiring me, he *noticed* those three steps, since they had bothered him too; they were in fact the first thing you saw when you came in, and although he didn't really want to spend money on a house in which he spent so little time, he was ashamed of those steps before his guests, who were as snobbish as he was. And so was Linda, whom in the first months of my employment I didn't trust at all, considering her a spy for her employer, which in a certain sense she probably was, and not only then, either—I even overheard Linda telling Nancy on the phone, ". . . He fixed the steps in the hall. . . . He does every-thing well."

I'll be damned if I didn't learn something from them—from Linda and from Gatsby, too. Both good and bad, depending only on how you look at it. "Don't trust anybody but yourself," Linda taught me. "Check on everybody—everybody! Start from the premise that the people you work with are lazy assholes; that's the only way you'll avoid mistakes."

She taught me not to trust anybody, and I didn't, whether it was the butcher, the proprietor of the Modern Age framing shop that mounted and framed our pictures and photographs, the watch repairman to whom we sent Nancy's gold and Ste-ven's ultramodern quartz and electronic watches to be fixed, the furrier Kaplan, or the opticians at the extraordinarily expensive optical shop of Clermont-Ferrand where I took Steven's no less ultramodern glasses, or whether it was the bartenders and wait-ers who came to assist at our parties, or the electrician John, or the many, many others. Linda herself said I was paranoid about the bartenders, whom I virtually frisked when they left, in my stubbornness thereby rescuing a whole case of champagne once. Nor, as a result, did I have an iota of trust for Linda either, and never told her anything she could use against me. I was a very capable and diligent pupil, dear Linda, and "trust nobody" meant *nobody*.

Once on a Saturday, a day when Linda doesn't come in, the mailman delivered along with a pile of junk mail a registered letter which he asked Limonov to sign for. I signed for it, and since it was January and a wet snow was falling, I asked the mailman in for a cup of coffee out of altruism and boredom. He passed through to the kitchen, leaving muddy footprints behind, and drank his coffee while we chatted for a while. Outside the snow was coming down in sheets. The mailman was like any other—nothing special, a moustached man of about fifty who complained about the weather and his salary just as they all do. As soon as he left, I went down to the basement for a rag and then spent five minutes or so cleaning up the mud he had tracked in. And you want to be a lover of mankind, I thought to myself, and then from boredom and curiosity I opened the registered letter, from which a check dropped to the floor.

I picked it up and looked at the figure and couldn't believe my eyes. Printed on the check in thick red numerals was the number 400,000—four hundred thousand dollars! Linda had asked me always to call her if there was anything urgent. I thought this was urgent enough to disturb her on her Saturday off, and I dialed her number.

"What's the matter?" Linda asked me in an indolent, homey voice.

"They just brought an urgent letter," I said cheerfully, "with a check in it for . . ." and then I faltered, since it was actually hard for me to say the number out loud—"for four hundred thousand dollars."

Linda understood, and started laughing. "I realize, Edward, that you've never seen a check for a sum like that in your life. Relax, it's nothing special. After you've worked for us a little longer, you'll get used to it. I started trembling and gawking too when I first started working for Steven eight years ago. Just put the check on my desk."

"Wouldn't it be better to put it in the desk?" I asked uncertainly.

"Well, then put it in the desk, if you want to," Linda agreed, losing interest in me.

I put the check in the desk drawer in her office and sat for a while on her wheeled leather chair between the IBM typewriter and the telephone, and then took the check out of the drawer and looked at it. The unlikely amount of $400,000.00 stood out blood red against the pale lettuce green of the check like a Soviet banner over a green Czechoslovakian town. I tried to figure out how many years I'd have to work to accumulate such a sum. I was earning nine thousand a year in cash; that meant I'd have to work for Steven for forty-five years to make that kind of money.

I thought that I would hardly live to be eighty, so I would have to think of some way to speed up the process. I hid the check and sat for a while longer, then took it out again and put it on the desk. After all, I wasn't expecting any guests that weekend.

Steven arrived for the first time in a limousine one evening in the middle of January—he had been skiing in Colorado— praised his servant for the steps, glanced at the book *The Women's Room*, which the servant was reading while sitting in the kitchen, and then asked the servant if he liked the book. I said it was terrible. Gatsby said he hadn't read the book, but he thought it would have to be terrible—neither employer nor servant were feminists, as you no doubt have already been able to guess, gentlemen. At that time, the inhabitants of the United States looked eagerly for either feminism or anti-feminism in every aspect of life, the feminist epidemic having burst on the scene even before the roller skating epidemic. Even people who had once seemed far from stupid to me suddenly turned out to be idiots whenever feminism was concerned. They all wanted to be liberal and ally themselves as quickly as possible with the latest liberal superstition.

I didn't say any of this to Steven, although I would have enjoyed talking to him. Except for Linda, I really didn't have many people to talk to in the millionaire's house either then or now, which is why I spend so much time in internal monologues. Gatsby remained in the kitchen no more than a couple of minutes to drink a glass of milk, and then he went off to bed. He never has time, or if he does, he prefers to talk instead of listen, as a result of which he misses a great deal, I think. If I should ever notice that I've gotten fond of chattering and that other people are actually *listening* to my words, I'll make an effort to look around and see if among my listeners there aren't at least a couple of quietly skeptical Limonovs.

When I came downstairs to the kitchen at 6:50 the next morning, it was still empty. I sat there by myself until 8:30, looking out the window and listening to every sound in the house, before I realized that the Flying WASP had already split.

I've since learned how to tell quite easily whether or not Gatsby's in the house on the basis of some very simple signs—every servant knows what they are. For example, if I don't find *The New York Times* by the front door when I get up, that means that my employer has risen before me, or that he hasn't spent the night in the house but has been off fucking somewhere else, and picked up the newspaper on his way in after taking a taxi home. He also has the habit of drinking white wine, the Italian Corvo, with his women before going off to bed with them, so that, as I've already mentioned, I always keep two or three bottles of it in the refrigerator for him and a case of it in the cellar. So, if there's a bottle of Corvo missing from the refrigerator, that almost certainly means that Gatsby has a lady with him. Around eleven o'clock in the morning, Olga brings the empty bottle and two glasses down to the kitchen with a regularity that I find touching.

Now I try to get up before Steven does, so that I'm already sitting and finishing *The New York Times* when he comes into the kitchen with his hair uncombed and his strong legs and bare feet sticking out from under his short robe. I always have his coffee ready or at least some boiling water so that I can make it at once. As His Majesty is sitting down to read the paper, I'm already serving him his coffee in one of the huge mugs we have in two colors, red and blue. If Gatsby has a woman upstairs, he doesn't stay in the kitchen very long, but takes his coffee, paper, and another cup of coffee back upstairs after asking me to make breakfast or not, as his mood or that of his lady dictates. If Gatsby takes the coffee back upstairs, it's almost certain the lady is Polly, a cultivated but slightly inhibited woman. But if in the morning Gatsby asks for a pot of tea, that means he's spent the night with the Tea Lady, as Linda and I call her. The Tea Lady is another of Steven's more or less regular girlfriends and of Asian origin, I think.

If Gatsby orders breakfast, I usually fix him a tray with something simple. He eats a lot at lunch and dinner, and so for breakfast he usually has just English muffins lightly browned in the toaster, butter, cheese if there is any, and jam. Only very occasionally will he ask me to make him an omelet. He drinks orange juice too, of course, as almost all Americans do, and it would be a strange thing if you too didn't want orange juice in the morning after getting sloshed every night, and I suspect Gatsby is in a pretty good state every night, since His Highness drinks all day, beginning with lunch, continuing with dinner and after dinner, and ending late at night with a bottle or two of Corvo. What amazes me is that he never takes the hair of the dog to relieve his hangover—just orange juice and cold soda water. We always have ten or twelve cylinders of seltzer on hand which are brought to us every Thursday by a funny little man from Brooklyn named Mr. Schuman, who looks like a mosquito. I always keep a couple or three of them in our gigantic refrigerator—so large in fact that you could easily fit a couple of bodies into it.

Gatsby almost always comes down to get the breakfast tray himself. He could make me bring it up to him, but he's too liberal to do that. Demanding that their servants bring the tray to their bedroom is the hallmark of bad bosses—our neighbors, for example, whose servants have told me what they're forced to put up with. But my boss is a good one, the best of all. If he doesn't want to come and get the tray, we simply use the dumb waiter. But that happens pretty rarely.

Whenever Steven's in New York, Linda arrives at the house at nine o'clock sharp, and sometimes even earlier. She always knocks on the kitchen door in precisely the same way. Not long ago I begged her to change the way she knocks for the sake of variety. She did for a little while, but now she does it the old way again. Linda's first question is, "Where is he?" If "he" is in the bathroom, she relaxes and sits down in the kitchen with me for a bit.

Gatsby takes a bath every morning, a bath being one of his principal pleasures in life, as his oldest son, Henry, told me. His bathtub is a very special one, large and deep, and custom made. I don't deny myself the pleasure of using his bathtub either, and from time to time luxuriate in it with a girl, or even two. And I always think, whenever I'm sitting in his bathroom, what would happen if he suddenly came in and saw me and my naked girls. But that never happens—we're too well organized. We have an extremely detailed schedule of Gatsby's activities, so that I always know ahead of time when to expect him. He surprised me only once when there were naked people running around the house, although fortunately I wasn't one of them.

Linda's second question is even more succinct: "Alone?" In our private language that means something like, "Did Gatsby spend the night alone?" If I say that he didn't, Linda's asks, "Who?" She wants to know who's with him, naturally. She and I are, in this, much like real servants: We love to spy on our employer and rummage in his dirty laundry.

I, as his butler, am required to sort out his dirty laundry in the most literal sense of the word, to take it out of the suitcases he brings home after his trips around the globe, to fish it out of the extraordinary mixture of papers, new books, medicines, notebooks, cameras, cassettes, pants, jackets, and phone messages on stationery from hotels from all over the world, and foreign currency in every conceivable form, size, and color with which his suitcases are crammed.

Now I take the lion's share of whatever currency I find for myself. It wasn't that I was afraid to before, but simply that I didn't know how he would feel about that kind of expropriation. Convinced by all the evidence that he had no recollection of those paltry francs and pounds (my God, he spent hundreds of thousands a year, didn't he?), I started helping myself. No, no, I'm not talking about hundreds of dollars, just small amounts—five dollars here, twenty dollars there. After all, a butler has to do a little stealing, or what kind of servant is he?

Employers are right to believe that all servants steal, but the good servants are the ones who do so within acceptable limits, whereas the bad ones do so impudently. I wouldn't let anybody plunder Gatsby's things, nor would I myself take even one object. When not long ago two little silver vases from a sterling service disappeared, I was overcome with self-pity and despair, lest Gatsby think I'd stolen his silver when I hadn't, but the forgotten bank notes justly belong to me, gentlemen, and no argument. After all, I only make a hundred and sixty-five dollars a week.

In answer to the question "Who?" I reply to Linda, "The Tea Lady," or, "Polly," or, "I think it's a new one." Linda is also interested in what kind of mood Steven is in that day. "Average" happens rarely; most often the answer is either "excellent" or "very bad." Armed with this knowledge and clutching an ashtray, Linda invariably goes upstairs to her room after pouring herself a cup of coffee and adding milk to it. She's been spilling milk on the kitchen table every day now for two years, just as I have been giving her reproachful looks for two years while she gets mad.

I wander idly around the house or sit by the kitchen window, my favorite spot, and look out at the street and think, while nervously waiting for Steven to make his appearance. I already know from the schedule, say, that there will be three people for lunch at 12:30. I've already set the table in the dining room and put out the silver bread-and-butter plates too. I haven't forgotten: Everything's ready, all our magnificence is on display, and there are new candles in the candlesticks, although I still don't know what Gatsby wants for lunch. I wait for him to escort his lady from the house and seat her in a taxi—for them to pass by the window, the lady in a fur coat and Steven without any jacket as usual—and then, as soon as he has returned to the house and before he has a chance to sit down in his office and make his first call, I deftly intercept him and ask, "Excuse me, sir [or Steven], what would you like for lunch today?"

And Gatsby will say, "Lamb chops. I haven't had lamb chops in a long time." But if he's had meat in the last few days, then he'll say, "Make something light, Edward. Let's have fish, salmon steaks, maybe, or Long Island Sound scallops." Or perhaps he will say in an irritable voice, "I don't know, Edward, make whatever you want. I'm sick of always having to decide and worry about everything." In the latter case, I always decide in favor of meat.

Having received my orders, I trot around to the stores as fast as I can, first calling the Ottomanelli Brothers butcher shop, if Gatsby has decided to stick with meat:

"Good morning! How's it going? This is Edward, Mr. Steven Grey's housekeeper."

And one of the butcher brothers, wiping his hand on his white apron, will say, "Great, Edward, what do you hear from Jenny? Has she had her baby yet?"

I'll say no, she hasn't, or later that yes, she has.

"What would you like today?" the Ottomanelli brother will ask me then, since they don't have time for long phone conversations—there are very probably about a dozen rich old twats standing in the shop who've come to pick out the best meat, and just as many maids who've come for the same purpose.

"Send me a dozen lamb chops for lunch, please," I'll say, "only hurry up this time. The last time your delivery boy was slow in getting here, and I had to serve lunch ten minutes later than planned."

"Of course, Edward. Don't worry, he'll be on time today," the butcher will say. "'Bye!"

At first this ritual amused me. Now I'm sick of the regulated order of my life and the huge annual schedule on the cork wall in Linda's office and the monthly schedule that hangs in front of her nose and that's tacked to the lamp on the desk in Steven's office. The fact that I know what Steven will be doing in six months, and therefore what I'll be doing, is repellent to me. I live for the present, for those moments when Steven isn't in the house, and knowing beforehand that he'll be here, say, for five days next week, I already begin to anticipate how tired I'll be. I plunge into his visits with trepidation, with my eyes closed, and I reemerge from them with joy. Maybe that's only because I'm not a real housekeeper but a sham one, or maybe every servant feels that way. Or maybe I really am a housekeeper, and the writing business is just something I've made up for myself, it occurs to me sometimes. The only part of my life that has anything to do with writing are the few lines I scribble down in cheap notebooks from Woolworth's and the phone calls I make from time to time to my agent, Liza, to find out which publisher she's received a rejection from this time. There are already more than a dozen of them now—a dozen rejections. That's my whole connection to writing, whereas I'm connected to the world of service all the time. Probably I am a servant. I'm a servant, a servant, and writing is merely something I play at, I think bitterly.

After buying groceries, I drag myself home loaded down with packages and bags, trusting Olga to put everything away for me while I methodically set about preparing lunch. I've learned to be precise—I know when to put the Brussels sprouts on and when to begin cleaning the broccoli, and the only thing that might possibly put me off schedule is the inordinate activity of Steven and his businessmen. From time to time one of them will come in and ask me to bring him a cup of coffee. I then have to take the sterling tray with coffee pot, cups, and milk and sugar to Steven in the office. I take it in, although it makes me angry. Steven thanks me, and I go back downstairs to my spacious kitchen, where I sometimes open the door and stand in it, cleaning the vegetables and thinking how nice it would be if all of them—Steven, and his businessmen, and Linda—would just leave me in peace.

Linda always claims part of the lunch for herself: "Edward, always order for yourself and me whatever you order for Steven," she reminds me.

"If they'd only hurry up and finish stuffing their faces," I mutter to myself, "and get back into their papers and arguments and so on, I can take my time clearing the table and worry about myself and my own thoughts."

I cook the meat over a grill for five minutes on one side and three or four on the other. The Italian brothers without a doubt have the finest meat in the world; it melts in your mouth like butter. "Steven likes everything around him to be very classy," Linda never tires of repeating, and I try to make it all as "classy" as I can: The vegetables and the meat are served on sterling too. The table looks impressive and beautiful, and if Gatsby is in a good mood, he may express his appreciation by saying, "Thank you, Edward!" But if he's in a bad mood, you won't get a fucking thing out of him, not even if you cooked him angel's meat for lunch. Actually, his words of praise don't mean that much to me. The best thing he can do for me is to eat his lunch in forty minutes and get the hell out of the dining room. But Steven sits at the table with his very important guests for an hour to an hour and a half on the average, and sometimes for three. And I nurse my antipathy in the kitchen.

After his guests finally leave and Gatsby returns to his office, I happily clear the table and then go upstairs to my room and flop down on the bed, sometimes even allowing myself to doze off with my clothes on for fifteen or twenty minutes or so. Frequently the doorbell rouses me, and then I race downstairs on the elevator. Gatsby won't open the door—why should he?— and Linda is more often than not on the telephone at any time of day, and however many businessmen there may be in the house, they won't make any effort even to open the door— that's my responsibility, or Olga's, but Olga leaves at one o'clock. I don't react to telephone calls during my brief afternoon nap; I just continue to doze and nothing more. Man is a highly organized form of life, and I endure the two hundred and fifty to three hundred calls that come into our house each day without going out of my mind as the rats of Professor Pavlov or whomever would undoubtedly do.

Linda leaves at six or seven. Sometimes Steven is still having a Scotch with his businessmen, but if he doesn't happen to see anybody around, he's capable of fixing it himself. At eight or nine Gatsby is already dining out somewhere. Either at the Four Seasons or some other "classy" restaurant. He very rarely stays in unless he's sick or the summer or winter Olympic games are on, since he loves sports. In my view he has too many interests in life. If he had fewer, I as his servant would have less work to do. If Steven were, say, to give up photography and making underwater movies, I wouldn't have to run over to Forty-seventh Street to get his cameras repaired or go to the Modern Age framing shop.

Actually, Linda is more to blame for my trips around New York. Steven often yells at her for spending his money like water—she issues the checks and takes care of Gatsby's bank accounts. So now the trusty Linda cuts corners in little things. She's started using me as a messenger, not all the time, but she still does it. Delivery service charges have jumped back up, and she's decided it's cheaper for her to pay my taxi fare than to pay somebody sent by a delivery agency. At the same time that Steven bought Nancy a necklace for twenty-two thousand dollars as a gift. At the same time that it cost His Highness more than ten thousand dollars just to ship his racing car from England to California so he could take part in a race. It's called economizing.

It's my own fault too. I gave in to Linda a little, not in everything, but enough for her to get the upper hand. I myself volunteered in the beginning to run whatever errands she wanted—I said I liked walking around New York and preferred to be active. And it really is pleasant sometimes to hang around in the area of Fifth Avenue for a couple of hours instead of sitting at home with Linda and Steven and his gaggle of arrogant businessmen who think they're the saviors of mankind, the key people in the world and the most important. The businessmen are firmly convinced that they're the ones who give us poor mortals our work, our jobs, and that if it weren't for them, the human race would soon be extinct. They've been taught their insolence by the American press, by books, movies, and television, but it's a delusion, an American myth. They're as proud of themselves as poets, these business gents. I used to think poets were the most arrogant and proud creatures on earth, but now I see that I was wrong; poets don't even come close.

I've also spoiled Linda by making lunch for her. Even when Steven isn't home I still make something, and around one o'clock Linda and I sit across the kitchen table from each other and feed our faces. It frequently happens that I don't feel like eating, and even more often that I don't feel like cooking, but I have to. I started that routine myself, hoping to predispose Linda to me, and I succeeded, and now she gets very offended if I refuse to make lunch for her. She's even picky about what she eats, gentlemen—can you imagine that? If I make tuna fish with onion, which is easy to do—the whole operation only takes me ten minutes—Linda complains about the lack of variety in our diet: "Not tuna again, Edward!" Several months ago we discovered grilled Polish sausage and ate that with enthusiasm. But now Linda doesn't want Polish sausage anymore; she's sick of it, you see, and it might be fattening.

I don't think it's the Polish sausage that's making Linda fat, but the fact that she's been working for Gatsby for eight years, and getting nervous, and losing her temper, and putting up with Steven's various moods, the moods of someone who's closer to her than her own relatives, and taking pride in him, and hating him. I even have a suspicion that she's in love with him—I mean it. Linda's been sitting in one place too long; she needs some fresh new air and new people. I can see it, and even Jenny could. Linda needs to tell the millionaire's house to shove it, and jump into life, and then she'll stop gaining weight. And leave

David, her fifty-year-old Jewish boyfriend of habit who's always complaining he doesn't feel well, and get herself a younger lover and start a new life.

Sometimes after one of her periodic arguments with Gatsby, Linda mutters about looking for another job, that she's had it, that eight years of slavery is enough, but it's still a long way, gentlemen, from fancy speeches to actually attempting to break out of a well-paying cage. She'll never do it, although I hope to God I'm wrong.

I can picture the old Steven Grey inevitably cut down by a stroke during one of his rages and stuck in a wheelchair (a wheelchair of the most modern construction, of course, with computer controls) and bickering in the millionaire's house with the old woman Linda. It's all perfectly clear: they'll never change. Gatsby will never stop, and he'll never give up "this fucking business," to use his expression, and take up teaching and become a professor, as he once threatened to do in my presence during a forty-five-minute access of sincerity. No, it's all perfectly clear as far as Steven and Linda are concerned, and the only person for whom nothing is clear is the butler Edward— what will happen to him, and where and how and in what capacity he'll meet his end. So that it's possible I'm wrong to complain. I'm unquestionably freer than they are, although less happy. But you have to pay for freedom, butler Edward, so shut up and stop complaining about slavery.

But let's get back to the lunches. Another reason why Linda insists on them is that she doesn't want to spend her own money. She's a bit stingy, as Jenny told me. Not that she's pathologically greedy—she asked Jenny and me out to restaurants more than once, and she and David paid their share without any fuss, and Linda gives parties at her home, but she's frugal. With Jenny she didn't have it as good as she does with me—a free lunch, just like the kids in school. Jenny baked bread and cooked, but not every day.

But I continue to feed Linda; I don't resist. Anyway, she

sometimes does things for me too, things I either can't do by myself or that are a nuisance for me to do. For example, she checks my business letters written in English from time to time and corrects my mistakes or even retypes the letters, which is very important to me. At the beginning of my career in Gatsby's house, she helped me make lunch; I didn't even know how to steam vegetables—all that asparagus and broccoli and those artichokes and Brussels sprouts—she helped me, and though she did introduce more fucking nervousness and fuss into the process than was necessary, her help was of great value, and I admit it. Moreover, when Steven wasn't around, she even tried to teach me correct English pronunciation. I quickly tired of that activity, it's true, but for a while I read her articles out of *The New York Times* I'd found interesting, and she corrected my pronunciation and explained the rules.

But Linda's principal merit is that she talks to me. Several times a day I go up to her office, sit down on the couch next to her desk, and if she isn't busy, gossip with her or talk about politics. But our main discussion club is in the kitchen, where during lunch we talk about the news of the day. I read all the international news in *The New York Times* without exception, and I regularly read *Newsweek* and *Time,* and for that reason am better acquainted with what's going on than Linda is; I'm a newspaper freak and Linda respects my knowledge.

After my private eighteen-month propaganda campaign for an equal and unified humanity, Jenny departed for Los Angeles a very different Jenny than she'd been when I first met her. She hadn't become pro-Russian or a great lover of communists, but after associating with me for a while, she realized that the human beings living on the other side of the globe are people too and not monsters. Weak, poor, intelligent, and stupid—people of all kinds, but people. . . . The realization that Russians aren't a 260-million-strong band of evil-doers and criminals was, gentlemen, no small thing for the mind of a girl raised in a country where the word "communist" had not long before been used to frighten children. An achievement, you might say.

Linda is a very skeptical person. She is, moreover, strongly influenced by David, who really dislikes Russians. He's a cultivated person, a stage designer, and it would be difficult to suppose that he's a racist, especially since Russians aren't the most appropriate object for racism. Most likely he's just a failure who has found himself a sufficiently remote target on which to vent his anger, since in my opinion he's a coward—hence his karate.

David, although he's friendly enough with me personally, half-seriously considers me a Russian spy. Linda certainly doesn't share that opinion—she's seen me scrubbing the kitchen floor on my hands and knees too many times, an image of me that has obviously displaced from her mind the image of Edward in a KGB cap being photographed with his fellow spy school graduates with the Kremlin in the background. But Linda is by nature a skeptic; she doesn't trust the world. She cautiously peers out from behind her skeptical armor, and at any little thing withdraws again.

We discuss international problems until we're hoarse, especially relations between America and Russia, although we always reach the same conclusion every time, namely that our peoples are decent and hard-working, and that it's the fucking politicians who are trying to make us quarrel.

"Suckers!" I say. "Suckers!" Linda answers.

Thus we talk if Linda has time, and of course she doesn't always, unfortunately, which is why she always sits in the same place in the kitchen next to the phone, since people call her during lunch too, which makes us both very angry; it interrupts our conversations. Angry or not, as soon as Linda picks up the phone, she's instantly polite. "Hello, Steven Grey's office! How may I help you, sir!" Even though she's just shouted, "Fucking bastards! Why do they always have to call me at lunchtime!"

Linda always sits with her back to the window, whereas I always sit facing it—I like to watch the street. Our kitchen is about three feet below the sidewalk, so that the feet of people passing by land at about the level of our table. Actually, those "passing by" aren't passing by at all but out for a stroll, since they don't walk by our part of the street but come to it: It ends at the East River. They are almost always the same people— either rich ladies and gentlemen from expensive neighboring apartment buildings, the most expensive ones in the city, or their children, or their servants out walking their dogs. Only occasionally does a chance romantic couple wander past to sit by the river, smoke, and fondle each other. The characters in the street show are always the same, and you can set your watch by some of them. Thus, seeing a probably crazy elderly woman pass by the window on the other side of the street with a springy martial stride, you can say with certainty that it is exactly four minutes after nine. And that after going in the direction of the river, she will pass by the window again two minutes later, this time on our side of the street and going in the opposite direction. The only thing that changes in the course of the year are her clothes. In summertime she wears an orange plastic visor, and in wintertime, a blue nylon jacket. I think she's an old maid who obviously lives somewhere nearby. During the year she never deviates from her schedule of 9:04 by more than a couple of minutes.

In the mornings our street belongs to the limousine chauffeurs waiting to take our bosses to the office so they can conduct their important affairs. Many of our little neighbor ladies have nice portfolios of stocks in companies with impressive, internationally famous names like Avon, Amoco, Texaco, and so on. Open the *Wall Street Journal* and run your finger through it, and you'll make no mistake: you'll find precisely the same company names that my neighbors gaze at with satisfaction every morning as they flip through their own *Wall Street Journals*. The limousine chauffeurs in their suits and caps polish their cars with rags or stand in groups, cautiously talking. Gatsby is one of the few on our block who rarely uses a limousine; he prefers taxis.

The reason for that isn't his liberalism but simply the fact that he doesn't live here continuously; he doesn't, however, hesitate to use his private plane to fly to his estate in Connecticut.

Our street is animated early in the morning not only by chauffeurs, but also by beautiful women—it's a favorite site of New York commercial photographers. The façades of our buildings are exceptionally respectable, and we have a view of the river, so that our block has an old English look to it. And so almost every day on our street you'll see a bus with half-naked girls inside being made up by fussy homosexual make-up men, while women with cigarettes dangling from their lips and dressed in trousers of the sadistic lesbian style hoarsely direct elegant young people where to drag the next case of camera equipment, and the photographer himself, most often a Jew, although Japanese are starting to turn up with ever greater frequency now, fiddles with his camera—the Jews anxiously, and the Japanese like brand-new automatons.

And I, the servant, gladly slip outside whenever the boss isn't around to check out the girls, who are forced to repeat the same scene a dozen times—an unexpected meeting on the street, say. Although stupefied with boredom, the models pass in front of the camera with happy expressions. Like it or not, their faces must depict, for one, surprise and envy at the new dress of her friend, and for the other, pride in that dress—all this the creative discovery of the photographer or the hoarse lesbian. The male models irritate me: they're always bull-like, boorish types who seem a bit stupid and uncouth. Actually, I haven't had that much contact with them, so maybe I'm wrong.

In addition to the limousines and fashion buses, there are always at least a couple of vans parked on our street. We're always being repaired and renovated and painted—at least it's a rare day that there isn't some van on the street belonging to Royal Plumbers or Green Air Conditioners or Sherlock Holmes Security Installations or some other very important representative of business on a smaller scale. Our house is serviced by a black man named Andy whose business is called King's Air Conditioners—the same style, as you see, as the other representatives of private enterprise. Andy frequently gives me a hand in critical situations. I call him, for example, whenever a pipe bursts in the basement or a water spot appears on the ceiling in one of our rooms, such unpleasantness usually occurring in early spring. Andy respects me, and I respect him, although we're both very different. Andy neither smokes nor drinks, and he has a wife and two children. I both smoke and drink, and I don't have a family. Andy wants to educate his children and go for a long visit to Africa someday; he's very interested in the land of his ancestors. I dumped the land of my own ancestors, and it's unlikely I'll ever go back. Yet for all our differences, we get along very well, and when we both have time, we have some coffee in the kitchen and talk. As I don't try to extend my life to all the other rooms, I spend the larger part of it in the kitchen, as is appropriate for a servant.

Sometimes Linda is overcome by a kind of neurosis. Her attacks usually coincide with Gatsby's visits and the insulting things he yells at her, that she's spending his money like water or that he's had it as far as she's concerned, that he's "fed up" with her and wants her to "get out of the way!" Whenever that happens, Linda unconsciously starts screwing me over, although I'm not supposed to be her subordinate—I have my own things to do. She can always find a pretext to criticize me; it's very easy in fact, since she hangs around the millionaire's house eight and sometimes even nine hours a day.

About a month ago, for example, two huge businessmen appeared at the house one evening. I had been warned they were coming and expected them. I warmly showed the husky lads where they would be sleeping, and for their part they asked me what I was writing in my notebook, since I always loaf about the house with a notebook whenever Steven's away. Gatsby had of course told them I was a writer; I was one of the attractions for his guests. After that we played a crazy computer game on the TV screen for half an hour, they as the representatives of the most advanced technical thought in the world naturally beating me. And then they humped out to dinner somewhere.

The next morning while the gentlemen were still in bed—they had obviously come back from dinner very late—Linda said to me in a businesslike tone, "Edward, describe to me which of them is Mr. Burdell, that is, what he looks like, since I have to give him a personal letter from Steven."

"One of them has a beard and the other doesn't. Both of them are tremendously tall, well-built guys at least as big as the boss. They're about the same age, I think, but I don't have any idea which one is Burdell," I told Linda.

"Edward, please be serious about your responsibilities here, and in the future please remember who is who!" Linda said nervously, straightening her jacket, which it's possible she had put on especially for the two businessmen, for all I know. "Please, Edward, you've put me in an awkward position. I have to hand the letter to Mr. Burdell; the other gentlemen is just his subordinate," she continued. "Always, always ask their names, and ask again if you don't understand. We could be in real trouble because of your carelessness."

"Listen, Linda," I said, "what are you getting so upset about? Give me the letter and I'll hand it to him. And if I make a mistake, what's so awful about that? I only saw the gentlemen last night for a half an hour at most, and they never introduced themselves to me. I just opened the door for them, helped them bring their luggage in, and we immediately started talking about something. . . . Let me have the letter and I'll find some way of handing it to him. I've got it, Linda!" it suddenly occurred to me. "I'll just say something like, 'Mr. Burdell, I have a letter for you from Steven' to both of them from a distance, and Mr. Burdell, and not the other guy, will answer and stick out his hand for the letter."

The whole Burdell business was terribly funny.

But do you know what she did? She didn't give me the letter but continued to grumble and called San Francisco, where the gentlemen were from, and asked Burdell's secretary what he looked like: "I'm sorry, dear, but I've got a problem here. . . ." Secretaries form a worldwide brotherhood, or rather sisterhood, an international sisterhood that knows no boundaries. Burdell, it turned out, was the one with the beard and the curly hair. Looking at me triumphantly, Linda exultantly put the letter from Steven, which she'd written and typed herself of course, on the very top of the half dozen or so leather portfolios that were lying on her desk.

And when the two big lunks finally appeared in the kitchen, yawning and stretching, Linda with a happy click of her heels walked right up to the one she needed and said, "Mr. Burdell, welcome to Steven Grey's house. I hope you slept well!"

I almost burst out laughing right there in the kitchen when she handed Burdell the sacred letter. A half an hour later I fished it out of the waste basket. Written on beautiful paper with Gatsby's name and our address embossed at the top was no more than:

"Hi, Charles! Welcome! I trust you and your companion will be comfortable in my home and your weekend will be a pleasant one. I expect to fly into New York Monday evening at 6:30, and accordingly should be home by 7:00, and we will, I'm confident, have an excellent evening together. I'll call if I'm held up. Yours, Steven."

I had at the request of Linda herself conveyed the very same message to the gentlemen the evening before.

But Linda must be given her due. On one of my first days at work, I think, she said to me, "Edward! If I ever start to get on your nerves, or if I get too insistent about telling you how to live, don't be shy about it; just tell me to fuck off! Work is work," Linda went on, "and our relationship may get pretty tense at times, but don't pay any attention to it, just tell me to fuck off, and I won't be offended."

And I have told her more than once, and she's told me, and neither of us has gotten offended. Work is work, and we're building capitalism, Steven and Linda and I, sometimes successfully and sometimes not so successfully.

Although I do try to slip out of it and am even a little intimidated by it, I like the kitchen. Everybody likes it in fact, including Nancy, who spends the better part of her day there whenever she's in town, and even Steven, who comes into it quite often. All the other rooms in a sense distract us from the kitchen, its allure being somehow more ancient, a vestige of the caveman's desire for a hearth, and a kitchen is in fact all anyone needs for life. Everything else is an outgrowth of civilization, and we only waste the precious time on loan to us from chaos in going idly from one room to another and mulling over our inessential, our non-kitchen, objects and affairs.

Once I was sitting in the kitchen next to the window, a servant-philosopher, while outside it was getting dark and two boys were throwing a Frisbee in the street and quietly squealing with pleasure. A sunny fall day was coming to an end. I was drinking a beer and waiting for the boss. Maybe I shouldn't have waited for him—Linda says I don't have to—but it was possible Gatsby didn't have his key with him. That doesn't happen very often, but it's always possible, and so it's better to wait.

I sat and lazily thought about how nice it would be if Steven's plane went down with him in it. He's a bright person, no doubt about it, but he takes up too much space in my life; after me, he comes next. We are all engrossed in ourselves, but Steven is the other center around which my life revolves. There's no reason for that, I thought. It would be a good thing if the plane went down; my life should have just one center—me. I at once felt guilty, however. Did I have the right to such evil thoughts, did I have the right to wish for my boss's death? But Steven, if he were to find himself in my place by some whim of fate and circumstance, would probably have been thinking the same thing with his crazy temperament, would have been sitting next to the window and waiting for his boss Edward and probably would have wanted him to crash into the Atlantic Ocean too. That thought cheered me up.

Rights, rights, I thought. Who gives anybody the right to do anything? Is it my fault that I was born among the long cold ruins of Christianity, in the middle of this century in a godless country (whether that's good or bad, I cannot say), and that I've retained nothing, not the least little thing, from the Christian code of behavior in this world, or of any other code, and for that reason am compelled to devise my own code and decide for myself whether my actions and thoughts are good or bad? Is that my fault? And as far as Jenny was concerned, should I or should I not have indulged my incomprehensible loathing for her and have thought such bad things about her behind her back and have seen her as bad—as ugly, lazy, and farting? Maybe I needed to close my eyes and not see that, intentionally not see what was bad in her—refuse to notice the bad and see only the help she gave me and simply be grateful to her for everything she did for me, voluntarily or involuntarily? Maybe I didn't have the right to see her as ugly and shouldn't have noticed that pimple under her nose?

But how? I thought. I did try to love her, I really wanted to, but in spite of myself I slipped back into my merciless way of noticing the pettiest details, slipped back to my terrible unforgiving sight, to my vile, graphically honest thoughts. That's the secret, it suddenly occurred to me. I want to be honest with myself; I *cannot* consent to illusion and falsehood.

And in wishing that Steven would fall into the Atlantic Ocean along with his Concorde, I was also being maximally honest with myself, selfish, but honest. His visits bring me inconvenience, physical weariness, psychological distress, and a general repression in my life. They force me to live differently from my own notion of the way I ought to live, and that's why I wished him death. Is it really so shameful to wish death on your jailer,

205

even if he's married and has children? When at eighteen I tried to persuade the paranoid Grisha to kill the orderlies so we could escape from the hospital where they were tormenting me, where they were injecting me with insulin, putting me in a coma, mutilating my psyche, and humiliating me, I was, biologically speaking, entirely in the right. Kill your tormentor!

I didn't want my boss to crash on land; that would have been too painful. It's somehow more innocuous and humane for a plane to fall into the ocean. In the ocean is better, I decided. . . . But then it suddenly occurred to me that if Steven were gone, the power would pass to his heirs, and Nancy would inevitably sell the house—exactly, since she prefers living in the country with her horses and cows and had been grumbling to Steven that the New York house is a completely unnecessary luxury— and I'd lose my job and the possibility as a poor man of living on occasion the life of a rich one—a possibility and life unique in their own way. No, I thought, let the boss arrive safely after all. He's a decent guy, and if he's a bit hysterical, well what of it? We'll manage, we'll get through it somehow.

I'm a realist. Even in little things I sometimes catch myself in the most vulgar realism. Thus I remember altering some pants for a certain old lady and wanting to overstitch the seams—as you're supposed to do so they won't fray. I'd already put the right color thread in the machine when I suddenly thought, but why should I; she won't be using the pants that long. She's old, and she'll die before the seams have a chance to fray. And I didn't overstitch them.

I extend my awful realism to myself too. I'm constantly aware of death now. Before I wouldn't remember it for as much as a year and lived as if I were going to live forever, deeply absorbed in the problems of the day and never glancing around, and only occasionally stopping to muse with terror and bewilderment. And then I'd forget. . . .

But now I think peacefully and tranquilly about death every day, and remember and count the time left. In essence, I've got twenty to twenty-five years of normal, active life before my body deteriorates to the point where it will be more a source of inconvenience than pleasure. Into those twenty to twenty-five years, I must squeeze all of myself—my thoughts, my books, my actions, and my sexual life, fucking the women I dream of fucking, and if (all of a sudden) I should want to kill men and women, I shall have to hurry if I'm going to do that too. If I should want to have children, then I'll have to conceive them in the middle of that period, and if I should have the lofty dream, say, of founding a party or a state or a religion, then, gentlemen, it must *all* be done by 2,001 to 2,005 years after the birth of Christ. I'm a corpse in the middle of his vacation. And that vacation is trickling away, gentlemen, and soon it will be back to chaos.

Faster, faster, while there's still time, and fan whatever delirium or fire there is in you; it's unimportant what it is, only that you do it while there's still time—I advise you too, reader. Before your meeting with chaos, before your sunny vacation is over and it's back to nothingness.

A couple of days after that I found myself sitting in the same place by the kitchen window repairing Steven's fur coat. He didn't ask me to. He merely threw the coat down on the chest in the hallway since winter was over and he didn't need it anymore, and I saw it there and realized the pocket was completely torn and the lining was coming undone at the seam, even though the coat was almost new. I could have sent it to Kaplan's for repair, or not have bothered about it and hung it up in the closet; yet I was sitting there and mending his fur coat, and taking great pains with it. I'm not moved by my own nobility; I'm just amazed at the different tendencies I find in myself—first wanting Steven's death, and then, like his mother, mending his coat. Probably that's as it should be. It may be that I'm capable of mending his fur coat, putting the mended coat on him, and then sending him off to his death. Or maybe it's just a manifestation of my fondness for order.

Send him off, send him off. It's what Steven deserves. After all, he's been terribly rude. Sometimes the instant he comes in the door. Yesterday when he arrived he announced he was going out even before he had a chance to shut the door. To which his servant replied in an ironically distraught voice, "Right away?"

"In fifteen minutes. Do you mind if I rest for a moment in my own house?" he answered, glaring malevolently at his servant.

I didn't mind. I had no objection. Rest, tired boss, rest, you neurotic old woman, I thought. I didn't expect him to blow up and start yelling at me. After Efimenkov's visit my stock has stood very high and solid with him, but I still cut out to my beloved basement where it was quiet, warm, and restful, and where nobody would come unless for wine, and sat down in the corner of the laundry room on a pile of dirty linen. A laundry room or basement is a good place to rest up after an escape from jail in damp and rotten weather, a place where after several weeks in the cold and wet you can cover your head with freshly laundered sheets and sleep and forget all about the rest of the world for a moment and about your own exploits and fame— where you can forget about everything except its slightly stuffy warmth and your own inhuman weariness. . . .

Steven, I thought abstractedly . . . Nancy . . . Sometimes, in those moments when I stop looking at my day-to-day life as an inevitable stage in my destiny without which the future simply cannot occur, I think in dismay, *Why am I a servant, why did I turn up here?* It's all so ridiculous—Steven, Nancy . . . the silver, the dirty dishes, how to serve meat and how to make sauce for crab . . . It's all so ridiculous and stupid, so what are you doing here, Edward? Long ago in the Soviet school system you read about your present life in the books of pre-revolutionary writers, never thinking that one day that past would suddenly become your own life. It's as silly as . . .

Escape from servanthood? Where to? Wouldn't I end up wasting the minutes and hours I waste on Steven on some other, even more pointless work, on other things I don't have any fucking use for either?

Thus I sat on the pile of dirty linen thinking about what to do next. After spending about an hour in that state and weighing all the pros and cons, I came to the conclusion that it made sense for me to go to work for Gatsby. What would I have been doing then in my apartment on Eighty-third Street, even supposing I had had the money to pay for it? I'd have been sitting there alone like an owl. At least here I'm surrounded by people, by conversation, language, books, and money, I thought, listing the advantages of the millionaire's house. Anyway, the whole family's going to Tunis for three weeks at the end of March, and then Steven's flying to Japan, I remembered happily, and got up from the pile of linen and went back upstairs.

After hanging around the house not fifteen minutes but an hour, Steven slammed the front door and walked past the kitchen window. But seeing me, he came back, smiled, and waved his hand, obviously ashamed of his rudeness. He's gone out dressed in nothing but his suit, I thought mechanically. He's not a bad person, I thought. Maybe someday he'll invest his money in the destruction of civilization. . . .

For some reason during my first winter and spring at the house, it happened that Nancy had pressing business in New York a couple of times a month, and she came down either alone or with the children or even with her neighbors from the country, usually staying for a few days and only rarely longer. I calculated that during the first months of my employment in Mr. Grey's house, Nancy spent much more time there than she had during the whole time I'd been Jenny's boyfriend. Nancy was clearly checking up on my suitability for the duties of housekeeper, and unaccustomed as I was to being checked on, I got fucking tired of it.

Nancy loves to cook; she's no mere lady of leisure. She almost always made breakfast herself and for their whole crowd—for her own children and for her country neighbors and their children. My own responsibilities consisted of helping her—hanging around the kitchen with her, getting one thing and another for her, and running to the store. If it turned out, say, that the kind of butter I used wasn't the same one Nancy used, or if she suddenly decided to make pancakes, and there wasn't any flour in the house, I slid off my stool and ran out to the store for the butter or flour.

Thus I remember myself that winter standing in the brightly lit kitchen early in the morning like the sleepy servant boy Vanka Zhukov in Chekhov's story, and setting the table for a dozen people, and putting out the napkins, and pulling back the chairs, all before the sky had had a chance even to turn gray— Nancy and her friends are residents of the country and get up at the crack of dawn.

Helping and being ready to run errands was a lot worse than cooking breakfast for them myself would have been; personally I prefer to cook. Nancy undoubtedly knows how to do everything and she's a deservedly celebrated hostess. At home in Connecticut she sometimes bakes insanely large cakes for a hundred people in the shape of a ship or a church or City Hall, and every time, the cakes are mentioned in the cooking section of *The New York Times*. The cakes are devoured by Mr. and Mrs. Grey's guests in the open air in a Connecticut forest meadow to the accompaniment of a symphony orchestra. I've already said they're fond of showing off; they may not eat, that little family, but they will show off.

Mrs. Grey cooked the breakfasts, for which I thank her, but after one of her forays, my kitchen looked like a peaceful little Jewish village after a pogrom. The fact is that she used as many dishes as she deemed necessary—three times as many as I would have. In Connecticut she had six servants to clean up after her, whereas here there were only Olga and I to form a living conveyor between the sink and the dishwasher, Olga rinsing the remaining food from the dishes, and I putting them into the diswasher. After lunch, I had to clean up everything by myself.

Once Nancy noticed I was rinsing the dishes before putting them in the dishwasher.

"You don't have to do that, Edward," she said patronizingly, obviously amazed by my stupidity or ignorance. "That's what we have the dishwasher for—to wash the dishes."

I said, "I'm sorry, Nancy, but the specialist who repaired the dishwasher about a month ago told me to, and so I'm doing it."

"Why?" Nancy said. "I have exactly the same kind of dishwasher in Connecticut and I never rinse the dishes before putting them in."

I shrugged my shoulders, while Nancy put the dirty breakfast dishes with egg yolk spread all over them into our unhappy dishwasher. Forty minutes later they all came out clean, except for the egg yolk, which was still stuck to them. She then sat down, her skirt spread out on the floor next to the dishwasher, and pushing her sleeves up, started digging around in it. She unscrewed several nuts, removed several pieces, and tinkered with the machine for a long time, repeating over and over again, "Why?" The stubborn and inquisitive Nancy. Then she was joined by a guest, one of her country neighbors, an extremely thin banker in his stockinged feet, who sat down next to the dishwasher and sank his hands into it too. . . .

From time to time I discreetly nudged Olga, who was present for that whole scene, and smiled ironically. We people from technologically underdeveloped countries don't stick our noses into areas we don't understand. The meticulous Nancy and the banker fiddled with the machine for about an hour and a half, however, getting greasy water and food fragments all over themselves, but with zero results—0. To this day we rinse the food off the dishes before putting them in the dishwasher, having been ordered to do so by His Highness the Specialist, a red-haired guy in overalls—the god of dishwashing machines.

I would earnestly ask Nancy how to *do* things, pretending I really was interested in how she made mayonnaise with dill or some other culinary crap. I asked her and even wrote down what she said, gentlemen. If you want get in good with somebody, be diligent, or at least pretend to be. I pretended with a vengeance. Nancy may not actually have believed I was interested in kitchen arithmetic and mechanics, but she didn't have to—we were playing our respective roles, she the mistress and I the housekeeper, and it all worked out very well. For some reason, I know how to make a superb chicken soup that is much better than Nancy's, which not only Linda has noted but Steven too. Many people in fact have told me that my chicken soup is the best they've ever had. Could it be that I make the best chicken soup in the world? I think Nancy respected me for my chicken soup and also for the fact that I didn't show off but accepted the rules of the game: I made an effort to seem diligent. And that's why she gave up her raids in the end and came to New York only when she actually needed to. Then in March of last year, as if summing up the results of her inspection, she said to me, "Well, Edward, you're doing just fine. The house is spotless. You have my thanks."

Now we live in peace, harmony, and tranquillity. Although it is in fact my feeling that the master and mistress only track dirt into the house and aren't really of much use—a housekeeper's point of view. After the raids by the wild bunch from Connecticut, now infrequent, thank God, Olga and I gradually put the house back in order. The children's rooms are particularly messy of course. During their short visits the inquisitive American children manage to accomplish a great deal: They glue together model airplanes and boats, cut up paper into small pieces, which they then spread all over the house, run on the roof, thereby making all the glass in the house vibrate, and tie ropes and wires around the banisters. . . . It would be impossible to describe the full extent of the havoc wreaked by the children; suffice it to say that each one of their visits costs Olga and me several days of labor after they're gone. The most offensive thing is that we are in fact cleaning up after the neighbors' children, since only the youngest of the Grey children is capable by age of participating and in fact does participate in these outrages. But I'm always so happy when the mistress at last takes off for home, that the consequences of her visits are unable to dim my joy.

Sometimes Nancy leaves somebody to stay at the house for a few days. Or else her Connecticut banker neighbor has some business in the city and he stays for a couple of days, or Nancy's lover, Carl, comes and stays. According to my agreement with Steven, however, I am not obligated to these people in any way. I may give them coffee in the morning if they come down to the kitchen, or anything I happen to have in the refrigerator, but help yourselves, dear guests. It's self-service.

Carl always turns up at the house within half an hour after Nancy arrives. The first thing she does, after parking her jeep in front of the kitchen window and leaving me and the older children to unload it, is to phone Carl. Carl is a youngish, rapidly balding man obviously about my age or even younger, but unlike me he has made a career for himself in the last four years. After starting out as the bookkeeper of a provincial yacht club in some remote corner of Connecticut, he quickly climbed up the social ladder, skipping two or three rungs thanks to Nancy's good offices, and now occupies the position of president of one of the largest of the computer subsidiaries that make up Gatsby's empire.

Learn, Edward, I tell myself every time I see Carl sitting with Nancy in the kitchen and talking with her in a cultivated way about nothing at all. He's an opportunist, the genuine article—unlike you.

Nancy is forty and a very attractive woman, tall, with a good figure. The only thing you can reproach her or nature with is that, like Jenny, she is the most perfect of mothers, the sort whose affectionate lap it's good for a child injured by life to curl up in. Regardless of the things that have happened to me, even in the most difficult times in my life, I've never felt the need to have a good cry in my mother's lap or on her breast. What I need are capricious and whorish young girl-pals, haughty and painted and perfumed, and have never had dreams of myself as a timid little creature descending into a gigantic cunt—I'm not Steven and I'm not Carl, and Nancy doesn't appeal to me. Even though I did, like a true opportunist, have thoughts about the boss's wife in the beginning, after considering all the pros and cons, I realized she wasn't my cup of tea. It is, of course, another question entirely whether she would have been interested in me, although I doubt that she would have been. There wasn't even one point of contact between us, though there wasn't any antipathy either. Moreover, I think that Nancy and I are the same type of people: we're both self-assured, enterprising, and given to action, and I've always taken my women under my protection and been a papa to them, even when they were older than me. That may in fact be the reason why Jenny and I never really got on together. She wasn't a tempting girl-daughter for me, but mama Jenny, and we didn't need a mama Jenny—no. I myself am a papa Limonov; I myself like to be the one in control.

Carl the opportunist is a quiet person, and when he stays at the house, he's neither seen nor heard. Sometimes in the morning I find him in the kitchen reading the book on etiquette by Amy Vanderbilt, obviously a kind of handbook for opportunists—who else would need it? Gatsby has no need of books like that; he already knows a little, and in any case his wealth and self-assurance place him above any etiquette. Gatsby is a representative of the upper classes and not a bourgeois like the former bookkeeper Carl. It's right for Carl to read a book on etiquette, and he reads it. Nevertheless, they share the same woman.

How odd that nature sticks different types of people wherever it can, not worrying in the least about the bodies, using the first one that comes along. And so here is the robust fellow Steven Grey, six feet two inches tall, and inside him the vulnerable soul of a little boy who seeks a mother in all his women and who chooses the mother—Nancy and Polly, for example, and several of his other women as well, all of whom give off a maternal aura. Whereas I, Edward Limonov, five feet eight and with the face of a child, have—just imagine!—the habits of a papa. I remember that only once during the whole of my life with Jenny, at a time when I was sick with a fever, did I play the child with her, and in that instant everything suddenly assumed its proper place for her: She pressed my head against her breast and stroked my hair, obviously not even aware that she was doing it, and started muttering affectionately to me. The next day she told me sadly, "How sick you were last night, Edward, but at least you were *human*. It's the first time since I've known you."

Whenever I see the severe Nancy kneeling in the garden in her long dress, her face tanned and without any makeup and her hair pulled back in a bun, as she concentrates on transplanting an azalea bush from a pot, I feel a certain masculine superiority over my employer. Because he needs the protective caresses of this strong woman, while to this day I still sigh in anguish every night and toss and turn in my bed remembering the unbalanced child Elena, who could drive me to a frenzy with her whorishness, that child who had grown completely wild. Elena had run away from her papa Edward and was doing shocking things—fucking bad men and behaving in whatever hoodlum way she pleased, instead of living like a good daughter the way her papa wanted her to. What could I do—nature made me that way. If I had been able to, I would with pleasure have rested my head on some woman's large breast—like a poor, tired little boy.

Oh, I would give a great deal to enter Steven Grey's bedroom and see how he does everything with his women. It's only the curiosity of an investigator, gentlemen, only the curiosity of an investigator—nothing dirty, no sexual thoughts whatsoever. I would just like to see who dominates and how. Steven and his girlfriends, by the way, use not only the master bedroom but also the guest bedroom next door. Either he and Polly hump each other on his bed, and then she goes to sleep in the guest bedroom (in which case I've had it with these spoiled WASPs), or else Gatsby feels it would somehow be unethical to fuck in the family's master bedroom with its photograph of the naked Nancy holding an equally naked baby—Henry, his first-born. I don't know what the answer is, but Olga, the black woman from underdeveloped Haiti, has more work to do thanks to the strange scrupulousness of our lord and master. And the yellow half-Tatar Edward has yet another excuse for grins and reflections.

Chapter Eight

Just a few days after I became the millionaire's housekeeper, or butler as Gatsby says, the energetic bureaucrat Linda put together a curious document for me, a very long document on which she had obviously spent a great deal of time. In order to give you an idea of the kind of semi-military order that prevails in our house, I cite it here.

Edward:

Attached is a list of Steven's friends and business colleagues, with which you must carefully acquaint yourself.

"P" after a name indicates a personal friend, and "B" indicates a business colleague. If nothing is indicated, then the person in question belongs to both categories. The countries following certain names indicate principal places of residence in the event that it isn't the United States.

This is by no means a complete list but includes only the most important people. Please try to become *familiar* with these names and their correct spelling, and so on, so that if they call, you can more accurately understand the tone of the message. By this I mean that it may not be necessary every time to track down Steven wherever he is on the globe, but that every message definitely deserves to be written down and given to both of us, that is to me and to Steven if he happens to be in the city. Please pay particular attention to messages coming from people who are going to be in New York only a short time while Steven's in the city.

I have another suggestion for you as well—that from time to time you look at my card file and gradually familiarize yourself with the names there. If someone calls who isn't on the attached list, a basic rule is that if you can find his name in the card file, he's entitled to have his message written down.

Two requests: Always tell me, please, if you give a message to Steven, in case he can't immediately answer the call himself and asks me about it later.

Don't trust people if they say the message isn't important, and please try to get their names and telephone numbers in all cases where that isn't all there is to the message. It may be a call for me about something I happen to be working on at the time.

IF YOU DON'T UNDERSTAND SOMETHING, ASK ME ABOUT IT REGARDLESS OF HOW TRIVIAL IT MAY SEEM TO YOU!!!

L.

P.S. If you can't find a name in the card file, it may be because it's listed under the name of the caller's company. For example, Carl Fink's name can also be found under "Norse Electronics." Thus, if it's not a personal call, you may feel free to ask for the name of the company the caller works for.

A list of about two hundred names followed. And the countries in which all those P's and B's lived really were scattered all over the globe.

Ghupta is a "P," that is, a personal friend of Gatsby's. Linda explained to me that he's worth around forty million dollars and works in the areas of oil and atomic energy. Ghupta is from Burma but received his education in England, although he's a citizen of the world, with homes in Rangoon, Kuala Lumpur, London, and in Texas, where he hangs out most of the time, close to his oil. Whenever he comes to New York he always stays with us at Steven's house, despite the fact that he has a permanent suite waiting for him at the Waldorf-Astoria. He's just more comfortable with us, you see.

Ghupta is about my height, maybe a little taller, and has about the same build. His dark Burmese skin may be the main reason he's a little more human than the other wealthy people around Steven, since at first sight, without looking into his pockets, he's just Ghupta, a colored man. In the Great United States extending from sea to shining sea, that fact still means something.

I'm even fond of Mr. Ghupta in my own way, maybe because we're both Asiatics, or maybe because he's the only one of all the "P's" and "B's" who *notices* me. That is, he's not merely distinguished by the courtesy of wealthy people—the two or three meaningless questions; he actually has conversations with me in which he sometimes gets very interested. Of course he's a cunning Oriental fox with sugary speech and very strong paws—I know that—but the very first time we met, when I was still Jenny's lover, Ghupta suddenly told me after a ten-minute conversation in the kitchen during which we laughingly discussed the wedding page of *The New York Times*, "Edward, I have no doubt you will be very successful." Even if he was merely flattering me, and Orientals like to be on good terms with everybody (even the housekeeper's lover—just in case), I still very much needed to be flattered then. I needed support. And I made a point of remembering him and told myself, Here's somebody who's alive. Maybe not a friend, maybe a completely different class of person, but enjoyable to be with.

Besides, Ghupta is somehow more with it. He dresses in a much more contemporary way than Steven does. He's capable of wearing, say, the best silk jacket from Saks Fifth Avenue with cotton pants bought on sale at the Gap store on Lexington for ten dollars—I've shortened quite a few pairs of such pants for him. He's right to get out among people and make friends; after all, I proved useful to him, and not merely as a tailor, as you will see. Ghupta has taught me practicality: He once took me to a sale at Saks and showed me how to buy expensive things at half the price. I learn with pleasure, and thanks to him, I now have a small but very impressive wardrobe of designer rags which I would never in my life have allowed myself to buy at the regular price. An opportunist should be well dressed.

He always gleams, my friend the millionaire Ghupta; he's always decked out like a schoolboy on the first day of vacation— white socks, a red knit alligator shirt, loafers, and cotton pants that are always of a light color. At his office, and he has one in New York too, Ghupta wears suits and ties of course, but they aren't the same suits and ties my boss, Steven Grey, wears. Ghupta somehow gives the impression of enjoying himself, although I am in complete agreement with Linda when she says that working for Ghupta is far from a piece of cake, and that he makes his bed soft but lies hard in it and has completely worn out his secretary. Yes, I say, but with Ghupta it's more fun; he may exploit you even more than Steven does, but I prefer the even-tempered, cunning, Oriental slyness with which Ghupta squeezes the juice out of his employees to the hysterical outbursts of Gatsby. Linda is an unconscious admirer of Gatsby's, but the best thing of all is to be your own boss and not have to serve anybody. Furthermore, Ghupta, who doesn't spend all that much time in New York, has hung around the kitchen with me a lot more than Gatsby has, and he's my boss. Judging from what I know about Ghupta's affairs, he's far from being the sort of person who pisses his time away, and is an even more successful businessman than my employer is, and much better at getting results. It follows that the puritan severity of Gatsby is quite unnecessary.

However strange it may be, Ghupta is also much more liberal. For example, he wasn't at all reluctant to invite me, a servant, into the living room when he was entertaining his country's ambassador and minister of commerce at our house. We all drank Dom Perignon together, the housekeeper Edward along with the millionaires and ministers, and politely engaged in small talk. After we had drunk four bottles, Ghupta called me into the corridor and asked me if I would mind going out to the liquor store for some more or calling them to have it delivered. It was a pleasure for the housekeeper Edward to run out to the liquor store for a man like that. "May I use the limo?" I asked him. The guests had naturally arrived in a limousine that Ghupta hired for them. "Of course, Edward!" he said.

I took my seat in the black lacquered coffin and rode the three blocks to the wine shop. It turned out to be a very pleasant thing to go for champagne in a limousine. The driver was a Russian, or rather a Jew from Russia, as I immediately deduced from his wooden accent as soon as I started talking to him, although I didn't tell him I was a Russian too. Why the hell should I? Except for the fact that we had both left Russia, we had nothing in common.

Coming back, I put the champagne in the freezer and sat down again in the living room with Ghupta and his company. Their ambassador in Washington had, as it turned out, been ambassador in Moscow before that; we had something to talk about. True, he had been in Moscow after I left. On top of that, one of the girls invited to entertain the guests, the one in fact who had been invited to entertain Ghupta himself, was a blonde model named Jacqueline who turned out to be acquainted with my ex-wife, and Jacqueline and I talked about the eccentric and from my point of view too well-known ex-Elena.

Gradually the guests and the girls wandered off to other parts of the house and garden, while I, deciding that I had participated enough in the social life of my friend Ghupta, withdrew to my room. But a little later the attentive Ghupta knocked at my door and asked me if I didn't want to join them again, for which I thanked him, but said no. Whereupon Ghupta, still standing in the doorway, confided to me that he had already fucked Jacqueline more than once and that he intended to fuck her again that night.

I couldn't even imagine Steven Grey in a situation like that.

With Gatsby I always feel out of place. Once, and only once, did he even take me to a restaurant with him after noticing that I was enjoying a conversation with a friend of his, the lawyer Ellis. "Ellis! Edward! Let's go. You can continue your conversation at the restaurant!" We did continue it, but it was extremely hard to do, since Gatsby wouldn't let anybody else get a word in, so that it was no longer interesting to me and I swore at myself for agreeing to go with them. Steven Grey loves to be the center of attention and he loves to talk, and everybody else is supposed to listen to him with their mouths hanging open. Uh-uh, that's not for me!

If I or Ellis or Birnbaum, another friend of Gatsby's, said anything, I noticed that Gatsby would instantly wilt; he was obviously bored. Maybe his hysterical thoughts were way ahead of us or maybe he just wasn't interested in what we were saying to him, I don't know. In principle I agree with him: most people aren't very interesting, but I consider myself, his housekeeper, a quite unusual personality, and the fact that he's never really had the slightest curiosity about me, that he hasn't tried to find out what's behind the taciturn but apparently friendly Russian who prepares his lunches for him—that fact compels me to hold him in not very high regard. Gatsby was, for example, interested in Efimenkov, who was a Russian too, but then Efimenkov was world famous, and Gatsby is a snob, gentlemen, and what do I want from him anyway? Nothing in particular. For me he's merely an entertaining personality, even an exceptional one for the circle he moves in. Just as Jenny was an unusual personality for the circle she moved in. And I'm interested in the reasons for things in this world. I'm curious, that's all.

Ghupta sometimes laughs at Steven. A great admirer of the opposite sex, Ghupta once told me with a sly grin that he wouldn't be able to get it up for even one of Gatsby's women, that they're all so terribly domestic. "I wouldn't either, Ghupta," I seconded him with an embarrassed smile, feeling a little awkward about betraying Gatsby that way. It was as if Ghupta and I were the real men, and Steven wasn't. I was even sorry for the miserable Gatsby. Poor Gatsby, Ghupta and I had first-rate women for whom we could get it up, whereas he had women for whom we couldn't. For some reason we were confident that Gatsby could get it up for ours.

That Ghupta could get it up for my women I am reminded by one of my jackets, a jacket he gave me the day after he fucked Tatiana. More accurately, Ghupta gave me a jacket from Saks in exchange for my having "given" him a Russian woman named Tatiana, who was somebody's estranged wife and even the mother of his two children. Tatiana is dark-haired and beautiful; she doesn't look Russian at all but Spanish. She turned up soon after I succeeded in publishing my long-suffering novel in Russian, a copy of which I immediately sent to Efimenkov—let him enjoy it. Thanks to the novel, Russian girls and women started hovering about me like bees and flies and wasps around something sweet. I had no objection. Tatiana was one of them.

Tatiana speaks in a quiet voice and considers herself very unfortunate. I, Edward, don't believe that she's all that unfortunate. She has a slender, sensuous body and a small moist cunt. It's pleasant to fuck Tatiana; she's delicate and adores being fucked, and during the act she sobs a little from pleasure. It may be that part of her misfortune, including her last husband, is explained by the fact that she can't resist a prick.

I had been fucking Tatiana since May, with only a brief respite after she supposedly discovered she'd caught an infection from me, although she hadn't really, and then she would secretly meet me at a bar on the West Side and sit there in a black shawl and weep and talk to me in a whisper. At first I even liked her crazy behavior and her black outfits and tear-stained eyes, but by September I was sick of her little quirks, which, for example, included paranoia. That's right, ordinary paranoia—she thought the CIA was after her. She had a certain basis for believing that; one of her lovers had in fact been a CIA special agent, although the distance between having a CIA lover and being followed is, you'll agree, not inconsiderable. But it's also quite possible that her lover was following her and possibly even using CIA resources to do so, for all I know. I've had enough problems of the detective variety in my own life.

But I was much sicker of Tatiana's carelessness than I was of her paranoia. A couple of times she failed to turn up at the millionaire's house when I was expecting her, and several times she turned up when I wasn't, once even scaring off a young cunt who happened to be staying with me at the time. Which is why I lost my temper with her, and one time when she called, I told her I was going to give the phone to Ghupta, which, despite her indignant protests, is what I did.

Ghupta spoke tenderly to her for a while, pronouncing her name with a Georgian accent for some reason, and managed to arrange a date with her, which was easy; all you had to do was pressure her a little.

Ghupta had seen Tatiana at the house several times and had liked her very much. Which isn't surprising—she's beautiful. "I'm tired of my own girls," he said while cooking up some vegetables for himself in a frying pan; he's a vegetarian. "American girls are fine, Edward, if you're going on a picnic with some friends, say; they're great company, they drink beer right out of the can, and they laugh loudly, but in bed they're all the same. There is something mysterious about your Tatiana, however, something romantic," Ghupta sighed hypocritically. It was obvious he wanted Tatiana. As far as I could tell, the majority of Ghupta's girls weren't Americans at all. He was fucking Jacqueline, who, despite her French name, was from Finland, and I'd also seen him with a Jamaican girl, so his so-called poverty was just a pretense.

Ghupta's attitude toward women is tenderly cynical and very practical, and I understand him; if I had a business life as demanding as his, I'd obviously have the same kind of sexual philosophy.

"All the beautiful girls in New York are actresses and models, Edward," Ghupta lectured me once, "and eighty percent of them at least use cocaine, which is considered very chic, and buying them cocaine is the quickest and easiest, although unfortunately not the cheapest, way to fuck them and hold on to them. You didn't know my girlfriend Letitia, did you?" he asked me, immediately answering his own question. "No, you couldn't have; Jenny saw her a few times. Letitia worked for Elite," he said, naming one of New York's best known model agencies, already aware that the interests of the housekeeper Edward were far from limited to the kitchen. "She really suited me and I enjoyed fucking her—you know how hard it is to find a bed partner who satisfies you, Edward. Letitia was, moreover, a very striking girl, and it was a pleasure to go places with her. I got so used to her, Edward, that I even started taking her on business trips with me. Once when we were going through customs, however, they found some cocaine on her. I used to give her money for cocaine, and I even snort it myself on occasion, although not very often," Ghupta added, "but here in the United States that form of entertainment is merely child's play, whereas there are countries where it is simply inconceivable, and I didn't let Letitia take cocaine with her on our trips. It's a good thing it happened in a country where I could simply pay the customs agents off. If it had happened in my own country, I would have been finished; we have very strict laws and my money wouldn't have helped, Edward," he said very seriously, and I sympathized with him. "I broke up with Letitia after that," he said. "She couldn't live without the white powder anymore, so what else could I do?" he appealed to me once more.

I think it was in fact for the sake of his girls that Ghupta at one time was obsessed with the idea of buying Isabelle's house, and it was an idea that was very hard for him to give up. "It's so

225

impossible to maintain relationships with women," he complained to me, "and how can I, if I'm only in New York once a month? When I suddenly come back a month later, my women have all made other arrangements."

Poor Ghupta. I don't understand what he's so nervous about. He has so many women in New York, they start calling him a week before he gets back to the city. He uses my telephone number, so I'm the one who gets the calls. Poor Ghupta, his eyes are much bigger than his stomach, and he wants them all.

On one of the following evenings Ghupta fucked Tatiana in our house—in my house, since I live here too. How do I know? I came home around midnight, and the light in the hallway and stairs had already been turned off, something Ghupta usually doesn't do, since it is Steven's and my privilege to turn off the hall light. The light was turned off, and from the solarium came the sound of classical music—Tchaikovsky, whom Tatiana adores and whom I can't stand.

It was obvious from all the signs that somewhere in the depths of the house Ghupta was at that very moment sticking his Burmese dick into Tatiana.

A couple of weeks later I was spending a Saturday evening at home with a large lady named Teresa whom I had been fucking the preceding night and all day Saturday, although without much success. Teresa had just returned to New York after living for more than ten years in Europe. I was seeing her for the second time in my life.

A writer with a very good figure and a face that was rather worn by the storms of life, Teresa was just about to leave, when the front doorbell suddenly rang, sounding, as it does in our house, like Big Ben or the Kremlin carillon. I wasn't expecting anybody that evening. Opening the door, I found Tatiana, dressed in black as usual and upset and a little overwrought.

I ceremoniously introduced the two ladies to each other, and since Tatiana said she wanted to talk to me about something very important, and Teresa had asked me to accompany her, I left the black apparition in the house and went with Teresa.

I accompanied her and then returned, smoking a cigarette.

When I got back, I couldn't find Tatiana at first; the house is a large one after all. I called to her, but she didn't answer. After wandering around the different floors for a while, I eventually found her lying on the bed in the guest room on the third floor. In the dark. For some reason she started telling me the story of her date with Ghupta and how he had fucked her, with all the details. While telling me, she held my hands in the dark and drank some wine, which she knew where to find in the house and had obtained during my absence.

Her hysterical story, told to me first in whispers and then in screams, ultimately came down to the fact that, not having bothered with birth control, this bold but careless Russian woman had of course gotten pregnant from the Burmese.

"Well at least it was nice for you—you enjoyed it, didn't you?" Edward asked.

"I did," she brazenly answered. "He's like an animal and trembled all over while he was fucking me. It was nice. He appreciates women—unlike you, Limonov."

I lay on my back and started laughing. What a bed of roses life is. After Jenny I had scoffingly decided I wasn't going to find happiness in love and stopped looking for it. I had served Jenny down to the last drop, a woman I didn't even love, a woman who in fact was not even to my taste, and who had broken me into little pieces.

I've long lived in the world as if in furnished rooms—I don't arrange it to my liking; I just use whatever happens to be available, women too. I've moved way beyond the passionate and crazy Edichka I was four years ago, whom I left to the world.

Tatiana was surprised to find I wasn't like Edichka at all. She said my book had made her cry, whereas I had, as you see, sold her to Ghupta for a jacket.

227

"You're an evil person, Limonov!" she sadly told me on the phone recently after I lost my temper with her over her paranoid delusions and told her that there wasn't anything between us except fucking and that she was a petite bourgeoise with neither money nor brains. Tatiana doesn't care about me either. She sees a writer in me, an author of books that make her cry. I interest her, but it's the interest of a consumer. She uses me to decorate her life. The same way that spices improve the taste of food, I make her life more interesting, a life that would otherwise be insipid. I, however, see Tatiana because I like fucking her, so that we in fact make very good use of each other, only I don't whine about it; I make jokes and smile and enjoy myself, while she whines and insists that I'm not "like Edichka." I already know I'm not.

I went to pee. I wasn't in the bathroom very long, but when I came out, Tatiana wasn't in the bedroom—one of her little jokes, her style. I called to her, looked for her, walked around the whole house, and then not finding her, I said the hell with it, and went out for a walk. I had almost been in the mood to fuck that unhappy, freshly impregnated woman, pulling up her black dress. She likes to go around in black. It didn't matter, I'd fuck her next time, or I'd fuck somebody else.

I always take the same route on my walks, going west on Fifty-seventh Street to Madison Avenue and then up Madison. I like rich Madison, particularly since you can always find beautiful women there. I walk without hurrying, gazing at the faces of pedestrians and examining the windows of the expensive stores, so familiar now that I've almost memorized them. I look at the faces of the men for the sake of comparison—to see if they're more interesting than mine. You'll say that it's difficult to be objective when comparing anything to yourself, but I try to be—the truth is important to me, and I want to find out if I have many rivals in my struggle. There aren't many. I see men who are much better looking than I am, but they lack that self-assured hardness, that peremptory decisiveness that appeared on my face around the time that I started working as housekeeper in the millionaire's house. It's strange, but the millionaire's house has given me a sense of assurance. Maybe I've been infected by Steven's nervous self-assurance and have acquired his confident habits—Steven who feels at home anywhere. That one time I went to a restaurant with him, I remember how he was the first to sit down, taking a seat in the most comfortable corner, the bastard, and putting his elbows on the table, comfortably and firmly in place and not giving a damn about anybody else. Maybe I did get it from Steven? I think, looking at the reflection of my face in a window. Before I was too embarrassed to stop on the street and look at my own face in the window; I was afraid of what other people might say. But now I don't care what they say, the pitiful failures, the suckers, the whole insecure and timid lot. "Don't trust anybody," I remember Linda saying. Don't worry, Linda, I never will. Why should I?

As you see, the buds of a new man, a new Edward, are urgently forcing their way out of me, pushing aside and supplanting the old one, just as green sprouts force their way into freedom from a potato, consuming it as they grow. Though flesh of my own flesh, a new Edward now walks along Madison Avenue.

The men, my rivals, understand something of this, I'm sure—there's probably a biological language that hasn't been forgotten even though it's been replaced in a way by words and speech. But a language of the body, of the eyes and facial muscles, still exists, doesn't it? In any case, before people used to ask me things on the street. You know, there's a special category of people who always want something from the rest of humanity—a quarter, a dollar, how to get to Lincoln Center, or just somebody to latch on to. But now nobody asks me anything; it's clear to them. My face obviously eloquently expresses everything for me: fuck all of you!

Behind Steven's confident appearance stand his millions. Behind mine is my newly discovered self. I don't need *anybody*; that's what I've discovered—not a mama, not Elena, not Jenny, not anybody. I'm strong enough to live proudly by myself. And there's no bitterness in my solitude, only joy.

I still look for the girl in chinchilla. If I should meet her on Madison, I won't recognize her of course, unless she's dressed the same way, but that doesn't matter. I'm looking for a type— that youthful charm, mystery, and inaccessibility, that alluring mixture of expensive prostitute and young girl, our civilization's highest achievement. When I write "prostitute," it's not at all judgmental; on the contrary. How many speeches have our kitchen mothers in aprons and slippers recited to us all with their hands on their hips, drumming into our heads over and over again the great value of gray, decent, virtuous women like themselves, of the kitchen slave, whom we at a certain time would have to, indeed were obligated to, bring into our lives. But I, thank God, have never believed in virtue and have never understood the value of those gray creatures. I have from child-hood always been fond of holidays and have continually found myself in conflict with humdrum everyday life. As a child I would ask my mother, "Mama, why isn't it Christmas all the time?" So why don't you all go stick it, mama and papa, and neighbors in Kharkov and Moscow, and friends and compan-ions, and residents of New York and London and Paris, and all of you who strain yourselves to the limits of your strength to support that heavy, gray, shapeless moral clod. Fuck all of you! I want to love whatever is beautiful, brilliant, sweet-smelling, and young. I don't want the decent, modest, and noble goose Jenny and those like her; I want the girl in chinchilla!

When I'm in a very bad mood, instead of Madison, I walk along Central Park South, where our city's most expensive hotels are drawn up in a line. In the spring or fall when it's raining, especially when it's raining, the entrances of the expen-sive hotels and restaurants present an unusual spectacle. Huge elegant automobiles drive up one after the other out of the mist, their chauffeurs obsequiously leaping out with big umbrellas, while absent-minded and imposing gentlemen assist their ladies from the dark warmth of the cars and fastidiously open their wallets to give the doormen a tip. Friends meet friends—they all know each other, these wealthy people—and at once kiss the little hands of their ladies there on the street, while a sudden breeze lifts the white scarf of one of the participants in that scene and carries to me, a modest passerby, the smoke of an expensive cigar and with it, the faint fragrance of warm feminine perfume.

I have in the millionaire's house the most expensive cigars and wines, wines that couldn't even be found, perhaps, in the cellars of the restaurants they frequent, and if I wish, I can open a bottle of Château Lafite Rothschild 1964 and drink it. But I'm a servant, and not one of their race. I know that sooner or later they'll accept me under the name of writer—it's inevitable. They won't be able to withstand my strength, and I'll descend on them and fuck their women, and their women will be wild about me and my masculinity and wickedness. That's right, my masculinity, for a wave of masculinity has for the first time in my life emerged on my face with its prominent cheekbones and taken it over. But how to survive the day and its humiliations; that's the hardest thing. I will endure it all, I think stubbornly, while examining the decked-out crowd around the Plaza—no, you won't have that pleasure, I won't go crazy and buy a Beretta from a pimp I know on Times Square, a little black instrument of death just like his, and bump off a congressman out of bitterness and hatred—a disgusting swine-faced congressman for all my sufferings, for all the sufferings of the pitiful failure Edward. No, I won't give you that pleasure. I will survive, survive and endure a great many more rejections from publishers, and many more years of empty evenings like this, and thousands of walks like today's. I will survive them and join you on the pinnacle as the most intelligent and malevolent. And not for your company,

231

which I'm sure will be only a bit more amusing than that of Jenny and her friends, and not even for your women, but for myself. I want to prove to myself that I *can*. The main thing is that I respect myself.

Returning to my refuge in the millionaire's little house, I realize that for many years I've wanted somebody to be waiting for me at my door. And I carefully glance ahead, seeking the doorway of our house in the darkness to see if perhaps somebody might be sitting there and waiting for me. But there's no one there. And that is yet one more small proof of the fact that in this world nobody cares about the servant. But then I don't have to care about them either, the servant thinks.

Tatiana turned up again several days later under the pretext of needing to talk to me. Her usual story. I immediately stuck a large gin and tonic in her hand, since she's much easier to deal with after she's had something to drink.

"You're the one who did this to me, Limonov," Tatiana said. "You did it on purpose so I'd get pregnant."

Such a declaration came as a surprise even from her. "Wait a second, how old are you, girl? You're thirty-one and you've fucked a lot of men, or at least you say you have, and you enjoy it, don't you?" I said. Tatiana was silent. I continued. "How can you screw around without taking birth-control pills or any other precautions, hm? It's dumb. It's idiotic. And doesn't it seem a little abnormal to you to blame me because you're pregnant by another man? Would I blame you if I got some girl pregnant, the village idiot, say?"

Tatiana looked at me with her Spanish eyes and said stubbornly, "It's still your fault. I didn't want to go out with him, so why did you give him the phone?"

"In the first place, you always said you wanted me to introduce you to a rich man. Didn't you? Why did you ask then? And in the second place, if you didn't really want to go out with him, all you had to do was say 'no,'" I said.

"But he was so sneaky about it, the animal," Tatiana continued, sipping her gin and tonic. "I had no idea he would attack me. We came back from a movie and he told me he wanted to take a shower and change and we would go to a restaurant, and then he took advantage of the moment and jumped on me. And he came inside me, the Burmese animal."

Thus did Tatiana lament, and I laughed uncontrollably. In the first place, I wasn't at all convinced she was pregnant. And I was also beginning to realize that getting into scrapes, both big and small, was for Tatiana a way of life.

"Tell me, where does he live?" she started asking me.

"Of course," I said, "I'll tell you right now; come on," and I took her by the hand up to my room on the elevator, and in spite of all her "noes" took her clothes off and started fucking her. At the height of that process, the phone rang, of course. Another time I wouldn't have picked it up for anything, but I was expecting a guest at the house, a Polish artist-friend of the boss's, and it could have been him calling from the airport. It wasn't. It was my boss, Steven, calling from God knows where to ask me to record a film about Vietnam on video tape for an elderly woman neighbor of his in Connecticut whose son had died in Vietnam. "It already started five minutes ago," the boss said in an apologetic tone.

Fuck the mother and her dead son! Why reopen old wounds? I thought, pulling my prick out of the warm Tatiana, putting on my pants and black shirt, and running downstairs to turn on the tape machine. They won't even let you fuck in this house! I inserted a sixty-minute cassette, pressed the record button, rode back upstairs on the elevator to fuck some more, and once again plunged my prick into the only slightly cooled cunt of Tatiana, who was almost in tears and kicking and howling something about the CIA and the KGB.

"And the CIA and KGB are all the same as you; they just sit there, the scum, and won't let me live either!" she screamed, although thanks to the action of my prick she soon quieted

233

down and merely moaned, while I laughed and softly and derisively said to her, "What's that, you pregnant whore, what did you say?"

When Tatiana's fucking she has an enchanting look about her, and her body, though slender, is very soft and what's called well-fucked in Russian. An hour later, after coming on her eyes and forehead, and in her mouth, I ran downstairs again to change the cassette. I got there just in time—it was down to the last few feet. I put on a new one, pressed the record button again, and then went down to the kitchen for a drink. Sitting in the kitchen was Gatsby's step-brother Mr. Richardson with a couple of guests, I don't remember who. I drank a glass of vodka, and after asking Mr. Richardson to turn the television off in an hour—the film about Vietnam was exactly two hours long, and I could hear explosions and machinegun fire coming from it—I took the elevator back upstairs and grabbed Tatiana again. The pregnant whore lazily told me that she had just that minute come again after masturbating while I was downstairs. "You didn't think I was going to wait for you, did you?" she asked insolently.

"All right," I said, "that means you're still hot," and pulling her bottom to me—she was lying on her side—I stuck my prick into her crack, which was already beginning to dry. When after a little while we were both starting to enjoy it again, the abominable intercom buzzer sounded, the same one that Efimenkov had used to wake me up in the middle of the night. What the fuck is it now? I thought without climbing off of Tatiana. The buzzer didn't go off again, but there was soon a knock at the door.

"Edward, somebody's ringing the front doorbell," Richardson's voice said.

"Well, could you see who it is?" I yelled angrily.

So they wouldn't even let me fuck. I went downstairs a few minutes later—they'd upset my rhythm anyway and dragged me away from the excellent fountain inside that crazy woman—I went downstairs and met the new guest, Steven's artist-friend Stanislaw, gave him an extra key to the millionaire's house, and told him he would be staying in one of the children's rooms, the other rooms already being occupied. I even had some vodka with him, and then went back to my room, where I rolled and lit myself a joint—the crazy Tatiana didn't smoke—and then grabbed her again in earnest. I remember almost crushing her large soft breasts, which she was usually ashamed of, and angrily thrusting my prick into her. We didn't stop till five o'clock the next morning. And she didn't say anything more about being pregnant or about Ghupta and the CIA.

The first time I heard about Stanislaw was from Gatsby, and I remembered that unusual evening very well. Gatsby was sick and had decided to stay home—probably the only time in his whole life that the stubborn Gatsby actually gave in and stayed home. He'd been sick for a long time before that, three weeks maybe, and was coughing so badly that I had no doubt that he was in the final stages of tuberculosis and that very soon I'd be without an employer. He was dying but stubbornly holding on to his insane mode of life—drinking Scotch with five ice cubes, running outside without a coat on even though it was winter, and so forth. By that evening he was at the end of his rope. The antibiotics he'd been taking weren't doing any good, and he had stayed home and was sitting red-nosed and miserable in the kitchen clad in his warmest robe and in warm pajamas under the robe and eating some of my chicken soup—Nancy had called from Connecticut with the special request to eat soup without fail—and panting for breath he told me one thing and another. I was sitting across from him; for the first time he hadn't sent for anybody, since he was obviously embarrassed about his illness, but he still needed somebody to talk to. A peaceful kitchen scene.

Why did we start talking about Stanislaw? I had asked the boss what I should do with the picture that had been standing in the TV room since Jenny's time. Should I hang it there in the kitchen? Gatsby objected to that, to hanging the picture in the kitchen, since Stanislaw, the author of that, in my opinion, ugly work, or at least one that overwhelmed me with boredom whenever I looked at it (a moon over mountains—abstract, a mere howl), might suddenly turn up, and it would be awkward for him, for Steven, that is, if the author found his gift hanging in the kitchen. Okay. I didn't say any more about moving the picture, but Mr. Grey didn't want to drop the subject, and he told me about Stanislaw. Mr. Grey was amazed by him.

"He's such an old goat, it's unbelievable!" said Gatsby. "He even tried to grab Nancy once, Edward, if you can believe that! What an old goat!"

I could believe it. Gatsby hadn't said what, what part of Nancy's body, Stanislaw had tried to grab—maybe it was awkward for him to tell his butler that Stanislaw had tried to grab his wife's ass? Or had in fact grabbed it, for what else could "tried to grab" mean? That he was merely thinking about it? How could Gatsby know what Stanislaw was thinking?

"He was visiting me in Connecticut, and he tried to grab Nancy," Gatsby continued delightedly. It was obvious that even if he didn't like what had happened, Stanislaw's audacity was very much to his taste. I didn't ask Gatsby how he reacted—did he pretend he hadn't noticed the satyr? I don't think he would have been reluctant to punch Stanislaw in the jaw, but he did have a certain respect for audacity in other people.

"He even went after Jenny," Gatsby continued, "and she complained to me about it. I said to him, 'Stanislaw, please, don't terrorize my employees.'"

Steven obviously used the word "employees" for my benefit. Telling the story to someone else he would probably have said "my servants."

"He's one of the Polish mafia," the boss continued. "You know, all those Polanskis and Kozinskis. . . ."

"And Brzezinskis," I added, and Gatsby laughed.

"An unbelievable old goat!" Gatsby summed up.

After such a testimonial, I was eager to make Stanislaw's acquaintance and observe him in action whenever he came to our house.

He looked pretty good for his age—slim, although his face was a little worn, it's true, but you wouldn't have said he was fifty—forty at the most. The only thing not quite right about him was that his clothing was out of date. He was dressed the way they dressed at the end of the sixties—in flared pants that fit tight across his ass, a close-fitting short jacket, and long hair.

I haven't dressed that way in a long time. I wear pants that are narrow at the bottom and wide in the seat, and my jackets are a good size with big shoulders, as if one or two sizes too large. My hair is cut now like James Dean's—you know, the famous actor of the fifties. The fifties are very "in" right now, as I'm well aware, and why shouldn't I be; after all, I'm a contemporary servant of the world bourgeoisie.

But let's leave me and return to Stanislaw. The Pole and the Russian got along well from their very first meeting, although I was busy with Tatiana and couldn't give him very much time, except for the glass of vodka we each had in the kitchen before I went back upstairs to fuck her, making my apologies to him and brazenly telling him I had a warm body in my bed. You know how we are, I thought complacently to myself; we fuck too and know how to.

The whole time Stanislaw resided in our heaven—he told Gatsby that he had come for just a few days, but thanks to my personal generosity and the fact that Gatsby was in Europe, he stayed more than two weeks—I had a body in my bed. And I gave him a terrible complex, an awful complex! I wasn't doing it just for his sake; it merely worked out that way. And here too the Poles lost, gentlemen, just as in the historical rivalry between Poland and Russia. During those two weeks he fucked only Marisza, the daughter of one of their Polish writers. Whereas I had, during the same period, at least six women, including the above-mentioned Tatiana, Teresa, the musician Natasha, and the Dutch girl Maria, and one evening Sarah dropped by, and in addition a married woman came specially from the state of Israel to fuck me—she'd read my book.

From time to time I made my appearance in the kitchen, in our club so to speak, where Stanislaw would invariably be calling all over New York, trying to get his old connections going again. He had come to New York from his home in Texas with a pile of pictures he was trying to peddle on his own—without gallery representation. I no longer respected people who didn't have a gallery; even I, a servant, had my own literary agent. You've got to be professional, Stanislaw, I thought, and it doesn't matter if you're a professional artist or a professional hit man. Thank you, Great United States; you have at least taught me something. And although Stanislaw maintained that he had no need of a gallery and showed me his portfolio with photographs of himself—Stanislaw with Roman Polanski, Stanislaw with Henry Miller, Stanislaw with Mary Hemingway—I began to discern in this cheerful Polish lecher and buffoon the all-too-familiar features of a failure worried that he was fifty and getting old.

I would creep down to the kitchen yawning and stretching—I was never fully rested, as is understandable—and Stanislaw would already be sitting by the phone and making calls. Not that he was hard pressed—not at all. In Texas they had built sculptures based on his designs. In a steel slab of extraordinary thickness young scholars enthusiastic about the project had made a hole using something like an atomic cannon. A hole ripped out just the way he wanted it. He was depicting holes. We live in a magnificent time, gentlemen, a time when everything is beyond our reach and nothing is forbidden—a time in fact for making holes. The *hole* may even be the symbol of our time—a torn and gaping hole leading nowhere.

Stanislaw had enough for meat and butter, but with artists, as with writers, if you're not among the first, you consider yourself a failure. The headlines in newspapers, the photographs, and the monographs are enjoyed by the few at the top. All that remained for Stanislaw was Marisza.

He would look and look at girls I would show him, and how could I not, since from time to time we would all sit in the kitchen, and his young friend Krysztof, a large, easygoing retired athlete, would come over too, and we would drink and smoke grass. Once Stanislaw couldn't restrain himself and started stroking Natasha's hair; she looks about twelve, gentlemen—you know, a small, blonde, rosy-cheeked creature with a white ass.

"Give her to me, Edward," Stanislaw said, as if joking.

I knew he wasn't really—I'd seen how hard he struggled to get back his lost connections again. But as the cunning and wise Oriental Ghupta had said, "If you're gone from New York for a month, all the girls are gone and have made other arrangements for themselves." It will be the same after our deaths, brothers, I wanted to say cheerfully to both Ghupta and Stanislaw—a few days after our deaths all our girls will have found new dicks for themselves, and the livelier ones will have made other arrangements the very same day. Nature leaves nothing of our sentiments behind, and all is reduced to dust and ashes, regardless of what you hold on to or use as your foundation.

"Take her," I said to Stanislaw. And I asked Natashka, "Would you like to go to bed with Uncle Stanislaw?" My girls are all very well trained now, and Natashka looked inquiringly at me.

She didn't need Stanislaw; she needed me, who could calmly send her off to the Pole's bed or anyone else's. He wasn't a bad sort, the Pole, and probably was a good lover, but she was mine. I didn't want her to go to bed with the Pole, and she said, "No, I don't want to."

As soon as I stopped paying attention to them, to my girls, they completely changed the way they behaved with me, and inflicted scenes of jealousy and outraged love on me, although without any response on my part. They love me and reproach me now, and are afraid of losing me. Whereas before it irritated them when I asked them where they went without me and whom they were seeing, now they get angry that I don't care at all what they do outside the confines of the millionaire's house—whether they're fucking somebody else or not. When they start telling me what they've been doing, my face clearly shows my boredom, as a result of which as a rule they suddenly stop in dismay and ask me, "Don't you care, Edward?"

"No. Why do you say that?" I ask. "Go on with what you were saying."

It's clear I'm not interested. It's always the same story, and how many have I heard in my dismal bedroom by the glow of cigarettes and to the background music of wine gurgling down my throat? Their stories are all alike, and even if I wanted to sympathize with what they're saying, I still wouldn't be able to, since it's all so trivial. Almost every one of them carries the burden of an unhappy love affair and some kind of grudge against the world. A grudge against her parents or, more often, against her husband or her lover. "He" is either mean-spirited or callous, and as a rule doesn't understand anything about "her" life.

They've devised the same kind of unhappy lives for themselves that I devised for myself with Jenny—we're all the same, only besides my prick I have will and talent, while they have their cunts and sometimes talent, but no will. Their lives are probably more tranquil in reality than they seem from my bed.

I don't treat them badly; oh no, I share everything I have with them—the house, wine, marijuana, money. I take them all to P. J. Clark's on Third Avenue, a former Irish bar turned restaurant.

There's nothing particularly special there, but the checkered table cloths, the old gravures, and the jerk-off waiters all create a sense of human comfort. Besides, they have very good steak tartare—not the slush they serve you at other New York restaurants.

I sit in P. J. Clark's with my girls and drink Beaujolais Villages.

We look at each other with friendly grins and touch each other's hands from time to time. Having just emerged from bed, we feel for each other the tenderness of animals who have been fucking each other, the affection of little dogs who have just fucked each other well. I always share with my girls my misfortunes, my ideas, and my little stories. I don't pretend my life is cloudless. "My agent called yesterday," I complain, "and told me another publisher has rejected my novel, a very progressive publisher that's published some good books in the past, but now that they've made some money, they've gotten lazy and are very careless about reading manuscripts. Liza doesn't want to drop me, she wants to continue working on it, but she admitted to me, 'To be honest, Edward, I don't know where to send the book anymore. Maybe you have some ideas?'"

Together my girls are like a wife to me—one woman with many faces and bodies. I can share with them my anger about my most recent setbacks, and I don't get depressed anymore. I can tell them about my feverish plans for the future, and they understand; they aren't all that normal themselves. For some reason they come to me almost immediately after their attempts to kill themselves, or from deep depressions, or even from psychiatric clinics. It's obvious I don't attract healthy girls, or maybe healthy ones don't interest me, or maybe, gentlemen, there just aren't any healthy girls in the world?

Love? I love them in my own way, only I allocate my love among them. Would it really be fair for only one to have it? I feel the same tenderness for them that I felt for Jenny when I looked at her for the first time in our garden—a tenderness for those creatures who are alive at the same time I am, the tenderness of a male dog for his bitches. I service them and protect them from enemies. I would live with them all in one house, but they rebel, almost every one of them wanting all of me and not

241

satisfied with merely a part. Then it's necessary to get rid of the rebels, to replace them with fresh young girls.

They often get drunk, my girls, because it's hard for them to have a normal relationship with me; they get drunk and take drugs for courage, and that's when they decide to rebel.

Even the little pianist Natasha rebelled against me in a way. I was sitting with her in a dark barn-like bar on the Lower East Side and drinking J & B, of course (their company should send me a case of whiskey once a month for the publicity I give them: "Edward Limonov drinks only J & B"). Natasha, as I've already mentioned, looks about twelve, an exaggeration of course, although she's almost young enough to be my daughter, and that isn't an exaggeration.

We were on a spree, although where we drank before that I don't remember. My girl, drunkenly puckering her little face, berated me for my indifference to life, for my lack of curiosity. The accusation of a lack of curiosity was unjust, but I didn't say anything: She wanted to fight. The fact is that all her grievances came in the end to something like, "You're special, you're unique, you can be, so why aren't you what I need?" Translating it all into normal language meant, "Why don't you love me?"

The bar was huge and cold and dated back to hippie days, and a gigantic bartender of about forty with hair as long now as it had been back then served punk boys and girls in leather jackets and multicolored tufts of hair. There were a few older types in the bar too, unshaven and with dark circles under their eyes. I said nothing, smoking one cigarette after another and drinking my J & B. As I get older I feel less and less the need to explain myself, especially since I know from long experience that you can't explain; everybody understands the words differently, and it's useless.

Natasha covered her face with her hands and then uncovered it and said I was empty and cynical and would never write anything interesting and would only repeat myself. She was angry and wanted to hurt me. I wasn't fucking her as much and was getting tired of her. I didn't object: probably I was empty and bad, and maybe I didn't have any future, either literary or human.

I went to the toilet. Its door was crudely fashioned from boards. Over the urinal somebody had written the words "Fuck you!" in bold letters. But a little below them somebody else's kind hand had written, "That's not nice." Exactly, it wasn't nice to write "Fuck you." When I came out, an affectionate ginger-haired dog was running around the bar.

My companion was already behaving a little better and started telling me very insistently that I should get myself roller skates and/or a car. There wasn't, she thought, enough speed in my life. While listening to her I drank another J & B, but I didn't get any drunker. But at least sitting with Natasha was better than drinking alone. After that we left, I first with my hands in my pockets, and she a little behind with her purse. For some reason I'd gotten interested in the purse phenomenon, and I thought to myself, a woman without a purse is always defenseless. That's why they all carry them. They have everything they need in them to make themselves up in the morning. Girls in jeans, however, have only their keys and a couple of dollars but no purse. As soon as they become women, the purse appears. Natasha has become a woman, since she's carrying a purse now.

She had become one, and with a vengeance. We went back to my place. Stanislaw was still there, I think, but I didn't want to see him, and so we went quietly up to my room and added to what we'd already had—we smoked a joint and had some more to drink. Then I think we fucked, although I don't remember. The next morning Natasha wasn't in bed with me. Well if she wasn't there, then she wasn't—she'd obviously left while I was still asleep. I shrugged and went into the bathroom to wash under the skylight. I opened the door, and . . .

The whole bathroom was spattered with blood. Lying on the floor were my knife and two pairs of manicure scissors covered with blood, and there was blood on some pieces of a razor blade that had come from who knows where. There was also blood on the floor and on the fluffy yellow rug and the tiled walls. My sandy-haired little girl, my little pianist, had obviously tried to kill herself or, more likely, had wanted to show me how serious our relationship was.

I sat down on the bathtub and thought. The little fool, I thought, why get mixed up with me, an angry thirty-six-year-old cynic? I certainly never had any desire to hurt her, but I live my life according to my own separate rules and, I think, separate from other people. I had told her at the start, "Watch out, Natasha, don't fall in love with me!"

"No, I'm the same way you are, Limonov; I've had a lot of men, as many as you like!" she had answered.

I called her at home and then at the school where she taught music. She was at school. I didn't get angry but only said, "Well, are you still alive?"

"Still alive," Natashka said self-consciously. "Forgive me, Limonov. I got so drunk last night and I shouldn't drink at all. I left a letter for you on the desk, but please don't read it, all right?"

Of course I read the letter; I am a writer. It was a long one; I think she spent the whole night writing it while I slept, bastard that I am.

Limonov [the letter began], since you usually don't pay any attention to what I say and don't let me speak and make bored expressions, here's a letter for you.

The fact that I made a pest of myself recently after drinking, saying you're not such and such and you don't do such and such, etc., whereas I'm "good," doesn't mean I'm in love or that I love you. No, it was because I was deeply offended by the way you treat me. And it isn't that I need you to love me or sleep with me. You don't really suit me as a lover at all—you're monotonous, unattentive, brutal, and ungrateful. . . . I'd very much enjoy coming over to talk with you and then sleep in one of the children's rooms, which is where my place is with you! But no, one has to pay for your attention by making a certain part of one's body available. Even though your attention is in fact directed at yourself, and I'm a spectator, a silent participant, which is very valuable to me, especially now, when I happen to be surrounded by so many worthless men and women.

I admire you, Limonov, but no more than that—I'm not a girl who's in love with you. I believe and feel myself to be someone who has excellent talents, and I like very much what you write, and I know why. Despite my age, I understand a lot more in general and have more taste and sensitivity than most of the people around you. For me you're not just a talented writer—otherwise there wouldn't have been anything to attract me to your person; I could have read your books at home—but I repeat, you're an exceptionally talented person, infectious, lively, and stand out to advantage from the feeble, silly, dreary people your own age.

The time I've spent with you has always given me the maximum pleasure, unless you start sulking and get depressed. What I'm trying to say is that I love you, or not even that I love you, but that I'm terribly curious about you, although you're not a man to me, Limonov, oh no! My attitude toward you is enthusiastically rational, I would say, and the pleasure I've gotten from you is of a purely intellectual quality. And I don't consider myself undeserving of your attention. I deserve it a lot more than those idiots around you who don't even have the sense to understand or appreciate you. It's incomprehensible to me the way they permit themselves to carry on around Limonov. You think the fact that they're older requires them to understand, although my age says just the opposite, but there are exceptions to every rule.

I'm a big fan of yours, Limonov, and of your books, both present and future, and I'd be happy to be of use to you, only not in bed; I'm not up to it anymore, unfortunately. I don't even want to get into bed with you anymore. You are really insulting in bed—unsatisfied and with absolutely no reason to be. If you don't want a woman, then don't fuck. Who do you think you're doing a favor? I get the feeling in bed that you're using one woman to revenge yourself on the whole female race. What I'd really like is for your Elena to finally come back to you so you could "live happily ever after and die the same day," and then Limonov would stop taking revenge on women as a group, and wouldn't be in such a hurry to take personal revenge on as many as he could, and would be kinder and more attentive and would write different kinds of books.

Excuse me for my hysterics, they're just temporary, and don't think they're because of you, Limonov! It's just that I shouldn't drink at all, and it's happened to me before that after I've got drunk I have for no reason started cutting my legs and arms, not to commit suicide but to hurt myself.

You're far from being the main thing in my life, in fact. I have my own life as a musician. You say I'm not a woman; I'm glad to hear it, since that would only interfere with my creative life. Because the music I play and care about doesn't include the lower part of the body, the sexual equipment, but the head and some organ of feeling in the chest. And it's a great thing if you can keep your sexual characteristics from interfering with your music. That's the reason you don't like classical music, in fact—there isn't any place in it for your prick—and why you like rock 'n' roll, where there isn't room for anything but your prick. It would be good for you, in fact, not to fuck for about two years; then you'd learn to like music and something else useful. Wouldn't that be nice!

I like to fuck, I like it a lot, but it's not all the same to me who I do it with, Limonov. And in bed it's not enough for me to have "cruel," dry orgasms. I also need lots of things I don't get from you, tenderness, for example, and I also need to have a desire for a particular man, and I don't feel that kind of attraction for you—I don't desire you and I never have.

I feel insulted by you. You've never even once asked me about anything and you don't know anything about me. You haven't even once looked in my direction with interest. But you're so sure that at twenty-one I don't understand anything, don't know anything, and am just a weak little infatuated idiot. My answer is that you're a conceited fool. It's just a lot more pleasant for you to have a girl like that around so you can surround your self with a picture of complete incomprehension and women who aren't worthy of you. I know I'm an independent and strong person. I have enough problems of my own. I'm alone, and I don't ask anybody for help, and I make all my own decisions by myself and suffer all my misfortunes by myself, and so I make some mistakes and have my disappointments, but I can say that I do understand something about life. I am, you could say, a kind of hero for my age and sex. It doesn't bother me that you don't have time for that—I'm interested in you and I don't care whether you're interested in me. It's just that it's unpleasant for me to have to listen to such baseless garbage about myself. You've found a little idiot who's also young.

I'm a musician, Limonov, a mature, thinking musician, and it isn't my profession to be a woman. My life is not for men, and I don't exist for them. And you've never been just a man with sexual equipment for me either. This is all true, which I think would have been apparent to you if you had paid a little more attention to me instead of just classifying me as a "twenty-one-year-old girl with a big ass."

Natasha

Natasha was wrong to say I never paid any attention to her. I did and was even very proud of her virtuosity on the piano, and often asked her to play for my guests, if any were at the house.

She was, moreover, a Russian girl, and I felt a sort of responsibility for her—I don't know before whom; all right, before God, although I don't believe in Him—a responsibility for my little sister Natasha, a girl from my own tribe. I tried not to hurt her. Sometimes she would spend several days at the house with me, and besides not having to fuck me, she played the piano for hours, and walked in the garden, and rocked in the rocking chair, and read if she wanted to, or listened to recordings of her beloved classical music, and in general had a good time.

Although many of the things Natasha accused me of were ridiculous and clumsy, I still gave her letter a lot of thought. The Limonov in her letter was after all very like his employer, Gatsby. That fact both pleased and troubled me, for I wanted to be both like Gatsby and not like him.

Chapter Nine

HENRY always stands off to the side in family photographs. He has a separate, naïve, but also slightly sardonic expression on his face. The other members of the family, and the younger children too, are much less refined than he is. He's as tall as his father, Steven, but extraordinarily thin, even for his seventeen years, so that it seems he is about to break in two at the waist. He has short blond hair like his mother, Nancy, and on his nose he wears the delicate glasses of a Parisian student. He hardly looks like a typical American boy.

Henry and I are friends. Not great friends; he doesn't live at the millionaire's house after all but goes to school, but in the ten or more times we have met, we've become fairly close. We even share certain enthusiasms—James Bond films, for instance.

At the end of April Henry came down from Connecticut accompanied by a dozen other boys and girls, his mother, Nancy, having called beforehand to warn me of their arrival and ask the butler Edward to look after the young people. As it turned out, there was going to be a children's costume party at our house to celebrate the end of the school year. Henry planned to shoot at the party, the final scene of a movie he was producing and in which he had one of the main roles. As you see, Henry was playing at being his father: Papa had been a producer once, and Henry had turned to the art of film too.

The children arrived as if on elephants in several large cars daubed with paint, and cheerfully started dragging their stuff into the house: costumes, a movie camera, bags, candles, blue lights, colored paper. . . . Along with all the other stuff there was even a large lemon tree in a tub. Henry ceremoniously introduced me to the other children—he was a polite boy. Their girls, the housekeeper remarked to himself, might easily have been mine. Some of them were even very pretty, and inasmuch as they all went to an exceptionally privileged and expensive private high school, they were all obviously from very good families; their faces were cultivated. Their school had been founded by the famous arms manufacturer Mr. X in order to atone to humanity for his sins. It would be interesting to count the number of people who perished from his primitive but reliable death machines before he was suddenly overcome with remorse and the desire to make amends. I've always been touched by innocent monsters like Mr. X, whose number includes the inventor of dynamite, Mr. Nobel, and the great altruist Mr. Sakharov, one of the fathers of the Soviet hydrogen bomb.

Apologizing with elegant good manners, the well-bred Henry told me his mama had said he could invite ten people or so to the party, "but we started counting, Edward, and there will be about fifteen or maybe even more, since if you don't invite somebody they'll be offended for the rest of their lives. I realize that means extra responsibility and work for you, Edward, but we'll be very quiet and afterward we'll pick up the whole house. Only please don't tell Mother, all right?"

Well, whatever I am, I'm not an informer. Seeing their rather meager supplies of alcohol, I even gave them a box of Corvo ripped off from Steven, and a couple of bottles each of whiskey, gin, and vodka, for which they were extremely grateful. I had the key to the wine cellar, and although the cellar is never locked, this time I locked it—the kids might get drunk and break all the expensive bottles.

To be honest, I looked forward to their party with great impatience. The fact is, I'd taken into my head the usual servant's desire—to fuck one of their girls. A little high-school girl, a blonde. To smoke some grass and then fuck her. A desire that was, if you think about it, more social than sexual. Taking one of their girls was the same as taking something from the world of my employer, as stealing something that didn't belong to me, a servant—as revenging myself, so to speak. Sex, as you've probably already guessed, gentlemen, was the only means of revenge available to me. I thought that in the confusion of the party, where, at a minimum, there would be twenty or more girls, I'd be able to get myself one of them. I was a man who knew what he wanted after all, whereas the most that boys of sixteen or seventeen would dare would be to grab a girl's ass, and so the evening would pass. Even boys of their generation—they weren't from the South Bronx or even Brooklyn, but the children of wealthy parents—were undoubtedly more "spoiled" in words than in action. So that while helping them set the table and make sangria and screw in their blue light bulbs (they didn't ask for my help; I offered it in order to ingratiate myself with them), I was beginning to get excited and looked forward to the evening with impatience.

Henry diplomatically asked me if I planned to go out that evening. "No," I said, "I prefer to stay at home. If somebody calls the police, Henry—not that they will—there will at least be one adult here with you." Henry said in a sincere tone that he would be glad to have me to join them, and maybe he was sincere.

And then the children-guests began to arrive. And what sort of guests didn't Henry have: sullen beanpoles twice my size in leather jackets with safety pins stuck in their ears and the faces of murderers, and polished boys with depraved faces and painted lips who were dressed in frock coats, bow ties, and top hats and carrying walking sticks—several such boys arrived together— and ironical young intellectuals in sweaters and glasses. One very beautiful boy came dressed in a wig, a black dress, and black stockings. And there were very solid and hefty round-headed lads in sturdy shoes and ties, in whom I saw large but unimaginative businessmen twenty years later—the owners, say, of supermarkets, or at least something connected with food. There was also a rosy-cheeked, red-haired fop in black patent leather shoes, striped trousers, and a broad white tie under an exceptionally lively and comic face, on whose arm affectedly reclined a slender, dark-haired little beauty wearing what were obviously her mother's furs.

To my dismay almost all the children arrived at the beginning in couples, boy and girl, but a half hour later what were simply noisy groups began to show up, and among them I was pleased to see several girls who apparently didn't belong to anybody. I had a strange feeling in that crowd, which seemed to grow and grow, so that even though there were already a lot more than fifteen people there, the flow of guests still didn't end. I felt that they weren't adolescents or children at all. I certainly didn't feel that they deserved to have any kind of allowance made for them—this was the normal world, and they were normal people. And just as in our adult world, they had their own hierarchy which duplicated our adult one precisely.

The guests were met outside the door by two guards, two large, powerful guys. Henry had dressed them in gold embroidered Persian vests which they wore directly over their naked torsos. Henry had found the vests in the basement, where we have dressers taking up an entire wall for storing old things. The muscular fellows were Henry's bodyguards, so to speak, and he ordered them around in every possible way and called them "my slaves," which they permitted without batting an eye. As you will see later on, "my slaves" were part of the setting of the movie they were making and connected with Henry's role in it—he was playing a certain Mostello, a modern Mephistopheles from the state of Connecticut. But apart from the film, those two guys with their simple faces really were his slaves and bodyguards and at his beck and call. I don't know whether they were from poorer families, or whether Henry simply lorded it over them thanks to his intellect and refinement, but I was present for one very unattractive little scene, gentlemen. Before the party actually started, it became clear they didn't have enough sugar for the sangria, mine already having been used up, since they were making an immense vat of it. Henry was paying for everything of course. Taking some money out of his wallet, he dropped a twenty-dollar bill on the floor, on purpose as it seemed to me. Instead of bending over to pick it up himself, he carelessly said to the older of his two bodyguards, "Pick it up!" and the latter obediently picked up the money and ran out to get the sugar dressed in nothing but his pants and Persian vest, from which his powerful shoulders bulged like stones.

Henry-Mephistopheles was playing his papa. He of course didn't have Papa's brutality—Papa humiliated people right and left. He used his wife's lover, the meek opportunist Carl, virtually as a chauffeur, and once in the kitchen in Linda's and my presence had irritably refused to drop Carl, who was sick with a cold, off at his house, although it was on his way. Carl, even though he didn't feel well, had just raced over with a car at Gatsby's request—had driven over one hundred miles with a temperature in order to bring an automobile to his employer and benefactor. The twenty-dollar bill dropped on the floor by Henry completely corresponded in the children's world to the adult situation that had also taken place in the kitchen.

The children gradually spilled into all the crevices and rooms in the house. On the door of my room the farsighted Henry had hung a sign with the words, "Edward's room! Do not Enter!" I circulated among the youths dressed in white sailor's jeans, a black shirt, and boots, and anxiously looked around. I wanted to pick out a girl ahead of time, or even better, several objectives, however tentative, so that after having had something to drink and smoke (in the living room several enthusiasts were delightedly adjusting the hookah which hangs on the wall there), I would then know which target, or targets if there were several, to aim for. I finished my preliminary survey in half an hour, visiting all the rooms and standing for a while among various groups of our merry and lively American youth, but with depressing results, I'm sorry to say.

No, I can't take that one, I thought to myself while looking over a rather pretty girl dressed as a nineteenth-century American lady and even carrying a lace parasol in her hands. A towhaired guy in a musketeer's outfit kept putting his arm around her waist possessively. . . . And not that one either, I thought, transferring my gaze to another objective, a ridiculously skinny girl-cameraman, who looked like Jenny's sister Debby and had come with the boy who was to be their director. They had slept together the night before, I think, and came into the kitchen in the morning in their pajamas, blushing and ridiculous—sixteen-year-old lovers. That one? A perfect woman of the highest class, well-bred, mysterious, with her dark hair piled up above a beautiful clear face whose features resembled those of the young Ingrid Bergman, was looking directly into my eyes with a brazen and provocative gaze. How did this miracle turn up at an adolescent ball? I thought. Is she really only fifteen to seventeen like all the others? That *can't* be. She not only looks more grown up; she is—a young woman and not a stump, not a pimply American female teenager swollen on doughnuts and sweet rolls or a big-chested, big-assed, and leggy cheerleader, the class beauty, but a young woman in fact, the kind they show in films about the English aristocracy. The stubborn, mad, and willful youngest daughter of the family, the one who reads philosophy books and wildly races around in fast cars. You see, reader, what vulgar stereotypes I think in, what banal myths nourish my servant's imagination.

I was intimidated by the stranger. Cold sweat even broke out on my servant's brow—she seemed so terribly unattainable to me—and the most frightening thing was that I realized she belonged to the same breed as the girl in chinchilla! Around the stranger, who had only just arrived, swarmed all the best of their boys. Even Henry himself came downstairs in a tuxedo and bow tie, and opening his arms wide like his daddy, greeted her and enclosed her in an embrace—behavior and gestures copied to the last detail from Gatsby the elder. I'd like to be in Henry's place and cover her in embraces myself, I thought enviously. Henry greeted her in French, if you can believe it, and the stranger answered him in French too in a voice that was strangely deep for someone so young. Fucking aristocrats.

My spirits sank. Just as they had when I was the same age they were now—a loss of strength and resolve in the face of beauty. Most often those attacks of uncertainty and stupefaction had happened at school dances. I always wanted the very best girl at the dance, naturally, and of course I always stood in the darkest corner of the hall, leaning against the wall and tormenting myself over my cowardice. No, I knew my value, I knew I was "good looking"—the girls had told me. But beauty plunged me into a condition of stupor and numbness. When I finally overcame it, it was already too late—some insolent clod with a budding moustache had already taken my girl by the hand and was telling her inspired lies. Neither then nor now did I doubt for a moment that I was far more interesting and alive than the young or adult clods who make up at least ninety-five percent of the masculine society of any dance, but what difference did that make? It's true that now, aware of the shameful sin of cowardice in myself, I have devised certain measures to overcome it. Thus, I'm fully aware that beautiful women plunge not only me into terror and stupor, but many others, and that they fall to only the boldest, usually the first of the boldest, and I therefore try to be the first. I usually cross the hall or living room with my eyes closed and in a state of utter terror, the main thing being to approach, to overcome the distance between you, and then as soon as I open my mouth, everything falls into place. It doesn't make any difference what you talk about in such a situation— the main thing is simply to emit friendly noises, since in essence we're just highly organized animals. Dogs sniff each other in situations like that or wag their tails.

The swine Henry didn't even introduce me. He had introduced me to a mass of completely useless girl-goblins, but he led that treasure upstairs to the living room without even a glance in my direction to get her some sangria. Walking past, the stranger continued looking at me in the same brazen way—no, no, it didn't just seem to me that she was looking at me; she actually was, which isn't surprising really, I being an adult man and she, despite her age, an adult woman, and the two of us face to face in that crowd of children. As she climbed the stairs, her young ass flexed under her black dress like the prancing rear of a fine young horse—forgive me for this cavalryman's comparison, gentlemen, but that's the way it really was.

After hanging around on the first floor a while for decency's sake, I made my way upstairs after Henry and the stranger. I was sure nobody was watching my behavior, so why the silliness? It was my natural cowardice before beauty that made me linger; when I'm afraid, you see, I immediately remember the proprieties. God knows what was going on upstairs. The children were sitting on the floor around the hookah and on the couches in a Frankensteinian blue and green light cast by the blue and green light bulbs they had screwed into Papa Gatsby's numerous lamps. Despite the fact that the living room in Gatsby's house is exceptionally large, it was covered end to end with a layer of adolescent flesh. They looked very happy, with contented faces all around, and why not—there weren't any adults at the party.

"Edward! Edward! Come on over here!" the children sitting around the hookah called out to me. Among them were several youths who had come down by car with Henry from Connecticut, and they already knew me, especially the boy-director and his ridiculous girlfriend. The general attention of the group fell on me for a moment when they called out. Stepping over torsos and bodies and across the legs and arms of the youths, the housekeeper made his way to the hookah where the children moved closer together to make a place for him on the floor. Someone stuck the flexible tube with a pipe stem at its tip into my hand. The smoking master was the same boy in the wig and dress and black stockings.

I inhaled with pleasure. Their hashish wasn't bad, not bad at all, and after taking his drag, the housekeeper grasped the pipe stem in his hand and passed it on to the person sitting next to him in the circle. Nearby the same mocking eyes were gazing at me. She was sitting on one of our rocking chairs, and ensconced at her feet was a handsome red-haired lad, the boy-actor who had the lead role in their film, the schoolboy Faust who is tempted by Mephistopheles-Henry. The kid was the very image of sleepy insolence and was hugging one of the young legs of my stranger and stroking it. A "youthful libertine," I thought with hatred, and passing her the stem and its hose, I smiled slightly at her from down on the floor. She smiled back—not too energetically, but mysteriously from a distance, a fleeting smile. . . .

Events hurtled on at a catastrophic pace after that, or, to continue the equine comparisons, like lathered steeds. Actually, there weren't any particular events to speak of. The housekeeper smoked the gratis hashish to the point where he lost all sense of reality, but they were all stoned without a doubt. These were wealthy children, gentlemen, and they didn't run out of hashish that night. The boy in black stockings tirelessly took out one piece after another from a little metal box. He was already chronically stoned and in a good state, sitting with his dress pushed up nearly to his armpits and his legs spread wide the same way that Jenny used to spread them while sitting, and you could easily see his quite impressive organ. He was a large boy, and from time to time I looked at his organ with dull interest. The stranger and I—I didn't know her name since no one had introduced me to her—passed little smiles back and forth, though somebody later squeezed in between us, and then somebody else's shoulder in a green tunic got in the way—it was a costume ball, remember—and I saw her, or more accurately I saw part of her dress, only through the spaces between other people's torsos and heads. Three boys were sitting at her feet now like pages at the feet of a Beautiful Lady, to which devotion she was in fact entitled.

"Our hookah crowd," as I came to think of it, continually changed form, with new faces turning up and leaving and then returning again, but its nucleus remained stable: the boy in the wig and black stockings, the boy director, the smaller of the two slaves, and me. We were only a small part of the noisy and excited sea of children-youths. Near the gigantic punch bowl of sangria (if only Jenny could have seen what a vessel of sin we made of the proper, domestic ceramic bowl she usually mixed her bread dough in) was its own group, a very active one— much more active than ours. They had, I believe, ultimately poured into their sangria all the whiskey and vodka I'd given them and added even more sugar—children, like the elderly, are fond of sugar. Later, after the party was over, Olga tried but was unable to restore that part of the floor; the sugary spots on it had apparently eaten through the parquet.

It was impossible to make out anything coherent in all that noise, smoke, and semi-darkness. The conversations all came down to something like, "Well, how do you feel, man?" "Great, man, incredible, I never felt better in my life!" "Nice hash, man!" "Yeah, great hash!" followed by pointless laughter and various observations that weren't funny to bystanders but that left us rolling on the floor. You must be stoned yourself to appreciate the pointless gaiety of people who've been smoking hashish or marijuana. "Great hash!" The well-to-do children around me spoke with the intonation and slang of the residents of the Hotel Diplomat, or at least they tried to.

The boy-director and his girlfriend had already undertaken to fulfill their primary responsibilities—they'd started shooting their film. I forgot to mention that they were supposed to shoot an "orgy" scene, a scene, that is, with Faust sunk in debauchery and consuming his life in the company of courtesans in a place (the millionaire's house?) he has been brought to by Mephi-

stopheles-Henry to be shown the world of pleasure. My stranger
was included in the "orgy" scene too, and was among the first to
be filmed, with the boy playing the main hero sitting at her feet.
The stranger obviously evoked in the youngsters the same tim-
idity she did in me. Later the children put on some of Jenny's
Arab music, and the two girls dressed in something like Arab
costumes started twisting like snakes not far from our hookah,
for which purpose we were asked to move temporarily. The girls
were depicting the houris of paradise, while the boy Faust sat in
a lotus position, smoked hashish, and indolently watched them
with "languor in his gaze." They'll have their film, I thought,
but what will I have?

The party gradually started to break down into groups in the
way that all parties do—some people left or went out for a
while, and other couples started quietly disappearing. I doubt
they all went off to fuck in the darker recesses of that house
entrusted to me, but many went off nonetheless. My stranger
disappeared from the living room for a while, stayed somewhere, and then came back again. Maybe I needed to get away
from that damned Oriental poison and the boy in the black
stockings with whom I already shared an understanding that
was not merely wordless but even motionless—a kind of
thought exchange across the distance separating us by means of
brain waves—but cowardliness and hashish had me pinned on
my back, and I lay there without twitching. Well, what could I
say to her, I thought, well what? She already knows I'm a servant—somebody's probably already told her. I had seen her and
Henry and some of the other children talking about something
and glancing in my direction. If only she weren't so stunning, I
thought, then I honestly wouldn't be so afraid. If she were just a
little worse and not so gorgeous. In short, I started having more
and more of a complex about it and even found myself sitting
there by the hookah immersed in melancholy thoughts about
how, in comparison to them, I was already old and lonely, and

that I didn't have any connection at all with that crowd of children. None whatsoever. They were separate, and I was separate.

I decided to rouse myself and stood up, casting a glance over the field of battle: the children had significantly diminished in number. Maybe they had gone downstairs, for all I knew. It was the first time I had stood up all evening, and my legs were numb and slow to obey me. It was only when I stood up that I realized how stoned I was.

It was force of habit alone that allowed me to move and not drop off to sleep or start vomiting. I decided I needed to move around and find somebody to drag off to bed. Even if my condition wasn't the most ideal for lofty philosophical discourse and was even doubtful for normal articulate conversation in any language, including the Russian language, gentlemen, it was for the bedroom quite appropriate and even desirable. And I went downstairs, making the rounds like a night watchman and housekeeper and checking every room along the way.

Everywhere were couples, paired-off teenagers in various stages of intimacy. True, there was only one instance where an indisputable sexual act was in progress, and that in the sanctum sanctorum, Steven's office, where one of the leather-jacketed beanpoles—I've always thought they're the most gallant—turned his flushed face toward me and grinned. Sticking out from under his arms and hanging on either side of his crew-cut head were the smooth legs of a maiden in high heel spikes. I couldn't see the young creature's head, since it had been shoved by the rascal's prick well into the corner of Gatsby's green couch, and only a piece of her rumpled skirt and a terribly indecent, very naked maidenly thigh was visible.

My turn around the rooms depressed me even more. It would have been better if I hadn't made it and had stayed by the hookah with the boy in black stockings who was now fucked up to the point of complete befuddlement, and smoked until I collapsed. More than half the kids had disappeared, and those that remained were energetically abandoning themselves to sin, or

were well on the way to doing so, while I shuffled like a foolishly grinning old uncle among the young couples—as I clearly
remember seeing myself at the time. Besides, I hadn't seen any
unattached girls, in fact not even one female figure by herself.
I'd let the moment slip by and hadn't used my device for outwit-
ting my own cowardice—hadn't gone to anyone first. After all,
there were a lot of good-looking girls among the children, I
swore to myself. Why are you such a blockhead, servant Edward, why didn't you find yourself a nice little pussy, young and
warm? They were friendly enough with you and didn't treat you
like a servant, did they? It was obvious Henry had boasted to his
friends that they even had a housekeeper who was a writer.
What the fuck were you wasting your time for? I reflected.
You're a weak little soul. A feeble little jerk, and you call yourself an opportunist! I insulted myself mercilessly.

   To top it all, as I was about to take the elevator from the first
floor back up to the living room, it passed me on its way down
to the basement, and to my horror I saw in the elevator's round
little window my stranger and somebody else in a white jacket.
My heart sank. They're on their way down to the basement, I
said to myself and then was lost in thought for a few moments,
struggling to understand what was happening. Why would a
man and a woman go down to the basement? Occasionally for
the sake of something exotic, I had fucked a few of my girls in
the stuffy warmth of the basement. I had in fact fucked them in
all the different parts of the house, in my boss's bathroom, on
the stairs, and once in the TV room while watching late-night
horror films on our huge screen. But that's me. It's all right for
me, I thought. My attitude toward my own sexual activity is
easygoing. But it was extremely painful to me for some reason
that my stranger—and I considered her mine, my young grace,
my girl in chinchilla—was going down to the basement to fuck
with the white jacket. I imagined that spectacle as something
obscene and awful, which is why I stood pondering a while by
the elevator, urgently trying to find a way out of the situation.

261

There wasn't any, as it turned out; I couldn't ward off the terrible thing that was about to happen. And what could I have done, anyway? I couldn't have followed them down to the basement, and even if I had, what could I have said? I imagined how that scene would look, and if they were fucking, then what? He obviously would turn his head toward me and grin the same way the leather jacket in Steven's office had, and she would do the opposite—she would turn away. . . . No, it would be even worse—that provocative young whore would undoubtedly turn her face toward me and gaze at me in an ironically mocking way while the white-jacketed guy fucked her.

At that instant the elevator passed me again on its way up, and immersed in my thoughts as I was, I didn't notice whether they, my stranger and the white jacket, were in it, or whether somebody had called the elevator from one of the upper floors and it had gone up empty. Attempting to introduce some clarity into my world, I plodded upstairs and went into the living room, but the only people there were a few remaining sangria drinkers and the stubborn boy in stockings who was still sucking like a leech on the hookah and lost in smoke. The distraught and angry housekeeper tossed off a couple of glasses of sangria one after the other and sat down with the boy. Exactly, they're in the basement, I thought, where else could they be? The only hope that the stranger wasn't down there was provided by the fact that when I went up to the third floor, the elevator wasn't there anymore. They had either proceeded up or had taken it back down, so that it was possible to think, say, that they had taken it up to the fifth floor and had gone out on the roof. They are standing romatically on the roof holding hands and looking at the stars, I consoled myself. But through the hashish smoke the devil gloatingly whispered to me, "Holding hands, little Russian fool, little Ivan Shitson? They tumbled onto the old mattress in the basement a long time ago, the one you yourself put in the farthest corner by the window behind the old ironing machine next to the hot water pipe, and the white jacket is fucking her dog-style with his robust prick, and if the children do lack sensitivity sometimes, they aren't without vigor—adolescents can always get it up. . . ."

Ugh, how stupid! I suddenly thought, coming to my senses. I, a cultivated person who only last night was working by the sweat of my brow on a new book and who is usually possessed of bright, clear thoughts, am sitting here like a suffering piece of meat with some young nymphomaniac on my mind. How fucked up, I thought, losing my temper, and rousing myself once again, I drank some more sangria and resolved to talk to the boy in black stockings.

I had overestimated myself, gentlemen. I was already in a state of utter weightlessness, and even though I was thinking more or less clearly, albeit not what I should have been thinking about, I was speaking the most complacent rubbish, which I realized at the time, although there wasn't anything I could do about it. I attempted to present myself to the boy in stockings as someone very important. I told him in confidence that I was not only a housekeeper but . . . but the bodyguard of Gatsby himself and tonight of Henry as well. It was an invention so extreme that I myself grimaced at its tastelessness, while telling it to the boy in stockings as we dully sat shoulder to shoulder on the floor. But the boy in stockings was in no better condition that I was, thank God, and merely said, "###," and then fell silent, continuing to suck on his pipe. For all I knew, he was at that moment crossing the desert with Lawrence of Arabia.

"Wealthy people in our time can't manage without bodyguards," I continued, talking more to myself than to the boy in stockings. "The many instances of kidnapping that have occurred on the territory of the United States have forced Steven Grey to hire me," I said, and then to my own surprise added, "I received special training when I was in the Soviet Union," thereby giving a certain piquancy to my own biography. The boy in stockings could take my words any way he wished—that I had perhaps been a dissident back home in Russia, or perhaps an even more alluring prospect opened before him—that I had graduated from a school for spies. . . .

Completely mesmerized by my own fantasy, I suddenly added right out of the blue in a nervous voice that I had a gun, and then was silent. The boy in stockings nodded off with the pipe in his hands. Perhaps he and Lawrence were now attacking, with sabers bared, somewhere in their Arabia.

Into the room walked a very drunk and, as it seemed to me, very lonely Henry, who informed me in an unsteady voice that he was going to crash. I at once became more lively; remembering that I was his bodyguard, I leapt to my feet, grabbed the unsuspecting Henry, and dragged him off to his father's bedroom, on the door of which, as on the door to my room, we had a sign reading, "Do not enter! Master bedroom." I pulled off Henry's jacket, undid his bow tie, took off his shoes and the rest of his clothes, and put him to bed. He muttered something in protest, but I was already overcome by the zeal to serve, and I put him to bed whether he wanted me to or not. I turned off the light in the room and went out, closing the door behind me. Henry plaintively tried to explain something to me in the darkness, but I didn't listen. Trusty bodyguard that I was, I took my seat by the bedroom door and remained in that position for a while, how long I don't even know.

When at last I emerged from my confused hashish-induced reverie, I found that the house was quiet. Looking into the living room, I saw that even the boy in stockings was asleep, his head resting on our hard Arabian cushions and the hookah's snake dropped from his hand. The others had obviously all gone to bed long ago. Like a proper servant, I decided to make a last turn around the house before going off to bed myself, and I went downstairs to the first floor. Several people had fallen asleep right on the floor and on the two couches in the solarium. I quietly passed through to the front door, which of course wasn't locked. I locked it and turned off the stairway light—one switch turns off all the lights in the hallway and stairs from the first floor to the fifth—and then took the elevator back up to my own fourth floor. Quiet snores and moans came from the fourth-floor guest bedroom.

I turned the knob of the door to my room and stepped into the darkness.

"Don't turn on the light!" a woman's low voice said to me. On my bed I made out a dark figure and the dim glow of a cigarette.

Now it already seems to me sometimes that it wasn't her, but some other girl I hadn't paid any attention to all evening, but looking into the darkness then, there wasn't any doubt in my mind. The blinds had been let down, which is something I never do, gentlemen. If I slept with them down, my boss Steven Grey would never get his coffee in the morning. The blinds had been let down of course by that young seeker of adventure.

"Come over here!" she said softly. The coal of her cigarette moved downward and broke into little pieces at the level of my night table. She had put out her cigarette, crushing the butt on the candlestick that stood there. I went over to my bed in the direction of her voice. I already understood what was up, quickly grasping, despite the abundance of hashish and sangria in my system, that this intoxicated young person, having read her share of erotic literature, had undoubtedly decided to broaden her experience, to experience new sensations, and get herself laid by a servant. We all think in clichés. Just as I had unconsciously sought a girl for myself there in classic cliché terms, wishing as a servant to revenge myself on "them" and fuck one of "their" girls and stick my prick into a warm crack belonging to one of "them," she too was playing out a classical variant. Lords and ladies, after all, had always fucked their servants, young barons traditionally humping their housemaids, and fifteen-year-old girls traditionally gazing with watering mouths at the pants of the butler or gardener. Here's a bold one, I thought in awe of her, much bolder than me, even though she had pronounced her "come hither" with a super-

265

fluous severity, a little bit too nervously, but a very bold seeker
of adventure all the same.

I went over to her. Though her face was hot, her lips were
strangely cold—she was, no doubt, very excited, almost
breathless, but in spite of her excitement and probably with a
sinking heart, she was doing what she wanted to. Finding my
face in the darkness, she stroked it with her hand, then moved
down to my neck and chest. Cool young hands, I thought. I
already knew what she was going to do. In a time when we
derive all our knowledge from TV and the movies for the most
part, I knew that she was going to unbutton my shirt, and yes,
as if obeying my thoughts, she did unbutton it—how many similar episodes had I seen in my life, in both the movies and reality. Anyway, what do you want; it's impossible to think up
something completely new in that realm, especially if you're
only sixteen or seventeen. However interesting a little tart she
was, my own experience was a great deal vaster.

While I was reflecting, the young scamp had already unbut-
toned the strap on my white jeans and was kissing my belly. Her
warm hair tickled my stomach and shut off my thinking mecha-
nism, thank God, and it suddenly became very pleasant and ago-
nizingly suspenseful, since I was anticipating that she would any
second touch my prick, with her hand. And then (and the idea
was even terrifying) take my prick, which had suffered so much
in the course of the evening, into her clean, maidenly little
mouth. Where it's nice and warm, the thought of an old libertine flashed weakly through my mind.

You're thinking, gentlemen, that the young creature departed
just a bit from the TV and movie version? Not at all. She
touched my prick with her hand, and she took my organ into
her mouth and diligently started sucking it, at the same time
stroking and pulling my balls with her other hand as one of her
older friends had perhaps taught her to do or she'd picked up
from some trashy pornographic novel, the dirty little rich girl.
The little tart.

I stood in front of her and writhed with pleasure, holding her for some reason by the ears, by her little warm ears, and from time to time moving her head onto my prick. She helplessly took my prick into her throat, but after two or three deep swallows, she started coughing and had to lick and suck just the head of my organ in order to recover her breath. Cocksucking is a great art, and not many master it. Try, do the best you can, I thought, rhythmically moving her head onto my prick. Her slippery little ears tried to slip out of my hands, but I held on to them by their tips, by their lobes.

She really wanted me to come so she could swallow the pungent semen of a Russian servant. Or whatever kind of pleasure and unbelievable humiliation it was that she was seeking. Maybe to smear my semen all over her beautiful face. And then to record in her secret diary, hidden under the rug far from the sight of mama and papa, that she had swallowed a whole "glass of the semen of an Eastern barbarian," or something in that spirit—"a glass of fresh semen." I'd bet an arm and a leg she wrote the episode down.

I didn't come from her cocksucking, though it did feel incredibly good, her enthusiasm more than making up for what she lacked in technique. Anyway, she smelled so charming, with young perfume of some kind and her bare arms and face gleaming in the darkness, that I was even beginning to find something mystically holy in that scene and imagine it as a kind of religious ritual. I was afraid to extend my thoughts about the two of us, lest I lose my erection, and I didn't lose it, but I couldn't come either. Besides the fact that it's always hard for me to come from cocksucking, I had swallowed so much hashish smoke that an orgasm was simply impossible, and realizing that we agreed to stop. I grasped her tender chin in my hand and stroked her neck, wanting to undress her and lay her down, but suddenly jumping up, she took my hand and said, "Come on!" She said it in a very brazen and merry way; she had calmed down, the little bitch, and now felt comfortable with the fact that she was engaged in sin with a servant. We groped our way out into the hall and got on the elevator, which was dimly lit with a blacklight bulb (!)—Henry had replaced the normal daylight bulb himself; the children wanted to have a real orgy. The young fiend went in first and I followed after her, gently shutting the heavy green steel door behind me, since on the fourth floor it makes a tremendous racket when it's closed, and we started moving. Where? Down to the basement, of course; where else would the little whore take me? I tried to talk to her in the elevator, and had opened my mouth to begin a sentence, wanting to tell her that I had intended to come to her all evening, but after the first sound of "I," she covered my mouth with her palm. I submitted.

We emerged into the darkness and stuffy warmth. I know my basement perfectly, and so I gropingly drew her toward the side where the mattress was, without turning on the light, but to my surprise she resisted and pulled me in the other direction. To the left of the elevator is a door leading to a small room containing the elevator drive with its dangerously turning cogged wheels behind a grating, but if you pass through that room to the other side, you enter another room heaped with old furniture, the most remote room of all, the same one where after my first and last argument with Gatsby I hid out and drank soda water.

The kid dragged me in there. It was very dark in the room, although a little evening light did penetrate from outside through a dirt-streaked basement window. We stumbled against things of every conceivable kind that had been piled on the floor there—boards, jars of paint, and parts of chairs. The lady pulled me all the way over to the window, where she came to a halt and then started moving about, releasing my hand. The place stank of old wood, with a slightly moldy smell given off perhaps by the cold, bare stone, not brick, with which the walls had been constructed. I finally realized what she was doing—she was getting undressed, and had taken her panties off herself, stepping out of them while hopping lightly on one leg and holding on to me and using her other hand to pull them off, since they had caught on her shoe. Her excitement had obviously returned, and giggling nervously she turned her back to me and bent over, resting her breasts on top of something and sticking her bottom out in my direction, and with a sudden movement flipped up the hem of her dress from behind and pulled it off, thereby revealing her unexpectedly large maidenly ass, which gleamed before me in the darkness with her legs descending like columns below.

I was even a little abashed by the brazen speed with which she did it all, until I remembered witnessing a similar scene in a porno film. True, that scene hadn't taken place in a basement and hadn't involved a servant, and the heroine hadn't suddenly assumed that position herself, but had been placed in it by somebody else. I glanced at what she was leaning on; it was a highchair—you know, a chair for infants with a special tray to keep them from falling out and hold the dish with their food. So there she was resting her breasts on that little chair, flattening them out on that childhood object and serendipitously using it for her own nymphomaniacal purposes. Bravo!

I of course use the term "nymphomaniac" ironically, gentlemen, for she was unquestionably a Seeker of Adventure, a wild and untamable spirit of the kind that's sometimes implanted in a woman, and let those around her beware! She won't leave anybody in peace for another forty years, a nymphomaniac by birth and conviction, I thought as I inserted my organ into her little crack. To top it all, her twat was prickly—she had shaved it, if you can imagine that. She had probably shaved herself clean that very morning.

I showed her everything I had, gentlemen, aroused by her charming lack of shame. I hope she still feels to this day that it's far more interesting to fuck a servant than a representative of her own class, that is, if she understands anything about it, since it's possible her curiosity was greater than her desire, that she had more a perverted imagination than a developed sexuality. I don't know, but if her sexual feelings weren't developed, then she pretended very skilfully. She moaned quietly and tenderly while my prick turned and moved inside her plump, cultivated little hole, and I hope inside all her hidden depths.

My cock felt so engorged with blood and so rigid that I thought its head was going to burst at the seams like an overripe banana. I had the delicious sense of having reached a limit, and when I roughly pulled her ass, well-fed on her mama's and papa's capitalist bread, toward me, moving it onto my prick, I felt that I'd gone as far as I could, that I'd reached one of life's limits, one of its most extreme manifestations—that warm, white flesh crammed onto me, embracing every inch of my prick.

I fucked her and fucked her, never doubting I would come inside her, and would even have killed her probably, if that was the only way I could have reached orgasm. I needed to hurl my seed deep inside her slippery depths, deep inside her little pink folds, somewhere near her heart perhaps, but I also wanted to reach the state where I wouldn't be able to stand it anymore and my whole prick would almost break off inside her.

I came inside her with such force that it seemed to me that despite the fact that that young whore had no doubt taken the world's best and most up-to-date birth-control pills, or whatever the very latest invention in that area was, my sperm would break through all the barriers and she would bear my child. A horse or a centaur perhaps, but definitely something hooved and proud.

We remained stuck together like that for a while, panting heavily, until I thought I would fall down, that my strength would all at once desert me, since my legs were suddenly in tremendous pain and cramping nearly to the point of convulsions. She and I had trampled my white jeans underfoot, almost tearing them apart, and they shone dimly on the floor. . . .

Somehow we separated, and she slipped off the highchair and made her way over to the wall and leaned against it. We groped at each other in the dark, reaching out our hands toward each other, each pulling the other closer, and kissed each other on the lips for the first time, and then stood embracing, still breathing heavily, and feeling very close to each other, she and I. I liked her unutterably, that desperate girl, oh how I liked her.

She was the first to start moving. "Go on upstairs to your room," she said hoarsely. "I'll be up in a minute." And then, in answer to my unspoken question, "Where are you going?" she added, "I have to get my things out of the kitchen; I don't want the other guys to know I'm still here." And gracefully putting her panties back on, she slipped out of one darkness into an even greater one. I groped my own way back to the elevator.

I didn't even ask her if she knew how to find the kitchen from the basement. Most likely she did.

I waited for her in my room exactly ten minutes, gentlemen, and when she didn't come, I went back downstairs, although to be frank, I didn't at all expect to find her there. It was perfectly clear: I had been fucked and discarded. Used like a servant and then thrown away.

Naturally she wasn't in the kitchen, how else? I was going to start checking the other rooms, and had gone into the TV room, where some of the kids were still asleep on the floor, but then I gave up that idea as useless and poured myself a glass of vermouth, dropped a couple of ice cubes in it, and went back upstairs to my room. I sat down at my desk, an old one that had once belonged to Linda and that I'd dragged up from the basement a day or so after I'd cleared out the last of Jenny's things from the room. A servant has no need of a desk, of course, but a writer does, and it has stood in my room by the window ever since. I raised the blinds, sat down at the desk, and gazed out the window. It was getting light in the garden, a rosy April dawn, and in the distance you could see the tip of Roosevelt Island, and beyond that a lighthouse on a rock and a foggy, open expanse of water.

All right, I thought, I had my pleasure too, if it comes to that, and what pleasure it was! But however much I tried to convince

271

myself that my own pleasure had been at least as great as hers, that arithmetic was of little use, and I was still depressed. The mere fact that she had been capable of such an adventure, the bold little whore, made her hopelessly attractive to me. Moreover, she had during the act been as passive as she could be, yielding to me and moving backwards onto my prick. My girl exactly, I continued my sad thoughts. She didn't make even one extra movement the whole time. It was all the way it was supposed to be, the way you feel it should be. And to lose a specimen like that!

And covering my eyes with my yellow comforter, with our yellow comforter, that is, I somehow dropped off into troubled sleep.

Naturally the next morning the house looked as if it had been turned upside down. Actually, after looking it over, I didn't find that any particularly serious damage had been done, except for one thing. Some jerk had tried to put his cigarette out on our TV projection screen, and a long and nasty hole gaped at its center. What can I do? I'll have to tell Nancy about it, only later—on Monday after Linda comes, I thought. I was, after all, concerned that morning with a problem of much greater significance to me—how to find out from Henry who that young creature had been, what her name was, and what she did, and maybe where she lived. I needed her, and nobody else.

Finding an opportunity as if in passing, I asked Henry who the girl in the black dress and bare arms had been, the very beautiful and mature one who had been sitting next to me in the living room when we were smoking hashish, and whom I'd been fucking in the basement, although I obviously wasn't able to mention the last part. Henry asked, "Which one do you mean, Edward? I seem to remember there were several girls in black dresses." I started explaining to him, but we got mixed up, since he, not surprisingly, couldn't remember who had been sitting next to me in the living room when I'd been smoking hashish. When I reminded him then how he had greeted her with open arms and then gone upstairs with her, he seemed to remember something, or at least his face looked like the face of somebody about to remember something, "Renée?" he asked, looking condescendingly at me, as it seemed to me. "The one who left with Gregory?" Henry was obviously getting bored with the conversation, but as a well-bred boy, he patiently explained that Gregory was the younger son of a senator from the state of X. "He came after everybody else," Henry said, "a tall blond guy in a white jacket."

For the first time in my life there wasn't anything I could do; it was beyond my power to unravel that story. If my stranger had been Renée, and she had left with the guy in the white jacket, and Henry confirmed that he'd seen them leaving together, then it followed that they had done so before I had put Henry to bed. But if she had left, then how did she manage to turn up in my room an hour or two after she'd gone? After pondering the question for a while, I realized that she could quite easily have come back, and even have done so without being noticed. The door had in fact been unlocked; I myself released the catch on it while shutting everything up. Door locks, as you know, have a safety catch on them, one position allowing the lock to be used in its normal way, and the other allowing the door to be opened from the outside by simply turning the knob. Whenever the eternally hurrying Gatsby runs outside to meet or accompany his guests, he always sets the lock in the second way. He doesn't want to be bothered with taking his key out of his pocket, which I certainly understand, but he almost always forgets to release the catch, so that it frequently happens that we sleep the whole night with the door unlocked. Anyone passing by could, if he felt like it, simply turn the handle of the door on the street and walk in.

I continued to struggle for a while against my fate, attempting to get "her" phone number from Henry, although obviously without asking him for it, but by pinching his notebook from his pocket. It was easy to do; Henry was even more absent-minded than Gatsby was. I took the notebook down to the basement, to my hideout there, and after a long search, since his notebook was extraordinarily chaotic, with first and last names and addresses running together, I found Renée's name and number but not her address. I had already begun to doubt that it was in fact Renée who had fucked me and dumped me; maybe it was another girl. I'd been stoned and drunk, and all the places we'd been together had been infernally dark. The only place where I had seen her "in the light" had been the elevator, if you consider that black, orgiastic lamp to be light. And in that moment, which lasted no more than a minute probably, since we could hardly have spent more time than that on the elevator, I didn't look very closely at the stranger. I had left my glasses in my room and was in any case occupied with something else, with my prick and my desire, and was kissing her on the neck, I think.

I called Renée, but her line was busy, gentlemen. My heart, my poor heart, was pounding. I started thinking hurriedly about what I would say to her. I couldn't just say, "Well then, my little adventuress, what did you run away for?" or "What's up, my little whore?" I called again a little while later, but nobody answered. And I called again that evening, once more without success. I've gradually accumulated my own list of grievances against telephones and have grown to hate them more and more. My call the next morning was answered by a maid. First she wanted to know my name and who I was. I lied that I was a friend of Renée's. Everybody tells me that my voice sounds very young. "Renée has gone to Europe with her parents and won't be back until October." And the maid mentioned the name of the town, in the south of France, I think.

I probably never would have been able to find her, if she hadn't wanted me to. And even if I could get her on the phone, what would I say to her, and even if I were able to summon up the audacity to remind her gently of what had apparently taken

274

place between us, she would simply tell me I was a crazy, insolent servant. And if she wanted to say more, she would call me a sex maniac and hang up. She could even make a lot of trouble for me, if she wanted to. She could call Gatsby and tell him that his housekeeper had lost his mind and was imagining . . . "Can you imagine, Steven, that I . . . ?" She wouldn't say "fucked him in the basement," of course, but she could say that I was sexually deranged and pestering her. Gatsby would in that event probably kick me out, and not even Efimenkov would be able to help, not with something like that.

She had unquestionably read all the books and seen all the porno flicks, which she'd probably gone to after putting on some old rags and making herself up to look like some impossible version of a whore. She went and probably even expected that somebody would fuck her there. She sat and trembled in fear while gazing at the backs of the men sitting by themselves, expecting that the owner of one of those backs would sit down next to her and put his hand on her knee or right on her cunt. It's unlikely though that she would permit anyone to do anything to her there, even if they did sit down. I understand her fear; you really can stumble onto who the fuck knows what there, even a psychopathic murderer. With me it was absolutely safe; she wasn't in a porno theater open to any creep who walks in, but in the house of a friend, a friend whose servant I was. She had probably heard something about me from Henry or from a couple of his friends, and even if she hadn't heard anything, it was clear enough from my appearance that I was a harmless but still healthy creature. "Cute," as Jenny and other women and girls have told me.

That case is closed, as far as I'm concerned; I never found the perpetrator. Or rather, excuse me, I never found the perpetratrix. To my great and everlasting regret.

My whole life over the last several years has been a yearning for "action." If, and this is something I long for, our civilization should in the next couple of decades begin to collapse, I would of course at once find myself an opportunity, and would probably be not the least among the bold and reckless of this world. For the time being, however, the only things that remain for me are sex and writing, the only two spheres in which a man, if he has the nerve, is still more or less free to show himself. All the other spheres have long been patrolled by civilization down to the least little byways and dead ends. Writing and sex have been placed in thrall too, and are under the control of civilization and social life, but there are still a few chinks in the machinery. Either there still are, or there already are. In any case, they still don't know how to control our thoughts; their geniuses in white coats still haven't found out how to read what's inside our brain cases. They've been listening for a long time to our telephone conversations and rummaging in our papers, but they still can't read our thoughts. Although I'm absolutely sure that feverish work is already under way in that area, and that the geniuses in white coats will eventually reach their goal—I have faith in human ingenuity. God grant I die before that glorious discovery is made, because after that you won't be able to write shit and you can fuck freedom goodbye.

Steven Grey's housekeeper hasn't been making very much progress with the writing part of it. The American publishers have one after another refused to publish my book. Maybe they've reached an agreement with my former girlfriend Sarah? Although I have long felt the itch to move on, although I have the ambition to proceed to the next rung in my life, I'm still compelled to remain here in service, and my life in the millionaire's little house, having now entered its second year, has in a way come full circle. It's all routine now and no longer interesting, and I've been looking around to see where I, the indefatigable Mr. Limonov, Edward, will turn up next. All those I started out with way back then have made their peace, some in jail and others with families, but in any case have come to a halt. Even Elena has grown tired apparently, and is married to her own European aristocrat, and only very occasionally permits herself little love adventures. But not I.

The publishers answer Liza in much the same way, with something like, "Mr. Limonov's novel is too threatening, and his hero too negative." Inside, deep in my heart, I believe they're right in refusing to publish my novel. I'm really their enemy, and books like mine destroy, if not civilzation, then at least faith in it, so that it's logical not to publish them. But the struggle is the struggle, and I therefore try with all my strength to win. I haven't reacted emotionally to their rejections in a long time. My agent just methodically sends the book off to those publishers who haven't been terrorized by it yet, and if Liza gets tired of the job, I won't die of a broken heart. I'll just find myself another agent and start over from the beginning. They're greedy when it comes to money, and they'll buy me in the end. I'm persistent. But unfortunately I'm also oversensitive, as my girlfriend Jenny once observed, and sometimes it all makes me sick to my stomach, and then, like a madman, I run off to the first place I think of, and more often than not I look for relief in sex.

The last time I got sick of it all happened quite recently, after the business with Natashka and the blood in the bathroom. And I got myself to a brothel. The reason didn't have anything to do with Natashka, and in fact there wasn't any particular reason for my mental upset, or at least no explicit reason. I obviously just needed to escape from my routine and from my struggle, which wasn't giving me any satisfaction. Maybe it was a full moon. My flight ended in a brothel.

Yes, I licked the cunt of a prostitute. But does that make me any less of a man? No. The cunt, when spread wide, turned out to be pink, and before giving it to me, she washed it while standing in front of a sink and raking water into it with her palm. Actually, "cunt" sounds crude. Paula didn't have a cunt, she had an Italian . . . what? I don't know; there don't seem to be very many affectionate or deferential terms for the female sex organ. In Paula, that place resembled an almost scarlet butterfly with its wings spread open. The scarlet area extended high and wide between her legs. It was probably irritation caused by her work, a sort of industrial trauma.

I hadn't been looking for Paula in the beginning. What I needed was a skinny blonde. But it isn't that easy to find skinny blondes on Eighth Avenue. Paula, who had herself stopped me, did not upon learning that I needed a skinny blonde betray the slightest astonishment, but only went to the edge of the sidewalk, put her hands to her mouth and, in her attempt to be heard over the rumble and roar of the cars, shouted, "Elsa!" And from the other side of the street came Elsa, maneuvering against the traffic. Her name clearly didn't suit her, and she didn't suit me either. She was small and skinny, and yes, she was a blonde, but not even a vulgar one, which would have been just right, but of the simple country-girl type. Her thin curly hair irritated me, a head of hair like a permanent, and so I said I'd look for another girl, and walked away. Apparently offended by my lack of interest, Elsa hurled after me, "He wants a skinny blonde! I weigh eighty-seven pounds! What are you planning to do, throw your skinny blonde up in the air and catch her on your prick or what?!"

After wandering around for another half hour and still not finding a skinny blonde, I returned to Paula on the corner of Forty-fifth Street and Eighth Avenue and settled with her. We went around the corner to a hotel. I had in fact invited her to the millionaire's house, but she turned me down, as they almost always do. There are a good many creeps wandering around Eighth Avenue.

Paula was a brunette of Italian descent. She was pretty, but in comparison with the rest of her body, her ass was a little bit plump.

On the gray but clean sheets in the room lay the little circle of a condom. On the ceiling a thin fluorescent circle glowed with a meager and foolish light. We got undressed, I lay down on my back, and Paula began licking and sucking my cock, after giving it a careful preliminary examination. That alone cost me thirty dollars, in addition to the ten dollars I had already paid to get into the room. I don't know how to haggle with them.

Though poor the room was clean, and as usual reminded me more of doctor's office in a poor Soviet village than a room in a hotel-brothel. Yes, it was both a hotel and a brothel. Coming in Paula and I had met a black mother and child in the hallway. I didn't feel sorry for that child living in a brothel; rather, I envied him—an interesting experience. Besides, when he grows up he won't have all those pitiful superstitions that have cost me so much effort to get rid of. The best thing is to be abandoned in this world, knowing neither your mother nor your father, so that you can then make of yourself whatever you want—vicious, without any looking over your shoulder. . . . In a word, it's a fine, liberating thing. And what a complex he'll have, I thought enviously. A person without a complex is like a new car they forgot to put the motor in. You can push it through life, of course, but it's incapable of propelling itself.

I stayed with Paula a long time, not having any place I needed to rush off to, and I paid her some more and we talked. I really laughed when Paula, obviously wishing to be amiable, suddenly picked up my Italian boots and said, "What beautiful boots you have, Edward!"—naturally, I'd introduced myself to her, how else? I recalled that the Marchioness Houston had once given me the same compliment. The Marchioness will, I hope, be pleased to learn that she and a prostitute have the same, the same . . . how shall I put it? The same grasp of the external world, or the same taste in men's footwear.

I told Paula I envied her profession. And I really did envy it. In addition to the fact that the work was interesting, and with people, Paula probably earned as much in an evening as I earned at the millionaire's house in two weeks, and maybe a lot more. I alone had given her a hundred dollars in all. Not everybody's as crazy as I am, and goes to a prostitute to soothe his mind, but even those who go to appease their flesh pay too, and so with her everything was just fine. She looked like a serious girl, neither an alcoholic nor an addict, and she was probably saving her money. I was neither a priest nor an intellectual jerk, and so I naturally didn't preach to her that her profession was sinful or even tell her that to live the way she was living was unhygienic, and I didn't try to persuade her to change her profession and stop selling her body. We simply smoked and chatted while sitting naked on the bed. Decent women also trade in their bodies; they also sell their cunts, although theirs usually go for a great deal more than a prostitute's does, especially in the first days and weeks of your acquaintance. You go to a nice restaurant, taking a taxi, and before that there are tickets for a show or you have to take the girl to a disco afterwards, and only then can you go to bed. And if you buy the girl cocaine, as Ghupta suggests, a gram alone costs one hundred to one hundred and fifty dollars, people! What's a prostitute next to a decent woman! When it comes to the art of robbery, decent women are much more professional and much better qualified than prostitutes are. . . . I'm not judging anybody, since my own is hardly the most virtuous of lives; I'm merely looking at life and turning it in my hands, and taking an interest in it and comparing it and analyzing it. I'm not satisfied with the verities of old books that call prostitutes fallen creatures. What's so fallen about this Paula, I thought, why she's more stable than I am.

I wrote down my phone number for Paula and then went back outside with her. I had gotten little sexual satisfaction from her, and in fact I don't really understand what sort of idiot you have to be to go to a prostitute for sexual satisfaction. You can get the same kind of satisfaction going to a urologist; he'll touch your prick for you too. But I did get spiritual satisfaction, as we may conventionally call it, from my visit to Paula, in the same way that a little hoodlum, suffering all day from idleness and boredom, is soothed only by doing mischief, by hanging a cat in the garden, say, or swiping his father's revolver from his desk and shooting his sister in the leg. . . . I was pretty sure Paula wouldn't call me—those girls are very cautious—even though I temptingly told her I was very rich and lived in my own house in Manhattan.

I walked back to my house, crossing Broadway and several other streets until I reached Fifth Avenue, where I went up as far as Fifty-seventh Street. Thickly inscribed with a black felt-tip pen on the wall of a bank on the corner of Fifth Avenue and Fifty-seventh Street was the proud invitation, "Rob me!" This is our special form of New York patriotism. Our New York robbers had been going to banks in record numbers those days. They'd robbed more banks than anybody else in the country, and so far that month they'd robbed more banks than they had all last year.

Go to it, guys! I thought. Let's make a real effort! We'll double the number of bank robberies! We'll double and triple it! I wasn't the only fan. Everybody in New York was keeping track; everybody was excited. The press was keeping a count, and we New York patriots were keeping one too. Thirteen bank robberies today, and more tomorrow, God willing, even if it's only fourteen. What excitement! Our bank robbers are the best and the boldest. Some of them are even women.

I walked calmly past the bank. No, I wasn't going to rob it; I've learned to keep my passions under control. Being a writer is much more profitable than being a bandit. I only have to be patient, to wait, and I'll get my piece and do my great deed. I'll be patient, although there's no doubt that inside I'm a bandit— what else? I'm no housekeeper or writer; I'm a bandit! That's my true profession, I thought wickedly.

Chapter Ten

THE BOSS was home. Five people from Kuwait were sitting in the living room. They had been sitting there for three hours.

The five Kuwaitis arrived in a limousine dressed in suits of Western cut and not at all in the Bedouin burnooses I had expected. "The four of them," said the boss's stepbrother and business associate, Mr. Richardson, as he skipped into the kitchen rubbing his hands together, "the four Kuwaitis are worth more than two billion, Edward!" *Two billion dollars!* That was a figure more appropriate to astronomy. A million I could still comprehend after a fashion, but two billion and even more? Only four of them were worth that, since the fifth, even though he was a Kuwaiti too, was a pauper and wasn't worth anything—he was only an interpreter. The interpreter, as I saw it, was a servant too, and so he didn't particularly interest me, but I was all eyes for the possessors of the two billion, and I tried to go into the living room as often as possible, pretending to be attentive.

When I'm attentive, I frequently overdo it. And I overdid it with the Kuwaitis and blew it. I put out alcohol in the living room, although not on the main table that Steven and his guests were sitting at, the mirrored one with the birds that Gatsby had cut out of a wall in Iran, but on a little table in the corner— some whiskey and rum and a few glasses. Even though I knew theoretically that people from Arab countries don't drink alcoholic beverages since it's forbidden by Muslim law, and that offering them something to drink is a great insult to them, or at least tactless. It was only by accident that I didn't shove the

282

alcohol right under their noses on the mirrored table. There fortunately wasn't any room to do so, since I'd just put out coffee and tea for them. Luckily for me I'd only been able to squeeze in our ridiculous leather ice bucket and in the process had seen Gatsby's face fall right before my eyes. He probably would have lashed out at me at once in the most obnoxious terms, if it hadn't been for the Arabs sitting around the table and for Efimenkov, my guardian angel, whom I think he kept constantly in mind, although only Gatsby himself knows that for certain. I left off what I was doing, naturally, although I didn't immediately realize what the problem was until Mr. Richardson came running in to me from the living room and worriedly informed me of my error. As soon as I got a chance, I took my bottles of alcohol away, and it's possible that not even all the Kuwaitis saw them, since most of them were sitting facing the other way. It occurred to me in the hallway that if I had made a mistake like that two or three hundred years ago, it would have cost me my housekeeper's and butler's life. Three hundred years ago a barbarian lord would have hanged me from the large tree in the garden next to the swings, although afterward he would perhaps have pitied his loyal butler, the victim of his wrath.

The Kuwaitis had been sitting all that time working on a deal with the boss and Mr. Richardson and two other businessmen of lesser rank. True, they took a break, during which they went down to the first floor to the solarium to examine and try out . . . well, what do you think? *A machine for instantly determining the composition of gold alloys.* The machine had been brought to the house two days before in a large case carefully packed in quilts, since it was one of only two or three such machines in existence, and our businessmen were very concerned about it. Externally, the machine looked like a small lathe with an electronic control panel from which various wires stuck out and a black box containing a screen and numerous indicators with needles.

After their break was over, and the Arab-American mob had

returned to the living room with its Persian carpets and cushions to chat some more and rustle papers, I stole down to the solarium to get a closer look at the machine. Lying on it were about a dozen oblong objects that looked like crudely made pastries. I picked up one of the pastries, and it felt abnormally heavy. Gold. It's gold, real gold! I said to myself while tossing the ingot into the air.

For some reason I was very happy. The weight of the gold was attractively pleasant. I thought for a moment how nice it would be to rake all the ingots into a bag, and I had just the one, and take off for distant lands. But how much gold could there actually be, how much was it worth? I weighed the pile of ingots with a glance. Not enough for me. Too little for me to give up my unpublished books and my agent, Liza, and abandon my struggle halfway. I often go to the bank to get cash for Gatsby, that being one of my duties, sometimes even several thousand dollars at a time, and occasionally the thought flashes through my mind to take off for Hong Kong or Las Vegas. But the difference between the big crook and the petty thief is precisely the fact that you can trust the former with even a hundred thousand. But don't trust him with just a million, Gatsby!

After returning the ingot to its place, I remained standing over the machine for a while shaking my head in amazement. That machine and the Kuwaitis and the house and my boss and the situation that day all reminded me of an episode from the adventures of Agent 007. The Kuwaiti-Gatsbian group looked like something taken from the silver screen, something right out of *Goldfinger*, and the only thing lacking was James himself. Actually, I could quite easily have played the role of James. Even mama Jenny had found it amusing to imagine I really was a Russian spy, and had suggested I open a Russian restaurant in New York and call it The Spy.

The Kuwaitis sat a little while longer and then at last went downstairs, shaking our already wobbly banister like masters of the house, and took their places in their limousine. I was grateful they had come between lunch and dinner, at a neutral time, so that I didn't have to make lunch for ten. Otherwise, I'd have been panting with exhaustion.

And then their asses were gone. After taking the fastest shower of his life, the boss at once disappeared after them; obviously he was running over to see Polly, his permanent New York woman. Does he have girlfriends in other cities in the world too, just like a deep-sea sailor? I wondered. Actually, I'm not so sure he did tear off to Polly's. That morning a van with the name "Tudor's Flowers" on it brought seven vases of flowers and plants, including a rubber plant. I almost sent them all back, since neither Linda nor I had ordered them. Fortunately Gatsby appeared in the doorway at that moment and with a sly smile suggested that they were a gift and that he had an idea from whom. Maybe he ran off to the woman who had sent the plants? To see the rubber plant lady, as I instantly named her? Most likely that was it.

All Gatsby did was smile and leave, whereas I wasted over an hour trying to find places in the house to put the flowers and plants and then taking them to different rooms. The full-grown rubber plant was particularly heavy; it was in fact a tree! I installed it in the living room, and the negotiations with the Kuwaitis had in fact been conducted underneath the rubber tree. Complain or not, it was my job.

Linda took off as soon as Gatsby went up to the bathroom; it was already after eight. I remained in the house alone, although I didn't feel free. I never do as long as Gatsby's in New York. I fixed myself a Scotch on the rocks and sat down in the kitchen and looked out the window.

Instead of the holiday life once promised me, I'm sitting in the kitchen, I thought bitterly. A man by a window. Outside, the Mystery of the Evening Dog Walk was in progress. I was interested in the women and the girls, not the dogs. My old girlfriend Jenny used to call dogs shit-producing machines. I share her point of view; it is, you'll agree, a practical one for a housekeeper or caretaker. Is it nice to have shit outside your window even if the dog's owner cleans it up? Bowing his legs outside my window, a big dog strained to push a large, dark turd out of himself.

At that moment my favorite appeared, although I of course had no idea who she was: a large yellow-haired woman with a ginger-colored dog on a leash. She was dressed in a slightly old-fashioned suit—a jacket and long skirt—and for some reason it was indecently charming.

That's what I need, a maiden wife with a yellow head, a big healthy girl like that, I thought. Then I'd be happy. And what's so good about my life anyway? All I do is sit in the kitchen by the window all the time or serve, while my employer goes off to restaurants.

I'm a human being too. I'd like to be happy too. You think my casual affairs satisfy me? I too would like to have coffee and a sweet roll *in my own kitchen*. Or lie in bed with a warm wife whose large pink bottom sticks out from under the blanket. I'm human too. (Turn on the music here.) I too would like to have a wife who is beautiful, who fills me with joy to look at. Don't I deserve that? But even now, after all the distance I've come from the Hotel Diplomat, I still don't have enough money to get married, or at least enough money to marry the kind of woman I want.

Who really needs me? Nobody. My boss is going to take part in a car race in California again, pulling a helmet down over his head and taking the steering wheel in his hands. He thinks he's a goddamn Paul Newman. During his absence I will of course be free to play and fill up the house with girls, but they still won't be the right ones. I want the expensive kind, like the girl-stranger who fucked me in the basement. Please forgive me my obsession with rich girls, gentlemen, but how could it be other-wise, since I measure life by women? They're the only ones who light up this world. There's nobody else. And they give the world its purpose, its excitement, and its movement.

What beauty is going to stand by and wait while I finally make the heroic effort to crawl out of this kitchen and become famous and maybe even rich? I thought sadly. What I'm striving for, the material part of what I'm striving for, Steven Grey has had since birth. No woman's going to take my stupid road with me. Who needs excuses like, "You know, I'm still a failure right now, but I'm very talented; wait, dear, just a little longer!" Why should she listen to my stories about the lunches and breakfasts I made and how I shined the boss's shoes and went shopping and suffered physically and spiritually, and sat by the window, just as I was doing then, and got depressed?

What woman is going to be interested in me when she can make the acquaintance of somebody who's already there, who already has something— of Steven Grey, six feet two, bearded, forty years old, and the owner of numerous elegant companies? "Who the fuck am I to beautiful women!" I yelled, pounding my fist on the table. The glass with ice fell off the table and broke on the kitchen floor. It was apparently the sight of gold that had brought on that little fit of hysteria, and the Kuwaitis, rich as swine, and the whiskey I'd drunk, very good and strong. "Who the fuck am I to them!" I repeated. Steven's rich and has a house that looks romantically out onto a garden and the river. What do I have? An old suitcase as old as I am given to me by my parents and a couple of obscure books in Russian I wrote in anger and disgust with the world.

Christ, how sick and tired I am of them all! I thought. I'd like to go into the dining room during lunch sometime, and instead of clearing away the dirty dishes and serving them salad and a cheese tray, spray the boss and his wine-drinking friends with a few rounds from an AK-47 or a no-less-celebrated Israeli Uzi! That day would have been a very good day for it—the fairy-tale Kuwaiti sheiks were an even more tempting mission than Steven Grey was. (The servant Limonov imagined the blood-spattered sheiks on the Persian cushions, imagined them slowly falling over onto the cushions.) It's possible that one of the Kuwaitis

287

even fucked my Elena, I thought, that he burst into her pink cunt with his black prick. Why not? It's very possible in fact, I reasoned to myself.

And what was it all given to them for, those billions? I tried to comprehend. I'm not exactly sure what for, maybe simply because there was oil on their land. Probably that's all. Mere luck? All right. And Lodyzhnikov got what he has simply because the bourgeoisie happens at present to like ballet—ballet has taken its fancy—and pays hard cash. More luck. My Gatsby was left money by his father, luck again, right?

That's a lot of luck, don't you think? And I for some reason haven't been so lucky. True, it could all have been different with me. If I had written different books, I wouldn't be a servant sitting by the kitchen window now; if I had exposed Russia and its social system in a talented way, if I'd helped America in its ideological struggle against Russia, I'd be sitting on my own estate like Solzhenitsyn. Or I'd be speeding around the streets of Hollywood in a Rolls-Royce, hopping from party to party, and since I'm still fairly young, I'd have as many of my beloved rich whores as I could want. What am I doing in the kitchen?

After my monologue I picked up the *New York Post,* which Gatsby in his haste hadn't had time to read, and immersed myself in that yellow rag. Jenny's brother Michael Jackson had warned me about reading such trash, but I still read it. The *Village Voice* is full of lies too, only liberal ones.

It turned out a lord had been murdered the day before, a cousin of the Queen of England. A handsome lord, old, tall, and majestic. A former admiral with connections to India—its last viceroy. The Irish killed him; they want independence from Britain. To live on their own. Obviously they think killing lords will immediately solve all their problems—the hunchbacks will stand up straight, all those who don't have money will perhaps suddenly have it, and the impotent will at once find their cocks suffused with the blood of life. The simple common sense of a housekeeper suggests to me that the hunchbacks will remain hunchbacked and that the national state will help neither the impotent nor the dispossessed, although those who guide those murderers will certainly take their places among the Big Brothers—without a doubt. They never miss.

A powerful bomb exploded on the lord's fishing boat. There were two pages of photographs in the *Post* devoted to the lord's life. Pictures of him walking majestically with a rajah, and standing like a tower to one side of an old man suffering from dystrophy and wrapped up in a piece of white cloth—the old Ghandi. And the lord's wife standing on the other side like another tower. And an Indian landscape in the background.

I averted my eyes from the newspaper and wondered why they regretted the lord's death by bombing so much. He would have gotten sick or expired of old age, bedridden and barely able to open his mouth, smelling bad and annoying his servants and no longer in possession of his faculties. Would that really have been better? This way he died like a soldier, the way he should have, blown up by a bomb. I envied him. A man ought not live to the point where he has to crawl. It's ugly and dirty.

A few pages later in the newspaper I found, by way of illustration for my thoughts, a picture of a hospital ward with several human bodies hooked up to artificial life-support equipment. The caption under the picture said they'd been lying like that for years. Vegetables. Why keep them going? What's the purpose of that degradation? I'd rip the hoses from everybody hooked up to life-support equipment. I'd go around to all the hospitals and cut the hoses or turn off all the switches. Cruel? No, honest, even noble.

Something we don't understand has happened to us, to people, to the human race. We've gone down a dead end, maybe, or we have developed in some mistaken way. I don't know what, but something's wrong, I told myself while rummaging through the paper. And then the telephone rang.

It was an acquaintance of mine, somebody whom I had inherited from Jenny and Martha and who at one time had been Martha's boyfriend. He's twenty-five to twenty-eight and works as an assistant manager at the huge Waldorf-Astoria. His name is James, James O'Brien. Even the disciplined and hard-working Martha used to call James a slave— Martha, who never missed a day of work! Probably James O'Brien deserved that epithet. James occasionally drops by the kitchen out of habit to chat with Linda and me for a while, just as he did with Martha. Linda and I don't encourage him, but we don't chase him away either. We tolerate him.

"Do you want to go to a movie, Edward?" O'Brien said over the phone. "I and my boss, Youssef, are going to one tonight. Several girls are coming with us." James has very refined manners, and so he added, "I'm sure you'll like the film very much, Edward; it's *The Seduction of Joe Tynan*. It deals with intellectual problems very important for our time."

I wavered. Another time I'd have refused without hesitating—I usually don't go out when Steven's staying overnight— but that day or the next was a damned full moon, and I was already a little crazy, or maybe it was just that I was getting sick of it all.

"All right," I said to O'Brien, "let's go to a movie." And attempting to find out more, I added, "And what about the girls, are they nice?"

"One of them is very nice and very intellectual," O'Brien answered with the voice of a robot. "She isn't going with anybody, and you can have her if you want, Edward." James is fond of words like "intellect" and "intellectual."

"Okay," I said. "We'll see how it works. Where are you meeting?"

The Egyptian Youssef was planning to drop by James's house, and so I set off there too, a place I'd never been before. James

lived, it turned out, not far from me or the Waldorf-Astoria—
on Fifty-fourth Street near the corner of Madison.

Despite his excellent address, I realized almost as soon as I set
foot in his apartment that I'd come to him from another life.
Everything in the apartment was shabby and of poor quality and
messy. A filthy couch, a couple of silly faded hassocks of indeter-
minate color, and a dark blue carpet which James had picked up
at his hotel for nothing, as he immediately bragged. He still
hadn't managed to put the carpet down, and I found him cutting it up when I came in. Either James was a jerk-off and
couldn't put his one room in order—and he could have made it
attractive; it even had a fireplace—or maybe I as a servant of the
world bourgeoisie had already gotten so spoiled by the millionaire's house that all life outside it seemed paltry and dirty. I
don't know, but the impression made on me by my visit to
O'Brien's apartment was disheartening, even though we left almost immediately after the Egyptian Youssef showed up.
Youssef, O'Brien's boss, was a short but very self-assured person, and he somehow calmed me down. He reeked of sweet
perfume.

We were supposed to meet the girls near the Little Carnegie
theater next to Carnegie Hall and the Russian Tea Room.
There's always a crowd of people there, including a lot of girls,
and as I strode down Fifty-seventh Street with O'Brien and
Youssef I tried to make out in the distance which ones were
ours. I was in for a disappointment, unfortunately. Ours were
the worst. Two short, frightful-looking girls carrying purses and
dressed in baggy jeans and something like slippers, with asses
that almost dragged on the ground, and both wearing shabby
velvet jackets. I got very upset, since I was wearing white boots
from Valentino's, blue and white striped pants, and a white
jacket. With my tan I probably looked foreign and very mysterious, and now I was going to have to walk down the street with
these eyesores. The girls felt awkward with me too, I think, but

who could have foreseen such a situation? James was always neatly dressed and wore gold-rimmed glasses, so there was no way I could have known he would have such eyesores for girlfriends. He worked like a slave, Mr. O'Brien, sometimes even two shifts in succession—twelve hours a day, and he was on his way up, hoping someday to become manager of the Waldorf-Astoria Towers. Millionaires always stay at the Towers, as do heads of state and their wives, and the world's few remaining kings. Come on, O'Brien, I thought, a careerist should have better girls.

"You're always in such good shape, Edward," O'Brien said to me in passing, his eyeglasses flashing. He obviously sensed that I was holding myself a bit aloof and was unhappy with the girls' appearance. "Do you exercise?"

What the hell would I need to exercise for? I thought. All I had to do was spend fifteen years of my life half-starved, so that now that I have enough to eat, I'm no longer capable of getting fat. I muttered something innocuous to O'Brien.

Our whole group, I thought, I, a housekeeper, and they, the employees of a fashionable hotel, remind me of the crowd that went around with Clyde Griffiths, the hero of *An American Tragedy*, a big two-volume book I read many years ago in Russia after discovering it in my parents' library.

The movie turned out to be extremely boring—about a senator and his personal life. The senator's wife leaves him. And she leaves him at the very moment he's nominated for President at a party convention. And his lover leaves him, and his daughter doesn't love him, only it isn't clear why. And the daughter's so hysterical, it's as if she's forty and not fifteen. But the senator's career is more important: he loves his work; he's a bureaucrat by calling. And even though he's unhappy in his private life, he's nominated as the party's candidate, and the crowd applauds, and even the senators who are his enemies applaud, and the balloons go up, and the music thunders and roars. And everybody in the

theater learns that the senator too is a human being. As for me, I
never doubted it, even without the film. A senator once stayed
with us briefly at the millionaire's house. Not for very long, but
long enough for me to understand that he too was a human
being.

The senator came from the airport one evening in a limousine
with a briefcase and bag. We briefly introduced ourselves to
each other. He said he was a senator; I told him I was the
housekeeper. In appearance he looked rather like a male
model—the face of an actor who does lotion ads. You know, a
very masculine face, tanned, with large, massive features. A "real
man." The first thing he asked me after putting his briefcase and
bag in the guest room on the third floor was whether he could
bring a lady to spend the night and where the cognac was, since
he was planning to come back late. He also asked me to show
him how to turn on our complicated television equipment. The
servant Limonov showed him how everything in our movie theater worked—which buttons to push and in what sequence. I
also showed him where the cognac was, not even forgetting to
point out where we kept the snifters, rarely ever used, since cognac makes the master's face break out. With regard to the lady,
the servant brazenly informed him that whether or not he
brought a lady back to the house with him was of course a personal matter the senator would have to decide for himself, but
that if I was not mistaken, Nancy was supposed to come down
from Connecticut early the next morning. "Nancy has urgent
business in New York," I cheerfully lied.

The limousine waited for the senator. I handed him a key and
showed him how to open the door. I had no intention of staying up for him; in fact, I planned to go to bed. Although already on his way out, he still stuck me with an errand—to call
Room 816 at the Park Lawn Hotel and say that the senator was
already on his way and would meet the lady in the lobby. I
closed the door behind the senator, went to the kitchen, dialed
the number, asked for Room 816, whereupon a sweet little

293

voice, redolent of perfume, and belonging, I'll bet, to an elegant young whore, drawled into the phone, "Y-e-e-s?"

"The senator has already left for the hotel and will meet the lady in the lobby," I said in the conspiratorial voice of a movie spy and hung up.

So I already knew something about senators. While I was watching the movie, I tried to think of an excuse I could use to leave my companions as soon as it was over. It was clear to me that it would be even more tedious afterward. We would go to the cheapest restaurant we could find, maybe even a coffee-shop, and after we'd eaten, O'Brien and Youssef and the girls would add up how much money each person owed, even writing it down with a ballpoint pen on a paper placemat, and there would be yet more boredom and awkwardness. By the time the movie was over I had come up with something. I told them I was expecting a phone call from Europe that night, that somebody was supposed to call me from France at a certain time, and I had to be home when they did. I left them at an intersection with a sense of relief. The Egyptian was unquestionably glad to see me go, and parted with me in a very friendly way. Now he can certainly fuck one of the draggle-ass girls, I thought. If I had stayed, he wouldn't have been able to. The Egyptian reasoned very practically—since a cunt was already there and indeed walking nearby, it remained only to bring matters to a conclusion. With me, aesthetics and social issues inevitably get mixed with the business of fucking. Thank God there are normal people too.

I went home by myself, independent and mysterious, went back to my own elegant East Side and as far away as possible from ordinary people and their petty lives. It was better not to be with anybody. Or to have only my professional relationship with my boss—I wasn't ashamed of him, at least. He's rich and healthy. I was ashamed of the casual acquaintances I'd just made, for some reason.

After I got home, I had something to eat and then wandered

around the house. As I'd suspected, the boss still wasn't home; he was obviously staying over at his lady's place. I sat in the TV room, flipping back and forth among the channels for a fairly long time. If the boss turned up, I would hear the door close and have time to slip up to my room. Not that there's anything in the house I'm not supposed to do. It's just that I like to avoid those evening encounters with him and his ladies for my own reasons, out of my own sense of delicacy. I went to bed at four A.M. feeling closer to Gatsby than to anybody else on earth—odd, isn't it, gentlemen? As I was falling asleep, I made a discovery; I suddenly understood the reason for my being in the millionaire's house. I needed the atmosphere of dreams, and the millionaire's house is the closest thing to dreams there is in this life. Further from normal life and closer to dreams, I thought and then fell asleep.

I was already up by six and sitting in a pine oil bath. Through the skylight above me I could hear that the birds had just awakened and were beginning to sing, and I too was cheerfully singing a song: "I wanna fuck somebody who is good. . . ." A busy day lay ahead, and here I was copying the boss, even down to the bath oil, which I'd swiped from his bathroom. Steven's bathroom is located downstairs right underneath my own, and opening the dumb waiter, I could hear radio music and water pouring into his bathtub too. We were both up.

At seven, the housekeeper Edward, dressed in black serving pants and a white Pierre Cardin shirt and wearing a quilted Chinese jacket, was raking up the dry September leaves from the terrace and putting them in a big plastic bag. The mornings had grown cool, but the garden was still very beautiful. Steven was expecting the president of Rolls-Royce for lunch, and I, energetic and thoughtful servant that I am, and knowing the boss's habits as I do, was sure that either before or after lunch Gatsby would take the president of Rolls-Royce and the other businessmen accompanying him out to the garden to sit in the late

September sunshine and drink coffee on iron benches right by the East River and go through their papers there. That's why the hard-working Edward decided to clear the terrace of the leaves that had already accumulated there in considerable quantities—so that they wouldn't hinder the hard-working businessmen.

At the height of my pastoral labors on the terrace, Steven came out with the newspaper and a cup of the coffee that had already been waiting for him in the kitchen.

"Good morning, Edward!" he said. "What a beautiful day!"

"Good morning, Steven," the servant answered. "It is beautiful!" And I continued with what I was doing—raking and putting the leaves in a bag. It was very beautiful that morning, just as in Germany, in Bavaria on the Rhine, and the variegated colors of the dying leaves put me in a festive mood. The air was heavy with the fragrance of dead plants already beginning to rot, tiny blue berries were falling in great numbers onto the terrace from the ivy on our house, and around the servant and his master, birds of an unknown species whirled, trying to grab their share of the morning's exchange of capital and labor. I like the pastoral life very much, and although it's usually hard for me to spend very much time in the country, I enjoy working on our terrace, and following Nancy's example, I even plant things there from time to time, say new azalea bushes wherever there are bare spots around its perimeter, and this fall I'll plant some tulips.

I was just sweeping up, while Steven, his hair still wet, read his paper, when the telephone rang for the first time. It was 7:30. My ex-wife Elena on the other side of the globe would just be going to bed. Steven answered the phone himself, reaching it before I was able to, and talked for a while, and then came back out onto the terrace and said it had been Nairobi calling.

"It was the man who may soon become the premier of Uganda, Edward," Gatsby boasted to me—there wasn't anybody else around.

I thought the boss would in that case probably be undertaking some sort of business in Uganda, starting rabbit or chicken farms there in order to develop their national economy, and would be feverishly trading with them, in oil maybe, since Ghupta had some. Only recently Ghupta and his attorney had been negotiating from my kitchen phone (!) for the purchase of a new tanker. They concluded their business at two o'clock, doing the figures on a calculator and calling from the kitchen all over the world, and the next day all the necessary documents arrived by express mail and they signed them. I wondered if Gatsby was aware of it. We could therefore transport oil to Uganda on Ghupta's tanker. Maybe Gatsby would even send me to Uganda to do something on his behalf, trading in some rubbish that was absolutely essential to underdeveloped countries. Anything was possible. I remembered Rimbaud wending his way to Khartoum by caravan, or maybe it was back from Khartoum. . . .

Linda arrived. Steven went upstairs to change from his bathrobe into a suit, and I finished my work on the terrace and went in to set the table, covering it with our cleanest and whitest tablecloth and putting out the flatware. We spend fabulous sums on laundry each month, and I have my own things done with Steven's, so everything I own gleams and I look as well-groomed and fresh as our silver and tablecloths do—not like my business affairs, thank God.

My business affairs were in a terrible state. Harper & Row had turned me down a few days before. Who hasn't turned me down? I thought. Soon there'll hardly be any left who haven't. Defeat after defeat on that, my principal front. It would be better to have a falling out with Gatsby; I could stand that somehow. The main problem is that I can't get involved personally in that fucking bureaucratic business of selling. I'm compelled to sit passively and wait.

I put out the glasses and continued the same line of thought: Waiting for decisions from unknown office forces, from people

297

you've never seen even once in your life and never will see is just like being condemned to death and sending your appeal to one court and having to wait months for an answer. In the end they send you a paper with a "no," and you then appeal to another court, since you can. And you wait again, and then after months have gone by, another "no" surfaces from the bureaucratic depths. You are on the verge of terror and hysteria and in despair, since you still fear death, and their decisions in those Kafkaesque inner offices have nothing to do with your work, or with who you are and what you have created. Houses of Terror and Fate—that's what publishers are.

Long gone are the simple patriarchal times when you took what you had written directly to the publisher himself, and said, "Hi, Bob (or John or Moses)! Here's my book. I'm convinced it will do well. Let's make a deal! I'm young and energetic, and this is my most recent work."

And Bob (or John or Moses) read the book and after scratching the back of his head, said, "Okay, Ed, I think this book will bring in something, it will earn us some money, although there's a risk of course, but all right, we're ready take it. . . ." Those were the good old days!

I knew a fair number of people in Russia who were willing to sit in prison for years just so their books could be published. Many got involved in the social struggle and came into conflict with the government for that reason alone. Does that seem like a normal situation to you? But the same kind of barriers are erected in the individual's path in absolutely every area of life, the servant thought, and such are the daily murders that civilization inflicts on us.

The nice thing about physical labor is that sometimes it allows you to give yourself up to your thoughts while you're doing it. I ordered lamb chops over the phone.

"All right, Edward," one of the Ottomanelli brothers said, "you'll get your lamb chops. But maybe you'd rather have sirloin? We have some excellent fresh sirloin today."

"No thanks," I said. "We're conservative. The boss wants lamb."

"Okay!" the Ottomanelli brother laughed.

I spent the next fifteen minutes or so trying to extract a check from Linda. She bounced around like a billiard ball the whole time as she took one phone call after another, half of them making no sense at all, while I sat disgustedly in the Chinese lacquered chair next to her desk and waited. There was no way Linda was going to interrupt one of her goddamn phone conversations just to write me a check.

"How much do you need?" she finally asked me in a suspicious tone.

"Give me a hundred and fifty," the housekeeper said.

"What do you need a hundred and fifty for? That seems like a lot. Steven's leaving tomorrow. You're not going to spend a hundred and fifty dollars on one lunch, are you? After all, you won't have to pay cash for the meat, Edward. Take a hundred," Linda said.

"And you, my dear, aren't you going to eat anything tomorrow or the next day? Aren't you going to have lunch too?" I asked her snidely.

She gave me a hundred and fifty. She's the boss's own Cerberus, that Linda.

I stuck the check in my pocket and leisurely set off for the bank. When you're around money, when you find yourself rubbing up against it all the time, you tend to have a certain unhurried confidence in yourself. Until I started working for Steven, I used to be afraid of banks and always felt like a timid pauper in them. I'm much bolder now. I even lost my temper once when a new teller asked me to endorse the back of a check for Steven made out, I think, for $1,500—cash for one of his trips. As I signed my name, I disgustedly told the bank slave, "Listen, you, I come here, at a minimum, twice a week, and sometimes more often, and nobody has ever asked me to endorse one of our checks before." For on its face the check carries the proud name of Mr. Grey. But I didn't say that to the slave. I thought it.

The produce markets in our excellent city of the devil are for some reason run by Koreans, just as in Moscow all the boot-blacks are Assyrians. A Korean girl with a flat intellectual face always greets me with a smile whenever I enter her store; I'm a regular customer. I picked out my invariable romaine, some asparagus, and whatever else I felt like, and with one hand in my pocket set off for home in the same unhurried manner. On the way I dropped in on the chubby Michael at the little shop Mad for Cheese to pick up some cheese and bread, the bread so fresh that Linda has been expressing her amazement with it every day for the past year and gobbling it up as if she were mad for bread. I walked back to the house very slowly, since it was still early, and the day was the kind I like. In general I like the fall. In the fall I listen to myself with particular attention; in the fall everything's clearer and makes more sense to me and is less confining.

That day it became clear to me for the first time that I would soon be moving out of the millionaire's little house. I still didn't know how, and it still wasn't even clear when, but the first signal had already reached me from somewhere. I didn't make any decisions about it then; I just continued my leisurely way back to the house in my old Chinese jacket. I picked up that jacket after Henry had left it, or perhaps it was left by one of his friends, and the host never mentioned it. I wasn't ready to make any decisions then, but I know myself well. I've moved around in my life so often and have completely changed the scene of action and the cast of players so many times, that I've learned that if I once start thinking about leaving, it means I will. Even the millionaire's house has outlived its usefulness. It will be three years next spring since I entered it, and that's enough. Other lands and countries and women, and other adventures, beckon to me. If I stay here I'll turn out like Linda, but I don't have the right to do that, to stay in the same place for eight years. I don't have eight years. I need to get my ass out of here, I thought with a happy smile, as I opened the door with my key. Nearby they were shooting a commercial, and a beautiful model—they just won't leave me alone—smiled at me as she straightened her hair while the photographer fiddled with his camera. Maybe she thought the house was mine.

The president of Rolls-Royce came in a Rolls-Royce. But not the elegant white-lacquered and chrome-plated kind that black pimps drive around Central Park with their white girls by their sides or that high-class drug dealers use. He came in an unpretentious silver-gray Rolls of medium size, the sort that doesn't require a chauffeur with a cap. The Rolls was driven by his business associate, and they both looked quite unpretentious. Steven even came out to meet them, something that doesn't happen very often. He sees his guests to the door, but I open it for them, or, less often, Olga does. I think Gatsby secretly despises the Rolls-Royce company for the slightly vulgar nature of its product, maybe for precisely the fact that pimps and drug dealers drive around in their cars. Drug dealers and pimps don't drive around in Steven's cars, even though they're produced in far fewer numbers than Rolls-Royces are (and cost almost as much). "Our" cars are as staid as an old English conservative tweed suit and don't look like much at first sight, but the expert will note their restrained severity of form and color and will appreciate it.

Upstairs in Steven's office I served the group coffee on a silver tray and, for the president, specially brewed tea in a silver teapot, or rather, I left it with them, letting them serve it themselves since they had already spread their papers out and didn't need my interference, and went back downstairs to the kitchen.

After a while Steven came into the kitchen and asked, "How's it coming, Edward?"

I said that if they were ready, I could have lunch on the table in five minutes.

"Excellent!" Steven exclaimed, and dove into the cellar to select a wine to go with the meal. You can always tell unerringly by the quality of the wine just how much value Steven places in his guests. He wanted these, as I guessed, to share a distribution network with him, that is, to undertake to sell his cars too. No doubt they have a very good network; indeed, as a powerful firm, why shouldn't they? It turned out I was right. Steven came back with two bottles of Château Haut-Brion, 1961. Oho, I thought, he's treating them first-class! Even the fact that Linda had warned me the day before to be sure to wear my black serving pants, white shirt, and a jacket ("Steven asked me to tell you," Linda diplomatically put it), even that fact underscored the importance of what was taking place.

I've gotten spoiled as the servant of the world bourgeoisie, and have even permitted myself to serve lunch to Steven and his people dressed in a T-shirt with the legend "Cocaine Is Hazardous to Your Health!" printed on it. Or else, East Side patriot that I am, I prance around in another shirt given to me by Bridget in her day with the words "IRT Lines" on it—the New York IRT subway line, that is, the main East Side line hidden under Lexington Avenue. That T-shirt had once belonged to Richard Hell himself, to our number one New York punk rock star. Bridget's boyfriend Douglas had once been Richard Hell's drummer. In that T-shirt, slashed here and there with a razor blade—intentionally slashed— Richard Hell had given newspaper interviews. And I, after sewing up just a couple of holes in that punk rock relic, wear it around Gatsby. My "fall" didn't happen all at once, but gradually. In the beginning, I dressed every day in black pants and a white shirt.

Gatsby and the Rolls-Royceans sat down at the table and I served them lamb and steamed vegetables, which I can't stand myself, and then whistled upstairs, by that whistle inviting Linda to assume her place at the kitchen table with me. Mr. Richardson was supposed to have lunch with Linda and me too, since he was at the house every day now, working on Gatsby's latest fantastical project. This one concerned the allocation of the Southeast Asian labor force. Gatsby, along with some big international corporations, wanted to put to work the unfortunate boat people who had been hacked to pieces by Malay pirates or by Thai fishermen. As you see, Gatsby thinks in global terms and strives to extend his power over mankind; he's a typical Big Brother. Usually Mr. Richardson has lunch with Steven when the latter's at the house, but that day was a special case. Mr. Richardson doesn't have any part in the automobile business, so he was having lunch in the kitchen with the secretary and the housekeeper.

Linda and Richardson came downstairs and took their places at the kitchen table. I sat down with them, chewing a piece of meat. I poured myself a bottle of Guinness and started listening to what they were saying.

"Perf!" said Linda, after trying a lamb chop. "Perf! You've really learned how to cook lamb, Edward."

"Perf" means "perfect" in Linda's private slang. She also uses the term "delish," short for "delicious" and no less important to her vocabulary.

Linda was telling Mr. Richardson with a serious expression that she had the day before reheated some spaghetti and that it was better reheated than fresh. I grinned ironically. I didn't actually believe that it was only the first time in her life that she had reheated spaghetti. She's probably lying, I thought, pretending she lives better than she really does. But I refrained from making any comment. Let Linda tell Richardson whatever she likes and play at the high life; what difference did it make to me? If she'd started lying about politics, I'd have gotten into it, but lying about food was harmless enough.

Linda then started describing to Richardson how she and her black belt in karate, David, had been invited for dinner the previous weekend at the house of some friends on Long Island. The dinner was a candlelight affair with classical music— Vivaldi had been playing in the living room the whole time. Right,

I thought ironically. Vivaldi is good for the digestion. Linda and her friends can't invite a symphony orchestra to assist with their digestion the way Gatsby does, so they eat to records.

I left to clear away the empty dishes for the boss and the Rolls-Royceans. "Tank yu verri mach!" Gatsby said to me with a Russian accent. The Rolls-Royceans thanked me too. Since the boss was fucking around, it meant he was in a good mood. The business had therefore gone well and they would be selling his cars. I served Steven and his comrades salad and after coming back to the kitchen gossiped to Linda and Richardson about how things stood. This gave them an excuse to shift the conversation to the boss, our usual topic, although from time to time Linda and I pledge not to talk about him, at least not while we are having lunch.

"Oh, Steven's in a very good mood," Richardson said. "I've noticed in general that he's become more human. Perhaps because he's getting older? He's much less irritable than he was a couple of years ago."

And Linda agreed that it seemed to her too that he was getting better. We all happily started talking at once. Why not, our savage was turning into more of a human being. Excellent! Marvelous! Fantastic! And then in the midst of our enthusiasm it suddenly occurred to me, Does that mean he won't get pissed off? And I went to see what the gentlemen at the table were doing. The gentlemen were still confabulating over the remaining salad and cheese. I asked them if they wanted coffee, and they happily consented. After clearing away their dirty dishes once again, I served coffee and returned to the kitchen. It turned out Polly had just called, and the conversation therefore passed naturally to a discussion of Gatsby's sexual capacities.

I announced: "I don't believe that Steven's sexual indices are that high. In my view, he's probably crude and primitive in bed. Even though he's a strong guy, it still seems to me that all he's capable of is very simple sex of the in and out type, and not even that for very long."

304

Linda seconded me and even generalized my thesis, saying that in her opinion all WASPS are uninteresting in bed, their puritan upbringing having deprived them of sensuality. For Linda this last remark had a particular point, since her boyfriend David was a Jew.

I didn't want to offend Linda, and so I didn't tell her that I didn't have that high an opinion of Jewish men either. And so we took up the case of Gatsby again, whom his relative Mr. Richardson defended. And of course not merely because he was Gatsby's relative, since he often referred to Gatsby ironically, but also because Mr. Richardson was a WASP himself; he was offended on behalf of all WASPs. Which is quite understandable. After all, who wants the reputation of being worthless as a man, especially if you acquire that reputation only because the nation you belong to is regarded as undersexed? The battle began in earnest.

I didn't really want to insult WASPs, but I did have my own stake in the quarrel. I would like to have told them that in my opinion artistic people were much more interesting in bed than businessmen. No question about it. But I couldn't. Mr. Richardson would probably be as offended on behalf of businessmen as he already is on behalf of WASPs, I thought. I had already tried once to talk to Richardson about Dostoevsky, stressing that the profession of writer is an exceptional one. To which Mr. Richardson answered in an irritated tone that everyone invests a part of his labor and talent in the world, and that as a businessman he, Richardson, did too. And then he brought in the usual businessman's propaganda—that they, businessmen, are important to the world, that they give people work. . . , and other such slogans from his arsenal.

I thought then that Richardson is Richardson and Dosteovsky is Dostoevsky, but out loud I merely said that a writer's possibilities are greater, since he deals with ideas, and since he does deal with ideas, he's a lot more powerful and even dangerous. But even my hint that a writer may be a villain couldn't dislodge Mr. Richardson from his firmly held conviction that the businessmen of the world constitute a special caste, a conviction that he well knew how to conceal behind demagogic assertions that everyone invests the same amount of labor in the world.

I remembered an idea of mine and decided to share it with Linda and Richardson. I was interested in what they would say. Linda sometimes listens to me. She pretty much regards me as a "crazy Russian," but sometimes I say intelligent things.

"Listen, comrade Americans!" (I always adopt a jocular tone whenever I want to speak to Linda about serious things.) "Listen," I said. "It seems to me that you, and please excuse the necessary generalization, always tend to take a mechanistic approach to the problems of life and mankind. That is, you approach man the same way you'd approach an automobile or a tractor. I'm not saying you don't admit the existence of the soul," I continued, laughing, "but you have the presumption to approach both the soul and its problems mechanistically. Even your methods of healing people, psychoanalysis, say, are at bottom predicated on repair, just like the repair of an automobile or a tractor. . . .

"Even your drug revolution," I continued, "with all its so-called radicalism, with Timothy Leary and the other prophets of LSD, hallucinogenic mushrooms, and other garbage for the salvation of mankind, hasn't introduced anything essentially new. It's also a consequence of this mechanistic approach to man as a machine. You want to be happy? Swallow an LSD tablet or gobble up some mushroom spores, and you'll be instantly happy. And all mankind will be happy too. It's quick, of course. . . ."

Here Mr. Richardson started protesting. I stopped him with my hand. "Sometimes it seems to me that you Americans—a generalization again; forgive me, but I can't help it—that you're much more steeped in primitive Marxism than the Russians are. The Russians are way behind you. You're always repeating the magic word economics. You explain everything in economic terms, and you persist in believing that every event in the world is attributable to economic causes. Both wars and revolutions— everything. I regard that as a naïve point of view that's at least a century out of date. There's no question that bread is a motivation in the world, but it's not the only one, or even the main one. Overpopulated India has been starving for all the thousands of years of its history, and yet it's never had any revolutions to speak of. There's something higher than bread, namely human spiritual energy. . . . Heroism . . ."

Suddenly realizing from Linda's and Richardson's faces that this new topic left them more indifferent than I had hoped, I leapt to another. "All right," I said, "forget heroism, and take the historical event that's closest to us, the Iranian revolution. How can you explain that in economic terms? The Shah improved the well-being of his country; there's no question about that. According to statistics, the population of Iran before the revolution enjoyed the highest standard of living in Iranian history. But the revolution still happened; it follows that it wasn't economics that caused the revolution, true? Perhaps it was something else then?"

Linda and Richardson started objecting. . . . They agreed with me on some things, and not on others. It wasn't that we were divided into two camps—a Russian against the Americans, two Americans against a Russian. America and Americans had long since ceased to be foreign to me. I had been living in New York going on five years, and I didn't have much sense of myself as a Russian, though, yes, I did feel like a European sometimes.

As in all our other kitchen discussions, we didn't reach a common view. They suddenly got tired of "politics," and Mr. Richardson started praising my English. "I'll admit when you first came here to work, Edward, I got a headache every time I talked to you on the phone," he said, laughing. "Now you talk like anybody else. You still have an accent, of course, but it actually gives your English a certain interest. The girls obviously find it charming."

"Edward's biggest weakness is pronunciation," Linda said. "His vocabulary is extremely large—sometimes he even uses words I don't know very well—but he can't use his whole vocabulary because he doesn't know how to pronounce the words. Get yourself a grammar book, Edward, and learn the pronunciation rules," she concluded. "I've been telling you that for a year. If you like, I'll get one for you; I'm going to Barnes and Noble next week."

"Sure, get one for me," I happily agreed. "I'll pay you back immediately."

"If you don't, I'll deduct it from your salary," Linda laughed. "Edward once managed to get me in a snit with his pronunciation," she told Richardson. She laughed and continued. "You remember last summer when they broke into the house next door, of course, the one that belongs to Mrs. Five Hundred Million. The thieves came through the garden, cut out part of the door with a saw, and broke into the house and stole her paintings and other valuables. The special alarm system she had in every room didn't do any good; they just cut the wires."

Linda told her story and Mr. Richardson shook his head in horror. He and his family live in Massachusetts, and it scares him to hear about our New York crimes.

"So the day after the robbery," she continued, "Edward came upstairs to my office with a newspaper," and here Linda tried to reproduce my accent: "'Leesen, Leenda. Zat is zee edvartizingh in niuspepper. . . .'"

I yelled indignantly that that wasn't fair, that I'd never spoken with such a wooden accent, but Linda dismissed me with a wave and continued, though dropping the accent. "'Send $399 and in two weeks you'll get a new machine gun cheaper than any life insurance you can buy. Insure your lives with our machine gun, Americans!' And the address," Linda concluded triumphantly, "was 'Kunoxville, Tennessee'!"

Mr. Richarson laughed long and sincerely. And after he stopped laughing, he repeated "Kunoxville, Tennessee!" and looked at me, smiling. I laughed too and looked at Linda; she loves to tell that story. I waited for the end, which contained my victory over Linda.

"I told him," Linda continued very seriously, "Edward! You don't say 'I kunow'; you say 'I know' with a silent 'k,' so why do you pronounce it 'Kunoxville'? Memorize the rule, Edward; if there's a consonant after the 'k,' the 'k' isn't pronounced in English. Or an even better rule is, if there's an 'n' after the 'k,' the 'k' is always silent. Always. Don't forget it, Edward, it's 'Noxville.'

"Do you know what he said to me?" Linda asked Richardson. This was the point of the whole story. Richardson didn't know. Of course not. "He said, 'Are you sure? What about those delicious little things made of dough? Knishes!'"

Mr. Richardson howled with delight. "Knishes! Knishes!" he repeated, and Linda looked at him in triumph.

"'Knish' isn't English, of course, but a word that's been taken from Yiddish," Linda said, "but it really is just about the only example where a 'k' standing before an 'n' is pronounced."

After he'd had a good laugh, Mr. Richardson asked me, "What did you want a machine gun from Kunoxville, Tennessee, for, Edward?"

"What for?" I said. "Before they broke into Mrs. Five Hundred Million's house, they robbed Mr. Carlson's house. They went through the garden the same way. And did you read in the papers about what happened in the Berkshires recently? An owner's twenty-year-old son and his housekeeper, a seventy-year-old woman, were killed by robbers. I want to live! I don't have the slightest desire to die for the sake of your step-brother's carpets and sterling. As you perfectly well know, our front door has only one lock. And your absent-minded brother leaves the doors open all night, both the front door and the door to the garden. Our alarm system has never worked, not even while

Jenny was here. And the two watchmen who are supposed to guard our block sleep all night. . . . I live alone in the house," I went on passionately, "and I'm scared!"

Richardson looked at me very seriously. "I had no idea that even on such an exceptional block with its own security it was still dangerous," and he shook his head.

The bitch Linda, who doesn't have to live in the house, said soothingly, however, "You're exaggerating the danger, Edward. You could be hit by a car on the street, and the statistics prove indisputably that a lot more people are killed in automobile accidents than by murderers. And anyway, you shouldn't be permitted to get your hands on a machine gun; you'd slaughter us all. Crazy Russian!"

Laughing, she said to Richardson, "Steven even suggested we put up a sign on the front door reading, 'Beware! Mad Russian housekeeper!'"

I laughed too. Linda had no idea that an excellent semi-automatic rifle with a scope has been standing in my room since last summer. In the closet, carefully hidden behind my coats and jackets. Carefully hidden in case somebody should come into my room, but there if I need it. I didn't send to Noxville, Tennessee, for it, however. A friend of mine brought it quietly from Texas in the trunk of his car. I had intended to register it with the police, citing the recent robberies of our neighbors and the fact that I live by myself, but then after thinking it over I decided that as a former Soviet citizen I wouldn't be allowed to keep it.

"It would be even better to keep a tank on the terrace," I said. "Just in case."

We all started laughing and roaring again, each trying to drown out the others. At that instant Steven came into the kitchen and looked at us in amazement. We shut up at once. Linda went back up to her office, back to her desk and the salt mines, I started clearing up the dishes, and Steven took Richardson out to the garden to introduce him to the Rolls-Royceans. I had been right; they did go out into the garden.

I cleaned up while a breeze blew through the kitchen—one of its windows and the door to the garden in the dining room were both open. It was the end of September, with a quiet chill in the air, and I thought about the fact that it was already a full year since I had worked in the country by the Hudson River, and that in the meantime I had gotten a lot stronger and more energetic and livelier, since I'd managed to give both Linda and even Richardson a really good scare.

Peering through the grating in the kitchen window was the smiling black face of Christopher, the cook from the baronial mansion next door. He had brought me a cake, as it turned out, an apple cake. Linda won't let Christopher in the house unless I'm in the kitchen. She doesn't have the patience to wait while Christopher gathers together the few English words he knows and explains what he needs. She unceremoniously sends him packing. "Later, come back later!" she says. The fact is that Christopher's from Martinique and speaks French, not English. Our acquaintance began with his knocking on my door one day in the middle of winter. I opened it and found a black man dressed in slippers, sailcloth pants, and a white T-shirt and hunched over from the cold. The man was mumbling something. I remember a little French from school, a couple of dozen words, and so I succeeded relatively quickly in establishing that he was the cook from next door, and that he had stepped out for a moment and the door had slammed shut behind him. And that there wasn't anybody home at his house, that there was food cooking on their gas range, and that if he didn't get back inside in the next few minutes, there would be a fire. He asked me to let him go through the garden so he could break one of the windows in their door and get back into the house. The windows facing the street in their house are, like our own, covered with heavy gratings.

Naturally I let him into the garden and even went with him to help break out the window. I still had a few window-breaking skills left from my youth. About ten minutes later the black man came back to thank me, and from his confused account I learned that he had knocked on several other doors before mine, but that all the other neighbors had been afraid to let him into the garden. "You are a very good man!" Christopher said to me. I explained that it wasn't that I was a good man—I insisted on that—but that our neighbors were cowardly to a pathological degree.

Whatever, after that episode Christopher became my friend. He's a real cook—not like me. I'm a fraud. Christopher's cakes are delicate and delicious. I don't much like sweets, and so my favorite is the apple, since it's tart.

I poured Christopher a whiskey on the rocks and sat and chatted with him awhile in a garbled mixture of French and English. While we were talking, the doorbell rang—Steven's suits had come back from the cleaner's, brought by another friend of mine, a forty-year-old Puerto Rican named Victor who looks between twenty-five and twenty-eight. I sat him down in the kitchen too and gave him a portion of the yellow elixir. We sat and talked. Steven wasn't likely to come into the kitchen before six, and even if he had come in, he wouldn't have said anything. I have my own responsibilities as housekeeper, and dozens of service people come by the house daily. At Christmas, we give them all gifts so they'll serve us better.

Linda came down to the kitchen and upon seeing my Internationale seated on white chairs, immediately started choking with laughter. I can't stand it when she comes downstairs to the kitchen to rinse her teeth, which she does noisily and at length several times a day, each time using a clean glass.

"Edward," she said maliciously after rinsing her jaws, "aren't you planning to go to Bloomingdale's? I hope you remember that Steven asked you to get him two dozen pairs of underpants; he's leaving tomorrow morning, you know."

Linda loves to spoil my fun. Actually, though, I didn't mind going to Bloomingdale's, especially since I planned to use the occasion to buy several pairs of underpants for myself and stick Linda with the bill. If I got away with it and she didn't notice the quantity but only the amount of the charge, I'd get free underpants.

I left the house with Christopher and the Puerto Rican and set off to Bloomingdale's in the cool autumn sunshine to buy my employer underwear. Linda used to do it before, and not Jenny, as I had assumed. Jenny, it turns out, didn't understand anything about Steven's rags. Now that duty has fallen to me.

Bloomingdale's smelled of expensive perfume and was filled with rich people strolling around with packages of the things they'd bought. In the men's department decency and severity prevailed. I took a long time making my selection, walking around very importantly and looking and sniffing. Shopping is a sacred affair, and must never be hurried. Obviously, I spent less time on his underpants than I did on choosing the nine pairs I got for myself. I even picked out some white ones for myself, and there were dark blue and black ones too. They were of an excellent shape, elegant and not too large. They should never be large—that's vulgar. Expensive underpants, obviously, and pure cotton. Mine were a size smaller than Steven's. I paid and walked away, happily pressing my purchases to my chest.

Coming out of the entrance to Bloomingdale's, the servant felt on top of the world and in command of his life, and he gazed haughtily and invitingly at the sleek, manicured girls and ladies he met. Step aside! Here comes a master of life! And I had only nine pairs of underpants. Three pairs per cylinder.

Admiring the fall, I walked back to the millionaire's house and thought about how much I love my New York and its perpetual nervous activity, and about how I've gotten used to living here, so that I hardly remember Russia anymore—a sweet childhood dream. And as I breathed in the dear autumn air, I thought too that if I had been born to wealth, I would have been a completely different kind of writer, maybe of the Oscar Wilde type, although my spirit would probably have been just as restless as it is now. The leaves were falling and an already very fresh breeze was blowing. The Rolls-Royce was gone when I got home, and I breathed a sigh of relief.

Our barbarian was taking a nap. He was tired. Linda and Mr. Richardson were wagging their tongues on the second floor while Linda automatically dealt herself a hand of solitaire, her one distraction from work. No, excuse me, I forgot her other passion. Whenever Linda has some free time, she carefully diagrams on a piece of graph paper a project for the reorganization of her "closet"—her storage room, that is. She diagrams the project over and over with a zeal that would have been the envy of the planners of the Aswan Dam or the Bratsk Hydroelectric Station. I laugh at Linda everytime I find her absorbed in that activity. Just like Noah and his ark, she is trying to put into her closet both the possible and the impossible: two file cabinets, shelves for paper and books, and even a small desk with drawers. The project's end is still not in sight. Linda laughs at herself too but stubbornly continues to devise ever newer plans.

I sat with them for a while. Richardson was telling Linda why a certain small firm had gone bankrupt, and I soon lost interest and went out to the garden. Flowers were blooming on the terrace and our stray garden cat was lying asleep on his back. When I came out, he opened an eye, saw it was me, and closed it again. The cat knows I respect his independence, and so he just went on dozing, expelling from his body and fur the moisture from the rain that had just fallen in great quantity. The cat basked in the September sunshine, and since he knew me, he wasn't afraid of anything.

Sitting on his haunches on the grass in front of his house was a Chinese man, a well-known artist, and he looked at the glass-covered house with a sadly astonished expression on his face as if he were seeing it for the first time in his life.

If only Steven would sleep a while longer, I thought, it would be so nice for everybody. Mr. Richardson and Linda could continue calmly chatting on the second floor, and I'd be able to stay out here in the garden. And then I started philosophizing. I decided that the Chinese man and the cat were invisible to Steven Gatsby. He meddles in life too crudely, whereas if you want to see something in it, you have to enter very carefully so as not to frighten it away. In fact, I thought, it's as if Steven doesn't even exist, since the Chinese man on his haunches and the cat are invisible to him. Whereas I, a servant, am more useful to the world, for I see the Chinese man and the cat and am able to tell about them. Steven sees only his papers and feels only his body, and his function in the world is basically to set things in motion.

I remembered Stanislaw once taking offense because Steven and Nancy hadn't invited him to a restaurant with them, and saying bitterly to me, "Steven wants very much to be creative, but he can't be. He's insensitive, although he has a very good brain."

Stanislaw wasn't being fair then; it was his hurt feelings speaking. I didn't want to be unfair, and so I thought that if Gatsby didn't own this house, I would never have met Stanislaw or seen the Chinese man and the cat, and neither would the garden have existed for me, nor the cool East River, and my life would have been more boring and blacker, as black as coal.

Having already completely justified Gatsby and having decided that everyone has his place under the sun, I suddenly remembered that on the day the angry Stanislaw had called Gatsby insensitive, the bitch Nancy had tried to humiliate me by teaching Steven how to use a little silver bell to call me from the kitchen. Steven and Nancy, their two children, and the country neighbors in Connecticut had just finished with lunch and were all still sitting at the table in the dining room. They had taken it into their heads to light a fire in the fireplace, and Nancy, obviously not feeling like making a trip to the kitchen, had rung the little bell instead. The ringing of little bells had never been heard in our house before, but I understood and went into the dining room. When I entered, Nancy turned to Steven and said, "You see how easy it is!" and then asked me to make a fire.

"I'm embarrassed," Gatsby said, and he really was embarrassed, and I think even ashamed for Nancy, and after that episode the bell was never heard again.

As a result of that memory the world once again collapsed into two unequal and diametrically opposed camps—servants and masters. The almost stilled argument within me was revived. About what? The same old argument about who was more important to the world, Gatsby or me. I produce books, I thought, things of more or less "immortal" spiritual value. What does Gatsby do? He oversees the production of money. Or more accurately, he oversees the manufacture and sale of ever newer things that from my point of view aren't really needed by mankind—automobiles and computers. His expensive cars and computers, I think, undoubtedly serve the cause of enslaving man's body and spirit. Whereas my activity is directed towards the liberation of that body and spirit, towards the awakening of human consciousness. At least, the couple of books I've already written promote the awakening of doubt in people.

Gatsby, Linda, Richardson, and the others, their group on the second floor equipped with telephones, typewriters, Xerox machines, notebooks, teletypes, and file cabinets, are constructing a new supermodern dungeon for mankind, while I, sitting by myself on the fourth floor or bent over in the kitchen with a notebook, am cutting out an escape route to freedom.

We are enemies, it turns out—if not personal enemies, then unquestionably enemies in the social sense. And we laugh together sometimes, just as if everything were fine.

I sat in the doorway to the garden dressed in wide linen pants. My nose was burned by the sun, but my ass was cold;

odd, isn't it? I love the freshness of life in autumn, the wind, the plants, the birds squalling something. The only thing that saddened me was that I was by myself, that there wasn't any being with me to whom I could say, "Look, listen to it, isn't it fine?" And then suddenly add, "You know, even though we're going to die, it's still fine, isn't it?" Nothing new here in essence, gentlemen, just feelings. . . .

There was somebody to say it to. In proof of that, a blonde adolescent girl wearing heavy knit stockings—it had already turned colder—came out into the garden from Isabelle's old house and strode with a ballerina's silly gait to the swing. She lazily rocked back and forth on it for a while, smiling thoughtfully and obviously unaware that anybody was watching her. Then noticing me, she immediately jumped down from the swing, walked over to the river and stood there for a while, and then quickly went back into her house. Why are people so afraid of each other? I wondered. It was merely my presence in the garden that had frightened her. Or not even in the garden, actually, since I was sitting in the doorway leading to our terrace. Whatever my gaze meant to her, she still ran away.

I went back inside too. Linda had gone, and Steven was awake; I could hear him filling his bathtub with water. I went upstairs to my room. The radio announced that the wind was increasing and that a hurricane was expected that night. Just in case, I closed the special storm windows in my room and went around the house, checking to see that all the windows were shut and closing the storm windows wherever we had them.

Steven went out. He always slams the front door so hard when he leaves that it's impossible not to notice. The energy seething within him bursts out and makes him slam the doors. The servant, however, took his place comfortably by the window, waiting for the storm, and started reading Che Guevara's *Guerrilla Warfare*. I wasn't really in the mood for it. Certainly we can dig tank traps, I thought, but it would be better if we had our own tanks. And the servant absent-mindedly concerned himself with less concrete details. As if summing up for the day my inner struggle with Gatsby, I thought with conviction: *There will always be oppressors and oppressed. And there will always be hope for the oppressed. And the inexhaustible light of a thousand suns of revolution will be obscured neither by the Jacobin Reign of Terror nor the Stalinist camps, for these are counterrevolution. Never! The proud revolution. The right to revolution is in every heart. Capitalism or socialism are human inventions, whereas revolution is a phenomenon of nature, like this approaching hurricane.*

I continued reading for a while in that and other books, and then fell asleep after pulling a pillow over my head, just as my army officer father had always done.

The storm woke me before dawn. Branches were flying about and the trees in our garden were cracking, and the plaster was falling from the skylight in my bathroom, so that I was afraid the glass wouldn't withstand the buffeting of the wind and the hurricane would burst into my bedroom. To my amazement, however, it withstood it.

The storm was still raging at eight-thirty or nine, and it wasn't until eleven that nature more or less calmed down. Lying in the garden were the corpses of two or three smaller trees and the branches of some larger ones. The obscene fence that separates us and our little millionaire's garden from the rest of the world had been stripped bare.

The master had apparently come home drunk in the middle of the night and had some white wine with his lover and other, unknown friends of his (there were several glasses on the table). The doors to the garden and the street were open when I went down the next morning at seven, and there were still wet footprints on the floor. *The New York Times*, although it lay under the front porch overhang, was soaking wet, and so I dried it over our gas range sheet by sheet, gradually acquainting myself with the events of the day before.

Chapter Eleven

THE WINTER PASSED. I've noticed that I don't remember winters very well. My memory leaves them out, with the result that my year has only three seasons: spring, summer, and fall. The only winter I remember completely and distinctly is the winter of 1967–1968, my first in Moscow. The hellish forty-below frosts were supplemented by the fact that I was undernourished. My flesh and all my muscles ached from the cold when, after pulling on everything I had to pull on—all my clothes—I ran to the cafeteria on the corner of Uhlan Lane and the Sadovoe Circle Road. That cafeteria, an iced-over basement heaven where I ate black bread and mustard for free after paying for the obligatory glass of compote, will remain frozen in my memory forever. Sometimes I would also sneak uneaten food left on the plates—a piece of hot dog and some mashed potatoes or hot dog skin peeled off by a squeamish taxi driver. What had been inedible for the taxi driver was eaten with pleasure by the poet. I lost twenty-five pounds that winter, so I remember it all.

The New York winter of 1979–1980 I spent fucking and working, but mostly fucking my girls, since Steven went skiing no fewer than three times. No matter what was happening in New York, he dropped his business affairs and left his papers lying around and unsorted, while Linda hissed and raged. I remember one morning in January when Steven, pink and cheerful after his most recent ski trip, came down to the kitchen in his bathrobe, and I asked him politely if he had enjoyed skiing at Aspen. The question was an innocent one, just something to ask the boss about, without any ulterior motives, but Gatsby was taken aback and for some reason started justifying himself to me.

"I wasn't just on vacation, Edward," he said. "I had three separate business meetings in Colorado, all in different cities."

I forced out a respectful "Oh!!" What else could I say? His meetings didn't sound that convincing. While unpacking his things and turning over the strata and rubble in his suitcases and bags, I had found not a single work document, only light reading—among others, a book called *The Last Convertible*, as I recall—and an indecent quantity of woman's things: stockings, panties, mittens, and even a couple of hats. Business meetings! Olga later washed his business meetings in the laundry room. Around that time a magazine came out with that article about Gatsby portraying him as a "working-class" millionaire. And people read it and obviously believed it. He spoke very intelligently and wearily with the interviewer. Steven is good-looking and inspires confidence; what else do readers need?

The New York spring began. With the appearance of the first green in our garden, the housekeeper Edward received a letter from Rome which left him beside himself with happiness. One of the best-known small publishers in America, Leonard Angeletti, wrote to say that he had obtained my address from a friend of his in Rome, the Russian writer Evgeny Efimenkov, and that Efimenkov had told him I had written a "great book." And that he, Angeletti, would be flying to New York in a couple of days and wanted to see me and get the manuscript of my book with the object of possible publication by his publishing house. Angeletti named the date he would be in New York and asked me to be home so he could call and arrange a meeting.

Sure I'd be home! Even if they had put me in prison that day, I would have escaped and crawled to the millionaire's house wounded and bleeding. My book was going nowhere; not a single publisher was looking at it. Liza didn't know where to send it anymore. A dead end.

I almost had a publisher last fall. Now, just by looking at his face, I would say that as far as publishing my book was concerned, he would sit on the pot but he'd never finish shitting, and that he was completely wrong for it anyway, but then, as it happened, I still didn't know a fucking thing about publishers. Malcolm had been introduced to me by an artist friend of mine on purpose, but as if in passing: "Let me introduce you. This is Malcolm, a publisher, and this is Edward, a writer." But mainly it was Malcolm who latched on to me and started asking me questions—what sort of book had I written, what it was about. . . . The fact was that until then Malcolm hadn't published very many books, and what he had published were mostly expensive gift editions. You know, books with glossy paper and good photographs of places of note or of minerals or flowers. . . . The sort of book, in short, that nobody except the publisher needs, not even the person it's given to. Token books. You give one of them to somebody, and then a week later he gets ready to visit one of his friends on his birthday and starts thinking about what sort of gift he himself will give. He doesn't really want to spend any money, and then his eyes fall on the book put out by the publisher Malcolm. Those books are always in excellent condition; frequently they've never even been opened. What's there to look at; they're all the same.

It was even written all over Malcolm's face that he wanted money very badly but was scared of taking risks. Only the housekeeper Edward preoccupied for six months with his problems could have believed, gentlemen, that that coward would publish his book, one ending with the words, "Fuck you, you cocksucking bastards! You can all go to hell!"

By that time I already had a complete text of the book in English. I'd paid the translator out of my own housekeeper's pocket—the main thing in my life being, after all, Edward the

321

writer and his books and not Edward the housekeeper and his problems. Let Edward the housekeeper stay home instead of hanging around restaurants or buying himself new rags on sale at Saks. He'd survive.

Malcolm gave the Russian text to a professor in the Russian department of a university I'd never heard of, but he wouldn't tell me the professor's name, obviously so I wouldn't be able to exert any influence on him, or bribe him perhaps. The professor's review was super-favorable. There are still people who can think for themselves, I thought approvingly. It's nice to know they exist. Among other things, my unknown friend wrote, ". . . the author emphasizes the dehumanizing character of both societies, maintaining that there is no place in either for the independent and creative personality."

Malcolm wasn't satisfied with that opinion, and gave the English manuscript to three other people to read, and in addition read it himself and gave another copy to a scrawny forty-year-old mouse named Barbara. Barbara was his colleague and assistant; she walked his dogs the same way Madame Margarita walks Lodyzhnikov's and did other things of that kind. Maybe Malcolm fucked her too whenever he was on a diet. Even the timid little mouse Barbara liked the book, and all his other hired readers did too, but Malcolm continued to stall and drag things out. He was still afraid.

I once asked him over to the millionaire's for a drink, thinking that perhaps we hadn't had enough personal contact, that perhaps if he saw me in my actual circumstances, he would understand me better, just as Jenny had after visiting me in my hotel. He would see that I wasn't just a temporary guest in the house of literature. After sitting a while with me over a glass of whiskey, he would realize that I was very ambitious and talented. And I thought that after that he would want to come to terms with me and publish my book.

He came over and we had a drink. True, he didn't stay very long—he had to run off to some dinner engagement he couldn't put off—but I learned more about him during that brief visit than I had in all my months of meeting him at his office. He examined our house very carefully and obsequiously, servilely admiring our walls and even the shabby rugs on our floors, and he praised all the things I detested; he liked the Connecticut landscapes and our antique dishes on the buffet and our living room picture window with its view of the river, and the dimensions of the living room itself. He even tested the mattress in Steven's bedroom with his hand. Instead of sitting with me and drinking Scotch as I had intended, he walked fawningly around the house and talked to me about my kitchen. And I got to know him. I know you, mask! I thought. You're a petit bourgeois, little Malcolm. He badly wanted to grab up a house like that for himself so he could become a fucking grand bourgeois.

He walked around the house and I followed and looked at his bald patch and his not so much fat but spreading ass bashfully covered up by his shiny pants. His velvet "intellectual's" jacket didn't impress me anymore—it was all too clear now. And when I mockingly said to him, "Malcolm, if you want a house like this, then buy my book!" it was just to spite him. I knew he wouldn't publish it; he didn't have the guts, little Malcolm. He didn't even drink Scotch—he drank wine. You bald pussy, I thought, you fat-assed little pussy.

Malcolm tried very hard to be high-society and decadent. Once he invited me to a dinner party among whose guests were some women who were finishing or already had finished dissertations on Proust and Yeats. The one who had written/was writing about Proust had nice white legs. Also present were: an old Mexican woman in broad Spanish skirts who had obviously not been fucked by anybody in about ten years, and an aging European beauty named Rosa who was supposed to be Malcolm's girlfriend, although I found that pretty hard to believe. It seemed to me that if he wasn't actually a homosexual of the very worst type—old, fat-assed, and bald—he was in any case something in between. Even though it was still February, I arrived dressed entirely in white and, like my boss, without my coat and in a taxi—ready for spring. When he opened the door, Malcolm paid me a compliment so incredible that I was forced to stay at his place a good two hours, although I ought to have left immediately, since it was already clear they were a waste of time. Malcolm said, "Oh, Edward! You look just like the Great Gatsby!" Thus was I compared with my employer.

While serving us dinner—stuffed cabbage prepared by Rosa—Malcolm apologized to me. "I'm sorry, Edward, but I don't have as much room in my apartment as you do in your house." What? I thought. Doesn't he know I'm only a housekeeper? Does his servility even extend to the point where he identifies me with the house?

Malcolm continued fucking with me until spring, and then in March he said to me (even here the whore couldn't be a man about it and give me a simple "no"), "It's not that I'm rejecting you, Edward—we're still considering your book, although you have to understand that things are very difficult right now in the publishing business—but I don't want to tie you down with any obligations. You might try your luck with some other publisher if you don't feel like waiting for us." To top it all, the fat-assed bastard asked me for Elena's address in Europe. It turned out he knew her, Elena having once been, you see, an extremely popular member of New York society. Malcolm was going to Europe. Naturally, I didn't give him the address. Malcolm was a sneaky little son of a bitch.

Writers always abuse their publishers. True, but I despise Malcolm not because he wouldn't publish my book, but because he was small about it.

"A holy place is never empty," as the Russian proverb has it. Malcolm was gone, and Richard Atlas at once stepped in to fill the void. That's right, the personage himself, Mr. Richard Atlas, publisher, of the house of Gerard and Atlas. I met him at a party given by Mrs. Janet Garrisson, the wife of the chairman of one of America's oldest panty hose manufacturers, who had started receiving me again. Despite all my dislike of rich old ladies, this was one I was even fond of. I had particularly good feelings about her after learning that she had once energetically and cheerfully supported herself and her daughter by making women's dresses. Labor is something I respect. I don't know whether Madame Garrisson supported herself on dresses alone, or whether she also supplemented her income with a little trading in her cunt, as women are wont to do, but I respect her. At the age of seventy or whatever, she's unbelievably cynical and for that reason a rare pleasure to talk to. The other reason I became enamored of her was that she liked my book—my whole life revolved around it, gentlemen, as you see. I had given Mrs. Garrisson a copy to read. The homosexual Volodya had long before wormed his way in with the Garrissons, and her enthusiasm for the book had been his work. I thought she would be embarrassed by it and dismiss all my strong feelings as "pornography." But she didn't; she was up to it. "I'm in raptures!" said Janet, looking like an old circus clown as she descended from her upstairs chambers to the living room where I was waiting for her. "Let me kiss you, my dear!" She kissed me, and afterward looked slyly at me and said, "In your next book you can write that I'm an old hag, a repulsive old hag." And so I have, as you see, but she's not an old hag; that's the wrong image for her. If I were a little older, and she about thirty years younger, I'm sure we'd have hit it off beautifully. As I was leaving her that day, she came out to the doorway of her house, between Park Avenue and Lexington, and said to me very seriously, "Watch out for Elena!" Elena was in New York then, and Madame Garrisson was, as you see, concerned about me and shielding me from that monster.

And so it was at a party at the Garrissons that I met Richard Atlas. A cocktail party, that is, with people coming and going. Andy Warhol was there with his retinue. I could have asked Madame Garrisson to introduce me to him, but what the hell for? To show him my two books in Russian? What else could I have done? I already believed firmly in the system and felt that until I had a book in English, I didn't exist. I could, say, have stood with Warhol and said some intelligent things to him, since I did know something about his work and his book *The Philosophy of Andy Warhol*, but I didn't want to bullshit anonymously; I wanted to speak as Edward Limonov and not as a nonentity, and so I didn't ask Madame to introduce us. There'll be time for that. I hope that Andy and I will both be around for a while.

Atlas started talking to me by accident. We happened to be together in one of those fluctuating groups that take form, break up, and merge with other groups countless times at any more or less large-scale party. I said something, he said something, and then he asked me what I did, and I brashly told him I was a writer. His interest piqued, he asked, "And what have you written, if you'll permit me to ask?"

There wasn't any mockery in his voice, and I permitted myself to answer: "Right now I'm trying to sell my first novel." I said it as modestly as I could.

"Interesting. If it's not a secret, what is it about?" he asked, taking his pipe out of his mouth. He was smoking a pipe.

"No, it's not a secret. Basically, it's an account, novelized obviously, of my own social and sexual experience in the United States," I said, trying to sound serious and literary and yet still be brief. I didn't have any idea who he was. Just a man between fifty and sixty, apparently. In a tweed jacket with a pipe. He could have been anybody; I didn't even care who he was. His face was simple enough. A businessman, perhaps.

"And have you sent your book to *my* publishing house?" he asked.

"Which one is that?" I asked in my turn. "Forgive me, but we haven't been introduced."

"Gerard and Atlas," he said. "Heard of it?"

"Yes, certainly," I said. "My agent sent the manuscript to Gerard and Atlas. That is, she sent an outline and three chapters in English. At the time only three chapters had been translated. The whole manuscript is in English now," I said.

"And what answer did your agent receive?" he asked, smiling.

"I don't remember exactly," said the writer Limonov, "but whatever it was, they didn't take the book." "They" had a very diplomatic sound to it.

"You say you have the whole manuscript in English?" he asked, filling his pipe.

"Oh yes," I assured him. "I got it back from the typist a week ago."

"I'll tell you what," he said, "send the manuscript to me personally. I'll take a look at your book myself."

"Who are you?" I asked in bewilderment and added, "Excuse me."

"I'm Atlas. Richard Atlas—the publisher," he said. "Send it to me, by all means send it—we publish Russian writers sometimes. Just today, by the way, I had a meeting with Joseph Khomsky. We're bringing out a volume of his poetry next fall. A magnificent poet, Khomsky, and an extraordinarily interesting man. Do you know him?"

"Oh yes," I answered hastily, "I know him."

"You can send your manuscript to my home address," Atlas added, and then he disappeared. Either somebody else came up to him, or somebody came up to me, but we parted.

It would have been odd if Volodya hadn't been there, and of course he was, and even introduced me to the wife of a Greek billionaire, a still very beautiful woman of about fifty, although she looked much younger. I drank for a while longer, stimulated by the billionaire's wife and my talk with the publisher Atlas, but still left around nine. The Garrissons weren't nineteen, after all, and couldn't put away cocktails until morning. Andy Warhol was still gleaming white in a corner of the living room. Next to him, the pretender to the Russian throne was trying to prove something to a Soviet poet. I went over and listened. The pretender was talking enthusiastically about his trip to Russia and defending the Soviet regime, while the overfed Soviet poet was running it down. What won't you find? I thought, shrugging my shoulders. And then I left.

I sent the manuscript to Atlas at once; I am in such matters exceptionally quick and exacting. I sent it and waited. I'm always waiting for other people. Everything that is required of me personally in this world, I do quickly and conscientiously. I'll sit up nights, but I'll finish the manuscript when I planned and promised to. I've been waiting for other people my whole life. Even as a snot-nosed fifteen-year-old kid I would be the first to show up at the agreed place at the cemetery where our gang used to meet before going off on a robbery, and I would have to sit and wait a long time for the others. As I see it, other people are fuck-offs and bunglers, careless, unreliable people who obstruct my life and my tempo, who get in the way of my energy, and who ultimately use me up. As you see, this view is similar to Gatsby's own view of "other people," and thus it turns out that master and servant have the same screwed-up temperament, and the world tries to slow them down. Gatsby is undoubtedly much luckier than I am: he can take the Concorde or a car or use his private plane. He has the illusion of speed, of movement and energy, whereas I'm left only with mindless waiting. To remain stuck in the syrup of a fucking daily routine devoid of odor or flavor, to remain locked in humdrum reality, while the months and years pass by, is truly heroic. To rush with a shout and the bullets flying and mount an attack (excuse me) in the teeth of popular opinion is a lot easier. It's a deed requiring only a momentary effort of will. I'm certain I could stand smiling with a cigar between my teeth and my hands in my pockets up against a brick wall before a firing squad. I'm not kidding, I could do it. I've got what it takes for the smile and the hands in the pockets and the cigar and the eyes wide open. But sometimes I think I haven't got quite what it takes for the ordinary, everyday crap; I become unhinged and do stupid things.

Occasionally it seems to me that nature has stuck me with the wrong destiny by mistake. I have myself interfered in my own fate more than once, and obviously not altogether intelligently, and because I have indulged certain features of my nature, I have completely neglected others, to such an extent in fact, that I have sometimes been quite different from what I actually am. At times it seems to me that my true calling—what I really am—is a colonel in command of an airborne division. Having seen the military bearing that suddenly came to life in me from God knows where when I recently put on a close-fitting dress uniform at a friend's house, I suddenly thought, my God! this is what I really am, a decisive military man in full-dress uniform, and not the feeble, poetical soul I've always aspired to be. And in fact I did want to go to military school once, so why didn't I? With my head and ambition, I could have been an airborne colonel by now. Then they would have seen something. . . .

Maybe there was in fact a little mistake? It doesn't matter, since the best reader I could wish for my books, both those that have been written and those I still have to write, is a young colonel, although majors and lieutenants won't be turned away. The national origin of my military reader is of no importance either, nor is the color of his skin.

But let us return to the rigors of my struggle. A few days later I received a saccharine letter from Atlas noting that my manuscript had been received and that I would be contacted without delay as soon as he read it. "I hope you were able to enjoy, and enjoy to the fullest, Mr. Limonov, the delightful atmosphere of the Garrissons' cocktail party after my departure." Signed, "Richard Atlas."

I did enjoy it, I thought, and since I didn't know whether I should answer that I had his letter confirming the receipt of my manuscript, I asked Linda about it. She said no, I didn't have to; all I had to do was wait.

I sat down and waited. Or rather, I lay down—on an ever renewed succession of bodies. Although my lechery had begun as a simple inferiority complex in consequence of my being left by a woman I loved, it had long since exceeded the limits of that complex to become a way of life. I took pains to drag rarities of every sort into my housekeeper's bed: a Brazilian singer, a Polish actress, a punk star (although admittedly not of the very first magnitude), an Amsterdam designer, a German model appropriated from the photographer Eric, and a young French writer sent to me from Paris by a friend. . . . More a cabinet of curiosities than a bed. That bed was sometimes even adorned by the mothers of children. I let one bring them with her to the millionaire's house, and while they frolicked about the bed, I reclined beside their mama and pleasurably fucked her, in full awareness, it's true, that I was inflicting irreparable psychic trauma on the kids, but I still couldn't help it. The devil triumphed, and installing himself in Edward, he forced gentle Eddie out.

I fucked away the interval before Atlas's reply in the same way, probably, that other people spend such times in drink—to pass the time more quickly.

About three weeks later I received a large package. I often receive large packages, and so I didn't think anything about it at first, but when I read the address of the sender, "Richard Atlas, Sr." I understood it all. An office worker had sent the manuscript separately. The letter came the following day. "How could that have happened, Linda?" I asked the expert.

"Very simple," she said. "A secretary mailed the package and then remembered the letter the next day."

Linda knows all about secretarial work, I thought sadly. Ask whatever you like; she has the answer. And I unsealed the letter:

"I very much regret, Mr. Limonov, that I cannot be of assistance . . . Your manuscript, unfortunately, is not for our list . . . I wish you every success . . . I am confident that you . . ."

Ah, you asshole! I thought dully. You publish Khomsky; he's

fine for your list, since he's a nice bourgeois poet. Meek. And more and more ponders the problems of life and death. And conducts himself with exceptional propriety, never saying more than he has to, and whenever he's called upon to judge Russia publicly, he doesn't criticize his new Motherland, he doesn't touch it—God forbid. His favorite poet is the Greek Cavafy, who quietly sat out his life, a man with a temperament like Joseph Khomsky's—both deep, private thinkers. For his obedient behavior, the poet Joseph Khomsky is certain in time to receive the inventor-of-dynamite prize.

And me? Next to the respectable Khomsky, the housekeeper Edward is a literary lowlife. On the housekeeper's desk is a portrait of Colonel Khadafy that even Efimenkov found shocking. It's not so much that I sympathize with the brand of Islamic socialism invented by the Colonel or with the rest of his views, but that I like his personality. He's a human being and not an asshole like the majority of rulers. He took power by himself, overthrowing his king and carrying out a revolution. I like his thirty-eight-year-old face. It's the face of a man. There was a time when I played at being homosexual out of despair and a love for the outrageous, and since there wasn't any place for my masculine face in Eddie, it surfaced in that picture. . . .

If I'd written a novel about intellectuals "suffering" in Soviet mental hospitals, or about the oppressed Soviet national minorities, I thought, I would have found a place on their publisher's list immediately. Without a doubt. Gerard and Atlas is a publisher of liberal-intellectual tendencies. It's exactly the same as with the Moscow publisher "Soviet Writer," where you're perfectly free to publish a book on the life of the American unemployed. All you have to do is avoid sex scenes. . . .

I didn't even get drunk. I had just paid off Bill the money I owed him for his translation of *Eddie*, and gritting my teeth, I started paying him to translate yet another book, *Diary of a Loser*, in order to begin a relentless general assault along the entire front and against all the New York and for that matter all the American Malcolms and Atlases, from coast to coast. I even started looking for a new literary agent. For that reason I became intimate with people I never would have made friends with. I felt it was either me or them, the Malcolms and Atlases. My own capacity for patience put me on guard; otherwise I would have had a nervous breakdown. It had begun four years since I'd begun trying to sell my book and gain a foothold as a writer, and I was afraid that I'd flip out, that I'd go to pieces and be finished.

It was at that moment that Angeletti's letter came. There is a God, I thought in jubilation. There is a God, Edward, there is! Angeletti's firm wasn't a large one, but he had published a number of very good things in the sixties, including a book by Jean Genet and another by the French surrealist poet Henri Michaux. True, he had also published a little volume of verse by a Soviet poet—tightrope walker, the same one against whom the pretender to the throne had been defending the Soviet regime at the Garrissons' party. But I immediately consoled myself by deciding that in publishing the poet, Angeletti was merely paying tribute to an international literary fad. Who is without sin? I thought.

Angeletti turned up promptly on the appointed day, notifying me by telephone that he was in New York, and I invited him for lunch—after taking the precaution of asking Linda's advice as to whether it would be appropriate to do so. Linda had forgotten who Angeletti was, but she said, "Why not? You could invite a prime minister to this house, Edward."

Angeletti arrived with a woman. He was a tall, balding old man with a beard, an old guy but still strong. The woman, whose name was Louise, was the sort men call a "nice broad." Not first-class or anything, but very nice: well-built, arms, legs, all there, all nice to look at, all the right curves. I didn't envy Angeletti his broad, but given the chance I wouldn't have turned her down either. Louise, however, had nothing to do with the business at hand. My relations with her were limited to her asking, "Are you a homosexual?" She explained her curiosity by saying she'd been told that I was a homosexual, although she didn't think I was. Angeletti was in the can at the time. I told Louise I was bisexual. And I said it, you know, proudly—not coyly but with pride: "I am a bisexual!" Afterwards it occurred to me to wonder just what sort of bisexual I was, given the fact that for a long time I'd been fucking only girls.

Before Angeletti's arrival, I had acquired several books on him and his generation and had looked through them and studied them. I had also obtained a book recounting how Angeletti had gotten started in publishing in order to show off my knowledge and demonstrate during our conversation my heightened interest in his publishing house. My boss, before any meeting with somebody he was seeing for the first time in his life, was always sent a dossier on the person in question from somewhere in the bowels of one of his companies. I imitated the boss and got together a dossier on Angeletti.

Initially we sat in the solarium. All the stories in the millionaire's little house begin in the solarium. I opened a bottle of Corvo for my guests, taking my cue from Angeletti's Italian last name. They partook of the cold wine, and Angeletti complained to me about how badly they had slept the night before.

"We're staying at the apartment of my old friends the poets Gluzberg and Kotovsky—you've heard of them, no doubt," said Angeletti, addressing me. "It's way down on the Lower East Side," he continued. "Gluzberg and Kotovsky have been living there for about thirty years, and have no interest in moving anywhere else, since the rent's so low. But it's a terrible neighborhood, and we couldn't get to sleep all night because the Puerto Rican teenagers down in the square never turned their radios off. But you have a very quiet neighborhood here, like the older parts of London, very peaceful," Angeletti suddenly announced, getting up from our green couch and looking out through the glass door into the garden.

"Too peaceful," I said.

"I haven't stayed over in New York for any length of time in twenty years," Angeletti went on thoughtfully. "I've stopped for a day or two on my way back from Europe on occasion, but always when I was very busy with meetings planned beforehand without a minute to spare, so I haven't really seen the city. Probably it's changed a lot?"

"Yes," I said. "Even in the five years I've been here, it's changed a great deal. Certain neighborhoods have come back, and others have gone under."

"Efimenkov spoke very highly of your book," Angeletti said, abruptly changing the subject. "He regards it as one of the best things written in Russian since the end of the Second World War."

"I don't know," I said. "Probably it's easier for him to tell. But the fact is it's been very hard for me to find that masterpiece a publisher."

"I'll take your manuscript, and if I like it, I'll publish it. We only bring out a few books a year, but what we do bring out we try to make as choice as possible." Angeletti said all this in a way that made it sound very solid.

"I would be very pleased if you considered it possible to publish my book," I said. I meant it. Then noticing that the wine was gone, I asked, "Would you like some more?" and went to the kitchen to get it.

I had prepared lunch beforehand—sliced steak, something I learned to do from Jenny, although it doesn't in fact require much skill. You sauté long strips of meat cut a little thicker than for beef Stroganoff in a skillet and serve them hot. That's it. I also had a salad. And wine and some Heineken's, and cheeses for dessert. There was plenty of meat and plenty of salad—what else does a person need? We ate in the kitchen just as we were, and I asked Linda to join us too, just as she was.

We ate and talked. Nothing special—just mealtime conversation. Angeletti didn't drop any pearls of wisdom, nor did I.

Linda didn't drop any either, and Louise helped herself to the food. I had the odd sensation that it was all very commonplace and ordinary. I had known Angeletti from photographs and books when I was in Russia. My poet friend Dmitri had translated his verse into Russian for me. And now he was sitting in my kitchen, and calmly eating. A mythological figure of world-class proportions. And now he'd just downed a large gulp of beer.

But why should he have been a superman? His friend Gluzberg, who had shaved off his beard for the first time only last year, was a quiet and gentle bookkeeper from New Jersey, an old, not overly tidy homosexual in spectacles who barely looked like the author of the snarling, howling verse he had been famous for in the fifties. (I generally don't like the way writers age; they do it in an ugly way.) Was Angeletti supposed to cast fiery glances perhaps? What did I want from him, anyway? That he be unique? Such were my thoughts as I gazed at Angeletti sitting in my kitchen.

Was it that I still hadn't completely rid myself of romanticism, of my provincial, Russian romanticism, or that I had anticipated a heated discussion in which certain mysteries would suddenly be revealed to me? But he was certainly no seer.

The whole "Angeletti operation" lasted three hours. Then taking my manuscript, they left. Angeletti promised to write as soon as he had finished reading it. I walked them to the door, closed it behind them, and then went upstairs to Linda and asked her, "What did you think of that person, Linda—your own opinion?"

Linda, tearing herself away from her papers, lifted her head and said without hesitating and with complete indifference, "I thought he wasn't too bright, Edward," and then stuck her head back in her papers. She was working on her closet plan, of course—Gatsby wasn't home.

It seemed to me that perhaps she hadn't formulated her opinion very precisely; I thought it was rather that Angeletti hadn't

335

been very interesting. But maybe uninteresting and "not too bright" were one and the same? The hell with it! I thought. After all, he has somehow published good books in the past. Maybe he'll publish mine too. Anyway he came here himself. It's a great honor when a famous publisher comes to see a writer himself.

I went into the TV room, sat down on the couch, and fell into thought, trying to understand the nature of Angeletti's visit. I recalled what Angeletti had said, and what Louise had said. Was I a homosexual? No. What difference did it make anyway? I wondered. Although for her it probably did make a difference, since she was a feminist writer, as Angeletti had told me when introducing her.

"Linda, how do you feel about feminism?" I yelled into the next room.

"Shit! Don't bother me, Edward!" she answered. I couldn't tell whether "shit" was an expression of Linda's attitude toward feminism, or simply an emotional response to the fact that I had distracted her.

Leonard Angeletti's letter arrived a month after his visit. Whether by ironical decree of the post office or of fate, his letter arrived after my long-suffering manuscript, as had been the case with Mr. Atlas. I was so dismayed when I saw the package extended to me by the mailman, that I just stood there without moving. "Take it!" he said irritably, shoving it into my hands. I slammed the kitchen door and tore open the package. The manuscript. Just the manuscript. Well-trained office personnel don't include letters with their packages; they send them in separate envelopes. But the return address testified irrefutably that the manuscript had been sent from Mr. Angeletti's publishing house.

A letter will undoubtedly follow, I thought, possibly even tomorrow, but it won't change anything. Essentially it's all clear: That sixties liberal isn't going to publish my book. If he had decided to publish it, he wouldn't have sent the manuscript back.

I didn't say anything to Linda; I was ashamed and afraid she might decide I was a failure. I recalled the words of Sarah's parting letter: "The reason nobody will touch your book here is that the United States has much higher standards for literature, and your book just isn't good enough. . . . You're a huge, gaping, empty zero."

The next day the empty zero received the letter. Another secretarial blunder obviously. The zero opened the letter and started reading. No, he hadn't restricted himself merely to apologies; he had written a long letter, sparing no pains. He wasn't even, as it turned out, refusing to publish my book. Rather Mr. Angeletti was suggesting that I cut it. Why not, why not cut it? I thought. A little bit here, a little there. After all it's my first novel. I had never rejected the idea of cutting it, although in the Russian version it was two hundred and eighty pages long, not what you would call a large book. I was just about to start celebrating when I got to the main part of the letter. Angeletti was suggesting that I change the novel's ending, introducing a "political murder." He couldn't publish the book with the ending I had now.

He doesn't understand shit about my book, I thought. My hero is trying with all his might to keep from killing himself. He wants to go on living, to continue his struggle, and accept his share of the blood and tears of this fucked-up world. A political murder in the form of a suicide. The hero struggles against his own suicidal tendencies and desires throughout the course of the book, and frees himself from them at the cost of considerable suffering, thereby shaping a new personality for himself. The hero decides to live, but Angeletti was suggesting a political murder. He didn't understand anything.

At the end of the letter was a P.S. "Now, living as he does in such a rich and beautiful home and possessed as he is of such a soft job, and no longer on the bottom of bourgeois society but

337

already to a certain extent accustomed to its blessings, hasn't the protagonist of your book become more loyal to that society and civilization, calmer and more contented?" Angeletti wrote, adding a question mark.

I was enraged. You goddamn whore! I thought. Why drink our wine and beer and eat our meat and salad! Why take part in our "upper bourgeois" blessings, if you're going to start in with this demagoguery, you bastard? You shouldn't have eaten or drunk if you want to be consistent. Soft job! Why, you bearded cunt! I thought bitterly. I'd like to make you stand around on your feet all day from seven until midnight, and then see how you'd look and see what your tune would be then. Soft job! I'd like to see you run around the way I do: "Edward, coffee!" a dozen times a day. "Edward, an ashtray!" "Edward, go get some orange juice at the Greek restaurant right now!" But Steven doesn't remember where the restaurant is, just that it's somewhere around Third Avenue and Fifty-seventh Street, and Edward runs over there like an idiot. "Edward, take Stanley to the bus station!" "Edward, go meet Mr. and Mrs. Buckley; their bags are very heavy." "Edward, where are Steven's yellow pajamas?" And at twelve I tumble off to bed and have just fallen asleep, when suddenly there's a telephone call from Japan or from an island, fuck knows which one. And once somebody called at five o'clock in the morning, identifying himself as "Rockefeller"! Soft job!

He reminds *me* about bourgeois society! The protagonist whom nobody has yet bought off. Mr. Publisher Angeletti obviously regards himself as a virtual revolutionary. But what about his money and all the books he sells? Are we to suppose that he spends his nights under a bridge with nothing but a quarter in his pocket? Obviously, if his publishing house has been in existence for over twenty-five years, he's no asshole when it comes to business; at least he hasn't lost any money, given the name authors he's surrounded himself with. But does he really have no sense of humor? Apparently not, if he could

338

send a letter with a P.S. like that to somebody who works as a servant, to someone like me who polishes the floor and shines the boss's shoes.

Soft job! Fuck you! I was starting to feel bad about the boss's wine I had given him and his feminist to drink. Why should the boss have to pay for all that shit? I suddenly thought, reasoning like a faithful and devoted servant to spite Angeletti. Angeletti reminded me of Jerry Rubin, another half-assed American pseudo-revolutionary, who in his book *Growing Up at Thirty-seven* admitted that at the same time he was a leftist student leader and rebelling against all the values of bourgeois society, he also owned stocks and even consulted the *Wall Street Journal* to see how his money was doing. He had inherited the stocks from his mommy and daddy. Great revolutionaries! They have neither shame nor conscience. The publisher tells the servant that he's too bourgeois. Well, well!

I was so disgusted and angry that day that I got drunk and even started fighting with somebody in the street, something I hadn't done for a long, long time. The next day I had a headache and had the Saturday *New York Times* stolen from my front door, since I didn't get up until around twelve. My well-regulated way of life had been upset. Instead of *The New York Times*, there was a bundle of letters lying on the floor, which the mailman, instead of waiting for me to answer the door, had shoved through the mail slot. Among the dozens of letters for Gatsby was one for me. An official letter, with the name PEN embossed on the envelope. I picked up the letter and unsealed it, my hands trembling from my hangover: "We have no doubt, Mr. Limonov, of the literary merits of your books, but unfortunately we cannot accept you as a member of the PEN Club given the fact that both your books have been published only in Russian. . . " followed by warm wishes and kind regards.

What? I thought. I went to them beforehand and called them several times and told them several times that my books had been published only in Russian. They had told me themselves that PEN is an international organization and that I should go ahead and send my books, but include annotations so they could understand what the books were about, and if I had articles about myself and my books in English, that I should send those too. I sent them a huge package. And I had been recommended to them by Joseph Khomsky, one of their own. And now they tell me I don't have any books in English. But they've given PEN membership to a whole crowd of half-wit Russian dissidents who call themselves writers. They can join, but I'm not allowed to.

You beat your head against the wall for four years trying to become a man of letters. You receive rejections on all sides—"We can't! We don't need you! You don't suit us!"—even though you know that you are needed and that you do suit them, that you're more talented than many others, and so if you aren't a fish with cold blood in your veins, you get mad. "The goddamn faggots! The fucking bastards!" I started yelling and kicked several chairs. Round and made of iron, they flipped over and rolled across the kitchen floor. "Bastards!" I shouted with angry tears in my eyes. The one time in his life a person tries to become a member of an Organization. And even the feeblest of them won't take him. "Sanctimonious liberal assholes! Murderers!" I shouted. "What the fucking hell was I thinking of in applying to that society of worn-out old women and insipid liberals! What the hell do I need them for? Why, they're even worse than the goddamn Soviet Union of Writers, the old farts. . . . Mothball minds!"

Weeping with rage, I poured myself some whiskey, Steven's favorite, twelve-year-old Glenlivet, and drank off the whole glass, which sent me hurtling into the wide-open spaces of my own mind. I took the bottle, got on the elevator, and went up to my room, where I quickly got dressed, not forgetting to drink, since that yellow liquid made everything easier. Much easier.

340

"Freaks!" I said out loud. It's you who are the freaks, not me. I'm a normal, healthy person who has the courage to see the world as it is, face to face. You hump-backed whores! You craven victims! Anybody with a passionate heart and an independent mind is doomed among you. You all conspire to put him down on every level, from bedroom to PEN Club. I'm not interested in playing your primitive little games, you bastards! I'm not going to change anything in my book for you, Angeletti, you jerk! And you senile old twats from the PEN Club will come to me someday, but I won't join your decrepit organization. Never!

After I got dressed, I suddenly couldn't understand where it was I intended to go. Thinking over my plans and continuing to drink, I sat down by the window and looked out.

Down below a garden party was in progress. Only because of my hangover, I couldn't understand whose it was. Very formally dressed men and women were trampling the young grass around our huge tree in the center. A few small groups were standing by the river. I watched them for a long time, trying to make sense out of it, and then I remembered that in a paper bag in my desk drawer I had a couple of pale violet tablets of mescaline left to me by Michael Jackson on his last visit—he had needed ten dollars. I was in such a screwed-up state that I got out the tablets and swallowed both of them, both the little crystalline triangles, knowing from experience that I would soon start vibrating like an overheated pressure cooker. But I was in such despair that I was willing to pay any price for a way out. Move into another dimension maybe, but escape. I had never taken two tabs of mescaline at once; I had been afraid to. I had been unable to calm down for a good twelve hours from just one, and had fucked like a beast without ever reaching orgasm. It seemed my prick would burst and my nerves would snap, that my whole body was crackling under the strain and would suddenly split open, coming apart like an old brick building. But I swallowed the two tablets anyway, having decided beforehand, it's true, that whatever I did, I shouldn't go out. That I must not go outside in that condition, or I'd perish for sure. Moreover, I was still drinking. And drinking on top of a hangover.

Downstairs in the garden pleasant conversations were taking place, and you could hear polite laughter and the murmuring of the crowd. I envied them: Unlike me, they weren't alone. I raised the window and tried to get a better look at them. But with shitty success; from the fourth floor, their faces were barely visible. I was most interested in the women, of course. I usually got the binoculars from Steven's room on such occasions, but they weren't there anymore; he'd taken them back to Connecticut a long time ago. He and Mr. Richardson were planning to go deer hunting. Mr. Richardson was a hunter; Gatsby wanted to be a hunter too.

But I found a solution. I stood up, opened the door to my closet, and took out my rifle. It had a telescopic sight. So as not to scare them in case they happened to notice me, I put a couple of green pillows from my bed on the windowsill, arranging the rifle on them, and then I lay down on the bed and started watching.

How could I not have guessed at once! I thought. There's no question it's a party given by the Secretary General of the UN. Who else would have such formally dressed guests and so many men in tuxedos? Before such affairs people with the characteristic faces of special agents always sweep our bushes with bomb-detectors. But they never check the houses, thank God.

The cross hairs of the sight moved from head to head as I sought the host. Aha. There's his old face. At that instant he was being asked to pose; a young girl-photographer was taking his picture. Even though he frowned irritably, he didn't turn away; the girl was pretty, and he let her take a picture. Though maybe she isn't a photographer, I thought. They would be unlikely to let reporters in; they have press conferences for that. The mescaline apparently hasn't started to affect me yet, I thought, except that maybe I'm being a little too persistent and taking too much time looking them over. Really, what the hell do I need them for anyway? At that instant the servile face of a flunky appeared in the rifle sight, a man carrying a tray of drinks. Champagne. They were champagne glasses. I hated to bring drinks to Steven in the garden, although there were times when I had to. . . . The poor flunky. How much effort that face must have cost him.

As I was gripping and turning the rifle and catching their faces in its sight, it suddenly occurred to me that if somebody in one of the neighboring buildings should see me lying in that prone position and call the police, I could get about ten years in prison for it. Try to prove afterward that you were just using the optical sight for binoculars and didn't have anything bad in mind. They'd make a new Lee Harvey Oswald out of me, I thought.

And I suddenly felt a chill that made my hair stand on end. I remembered that I had the same kind of slash marks on my arms that Oswald had, and I remembered my morbid interest in political murderers and terrorists. And then a crazy thought flashed vividly through my mind: If you pop off the Secretary General of the United Nations right now, that would be no worse, in fact, it might even be better than taking out the President of the United States! The worst part was that it would have been childishly easy to do so. After all, I was already lying in a window open onto the garden where their party was taking place. And while at the moment I had the telescopic sight fixed on one of the branches of our large tree with its spreading greenery, it would have taken no effort at all, a mere thirty seconds, to find the requisite old head of the Secretary General in the garden. At a distance of no more than fifty yards, it would have been virtually impossible to miss, even if I hadn't practiced every day at a shooting range the way Oswald had.

I froze in that position, afraid to move and completely overcome by an already icy chill. That moment I had never even imagined and had never sought, that chance encounter with someone else's fate, chilled me to the bone. This will be no homespun provincial Rodichka Raskolnikov going after an un-

343

known old woman with a hatchet. This will be worldwide fame, instantaneous and sinister fame! I thought. By tonight the whole world will know my name and peer at my face. My picture will be in every paper. The world, which has pushed me aside for so many years, will speak only of me! All my diaries, my poems, my novels will be published, as will everything else I've ever written, down to the very last line, and before they put me in the electric chair, although maybe they won't, I'll bask to my heart's content in the attention of this fucking world. . . . What's poor Lee Oswald next to me, who will pass himself off as a political murderer who acted on principle! And I won't even have to pass myself off—my *Diary of a Loser* alone, with the part where it says, "Kill them all! Kill them all!" will tomorrow become a manual in the struggle of thousands of failures, and from the obscure housekeeper Edward, I shall make a figure of history.

I gasped from horror, from fear of myself. My right hand lay on the rifle stock, and my fingers moved quietly toward the trigger. I'm not exaggerating. A sort of autosuggestion, animal magnetism, a demon in love with terrible events—I don't know what pushed me to it, but my hand moved toward the trigger.

"It's the mescaline!" I said out loud in a suddenly sober voice. The mescaline, Edward! Have you forgotten you swallowed two tablets? You did, don't forget it!

My future began to pass very quickly before my eyes in movie frames. Not my past, but my future which I myself shall achieve by my own labor and perserverance, step by step, in about. . . I saw the bright covers of my books now finally published and in the bookstores. The publishers won't always reject me, I persuaded myself. I saw the faces of beautiful women, my girlfriends, whom I would have there at the top as a reward for all my trials and tribulations after I'd become successful. . . .

But part of my mind, the criminal part, the same part that makes me cast sidelong looks at the open holsters of policemen on the streets, and that invariably reminds me, whenever I pass a bank, that it can be robbed—that part cried, That's all bullshit, Ed! That's the way of timid souls. You're destined for something else. Squeeze the fucking trigger, and the world will at once take form, and people and things will arrange themselves in a shapely pyramid reaching to the sun, and you will be at its apex. And the electric chair, even if it means the electric chair (I tried to put that out of my mind at once, or at least shove it into its darkest corner), well, we all have to die sometime. Sometime—if not today, why then tomorrow! On the other hand, you'll determine your destiny and your future in an instant. Doesn't the hero of *Diary of a Loser*—you yourself—kill a president in his dreams? So is it really such an accident that you're lying here right now? And since you're already here, fuck it, shoot! Shoot, Ed! You still have a lot of life ahead of you, it's true, but aren't you sick of the world and all those faces, and your dreams, and the sunrises and sunsets, and the cocktail parties, and the world's timid politics, and its girls for sale? And what's next, anyway? You'll get old and slip back down, and they say it happens very fast. You already have a few wrinkles on that long, beautiful neck of yours which your girlfriends like so much. Can you imagine how pitiful and shitty it is to be old, even for a famous writer? After all, if you go out today at thirty-six, you'll be young and passionate forever. You'll be a hero, a black angel maybe, but still an angel. Didn't you inscribe one of your books once, "From the dark angel of literature"?

I grew rigid conversing with myself like that, blurting it all out like that to myself, and lying there in a position that belonged to someone else, and facing a destiny that wasn't mine either, and holding someone else's solution in my hands. I needed to make a decision, but I was rigid from all that mysticism, paralyzed by it. I remember the same thing happening to me many years ago when, as an eighteen-year-old poet, I had slashed my veins, and my legs and arms grew cold as the blood flowed gradually out of me. And my heart sucked noisily, and the warmth gathered in my chest, until I lost consciousness. . . .

The telephone rang. I leaped to my feet and ran to pick it up. I was, it turned out, expected at Anna's that day, Anna, my new girlfriend, my new cunt.

"I made dinner, Edward. We had a date. But if you don't feel like coming over here, then I can come to you," said the complaisant Anna.

"Stay where you are, don't move!" I said. "I'll take a taxi and be right there." And I skipped out of the house without looking back.

When on Saturday mornings I appear in the doorway of the five-story mansion in the best and most expensive neighborhood in New York, dressed in my customary snow-white shirt, blue and white striped pants, and elegant white boots of Italian make, and with round glasses in a thin frame resting on my nose, those passing by look at me with unconcealed curiosity and envy. Some of the young girls smile flatteringly. Sometimes the old women smile too, perhaps from a polite and cautious respect for the house I've just come out of. I am for them an unexpectedly live representative of that unattainable, extraordinarily sweet life they read about in the picture magazines.

With an unhurried gait and freshly washed, carefully cut hair combed à la James Bond, I set off for a walk. How could those passersby, out walking themselves and their dogs by the fresh East River with its link to the sea, how could they, mere pedestrians, know that the sleek and dignified man with the tranquil face is just a servant in the millionaire's five-story house, and that his aristocratic custom of a morning walk is due simply to the fact that on Saturday and Sunday his employer is never at home—that the multimillionaire employer invariably spends his weekends at His Highness's multimillionaire estate in Connecticut, and that that's the reason the servant plays master on Saturdays and Sundays.

The day is already warm, and as I walk in the direction of the beautiful windows of Madison, calmly and superbly playing my role, a New York springtime breeze pleasantly plays with my hair.